"Mike Cooper's debut novel, *Clawback*, is a frenetic, no-holds-barred thriller. The writing is taut and muscular, and like the character of Silas, I hope we'll see more of it."   —Hallie Ephron, *The Boston Globe*

"A fast-read suspension of disbelief that benefits from [Cooper's] background in finance. *Clawback* will appeal to anyone who thinks that many CEOs of big companies still don't earn what they get paid and that Wall Street is still without parental supervision. It's easy to enjoy."   —*The Wall Street Journal*

"*Clawback* has intriguing characters, knowing insights into the Wall Street demimonde, a blistering pace, lots of action, and some over-the-top derring-do that may attract Hollywood. . . . Will thrill crime-fiction-loving 'peasants' afflicted with schadenfreude toward the masters of the financial casino that continues to cause so much hardship."   —*Booklist* (starred review)

"Mike Cooper's *Clawback* is fantastic. If Tom Wolfe could channel Robert Ludlum, he would have written this novel. Think *Bonfire of the Vanities* meets *The Bourne Identity* and then kick it way, way up. Action, suspense, and tons of insider information. This is my kind of thriller and I can't wait for the next one. If you like Nelson DeMille, you'll love Mike Cooper."
                            —Brad Thor, #1 *New York Times* bestselling author of
                                              Black List and *Full Black*

"*Clawback* is a guilty pleasure. It has vivid but convincing action, a sympathetic protagonist with a specialty we haven't seen before, and plentiful antagonists we all have reason to despise. Buy it."
                          —Thomas Perry, *New York Times* bestselling author of
                                              Vanishing Act and *The Informant*

"Intriguing . . . *Clawback* is definitely worth the investment."
                                                      —Associated Press

"There's much snappy, half-cynical repartee reminiscent of 1930s Hollywood cinema, including snarks about the necessity of gun control and a firefight aboard a mega-yacht followed by a jet ski–Zodiac water pursuit. Cooper sets the action in New York City, a locale he has down pat, from neighborhood diners to the only place it's legal to live on your boat. Arm a Hollywood hero with a Beretta and disposable cell, point him at a Gordon Gekko–type, and this book's big screen ready."   —*Kirkus Reviews*

"Sharp, invigorating, and remarkably assured, Mike Cooper's financial thriller *Clawback* makes Oliver Stone's *Wall Street* look downright naive."
                                      —Josh Bazell, author of *Beat the Reaper*

"A pleasing mix of action, sleuthing, clever tricks, a slow-developing romance, and far-out chase scenes. A great start for what one hopes is a series character, this will appeal to anyone who likes a fast-moving thriller leavened by wit."
—*Library Journal*

"Better than a bank with wheels, *Clawback* reads like a roller coaster on a financial graph! Mike Cooper's debut novel has a narrative that's breezy and light, kind of like the fire that backdrafts under a door before it blows off the hinges."
—Craig Johnson, *New York Times* bestselling author of the Walt Longmire mystery series

"Financial thrillers—once the least interesting category of mysteries—now flourish, thanks to vivid storytelling and an economic downturn that shows how high the stakes can be. *Clawback* mixes high-octane action with the details of banking and money management for a solid plot."
—Oline Cogdill, *Sun Sentinel* (Fort Lauderdale)

"*Clawback* is smart and savvy, and paced like a bull market rally! Silas Cade is part Jack Reacher, part Seal Team Six in the Madoffian canyons of power and greed."
—Andrew Gross, *New York Times* bestselling author of *Eyes Wide Open*

"*Clawback* mixes high-octane action with the details of banking and money management for a solid plot."
—*Mystery Scene*

"Engaging . . . Cooper clearly knows the investment world."
—*Publishers Weekly*

"*Clawback* races along at a relentless pace. It would be a loss to crime fiction if [Silas Cade] weren't to return."
—*Mysterious Reviews*

"One of the most interesting Wall Street crime novels to come along . . . Cooper has his finger on the pulse of Wall Street and does an excellent job show-casing the herd mentality (both on Wall Street and within the mainstream press). For those who love action scenes, this novel has some of the best. . . . Excellent . . . An action-packed tale made for the moment."
—*Reviewing the Evidence*

"It had to happen: mix guns and greed, and Wall Street warfare takes on a whole new meaning. With nonstop action, accessible insider maneuvers, and a distinctive, fallible lead, it's a smart and sassy debut for this former Boston financial exec. Here's a hot tip: Get in on the ground floor with Cade and Cooper."
—*Winnipeg Free Press*

PENGUIN BOOKS

CLAWBACK

Mike Cooper is the pseudonym of a former financial executive. Under a different name his work has received wide recognition, including a Shamus Award, an International Thriller Writers Award nomination, and inclusion in *Best American Mystery Stories*. He lives in Boston.

MIKE COOPER

CLAWBACK

A SILAS CADE THRILLER

PENGUIN BOOKS

PENGUIN BOOKS
Published by the Penguin Group
Penguin Group (USA) Inc., 375 Hudson Street, New York, New York 10014, U.S.A.

USA | Canada | UK | Ireland | Australia | New Zealand | India | South Africa | China
Penguin Books Ltd, Registered Offices: 80 Strand, London WC2R 0RL, England
For more information about the Penguin Group visit penguin.com

First published in the United States of America by Viking Penguin,
a member of Penguin Group (USA) Inc. 2012
Published in Penguin Books 2013

THE LIBRARY OF CONGRESS HAS CATALOGED THE HARDCOVER EDITION AS FOLLOWS:
Cooper, Mike.
Clawback / Mike Cooper.
p.   cm.
ISBN 978-0-670-02329-5 (hc.)
ISBN 978-0-14-312273-9 (pbk.)
1. Finance—Fiction.   2. Murder—Investigation—Fiction.
3. Wall Street (New York, N.Y.)—Fiction.
I. Title.
PS3603.O58284C53   2012
813'.6—dc23
2011036310

Printed in the United States of America
1   3   5   7   9   10   8   6   4   2

Set in Walbaum MT Std
Designed by Alissa Amell

Publisher's Note
This is a work of fiction. Names, characters, places, and incidents either are the product
of the author's imagination or are used fictitiously, and any resemblance to actual persons,
living or dead, business, establishments, events, or locales is entirely coincidental.

For Lisa

CHAPTER ONE

Y ou'd think imminent arrest for a forty-million-dollar fraud might slow a guy down, but nope, there he was, wandering out of Bazookas at midnight. By himself, conveniently. I'd been one step behind for twenty hours, chasing Hayden Pennerton across the hedge fund demimonde: Greenwich estate to Park Avenue offices to midtown soju bar to East Village nightclub, and numerous meetings between. Finally, long after dark, back to Connecticut—stopping off at a strip club on the way home, like it was any other workday.

Hayden was so obvious a flight risk I couldn't believe the Stamford PD wasn't standing in line.

A dozen college boys got out of their cars, dome lights glowing and radios blaring as they slammed the doors. Light traffic passed on Richmond Hill Avenue. The parking lot was well lit, the air warm for early October.

The sort of night you felt comfortable, at ease. Safe.

"Hey," I said, friendly like, when Hayden walked past. "How are the girls inside?"

"Easy on the eyes." He was thirty-six, gym fit, not too drunk and a Master of the Universe. What did he have to fear from me? "Nice, too."

"I hate wasting my money, you know what I mean?"

I was no older than him, respectably dressed in gabardine and button-down. My knockoff Breguet was good enough to pass. Hayden saw what he expected to see: another rich asshole, a man of his world.

"The way I figure it," he said, "cash money is never wasted on a naked woman."

"Truth."

The Yalies disappeared inside, pulling out their fake IDs. For a moment we had the parking lot to ourselves.

"May I?" I stepped up to Hayden, locked his right arm nice and smooth and put the Sig into his side.

He froze.

"I'm pointing this away from me," I whispered, about six inches from his face. "If I pull the trigger, half your internal organs splatter the pavement."

"What—?"

"To your car, please. Silver-gray Audi S5, right?"

"You're fucking *jacking* me?"

"No," I said. "Beep the remote on your keychain."

That was tradecraft—give someone a small illusion of control, and he'll be more willing to go along. It also occupied his free hand, inside his pants pocket. If he expected to drive, which always seems to happen in the movies, so much the better.

We edged over to the Audi. Too much tension in Hayden's muscles. He said nothing, but his breathing shortened, and the movement I could feel in his arm was too obvious.

"The door," I said.

He leaned forward, opening a little space between us, then twisted, shoved and broke the armlock.

All much faster than I expected.

"Shit." I stepped back, even as he swung a pretty nice left. By luck or design the punch struck the median nerve, right below my shoulder. A shock wave of pain down my arm, and I dropped the pistol. Oops.

I guess he *was* a gym rat.

Hayden jabbed again, then crossed. I blocked but the blows hurt. This was taking far too long.

"Gonna fuck you *up* now!" Grinning, teeth bared.

"Right," I said, waiting for his footwork to align. The instant it did, I kicked him sharply in the knee. He stumbled, face going white. I slipped inside, punched his sternum—hard—and followed with an elbow in the neck. He whooshed and fell backward, onto the Audi's hood.

I picked up the pistol, flexing my other hand. It hurt.

At least no one had seen us.

A minute later Hayden was more or less conscious again, groaning in the back seat. I'd flexicuffed his ankles together and his wrists to the steel bucket seat supports, one on each side of the car. This left him leaning forward, arms locked out and down, his torso bent over his knees. The position made it hard for him to breathe in fully, and therefore hard to yell.

Not that I was worried about noise. Audi soundproofing is top-notch. I sat in the passenger seat, keeping the handgun in sight.

"Just to be clear," I said. "I don't want your wallet or your house keys or this car—though the leather is very comfortable." It had that new-car smell, even over Hayden's sweat.

He grunted and glared.

"This conversation could have gone much easier, you know?"

No response.

"Oh well." I tapped him on the nose with the gun barrel. "I represent one of your investors. He wants to remain anonymous, so I'll just call him Mr. Green."

Another labored grunt.

"'Green' for the best kind of negotiable instrument, get it?" I allowed a demented chuckle. "No?"

It helps if they think you're crazy.

Hayden finally spoke. "What do you want?"

"Mr. Green is unhappy."

"What does *he* want?" Considering his position, Hayden was more defiant than most sensible people would be. I shook my head.

"Mr. Green has become distressed by rumors of a liquidity crisis in your operations."

"Hey, that's all bullshit."

"Oh? That leak from the Manhattan DA's office was solid enough for the *New York Times*. How many counts in the indictment—twelve, was it?"

"She's up for reelection. What do you expect?"

I thought about hammering his skull with the Sig. "In any event, Mr. Green has decided to accelerate his redemption request."

"Huh?"

"Think of it as clawback." A term of art, referring to the mandatory return of compensation paid on a deal that later goes bad. Sometimes the *claw* part is literal. "Mr. Green is now at the very front of your creditor queue."

I swear, you could see the gears grinding. But when Hayden finally spoke, he was way out in the tall grass.

"Which fund?"

"Which *fund*?" It was true Hayden's little shop ran three or four different investment vehicles, but I had to laugh. "Let me explain something. Making the proper journal entry is *very* low down on your to-do list, right this moment."

The Greenwich grapevine believed Hayden's hedge funds were rotten clear through. He'd bet the wrong way on Spanish sovereign debt, doubled down by selling CDS positions at the peak of the crisis, and then covered everything by falsifying statements and paying interest out of capital for six months. Even the SEC had gotten involved, Johnny-come-lately as usual.

My client, reasonably enough, wanted to get his money out before Hayden went to jail and every last asset froze up in a decade's worth of litigation. Because Hayden wasn't taking calls, he'd hired me instead. I wasn't even on fee-for-service—as the last available option, I was able to negotiate a generous contingency instead.

Now all I had to do was collect.

"You should have returned Mr. Green's calls," I said. "But that's water under the bridge. Let's talk numbers."

"No."

"No?" I nodded. "I'll start, then. Ten point six million dollars."

He squirmed. His face was hard to read, dark in the shadowed interior.

"You said it." Hayden's voice was hoarse. "Liquidity crisis. There's no cash. Mr. Green's out of luck."

"Hmm."

"I mean, I understand. Look, I'll be paying everyone back, in order. What does he have, A shares?"

"Don't bother. The ten point six isn't going to help you figure out who he is either—I adjusted the amount."

"Okay, okay." Another pause as he thought things through. "Look, we can work this out."

"Yes. Very easily. You give me the money and you never see me again."

"Exactly!"

I hesitated. "Good . . ."

"How much do you want?"

"Oh, for fuck's sake." If I ever took a bribe, I'd never get work again. "Don't even go there."

"Hey, I didn't mean—"

I lifted the pistol slightly. "Let's discuss your options."

He winced but shut up.

"Here's one approach I've found effective in the past," I said. "I shoot you in both ankles. Then both elbows. Then I cut off one ear."

His eyes grew large. "That's—"

"Only one ear, right. You need the other to hear me continue the discussion." I paused. "And to make the necessary phone calls, of course. Hands-free is nice, but they're not making *ears*-free headsets yet."

What can I say? If you don't enjoy your work, you're in the wrong job.

Hayden's brave front was cracking.

"There's nothing I can do!"

"I hope—I really hope—that's not true."

The club's door opened and two men exited. They walked past, thirty feet away, while I sat quiet, ready to silence Hayden if I had to. But he didn't even look at them.

A good sign.

"However," I said, "you'll be happy to hear that option one may not be necessary."

"No?"

"No. Because a few hours ago I spoke with Walter Smith."

He froze again.

"Walter told me all about your business arrangement."

"What arrangement?" But it was barely a question.

"Walter understands how life works. See, we're in the same world. We run into each other now and then. Me, he's going to see again." I shrugged. "You, on the other hand, . . ."

"He sold me out?" Hayden actually started to get angry. "I already paid the son of a bitch!"

"There's that, too, of course. You should always hold a little back."

Despite what I'd said earlier, I don't really like the Dick Cheney interrogation style. That was all for show. You can always beat a lie out of someone, but the truth? That takes psychology. In Hayden's case, psychology suggested that gruesome threats might be helpful, as they often are with small minds.

As for how I found Walter—well, that's the sort of inside knowledge my client was really paying me for, even if he didn't know it.

I'd gotten the assignment late last night, which left zero time for backgrounding. No problem, because Hayden was cutting public tracks everywhere. Two phone calls and twenty minutes on Google revealed a man living far too carefree for a fraudster with the wrath of a powerful, politically ambitious New York prosecutor poised above his neck. Dinners at Masa, a chartered helicopter to Mill Neck, a front-row runway seat at the Chloé show—Hayden acted like someone beyond suspicion.

Or like someone with other plans.

Suppose you're a corner-cutting hedge fund manager who's made a killing the easy way—by cheating—and the law's about to come knocking. Chumps like Madoff give themselves up, confess and spend the rest of their lives in prison. Smart guys, on the other hand, pull a Kobi Alexander and flee with every penny, to spend their lives like kings in nonextraditing corners of the Third World.

The problem is getting out. Hayden would have no problem funneling the cash offshore—half his job had been glorified money laundering cum tax evasion anyway. But slipping past U.S. border authorities himself? That's a different story. How many document counterfeiters do *you* know? Are any of them good enough to forge an RFID-equipped U.S. passport?

There aren't many, and on the midtown-Greenwich axis, the number's even smaller. Wherever Hayden got the tip, Walter was one of only two or three possibilities.

"So here's how it's going to work," I said. "Walter gave me details and photocopies." Not traceable to him, naturally, but that didn't matter. "If you don't cough up my client's balance, those copies go to the DA's office. Not only will you remain in the United States, I doubt the judge will even grant bail. You'll never see sunshine without bars across it again."

And that was that. Hayden blustered and complained and argued, but we both knew he'd come through.

The transactions were finally completed at two a.m. We managed everything from Hayden's iPhone—good thing he had a charger in the dash—except a confirmation, which I dialed from mine. When I provided my client's bank details for the transfers, Hayden noticed it was based in the Caymans, and I could see him start to say something.

"Hayden," I said, "I *hate* irony." And we buckled down and finished the job.

When I opened the passenger door, grateful for the cooler night air, Hayden spoke up.

"Hey, you're going to cut me loose, aren't you?"

I thought about it.

"Let's do this," I said. "The girls inside, did you tip them okay?"

"Uh, yeah."

"Good. They're earning a living, they deserve decent pay."

He looked at me. "Sure."

"This is about the time they finish up." Connecticut bars close at two—thanks, blue hairs! "So they'll be coming through here soon. Just holler."

"But—"

"Since you treated them well, I'm sure they'll help you out."

He started to splutter, and I closed the door.

CHAPTER TWO

I f I had one, my logo might be a green eyeshade crossed by a 9 mil.

It's a small niche, though a necessary one, especially in economic times as difficult as these. Straightforward accountancy is all well and good. But sometimes you need someone packing a P226, not an HP-12c—if you know what I mean.

My own background? Military, of course, and I can't say much more about it. When I got out, most of the guys I knew were going over to Blackwater, but I wanted something quieter. Benefits paid for some college, I took the CPA exam because a girl I knew was doing it, and I kind of drifted into independent consulting.

You hear all about how cutthroat American business has become. As if Wall Street is worse than Blofeld's shark tank; like guys get shivved in the coatroom at L'Atelier. Now, at a few places that's true, I admit. The way the *mafiya* has moved into penny-stock fraud, for example, I wouldn't go near a boiler-room brokerage without a machine gun. But come on—mostly we're talking about guys who haven't been closer to combat than ducking a swing from a drunken panhandler they insulted outside Grand Central.

When you find out someone's been fiddling the books, you've got options. You can issue a restatement and a public apology—ha-ha, just kidding; *nobody* does that! You can take it to the U.S. attorney and prosecute in the full glare of God and everyone. You can buy the guy off. Or you can fire him and cover up, although that's harder nowadays, what with all the reregulation.

But when you need the problem solved fast and permanent, you call me.

———

I thought my night was over, but when I dialed Tom Marlett—the client—to let him know Hayden had come through, it rang with no answer. Not even voicemail, and that was odd. Okay, three a.m. and all, but I'd told Marlett I expected a resolution, and he'd demanded to hear as soon as it was settled.

For ten million bucks, I'd stay up all night, too. Something didn't feel right.

His home wasn't far away, especially via the deserted roads of suburban Fairfield County. I had the windows down and night air washed through the car, bringing that early autumn smell of fading leaves and dying flowers. A good smell. I flashed past estates and horse farms and conservation land, dark and lonely, wondering if Hayden was still cuffed to his backseat. Even odds, I figured, that some opportunist would have stolen his phone and wallet by now, rather than releasing him.

I had to slow down, going through Old Ridgefork's town center, and just as well. A hundred yards after bumping over the railroad tracks, where the blacktop curved around the old cemetery, blue lights appeared down the road. A moment later an ALS ambulance shot past, lit up but no siren, going at least twice my speed.

Uh-oh.

Sure enough, all the excitement was at Marlett's outsized "farm-house," as he liked to call it. I drove past slowly but without stop-ping, staring over the low stone wall edging his property line. The ambulance had joined three police cruisers and a fire engine, all at the top of the mansion's long gravel drive. A uniformed officer in reflective striping stood at the estate's entrance, arms crossed, doubt-less posted to keep out bloggers and gawkers and oddballs who'd be drawn like moths to the flame of celebrity misfortune.

Well, what else could I do? Before the lights had disappeared from my rearview, I was speed-dialing my pal Johnny, who runs a three-billion-dollar incremental fund downtown.

"Wake up," I said.

"Fuck." His voice was groggy. "The after-hours just kick you out?"

"You've got fifteen minutes, tops."

"What?"

"Emergency vehicles and an ambulance at Tom Marlett's house. Police are standing guard on the perimeter. The 911 probably went out less than ten minutes ago."

A pause, but only for a few seconds.

"Tom Marlett's dead?"

"Or badly hurt. Or someone else in the house."

"I thought he was between wives."

"Yeah, you're right—number three went a few months ago." It's a small playground, our overpaid corner of the financial world, and gossip about rich people you sort of know is a lot more interesting than gossip about celebrities you don't. "Doesn't matter, does it? Three police cars tell me all I need to know. It's the morgue or the ICU or jail for Marlett. Either way his firm is about to go through the guardrails."

"Yeah." Johnny fell silent for a few moments as he sorted through options. "Shit. I can't do anything with it."

"What?" I slowed at a crossroads and turned right, aiming to get back on the Merritt. "Why not? This is the tip of the year, for Christ's sake. Beat the vultures to it."

See, Marlett basically ran a one-man band. Typical for a small investment shop, the kind of firm with a billion or two under management, mostly for other rich guys and some banks and so forth. He was a dabbler: a little private equity, a little trading, a little debt arbitrage. That deal with Hayden was the sort of one-off that would scare any sane investor away from a Marlett prospectus, but he found his investors on the golf course and the yacht club. You know, places where due diligence didn't run much further than seeing if Marlett picked up the bar tab.

Which meant that Marlett Capital's returns depended entirely on Tom Marlett himself. Whatever happened a half hour ago, the short-term outlook for his investors was a flashing-red SELL! I thought Johnny could use the information to get in and short Marlett ahead of the crowd—a sure bet on the rigged roulette wheel of Marlett Capital's forthcoming swan dive.

"It's not a public company," said Johnny. "There's no stock to sell short."

"Jesus, I know that." What was I, an idiot? "So go after his debt. Or whatever deals he's got cooking—it's all going to tank as soon as Wall Street wakes up this morning."

"The problem is he's *already* in the basement." Johnny laughed. "The sub-subbasement, in fact. With rats and sewage and broken utility mains."

"I didn't know it was that bad." True, rumors had been zipping around, especially after Marlett had delayed his quarterly performance letter. I'd figured that was why he was so keen on recovering the ten mil from Hayden. But because I was on a contingency funded directly by Hayden's cash, I hadn't done any kind of liquidity check. "What do you know?"

"I heard from a guy that Marlett's going to announce a seventy-eight percent loss for the last quarter."

"What? Wow. That's awesome!"

"Yeah."

And if Johnny knew, so did enough other smart money. I could see the problem—no one was going to touch Marlett, no matter what Johnny offered. All that first-responder excitement I'd seen was just icing on a cake that had been scavenged down to crumbs already.

I didn't bother asking "What guy?" either.

"Wait a minute," Johnny said. "How do you know about this?"

"I was driving by."

"Is that *all*?"

He was a longtime friend, so I could overlook the implication.

"Nothing to do with me," I said. Which I thought was true—I couldn't imagine any connection to Hayden, who was probably still in the Bazookas parking lot. And who had no idea it was Marlett who'd hired me, for that matter.

"Uh-huh. Come by tomorrow, we'll talk."

A sign for the Merritt Parkway appeared in my headlights, then the on-ramp itself. At the top of the incline, merging on to the mostly empty highway, I could see a faint glow of false dawn in the rearview mirror.

"Sorry to wake you up," I said.

"Nah, still good to know. Maybe I'll call around. See if I can find anyone who's still exposed to Marlett—salt the wounds." He would, too. Inside knowledge is always good for *something*, even if only to talk smack.

On the way back to Manhattan I considered the ten million Hayden had grudgingly coughed up earlier. I'd already extracted my cut, of course, but Tom Marlett might not be needing all the rest. Maybe he wouldn't even know about it . . . When I got home, and had access to a securely anonymized computer connection, I would see if the recovery was still sitting at that bank in the Caymans.

Even if Johnny couldn't profit from Marlett's misfortune, maybe I could.

CHAPTER THREE

I slept until birds woke me up. Midmorning sunshine slanted through the window slats. Pigeons don't chirp, but what the hell else lives in the city? Every year some nature-loving reporter runs a story on peregrine falcons roosting on City Hall or Trump Tower, but I don't think they chirp either. Sparrows? Robins? Where's John James Audubon when you need him?

If the falcons moved uptown, maybe they could eat the sparrows. I'd have to write a letter to the editor.

First thing, like every morning, the news. Still lying on the futon I pulled my laptop open:

"MILLIONAIRE BANKER KILLED IN DAWN ATTACK!"

Good job, Rupert. At least two errors were obvious in the single headline: Marlett was a fund manager, not a banker, and the attack had occurred hours before dawn.

But he really was dead. The news aggregators all said the same thing: Marlett had died on his doorstep, shot between two and five times by an unknown assailant.

Nothing to do with me, thankfully.

I hadn't been able to get Marlett's cash out of the Caymans bank, six hours earlier, because it was gone by the time I logged in. Sadly, that kind of cash will always find a new home as fast as it needs one. But the day wasn't lost. Once I got out of bed I found a new-business call on my voicemail.

"Silas Cade? Are you there? Don't you ever answer the phone? I've tried three times now. Call me back."

Well, in fact, no, I never *do* answer that phone. It's a voicemail–only number at Verizon, which I signed up for years ago, back before customer-verification rules became stricter. They don't know who I am, and I pay with a money order sent through the mail every six months, so they never will. I call in to collect my messages now and then—once every few days unless the wolf is at the door.

Presumably, my new lead had gotten the number from a previous client or the grapevine or who knows? Like Walter, I have to rely on word of mouth, which means I need a permanent contact number. But I use it strictly for first impressions. After that I buy a prepaid cellphone, one for each job, and throw it in the East River afterward.

You can't be too careful.

I still had the mobile I'd used with Marlett, but I couldn't use it anymore—the job was over, he was dead, the phone had to go. I'd leave it in a dumpster somewhere later. Fortunately, I'd stocked up on throwaways from the 96th Street bodega recently, and found one in the kitchen drawer. I powered it up, verified the balance and called my possible new client. In as few words as necessary I set up an appointment that afternoon: "No, don't tell me where you got my name. Yes, I'm glad for the reference, but . . . no, forget it. Let's not talk about . . . yes, I'm happy to meet."

They always need to see me in person. Evaluate my trustworthiness, see if they can spot the handgun, who knows? Privacy can be hard to come by, since they're usually C-level executives or millionaire business owners. But this guy—he called himself Ganderson—suggested the Willow Haven Country Club.

"What?"

"It's in Bolingbroke, do you know it?"

"Sure, but isn't that kind of, I dunno . . . public?"

"Don't worry about it. I'll see you on the range. Ask the girl at the front desk."

I started to say something about not having golf clubs, but he'd already hung up. Well, I could stand around while he practiced his drives. Maybe onlookers would think I was the caddy.

There were coffee beans somewhere in the cramped kitchen of my apartment, but a warm breeze was coming through the window, and it looked like a cloudless sky over the next building's roofline. A takeout bagel from Amir's seemed like a better plan, and I could walk down to Carl Schurz Park, find a bench and read the market blogs on my mobile.

Self-employment does have its advantages.

Going down the stairs I passed my neighbor Gabriel, shirtless, tattoos dark on his shaved head, hauling up a laundry basket. He nodded in a friendly way.

"Hey, Silas. Nice day, huh?"

"Global warming."

"Whatever."

In the tiny vestibule I checked the mailbox—nothing, which was good—and sighed. I'd had the place for less than a year, but it was getting time to move again. I don't like people knowing who I am, even a little. Not where I live.

And I'd gotten to like Yorkville. Students and people in their twenties, mostly, north of 80th and east of First. The closest subway was blocks away, which kept the rents down, and residents tended to come and go but without the seedy transience and heavy police presence of, say, Alphabet City. Most buildings were only three or four stories, so there were no doormen or concierges to keep a gossipy eye on the streets. I blended in—told people I was a freelance content management specialist or graphic designer or day trader, and they nodded and didn't care.

I'd even found an off-street space for my car for only five hundred a month, cash.

As I pushed through the vestibule entrance, I decided I wasn't done checking the mail. Rarely, but not never, someone I actually need to hear from writes me a letter. They don't send it to a real address, of course—I use a double-blind, with forwarding out of Nevada provided by an edge-city guy who thinks I'm Russian *mafiya* but who's paid well enough to be reliable. He sends it along to a box at the post office on 109th, up in East Harlem. I hadn't been there to clean out the junk mail for a couple of weeks, and this seemed like a good opportunity. It was only three stops on the Lex. Amir's could wait.

The building's heavy glass-mahogany-and-steel-bars front door swung shut behind me as I went down the worn terrazzo steps of the stoop. It really was a beautiful day. Sunshine, clean air, those damn birds, red and gold leaves in the gutters from trees down the street. Who *wouldn't* want to live in the world's greatest city?

"No change," snarled the helpful MTA employee from behind her scratched lexan, and went back to her cellphone conversation without drawing breath.

"But I only need two rides." I held up a twenty. She just looked annoyed and pointed at the ticket machines again.

I don't like the MetroCards, naturally. Trip history is stored centrally, and the MTA is happy to share data with police. Sure, they're anonymous—unless you're stupid enough to top them off with a credit card—but they can still match you to every trip on a single magstripe. So I try to buy only a ride or two at a time, which is hard when of the three machines, one is credit only, one is broken and one is flashing USE EXACT CHANGE. I sighed and gave up the twenty.

The post office was busy, like most weekday mornings. A long line, two clerks working the counter, the floor already littered with scraps of paper and torn labels. I found my box and had just turned the key when my mobile rang.

I stopped dead, pulled it out and stared at the screen, which was only giving me "Number Blocked."

See, the way I live, other people don't call me. I call *them*. I'm constantly switching phones, as I mentioned, and it all gets too confusing. Clients get a number until their job ends, and friends might get another, but never for long.

But worse, this was the phone I'd used with Marlett. He was the only person in the world I'd given the number—and I didn't think he'd need to be calling now.

I should have gotten rid of the damn thing immediately.

"Hello?" I took my mail, the usual stack of mass-distribution flyers and a couple of envelopes, and stepped outside.

"Hi," said a woman's voice. "Silas Cade?"

———

Okay, my first reaction might not have been the best.

I didn't know the caller. She said her name was Claire Something—no bells. She didn't mention another name, like, say, a mutual acquaintance, to validate the contact. And she wasn't asking whether I wanted a job.

So I immediately clicked off, and while walking directly back to the subway, I pulled the battery. Waiting at a red light on Third Avenue, I set the phone at the edge of the curb and smashed it with one boot, then swept up the pieces and dropped them, one by one, into garbage bins as I passed. The last one went into the MTA's massive, metal-bound, bombproof trash can on the downtown platform.

Dumb.

I should have held on to the phone to try backtracking the call. For a moment I looked back at the trash barrel—but no, that was too far beneath even my dignity, not to mention the possibility of drawing attention. Even in East Harlem, transit cops occasionally got out of their cruisers long enough to walk a platform.

My only activity lately had been running Hayden down for Marlett. It didn't have to mean a connection, but that old guy, Occam? He had a point.

I suddenly needed to know more about Marlett. A lot more.

A train squealed in, people got off, people got on. Not too crowded this time of day. I stood at one end of the car, swaying as it started up, eyeing the other passengers. At 103rd I stepped out, then slipped back in again, right before the doors closed. Old habits, easy to revive. It's no way to live, not all the time, but paranoia holds its own deep comforts.

Back aboveground at 86th I circled some blocks, zipped through an office building's atrium, then stopped abruptly at a sidewalk vendor's pretzel cart.

"What'd you like, chief?"

"No butter, extra salt." I stood a few paces away and ate it standing, squinting up and down the sun-washed street.

You know, being careful.

On the other hand, the NYPD had recently begun to deploy miniature camera-carrying dirigibles, operated by remote control, far enough above the city streets to be invisible to pedestrians and low enough to be out of traveled airspace. UAV surveillance technology, developed for the sandy battlelands between Afghanistan and Pakistan, and more recently Mexico and Texas, is now in service above the metropolis. Or so the bloggers say. You can't really be off the grid anymore, anywhere.

When the pretzel was gone, I continued another block to the Shale Building and walked down into the parking garage. Not so grand as it sounds—the building was a poorly maintained hulk from the 1940s, housing skeevy small-business offices and the sort of residential tenant who was required to pay weekly, in cash, direct to the super. The garage's striped exit arm was up, the attendant's booth locked and empty. I could see a Styrofoam cup of coffee on the tiny desk next to the credit card reader, though. Goldfinger was around somewhere, in the bathroom maybe.

I waited five minutes before I decided that loitering might become suspicious. Goldfinger must have gone off on one of his pointlessly mysterious errands. I found a scrap of paper, scrawled a note and pushed it through the cash window, to land next to his coffee.

"Where the fuck are you? Got an inquiry. Back later."

It was the nature of my job, sometimes, to depend on such stellar colleagues. I found my car, did the usual thirty-second check for bombs and bugs, and drove out.

Perhaps my new client would be a little more classy.

CHAPTER FOUR

A faint haze had dimmed the sun slightly, but it was still warm and bright. I took the inland route again, back up the Merritt eight hours after coming down it the other way. Now the four lanes were choked with traffic. Every car seemed to have open windows, stereos rattling the frames. Nothing like summer weather in October to put the city in a good mood.

Even my twenty-year-old Tercel seemed to perk up. It was the most reliable vehicle ever built, unprepossessing, perfect for the rough streets of urban America, but only on days like this could you say it was a pleasure to drive.

At the Willow Haven gates a guy in a red jacket waved me into the parking lot. The flawlessly paved blacktop was filled with open-top German two-seaters. Men with golf bags and women carrying tennis gear walked along the shaded veranda of the clubhouse. I felt as out of place as the sullen-looking teenager sitting on a wicker rocker, arms crossed, glaring at nothing. No doubt his parents had brought him along—quality time—but he clearly wasn't with the program.

Somewhere in the distance I heard a familiar *pop-pop* sound. For a moment I hesitated, then shook my head.

It had to be something else. This wasn't Kandahar.

"Ganderson," I told the woman seated at a gleaming table inside the doors. "I'm meeting him on the driving range."

She clacked the keyboard of a surprisingly discreet laptop. "I don't believe Mr. Ganderson has reserved any—oh, here he is." She looked up and blinked. "I'm sorry, were you expecting to play golf today? Because Mr. Ganderson has signed up the two of you for the *shooting* range."

"Shooting?"

"Skeet and target practice." She studied the screen. "No, not skeet. He's only marked down for the handgun lanes today."

I hadn't realized the NRA was running blue-blazer outreach. "I see. Can I check out a Glock?"

"I'm sorry. We don't provide the armament."

"No problem. Maybe Ganderson has some chrome I can borrow."

"Are you range qualified, sir?"

"Oh yes." I couldn't tell if there was a current of irony in everything she said or not. "Ganderson and I plink tin cans all the time."

"You'll fit right in, then." She gave directions, and I wandered back outside.

So that explained the gunshots. The jaded rich always seem to need new hobbies—why not small arms? Or maybe they'd begun to take "class warfare" more literally. Either way, once I found the range, with its measured lines and pop-up silhouettes and steep backstop, I felt right at home.

Quint Ganderson was a tall, jut-jawed, broad-shouldered cliché in lane five, wearing clear Oakley shooting glasses and a SWAT cap. He saw me coming but finished off the entire magazine of his matte-black submachine gun before putting the barrel up.

"Nice shooting," I said. His target was shredded. Bullet holes all over the place.

"Silas Cade?" He let the weapon fall forward in his left hand and reached out to shake with the other. "Didn't bring a gun, did you?"

To Connecticut's third-most-expensive country club? "I never carry unless I'm prepared to kill someone," I said.

"Haw! You never know, with these assholes." He waved vaguely at the other guys on the range. "You brought your own muffs, though."

I had on a pair of big Mickey Mouse–style ear protectors. At the gate a small brown man with "Rangemaster" embroidered on his shirt pocket had offered them to me. Not stylish, but I do value my hearing.

"Loaners."

"Good enough. Look, we'll find you something. I want to get another hundred rounds in."

So we stood out in the sun, tapping away. Ganderson let me use a customized Model 1911—someone had done a nice job with the barrel and action, but the laser sight was so embarrassing I had to double-check that I didn't recognize anyone else on the range.

"We've got a problem," Ganderson said, during a reload.

"Yes?"

"It's complicated."

Of course.

I'd looked up Ganderson online before driving out here. He was yet another investment banker. Managing director at Aldershot Capital Partners, a boutique M&A firm. Nothing exceptional, and nothing in recent news suggested he was dealmaking in choppy waters. But I noticed that his name collected more hits than one might expect—far more, given the modest size of his company. Advisory committees. Business roundtable position papers. Congressional testimony. Ganderson seemed to have an informal role as industry grandee.

"A number of us in the financial services industry, we're concerned," he said. "The public, the way they think about bankers and investors—not to put too fine a point on it, they seem to hate us."

"No, really?"

Ganderson grinned. "They hate our business, even though they don't understand any of it." He pulled a new magazine from a ballistic carryall on the ground, checked the load and racked it into his MP5. "They hate our companies. Our partners." He swung the weapon up and sighted down the range. "Our acquisitions. Our investments. Our families. Our boats. Our *dogs*."

BRRRAAAAAPPPP. He fired a long burst, obliterating the paper target, and turned back to face me.

I looked at Ganderson's face, cheerful under his SWAT cap. He may have thought the world was full of class enemies, but it didn't seem to bother him. Loose brass littered the ground at his feet. He wore leather shooting gloves, and I noticed he still hadn't brought his finger outside the submachine gun's trigger guard.

Careless.

"They hate us, our money, and everything they think we stand for," Ganderson said. "It's become something of an identity issue."

"No argument. But—and I hate to say this—there's not much I can do about it."

"Of course not." He shrugged. "Who cares? Comes with the territory. It's mostly just talk."

"Right."

Ganderson peered at me through his high-impact lenses. "Except when it's not."

"Oh?"

"Someone's gone beyond talk," he said. "Starting last month. You *know* what I'm referring to."

"Ah, . . . the president's blue-ribbon commission on banking regulation?"

"What?" He looked puzzled.

"I have to say, you want to start kneecapping senators, I might not be the best—"

"Haw!" Ganderson laughed again and waved his MP5. "No, no. No need for that. Why bother? We just bundle a few hundred grand every election cycle and they're our friends forever. No, I'm talking about the other assholes."

"Um . . . ?"

"The ones who've started killing us." Ganderson's voice deepened. "Jeremy Akelman. Betsy Sills. And Tom Marlett."

"Oh."

I finally realized what planet Ganderson's rover was on.

"Akelman was a hit-and-run," I said slowly. "Late-night training jog—he was a triathlete, something like that? No reflective vest, on a dark road in Greenwich. The cops figured it for a bad accident."

"That's what they said on TV. But they never caught anyone."

"Sills was that mutual fund manager. Freeboard Investments. She fell off a yacht charter in Jamaica."

"You do follow the news. Good."

"And Marlett, last night." I ejected the pistol's magazine, locked the slide and set it down on the carryall. Maybe Ganderson would take a hint and disarm himself, too. "Okay, three funerals, all in the last month. But two of them were accidents. How many people work in finance, just in the New York area? A million? On statistics alone, this is nothing unusual."

"You need the background." Ganderson left his MP5 in a firing grip.

"Um, okay."

"Freeboard has something like two hundred mutual funds. When they published last year's results, Sills was at the bottom."

"Ah . . ."

"Of the rankings. One hundred and ninety-nine managers had better results than she did."

"That bad?"

"The absolute rock bottom. Her one-year return was negative seventy."

I made a brief quiet whistle. "Okay, I'm impressed." And I was. Any piker can inflate their 12(b)-1 fees, but it takes real effort to burn off two-thirds of your capital.

"Akelman didn't do any better." Ganderson said. "He was a specialized commodities trader. OTC markets, third world mining—you can imagine. The last few months weren't kind to him."

"Rare earths." I remembered now. "He went all in on neodymium and the Chinese flattened him. His firm was one step ahead of receivership when he died."

"That's right."

"Well, I'm sure the lawyers involved are doing all right for themselves."

"And the Chinese." Ganderson glanced downrange, at our neighbor's target, then back to me. "As for Marlett—last quarter his hedge fund lost seventy-eight percent of its assets."

Same as Johnny had told me. "Got it. Three really lousy money managers." I paused. "You don't think they died in accidents, do you?"

"It's an impossible coincidence."

"The bottom-ranked mutual fund. The worst hedge fund return I know of, for three years at least. And the biggest commodity loss since Brian Hunter blew up Amaranth." I almost smiled. "I'm seeing a pattern here."

"Kind of jumps out at you, doesn't it?"

"No one else has figured it out yet?"

"We've had some calls." Ganderson finally took his trigger hand out of ready. "So far we're dealing with it."

I bet. "So who's up next, do you think?" I said. "You must be running a pool—can I get in?"

"Don't be a jackass." He cleared the submachine gun's action, hands moving with the automatic familiarity of long practice. "Marlett was a friend of mine."

I considered that for a moment. "No, he wasn't."

For a moment it could have gone either way.

"How would you know?" Ganderson said.

"Your friend is killed by gunfire, and a few hours later you're here, plinking away? Even for"—I hesitated—"ah, our line of business, that's cold. I don't think so."

"Well, I met him once."

Which actually could count for friendship in this world. "Whatever. So we're looking at . . . a more rigorous implementation of performance-based incentivization, maybe?"

"What?"

"Cash bonus is all good on the upside, but if you fuck up on the downside, Machete comes to call? I have to say, I like it."

"And the idea has certainly been floated, more than once." He might have been kidding. "But that's not what's going on. Not that anyone knows about. Anyway, it's against the code of ethics."

Really? *Section 4: You may not kill staff for bad performance.* This time I didn't bother trying not to smile. "Right. So . . . what do you want me to do about it?"

"Go find the murderer, of course."

I thought about it. "Losing so much money—lots of suspects out there, don't you think?"

"Not necessarily. Disgruntled investors usually don't pick up a MAC-10." Neither does anyone else with an ounce of sense, of course, but the firearms training at Willow Haven probably wasn't up to Fort Benning standards. "Still, as I said, everyone hates the bankers. Like it's all *our* fault somehow."

"It isn't?"

"If you have money in an underperforming investment, it doesn't do any good shooting the manager—everyone loses everything that way."

"So maybe it's just some little guy who finally couldn't take it anymore."

"Exactly." Ganderson finally set down the MP5 and pulled off his cap and shooting glasses. "Everyone's retirement depends on the stock market. Social Security's a goner and big companies are bailing out of their pensions right and left. On top of that, market data is everywhere—you can't escape. It wouldn't take much to push some unstable personality over the edge."

If an underfunded 401(k) were my only hope of not spending my golden years running a Burger King register, I might be pissed too, but I didn't interrupt. Ganderson seemed to have been practicing for interviews.

"Shooting a few investment managers with bad records is populist theater of a very high order," he said. "A hundred years ago anarchists threw bombs at robber barons. Today they might be looking for other scapegoats. They might be coming after us!" Obviously not meaning me, but I let it go. "I fear—" Ganderson's voice dropped. "I fear we may be seeing the beginning of our own Red Terror!"

"Wait a minute." I tried to follow the logic. "Terrorists, okay, sure. But why would they kill your guys?—who, let's face it, were doing a pretty good job undermining trust in the capitalist system all on their own."

"Oh, come on." He frowned. "If you're a madman with a gun, you don't have to make sense."

I guess I could go with that.

"That's how it'll probably play, anyhow," Ganderson said, and suddenly his voice was back to normal.

"Okay." I nodded. "So you're looking for some kind of Munich operation. Hunt them down, demonstrate the rule of law."

"Not exactly. We don't care about the rule of law."

Now *there* was a refreshingly honest statement. "Can I quote you on—"

He cut me off with a laugh. "Forget it. What we want is—we just need this to *stop*."

"Can't the police handle it? Or call the FBI. I'm sure there are interstate angles they can use to assert jurisdiction. Once they think this is some kind of direct-action Marxist conspiracy, they'll field a hundred agents. Wat Tyler won't stand a chance."

"Wat—?"

"Never mind. Look, I don't understand. What do you need me for?"

Ganderson rubbed his eyes. Someone probably woke him up in the middle of the night when the Marlett news broke.

"We can't let this turn into a circus. If the public gets the wrong storyline . . ."

"Does it matter?"

Some paper scraps from an ammunition box had escaped the Willow Haven grounds crew and were blowing across the manicured grass of the range. The rangemaster announced on a loudspeaker that they'd be moving the line to seventy-five yards, and the firing from the other lanes petered out as other shooters stopped for the break.

"You probably don't believe me," said Ganderson, "but it's not just the bad publicity I'm thinking about. Like I said, populist rage is too easy to stir up. What we want to avoid at all costs— besides this lunatic continuing his spree—is a proliferation of copy- cats."

"Ah."

"A wildfire, whipped up by demagogues."

"Now you're making sense," I said, and he was. Finally. "Open season on bankers. Talk about negative optics."

"Exactly."

"Can I ask you something? Is that the reason for all this?" I ges- tured at the range, the other shooters, the guns at Ganderson's feet. "Finance isn't usually where you find a lot of Second Amendment enthusiasm."

"Some of us have been serious for years." Ganderson glanced sourly at a young man two lanes away, holding his Beretta 92 in a sideways grip like some idiot video gangster, half his shots missing the target entirely. "But yes, ever since the economy went south, personal protection has been a concern."

Not that Wall Street had anything to *do* with the economy going south, of course. "So everyone's strapped now? You go into a meet- ing, sit around the conference table and chitchat about handloading and trigger pull before getting down to business?"

"Sometimes. Can we get back to the point?"

"Sure." I nodded. "You want me to find your killer. I can do that."

"Good." Ganderson began casing his guns, tossing the cartridge boxes into a duffel.

"Or them. Or her, for that matter."

"Let's hope there's only one."

We negotiated a reasonable fee on the way back to the clubhouse, figured out logistics, traded direct cellphone numbers. Ganderson headed for the front doors.

"You're not going to get in some golf?" I asked. "Air out the gunsmoke?"

"I have to run my son up to Highfield." He sighed and glanced down the veranda. The unhappy boy I'd noticed earlier was still in the rocker, head tipped back now, eyes closed. "He's working on a farm."

"Oh."

"A *goat* farm."

"College applications coming up?"

"Yes, but this is hardly going to help." Ganderson hefted his weaponry bags. "I told him I'd send him to volunteer anywhere in the world. And not just the rat holes! He wouldn't have to dig latrines in Haiti; he could sit on a beach in the South Pacific and teach the natives how to make piña coladas. But no—he wants to shovel goat shit a half hour from home."

"Well, I hope they're angoras."

"He brings home milk. I had to tell the cook to throw it away when he isn't looking." Ganderson shook his head. "And he's only managed a probationary license, so we still have to drive him everywhere. I swear, I don't remember giving my father so much grief when I was his age."

"Go bond," I said. "I'll take care of the Wall Street avenger."

"Good." We shook hands. Ganderson still hadn't removed his shooting gloves.

"I don't need to hear the details," he said. "I really don't."

"That's why you're hiring me."

"Just make sure Tom Marlett's funeral is the last one I have to attend."

"You got it," I said. "Either his—or mine."

They love that kind of stuff.

CHAPTER FIVE

Goldfinger's booth was empty when I finally got back, close to four. A few leaves had blown into the garage, out of place on the oil-stained concrete, and I stepped on one walking out. The coffee cup and my note were both gone.

I'd catch him later. It's not like he had a life outside the garage, particularly.

The day was still bright and warm, drawing out the strollers, the loiterers, the goof-offs, the students—everyone who didn't have to be inside wasn't. I walked back to my apartment at a meandering pace, enjoying the brilliant afternoon, the blue sky, the music from cars and windows and overamped headphones. Turning onto my block, I dodged a blader, glanced at a woman scooping up after her Labrador, heard a horn at the far intersection—

Trouble.

At a glance, she was a few years younger than me, maybe thirty. Light brown hair, cut short and stylish, and deep dark eyes. Average height, in a white T-shirt tucked into cargo pants over ballet flats.

She had a faded courier bag on one shoulder and sunglasses pushed up above her forehead.

Perfectly normal for the neighborhood. The problem was, without training and practice, it's more than difficult to stand and wait unobtrusively on a residential street. If you're not moving, you stick out.

All the worse that she was watching my building, and when I caught her eye, she stepped off the curb to cross the street, straight toward me.

I looked away and kept moving.

"Mr. Cade? Silas Cade?" She came up to my side.

"*Ayna ep hamam*?" I said, glancing at her but not stopping.

"What?"

I shrugged. "*Oreedu litr al-benzyn.*"

That should have done it, but she just frowned and kept up as I turned the corner. "I have no idea where the restroom is," she said. "And why do you need petrol?"

Fuck. I sighed again.

"Um . . . just practicing today's phrases."

"Well, your pronunciation is good, for Modern Standard. A little too textbook, maybe."

She seemed determined to have a conversation. Halfway down the next block—far enough from the interception point to complicate any plans a contact team might have had—I stopped and faced her.

"What do you want?"

"I'm Clara Dawson." She held out a hand. I shifted slightly, rebalancing my weight before taking it, but she just shook normally and let go. "Nice to meet you."

She'd called me. Not Claire, Clara.

I said nothing, just looked at her. The moment stretched out.

"Your neighbor? Guy with tattoos on his head? Told me he saw you this morning, what you were wearing. So I waited."

Well, I couldn't order Gabriel not to talk about me.

"What do you want?" I said again.

She shrugged.

"What's your connection to Thomas Marlett?"

"Who's that?"

"A dead hedgie."

Tough girl. "How'd you find me, Ms. Dawson?"

"It wasn't easy."

"Maybe, about now, you need to show me something."

"What?"

"Official ID? A badge? Court papers?"

"You're a suspicious man, Mr. Cade." She grinned. "In both senses of the word. That must be why you were so hard to run down."

I looked around. Parked cars, apparently empty. No panel vans. The pedestrians were all wearing shorts or flip-flops or tank tops. A post office truck drove down the street, but that was okay. They're never used by law enforcement—the USPS is notorious for refusing to cooperate with other agencies.

"Who are you?"

"An independent researcher and reporter."

"Ah." That seemed possibly true.

"I've been working on Marlett for two months, but now that he's dead, I need to get a story out, like, yesterday." She made a serious face. "We can do it all on background if you want."

"Oh?"

"Or I can publish what I know," she said. "Including your name."

A teenager went by on a skateboard, loud and oblivious.

Tough girl. "All right," I said, and looked around the street once more. "How about we sit down at Amir's?"

―――――――

"Where'd you learn the Arabic?" I asked. I'd chosen a booth by the front window for us. Not coincidentally, the late afternoon sunlight coming through the glass was in Clara's face. Also not coincidentally, I could see the street, the door and even through to the kitchen, past the end of Amir's linoleum counter. The place was quiet, mostly empty before the dinner rush. Scratchy subcontinent pop drifted out from the dishwasher's radio.

"Junior year in Cairo. You?"

The Defense Language Institute, but I didn't feel like sharing my résumé. "I'd really like to know how you tracked me down, Clara."

She drank some tea. "From Marlett's phone records."

"No way." Not after all those warrantless-wiretapping lawsuits. The national security horse was long gone, but the barn door was locked up tight. "Pretexting's dead."

"Interesting."

"What?"

"That you know how to con a pen register out of Ma Bell."

Oops. I frowned.

"Hypothetically," she said, "because we would never do something illegal, you're right—customer service *is* too hard to social-engineer anymore. But hypothetically, I might have used a star-seventy-two scam."

Aha. She tricked Marlett into forwarding his phone, and got the rebill delivered to some anonymized internet number. Clever. This time I tried to keep a poker face.

"I don't know what that means, but it sounds like your research expertise is, ah, usefully esoteric."

"Just legwork." She flipped her hand dismissively. "Most of his numbers were easy to eliminate—obvious business calls, his attorney, car services, the executive jet timeshare, the country club. A few stood out, though."

Including, apparently, mine. Marlett had called two: the cellphone, which was a one-off, and my anonymous contact number, at the beginning. But neither should have brought her to my door— like I said, even Verizon doesn't know it's me using that voicemail box. I was torn between pretending I couldn't understand what she was talking about, or immediately wringing out of her how she'd broken what I thought was an impenetrable firewall.

She laughed, apparently at the conflict playing out on my face. Jesus, was I such an open book?

"You did all that today?" I said.

"No. Over the last few days. Just backgrounding." Totally illegal, but whatever. "This morning, though, when I heard he'd been killed, I realized the list might include potential leads."

"Uh-huh."

"So I googled the numbers, and with one of them, your name came up."

Holy shit. I stared.

Clara shook her head. "People will put anything on the internet nowadays."

Could that be true? Had some idiot fucking client of mine gone and *blogged* about what a good job I'd done?

Amir came around the counter to drop off my plate of rice and beans. Also the jar of habanero sauce, and I didn't even have to ask—which was nice, but, sadly, another sign I was becoming too familiar in the neighborhood.

"I'm surprised you never checked," Clara said, buttering a corn muffin, left over from the morning. "Doesn't everyone search themselves now and then?"

I guess I'm just not vain enough, but it was sure as hell going on the checklist now.

"Because I have nothing to hide," I managed to say, "I would never think of it."

"Well, if you're curious, I didn't find much. Actually, nothing but your name and the phone number, to start. Which is kind of odd."

"Oh?"

"That's a *really* thin digital trail, for, like, a real person." She chewed on the muffin. "We wouldn't be talking right now, in fact, if you hadn't subscribed to some magazine under your real name. That got it into the public mailing databases."

"I see."

"A ten-dollar search." More muffin disappeared. "Which I can write off."

Myself, I'd stopped eating, the beans like cement in my throat.

You can't live off the grid, not if you spend any time in society whatsoever. Who wants to emulate the Unabomber, in his isolated shack? Rather than go survivalist, all barter and paranoia, I'd simply tried to keep my vocational activities totally secret. Compartmented. The rest of my life I lived more or less normally, just like everyone else. Until now, it had worked.

The voicemail number was the only link between my two worlds. Clara had broken it open.

"What's your story about?" I asked. I wasn't interested, not anymore, but I had to pretend long enough to figure out whether this woman was a threat or not. "Is he really dead?"

"Four .338 rounds through the heart, two in the head. The houseboy found him on the doorstep at two in the morning."

I squinted. "You know ballistics?"

"Nothing. But the Old Ridgefork cops were first on scene, and they aren't as practiced as the troopers in message control." She grinned. "I took a box of Boston Kremes down to their station this morning, and they rolled over like puppies."

"Who did it?"

"A sniper. Didn't you even look at your computer today? It's on the news everywhere."

"Sniper," I said. "Uh-huh. Sure."

Though to be honest, .338 *was* a sniper's caliber, popularized in Iraq and Afghanistan. It was just hard to see its place in the leafy suburbs.

"They found where he was standing, a hundred and fifty yards across the road in the cemetery. Tripod marks, used bullets, I dunno."

"Old Ridgefork isn't exactly Mazar-el-Sharif."

"And Marlett wasn't exactly Taliban." She finished the muffin, dusted crumbs onto the plate, held her cup in the air toward Amir. "Though his investors might have thought so."

"Huh?"

"He burned through three-quarters of his capital in just four months. Seventy-eight percent, gone."

She knew precisely what Johnny knew, and it was still a remarkable statistic. You really have to *try* to lose that much money. Russian penny stocks? Zimbabwean currency speculation? Marlett must have been a genius, in his way.

"In fact," said Clara, "it's possible that Marlett achieved the lowest return in the entire hedge fund universe."

"So he hit the record book on his way out the door." A thought occurred to me. "That ranking—who says?"

"Morningstar."

A moment passed.

"Those numbers haven't been released yet." And until then they were treated like nuclear codes, or USDA crop statistics. Clara, whoever the hell she was, had some serious research skills indeed. "Not for last quarter."

She winked. "That one took *two* boxes of donuts. Anyway, Marlett was right at the bottom. The absolute worst hedge fund in the country. His investors would have been better off pouring gasoline on their cash and tossing in a match."

Nice. "Maybe you can write their next management letter."

Amir came over with a kettle and refilled our cups. A customer wandered to the cash register at the end of the counter, and Clara waited until Amir had returned to ring him up.

"So you can see why I'm interested," she said. "What was going to be a feature piece on a lousy money manager is now, like, investigative journalism. Marlett loses a boatload of money, and someone shoots him. Pissed-off investors, maybe? Financial vigilantes? Wall Street cratered the world economy not too long ago—are the little guys finally taking matters into their own hands?"

I'm not sure Marlett's investors, who would have had to meet the SEC's million-dollar net-worth threshold for hedge fund participation, could be accurately described as "the little guys." But Clara had a point.

"People are angry," I agreed. "I'll give you that."

"They had a right to be angry at Marlett."

"Maybe." I pushed beans around on my plate. "You know, every trade that Marlett lost money on had a counterparty. Someone else got rich off his bad picks."

"True." She put down her cup. "So what did you do for him?"

That was an abrupt transition. She'd had practice interviewing.

"Tax advice," I said.

"Oh. You're like, what, H&R Block for plutocrats?"

I counted to three. "I help out with certain arcane issues in estate planning and tax management. In Marlett's case, well, I'm afraid client privilege survives his demise. But it wasn't anything you'd find useful."

We went back and forth for a few minutes. I could see Amir watching from his perch down the counter—watching Clara, probably. I wasn't nearly as eye-catching.

"So who do you write for?" I asked, finally.

"Well, . . ." She hesitated, twisting a band of hair around one finger. It was the first uncertain gesture I'd seen her make. "I used to freelance articles to the financial press, but now I'm trying to publish an online weekly. Original analysis, investigations, sourced commentary. A finblog with depth."

It's not like I've heard many elevator pitches, but even to me that sounded weak. "How's it going?"

"Slow." Clara sighed, and looked directly at me. Her eyes were an unusually dark blue, and unblinking. "Real slow."

"I think I'm getting the picture. Marlett's your ticket to fame, right?"

"One good story is all it takes."

"And Marlett's got it all."

She nodded. "Scandal, greed, a spectacular Wall Street crash and burn—and then the guy's *assassinated*? By some sort of avenging ninja? Reporters would *kill* for this opportunity."

"So to speak."

She smiled. "I'm three-fourths there, because I've been working it so long already. If I get the entire story . . . that's it, I'm *made*."

We'd both finished our plates. The coffee cups were cold. Amir was in the kitchen, yelling cheerfully in some foreign language at the dishwasher, who kept interrupting him.

"I'm not part of your scoop," I said. "I had some small business with Marlett, and it wasn't interesting at all." Clara started to talk, and I held up my hand. "No, I know you don't believe me, even though it's true. So here's what we can do. I'll help you dig up the real dirt."

"And in exchange, I leave you out."

"You don't want to waste your time looking at me." There was another entendre there, which I tried to ignore. "Just by convincing you not to, I'm helping you close in on the Pulitzer."

"Pulitzer? That is so dead tree."

"Well, then, synflood—level traffic monetization. Whatever you want."

"Okay." Clara held out her hand. This time her grip seemed warmer, and I admit I held it a few seconds longer than was strictly necessary. "Deal."

"Good," I said. "What's it called?"

"What?"

"Your blog."

"I like to think of it as a journal. 'Blog' sounds amateurish."

"Sorry."

"*Event Risk.*"

A phrase from bond-prospectus boilerplate. "I like that."

"Thanks."

I dropped a twenty on the table and we scooted out of the booth.

"Stay in touch," she said.

"You, too." I gave her the number of another of the so-far unused prepaid cellphones. "Those other digits—don't use them."

"Why not?"

"They won't be working."

"Uh-huh." She gave me a knowing smile and started out.

"Hey," I said. "I hope I hear before you write about it."

"About what?"

"Whatever happens next." I held the door open for her. "It's sure to be interesting."

CHAPTER SIX

"Abandit," said Johnny, generously giving me about a third of his attention. It was next morning, early in the business day. His eyes stayed on the five monitors—no, six, he'd added another flat-panel since I last visited—that were streaming market data, news, and blogosphere rants across his desk. "You were right—it was a great tip. And some fuckwad figured it out before me."

"No way. Someone out there's smarter than *you*?"

"Hard to believe, isn't it? And early yesterday morning, several million richer, too."

"I was thinking maybe you'd kick me back a finder's fee."

"Hah." He looked up. "Marlett was on spec, huh?"

"Never mind."

Johnny and I go way back. High school, believe it or not. He was baseball, I was football, we sat in the same AP classes—though that wasn't saying much in small-town New Hampshire. His ticket out was UVM and a Wharton MBA. While I was learning how to jump out of airplanes and field-strip a .50-cal, Johnny was clawing his way from entry-level i-banking to, eventually, running his own hedge fund.

Who made the better choice is a topic for another day.

I'd come down to his Beaver Street offices, where he oversaw a floor-to-ceiling panorama of the East River skyline, a roomful of twentysomething traders, and three billion dollars of alternative-asset allocations. The traders all seemed to have ADHD. Johnny's style was incremental: he could go in and out of positions in less than thirty seconds. Breakfast and lunch were catered every day, but the food mostly sat around getting cold, and the only consistent nourishment seemed to be cans of Red Bull and Jolt.

In these days of algorithmic technical strategies, it was all quaintly retro.

"I thought you said Marlett was down to fumes." I tried to get comfortable in the cheap plastic chair Johnny provided his guests.

"He had one last deal going, it turns out—the York Hydro acquisition." Johnny looked almost in pain. "I can't believe I forgot about it."

"Doesn't sound familiar."

"Canadian electric generation. The Conservatives went on a privatization binge a few years ago. Carlyle and those guys snapped up the good ones, but some of the smaller utilities went straight to market—just in time for the world economy to collapse. No more liquidity, so they need a new buyer, bad. Marlett was actually on to something."

Johnny couldn't have known any more than I did about North American power plants, but utilities are capital-spending pigs, so the financial picture was clear enough. York must have had cash flow problems, and with credit markets barely thawed, they couldn't borrow. That meant one option—a distress sale.

"York's stock went up thirty-four percent on the announcement of Marlett's interest last week," Johnny said. "But with Marlett dead, it fell right back down again. Someone was on the other side of that trade this morning. They probably needed a forklift to handle the bales of cash they earned."

"That was the motive." My kind of story. "Someone killed Marlett to win the trade."

"Could be. Not provable, of course."

"Who was it?"

"Nobody knows." He frowned. "It was all small-lot, anonymous transactions."

"Wait a minute." I love a conspiracy theory as much as the next guy, especially when it's about someone cheating the markets, but this didn't seem like a proven case. "If they were all small trades, how do you know one person was behind them all?"

"They were too even. A hundred shares here, fifty there, ten or fifteen trades a minute. I dunno. It just felt staged."

Well, Johnny was worth a hundred million and I wasn't. I probably ought to respect his instincts.

Out on the floor one of the traders must have hit the jackpot. He jumped out of his chair, pumping his hands in the air, yelling. The other guys threw wadded paper and staplers at him. I could see why Johnny had walled off his office with heavy glass.

"Let me ask you something," I said. "Three names. Tell me what you think."

Johnny raised an eyebrow. "Shoot."

"Free association, now . . . Jeremy Akelman, Betsy Sills, Tom Marlett."

He looked blank.

"Here's a hint," I said. "All three ran other people's money, and they did so *really, really* badly."

"Sounds familiar . . ."

"And now, they're all down for the dirt nap."

He finally got it.

"Three dead money managers! They're *connected*? Shit." Johnny laughed. "Deranged madman? Or are the peasants finally rising up?"

"My new client would really prefer Door Number One."

"New client—no, forget I asked." He knew I wouldn't share the details anyway. "Do the police see it like that?"

"No idea. Probably not—otherwise they'd have leaked it by now."

I knew what Johnny was thinking: *How can I profit from this?*

"So you're going to find the lunatic," he said.

"And persuade him to stop."

"Hell, plenty of people, they'd tell you, give him more ammunition."

"That's kind of the problem, don't you think?"

Johnny drifted off in thought, staring half focused at his screens. Something caught his attention for a moment, and he tapped a few keys.

Somewhere a day trader just got wiped out.

"If you can't stop him before he does it again," Johnny said, "maybe you could let me know ahead of time?"

So he could piggyback on to the killer's trade. Right. "Don't be a ghoul."

The bullpen had settled down, chairs returned to upright, traders at their desks again. Rain spattered silently on the window glass, the cityscape beyond dim and misty.

"Hey." I had a thought. "You pay attention. Ever heard of a financial blog called *Event Risk?*"

"No, but that doesn't mean anything." He went back to the keyboard, and a minute later had found Clara's journalistic endeavor. "Interesting."

"What do you think?"

"Contrarian." He read for another minute, flicking down the posts. "Not macro, not trading tips. Analytics. He must have an accounting background—there's a lot of balance sheet this, income statement that."

"She."

"Oh?" He clicked around until he found the About the Author page. "Whoa, you're right. Look at those—"

"Hey."

Johnny glanced over, grinning. "Friend of yours?"

"She knows me."

"I was only going to say, look at those sources. Sounds like she was in the industry."

"Just journalism, far as I know."

"But hardly any snark. What does she see in you?"

Johnny was already being pulled back to his trading. The blog disappeared, replaced by a set of charts. Inflection points blinked green and red on dense yellow pattern lines.

I was lucky to get even ten minutes out of him while the exchanges were open.

"See what happens on York," I said as I got up to leave. "I'd sure like to know who had advance knowledge that Marlett was headed to the big trading room in the sky."

"Yeah, me too," said Johnny. "He'd be a good contact."

CHAPTER SEVEN

Leaving Johnny's office, I had some free time. I'd caught him not long after the market opened, so it wasn't even ten a.m. Rain had fallen earlier, and judging from the overcast would be falling again soon, but for now it was all drizzle and mist. The canyons of the financial district were gray. Here and there people stood in doorways, taking cigarette breaks.

Walking along, I pulled out a cellphone. Oops, wrong one—brand new, and I hadn't used it yet. I went through my pockets until I found the one whose number I'd given to Clara.

"Hi, it's Silas," I said.

Some garbled noise, not comprehensible as human speech.

"Hey, I didn't wake you, did I?"

This time her voice came back crisp. "No, I was brushing my teeth."

And she answers her phone? The life of a blogger. "You're in the bathroom?"

"Don't ask what I'm wearing."

"I'll use my imagination." And I was, too. "Do me a favor, don't flush while I can hear it."

"Yeah, yeah. What's up?"

"I heard something you might want to look into. About Marlett's business before he died."

"Yes?"

"York Hydro."

"I know all about it."

"Did you check the stock activity yesterday?"

Finally I'd thrown her. A pause stretched out for several seconds.

"What are you saying?"

"It went up, it went down . . ."

"Damn." A clatter and some air noise. She must have been sprinting through her apartment for the computer. "Something happened? You think people heard about the shooting and started looking for angles?"

"Maybe. Why don't you check and see what you think?"

"I'll do that," she said. "I'm going to work soon. I'll follow up there."

"You have an office? I thought you said—"

"I can't sit around in my pajamas all day, wandering to the refrigerator and back."

"So where do you work?"

"The Thatcher Athenaeum."

"A literary café?"

She laughed. "More or less. Tell you what, why don't you come over? I'll see what I can find out about York, and you can tell me where the tip came from."

"Sure." I took the address. It was off Third Avenue, near Gramercy Park. "That's not far. When are you going to be there?"

"Well . . . make it eleven-thirty."

"See you then." I clicked off.

After a minute I realized I was grinning, stupidly. I wiped my face back to a scowl and considered.

That was an hour from now. Standing under a tree growing from an iron-fenced patch of dirt in the sidewalk, watching pedestrians and street traffic, was good, but not for sixty minutes.

Fine. I could do some research of my own.

I walked over to Broadway, then uptown until I found a coffee shop with free wi-fi advertised—and a bar right next door. The coffee shop was bright, with shiny chrome behind big plate-glass windows. The bar was dark and gloomy, and its door-side chalkboard, barely readable from smudging and dust, advertised deep-fried wings and Stroh's on tap.

You can guess which one I entered.

Settled at a table by the wall, a cup of burned java at hand, I opened my laptop and connected to the coffeeshop's network. It was time to find out just how badly I'd been compromised by the intertubes.

Like I'd choose the bar for the ambiance? No—I'd be happy sitting in either one, but this way I had an internet connection that was one more step concealed. You just can't be too paranoid. Not in an age when Google has partnered with the NSA, when the carriers legally tap every kilobyte of traffic traversing their wires, when Acxiom aggregates every public scrap of data about you and sells it to anyone who asks. I don't wear an aluminum-foil hat, but I don't want my life recorded and available to anyone with an interest, either.

And *son of a bitch* if Clara wasn't right: the third hit on my voice box number had my name, right there. Good God.

I clicked through, and discovered that some moron had put his entire address book online, using a cloud service called—no lie—GerbilWheel.com. Trawlers had found the database, which the owner had made public from either ignorance or carelessness or both, and converted it into an HTML list. Then cached it. Which mattered, because another five seconds revealed that GerbilWheel had gone bankrupt in 2010, and all formal records of its existence ended there.

The address book list had no headers, and no supplemental detail, like the owner's name. But it was clear enough from the database's original URL:

www.gerbilwheel.com/svcA7/users/profile/nleeson/08.1135DR.dat

Nobby fucking Leeson.

Bad memories washed up. Nobby Leeson was an ex-Marine rock-head I'd had the extremely poor judgment to take on as a partner in a job a few years ago. He tried to double-cross me, things went south, there was a sniper duel . . . well, the details don't matter. Leeson was dead, and I thought I'd left his bad karma behind long ago. But now here he was, laughing at me from the grave.

At least it was just my name. No address, no other detail, no job title—I was surprised Leeson didn't fill in something like, "Silas Cade, Hitman Accountant—Attn. FBI!" But even the name was too much, as Clara's sleuthing had revealed.

I saved the file to my computer—I'd have to study it later, to see if Leeson the Fuckhead had recorded other useful data, like on my competitors—and ran through the remaining search results to see if there was anything else on me. Nothing, fortunately.

Sipping the coffee, wincing a bit, I tried to think of any way to eliminate Leeson's data trail. Unfortunately once something was on the internet it was basically there forever. Like a recent college grad discovering in job interviews that he really shouldn't have posted all those *hey-I'm-drunk!* photographs on Facebook, I was trapped by the tenacious packrat permanence of the web.

Maybe it was time to lose the phone number and switch to an anonymous email address hosted by some hacker haven in Russia or Moldova or something. Nobody really uses voicemail anymore, and IDTheft.com's customer service couldn't be any worse than Verizon's. But then I'd have to advertise the new contact information . . . just thinking about the logistics, I finished the rest of the coffee without even noticing. Too daunting.

I went to get a refill.

"How's the novel coming?" the bartender asked, pouring from a scorched glass pot.

"What?"

"Everyone in here with a computer, they're working on a book."

"Oh." I handed over a five and waved off the change he half-heartedly made to return. "Actually, I was looking at naked women."

He laughed, which meant I'd tipped too much. "At least you're honest about it."

"This place doesn't have a payphone, does it?"

"Not for ten years. At least. What happened, lose your cellphone?"

"Nah, I wanted to call my drug dealer."

This time he wasn't sure if I was joking.

"Just kidding." I took the coffee back to my table, sat down and found the new throwaway. I had another appointment to set up.

I switched on the new phone. While it powered up, I noticed I was still carrying the mail I'd collected from the PO box yesterday, before the call from Clara. I uncrumpled the flyers and glossies and envelopes on the gritty table.

The phone beeped ready, and I dialed.

"Hey, Walter," I said. "How's the fishing?"

"Who wants to know?"

"The fish?"

While we talked, I sorted the mail. USPS service notice, cancer charity solicitation, credit card offer—I guess the financial crisis is solved, if they're trying to sign *me* up again—Gall's catalog, *Shotgun Digest* renewal . . .

And a hand-lettered envelope. Addressed to Silas Cade.

"Got to go," I said, cutting Walter off. We'd already confirmed a time. He hung up.

I never get personal mail.

Even my foster parents, still in their same old house in New Hampshire. They have the address, and they never use it. I send them a Christmas card every year, but I do it through "letter from Santa" forwarding—mail a preaddressed envelope to North Pole, Alaska, in November, and they'll postmark it "North Pole" and send it on. It's for gullible children, of course, fooled by their duplicitous parents, but works great as a blind forwarding service. At least if you need to mail just one letter a year.

Which is about right for keeping in touch with the people who raised me.

I examined the envelope, found nothing suspicious and carefully tore it open from the bottom end. A plain sheet of paper, ink-jet printed.

Hey Little Brother—

You're surprised, right?

Because if you already heard, for sure you would of tracked me down. I know it.

The state split us up when we were babies. Least you were a baby—I was one or two. Of course I don't remember, but my family told me later. I ended up staying with them the whole way through. I guess that wasn't how it went for you. New Hampshire DHHS gave me a little information—I had to hire a lawyer and file all these papers but they came through with the basics. I wrote to your last parents, and they gave me this address.

Also they told me a little about you. CPA—how about that! And in Vegas, too. Guess I know what kind of accountant that makes you, huh? Working for the casinos. I was out there, few years back. But not too long. Back east is home for me.

I fix cars, do a little welding, that kind of thing. Racing, sometimes, on the weekend—dirt track, kind of like you got out there. Not the Speedway, of course, more like Battle Mountain. I do all right. Got two alimonys to pay, though, you know how that goes.

You and me should talk sometime. Catch up. We don't have any other blood relatives, not that I heard about anyway. It's just you and me.

I looked for you on the google, I don't know, computers aren't my thing. You call me instead. I got some ideas.

Your big brother,
Dave Ellins

Okay. Um.

I put the paper down, drank off the coffee and read it again.

A brother?

He'd added contact details: an address in Pennsylvania, an email, a phone number. I checked an online map, found Derryville in the mountains east of Pittsburgh, near Latrobe. I also found Dave Ellins himself, on a local auto-racing website and some fan blogs. Dave raced cars, just like he said, on backcountry tracks. Photos showed his vehicle, which was low and dangerous looking, all custom metal and roll-bar framing, covered in dust.

Did he really think I lived in Las Vegas? It was just a mail drop. If he knew anything more about me—anything at all—he'd be looking for angles.

I had to wonder exactly what kind of "ideas" he was talking about.

Of course, my first thought was: *oh shit*. Someone has tracked me down and is running some kind of scam, trying to lure me out. I admit I've made a few enemies along the way—they all deserved what they got, naturally, but not everyone achieves satori about that sort of thing.

But the blogs hadn't just posted pictures of Dave's cars, they showed the man himself. I clicked on several, staring at the slightly higher resolution.

He looked just like me.

CHAPTER EIGHT

The Thatcher Athenaeum turned out to be a private library in a grandly maintained Beaux Arts building. Walking up from the subway, I noticed its obvious architecture from a block away. Closer, I could see a pair of ten-foot outer doors folded back, their wrought iron shiny in the drizzle. Overhead, the institution's name was carved into an original lintel.

I'd never heard of the place.

Clara met me at the door and led me in, past the guard's desk. Ceilings of plaster relief painted in gold soared above carved oak bookcases. High windows let in murky light, illuminating tables that looked as if they'd been taken from a sixteenth-century abbey. Three men and one woman sat apart from one another, at work, intent and quiet.

"I have a spot on the mezzanine." Clara kept her voice low. I noted the hair pushed behind her ears, small platinum studs, the curve of neck into shoulder.

"I'm impressed."

"Thanks."

"How can you afford membership? I mean—"

"No, you're right. Even if I had the thirty thousand annual fee, I probably wouldn't have made it through the screening."

"Old money, then."

"*Old* old. Family connections to the Astors would help."

"I see," I said, not seeing. "They have a special category, then? Youthful charm and energy, something like that?"

"I'm an employee."

"Ah."

Now it made sense. Hardly any bloggers made enough to live on, after all. Waiters used to be struggling actors; now most are struggling online entrepreneurs.

A walkway ran around an upper level. We ascended a carved wooden stair in the corner. Clara had taken over one of the alcoves, books and papers overflowing an ancient desk and chair.

"One of the perks," she said, gesturing at the workspace. "I shelve books for eight-fifty an hour, every Friday. But I can sit here as long as I want the other days."

"It seems . . . quiet."

"I have roommates at home. This is better." Clara opened her laptop and waited for the screen to light up. "Here we go."

"What?"

"I already published the story." She turned the computer my way. "Want to see?"

"That was fast."

"Maybe not fast enough. *StreetWire*'s had something up since eight this morning."

"York Hydro, all that?"

"Yes. Marlett's death—someone really did make a killing on the killing."

"So to speak."

She grinned. "By the time the sellers realized they'd been taken, it was too late."

I thought about Johnny. "Who was it, then?"

"You don't know?" Clara looked surprised. "That was going to be my next story."

"Sorry."

"I was counting on—wait, I get it! You were trying to get me to do your job *for* you."

I had to laugh. "Just like you."

The athenaeum was as still as a bomb shelter. Sound died against the massive stone walls. We could have been in the Fed's gold vault, eighty feet underground and dug into bedrock.

"How do you stand it in here?" I asked.

Clara stood up. "Want to see where I work?"

We went through a narrow door between glassed-in shelves holding old—really old—leather-bound books. Behind it a corridor of disappointingly mundane style led deeper into the building.

"I don't know where Kimmie is," Clara said. "Probably out on the fire escape."

"Kimmie?"

"She does her buying right down in Union Square, even though I've told her the prices are totally ponzi there. But it's her money, right? Come on."

Down the hall were two rooms, both with metal shelves, some carts parked higgledy-piggledy and books everywhere. No people.

"Lockerby might be out there with her," said Clara. "They both like their blaze."

In the rain? "Isn't that kind of . . . unprofessional?"

"Days get long in the shelving room. You need to liven it up. Speaking of which——" She moved some paper and uncovered an iPhone on one shelf, docked between two speakers. A few taps and Ninja Angel suddenly blared forth, echoing in the hallway.

I had to raise my voice. "Won't that music bother your patrons?"

"No, the soundproofing's good. Two-foot walls." She cut some dance moves coming out.

Library science might have more going for it than I thought.

"What the *fuck* are you doing?"

I turned, fast. Saw wild hair, a glare, a rumpled jacket—and a long wicked knife, point up, gleaming.

"Yaaa!" A combat yell, automatic. In a half second I went low and kicked sideways, snapping my heel back as it extended.

Never go for a blade with your hands.

My foot struck his forearm, not the knife itself—luck probably, but hey, I'll take luck any day—and it went flying. The man looked astonished and jerked backward, out of range.

"Stop it!" Clara's voice cut through. "Stop! Lockerby!"

I kept moving, away from the knifeman, trying to watch him and Clara at the same time.

"Hey." My attacker was rawboned and knobby, frowning as he stared first at me and then the knife on the floor. "What the hell was that about?"

For a moment the hallway was still. Ninja Angel hammered some power chords.

"Yeah, Christ, Silas," said Clara. "What the fuck?"

I straightened up. "You, uh, know each other?"

"Lockerby's the library's restoration specialist."

"Oh."

She picked up the knife, holding it carelessly, like a folded umbrella. The thing looked designed to disembowel sharks. "I think he cuts leather with this."

"Sorry. I'm, ah, kind of on autopilot around weapons like that."

"No problem. I guess." He looked at me dubiously, then took the knife back from Clara. "I was working at the bench, and when that pissant boy band started up all of a sudden, I about took my thumb off."

"What?"

"I *hate* Ninja Angel."

We sorted out introductions. Lockerby's handshake was firm, not the bone-crushing assault I'd expected. I apologized, he apologized.

"Hang on," he said, and went into the shelving room. The music stopped midchord, and a moment later something rawer and less intelligible came on, even louder. Bass thumped through the door.

"Oh, that's *much* better," said Clara. "Swedish death metal?"

"At least he's old enough to tie his own shoes."

Lockerby had his own room—a well-lit space, with a long worktable and racks of projects in various states of completion. I was surprised how many sharp, dangerous tools bookbinders apparently required: awls, knives, even small saws and a spokeshave.

"What's going on?" A woman in her twenties looked in, carrying a heavy volume in both hands. She wore a dark blazer with brass buttons, a tie-dyed cotton blouse underneath.

"Hey, Kimmie." And Clara went through the introductions again.

Kimmie set her book down and looked me over. "How do you know Clara?"

"Business connections."

Lockerby filled two paper cups with water from a cooler by the door and offered them around. Kimmie and Clara shook their heads, so I took one.

"What business would that be?" he asked.

A buzzer sounded, painfully loud, saving me from answering. Kimmie sighed loudly and went out. I looked at Clara.

"Someone needs a book," she said. "They're waiting at the desk. Kimmie'll find it for them in the closed stacks."

"Ah." I turned back to Lockerby, who dropped into a worn leather chair. He shrugged out of his jacket, tossing it onto the bench, and below the sleeve of his T-shirt I noticed a tattoo of two Chinese characters: 火力.

"I've seen that before," I said.

He nodded. "Uh-huh."

"'Firepower,' right?"

"Yeah."

"A sniper I knew once, he had the same tat."

"Marine?"

"No." I shrugged. "Was that you? A jarhead?"

"Eight years. Yourself?"

"Truck mechanic."

He studied me, then laughed. "Right."

"Really."

"You don't have that fobbit look, somehow."

"Mostly I dug holes," I said. "Then when the shooting started, I jumped in."

"I wish I'd had that kind of sense."

Clara got her own cup of water and leaned against the bench, next to me. "Silas is in finance, too. CPA and everything."

"Yeah?" Lockerby looked interested. "Investments?"

"Mostly auditing," I said. "Statement oversight. Compliance verification. Like that."

"But you understand all that money stuff."

"Well—"

"Because I've been wondering." He leaned in. "You know, I follow the news and all, but—let me ask you something."

"Sure." I suppressed a sigh.

See, I knew what to expect. Tell someone you're a doctor, they'll ask about *this funny rash I have on my stomach; can I show it to you*? If your job is to deliver soda to movie theaters, they'll tell you *it's total robbery Adam Sandler wasn't nominated for an Oscar; what's up with that*? And if you work anywhere near Wall Street, it's always *what do you like? Got a tip*?

"What I don't understand is why would anyone ever put their money anywhere except a lowest-fee index fund?"

I blinked. "That's a good question."

"Everything else just seems like you're letting some asshole skim."

"Well . . . yeah, that's about right."

"Lockerby wants to understand Wall Street," said Clara. She

patted him affectionately on the head. "Unfortunately, he's taken his understanding to the logical extreme: the market is completely rigged, so it's pointless to participate."

"You're all in what, then," I asked. "Gold?"

"In?" He laughed. "Rent, mostly. And food. And bicycle parts."

Kimmie wandered back in. "It's still raining," she said.

"Slow day," said Clara. She glanced at Kimmie, then at an old-fashioned clock on the wall above Lockerby's bench. "It's after noon."

"Yeah?"

"You got anything left?"

It looked like chasing down Ganderson's avenger was going to wait a while.

CHAPTER NINE

"I can't believe you're out here in the rain." I still didn't have a hat, and water seeped steadily through the collar and down my back.

"The fish bite better."

"What do they care?"

Walter shrugged. "It's true."

We stood at an iron fence behind a shuttered warehouse, where a seawall from the nineteenth century crumbled slowly into the East River. A few blocks north the shoreline park started, with mowed lawns and a stone river walk. The Parks Department encouraged fisherman there and on any number of the city's other, well-policed piers. But Walter insisted the fishing was better farther down, under the remnants of the Lower East Side's industrial past.

And he wasn't the only one. A handful of other guys leaned on the rail, stolid in the drizzle, next to their poles and bait buckets and tackle kits.

"The runoff has all kinds of garbage the bluefish like to eat," said Walter. "And the raindrops aerate the surface of the water, which makes them friskier."

"Then why haven't any of you caught anything?"

"We throw them back."

"What a great hobby."

Walter was at least fifty but tall and wide, with a thick mustache gone gray. No glasses. He looked like a North Sea trawlerman, not a counterfeiter. "So what's up?"

Meaning, why had I tracked him down, on his day off, in the one place he deserved to be free of life's usual crap.

"That guy Hayden," I said.

"Ah."

"I'm going to send the copies to the DA." And the key question: "If it's okay with you."

"Hayden didn't give you what you wanted?"

"He did, actually."

"So?"

"He's an asshole."

Walter considered that. "Most of them are."

"Who?"

"Your clients."

"What?—Hayden's yours, not mine."

He shrugged. "Wall Street. Listen, photocopy the sheets twice over, and send the final copies."

I'd met Walter years ago, when I was starting out, so I was forever and always an amateur to him.

"At the library," he added. "Or Mailboxes USA."

"I was going to scan it, convert the file to a low-res JPEG and email it."

"Uh-huh. That might work, too."

Twenty feet away one of the other fisherman picked up his pole and twitched it, experimentally. The line tautened and jerked. Everyone turned to watch.

"Hayden's not wrapped up with those dead bankers, is he?" Walter's voice was quiet, but his eyes focused on me.

"Dead bankers?"

"Three at least. That's what I hear."

No use asking where that bit of gossip had drifted up. Clara and her fellow newshounds might not have published the link between Akelman, Sills and Marlett yet, but it wouldn't be long. Ganderson's news blackout didn't have a chance.

"So far as I know, Hayden's clear," I said.

True enough—but I wasn't. A little bad luck could drag me into the official Marlett investigation. The police would be keenly interested in placing someone like me at the scene around the time of his death. Painful though the prospect was, I needed Hayden around as a prospective alibi. "Though, it would be good if he stayed in town for a few more weeks."

"Might be a lot longer than that." Walter still didn't look satisfied. "You *sure* he wasn't involved? Maybe just the last one?"

"Marlett?"

"The sniping."

"He has a rock-solid alibi," I said. "At the time Marlett got shot, Hayden was three feet in front of me, chatting away."

"Chatting?"

"You know these guys—can't stop talking about how smart they are."

But a small nagging suspicion wouldn't die, not completely.

Hayden one day, Marlett an hour later—too damn close. James Jesus Angleton had it right. Sometimes those odd little synchronicities *mean* something.

The guy working his line had reeled it almost all the way in. A moment later he flipped the pole up and landed a squirming, silver-gray fish with a dirty back, close to a foot long.

"Striped bass," said Walter. "Pretty good for the river here."

"Seems a shame not to eat it."

"Some of those restaurants in SoHo, you probably are."

The conversation drifted to business, which, like anywhere, mostly meant sharing invidious and poorly sourced gossip about people we worked with. White-collar enforcement is a small field, like I've said. It's not the rackets, where mobsters are constantly gunning one another down and going to jail and disappearing into WitSec. Hell, even the rackets aren't the rackets anymore, not unless you speak Fujianese or Lao.

"I'm thinking of getting out," Walter said.

"You tell me that every three months."

He shrugged. "I might actually do it this time. I bought a nice condo down in the Keys, did I mention? A foreclosure. And the boat's almost paid off. Who needs this shit?" He lifted a shoulder toward the river, the rain, and the oil-slick trash edging the shore.

"Spend your days bonefishing? Sounds nice—for about a week. You'd go bananas."

"Business is a pain in the ass. And there's new competition, too. Any punk with an iMac and a digital SLR thinks he can undersell me."

"If it's that easy, maybe I should try it. A quiet life, for a change."

"Is that what you think?"

"Nobody pulls an automatic rifle on the forger."

Walter laughed. "You'd be surprised."

"Maybe." I realized my jacket sleeves had gone a wet, rusty brown where I'd been leaning on the iron rail. "I've got competition too, though—if the vigilantes have really started hunting down rogue financiers."

"Is that what you do?"

"Not exactly. But they're diminishing the client base."

The drizzle eased, but the sky was darker than ever.

"Saw Zeke the other day," said Walter. "He asked about you."

"Asked about me." I thought about that for a moment. "In a good way? Or do I need to start carrying an M16 around?"

"Just social." Walter raised one hand, like, don't worry about it. "You know. Wondering how you were."

"Wet." I tried to rub the rust off one sleeve, and gave up. "But now that you mention it, maybe I should talk to him. Possible sub-contracting. Where's he been?"

"The same as always. Volchak's, behind about three empty pitchers."

"I'll try early in the day, then."

Down the row one of the fisherman had managed to light up, under his Mets cap. Smoke drifted in the mist.

"Got to go," I said. "Nice catching up, Walter."

"Throw Hayden off the sled if you want," he said. "Okay by me."

I guess he'd been paid already, too.

CHAPTER TEN

Clara was in the phone book. Too easy.

Not her cellphone, of course. But the *Event Risk* website had a fax number on its Contact page. Even modern, all-electronic journalism is still chained to its Pleistocene era. I looked up the number in a reverse directory online and *voilà*: an address for "C Dawson" on 90th, west of Second Avenue.

No wonder Clara had bothered to find me in person that first day—she apparently lived right around the corner.

It was early evening. Her home was five blocks away. Why not?

Dusk, cool and damp. I wandered along 90th Street at little more than a meander, examining the buildings and cars and faces.

Old brownstones, with a few tearouts mixed in: ugly aluminum and concrete flatfronts from the sixties, before the Planning Commission stepped up. A pizza deliveryman went by on a bicycle, passing a Chinese takeout guy just stepping from his double-parked hatchback. A light breeze drifted up from the river, three blocks east.

Fifty yards away, just as I'd recognized Clara's building from the

Street View image I'd checked earlier, the ace blogger herself emerged. She was dressed in a close-fitting T-shirt over running shorts, her hair pulled into a ponytail.

"Yo, Clara!" I called out, but a truck was passing and she hopped off the steps and took off down the street without looking in my direction.

I didn't try to catch up. She was headed toward the river. I walked briskly after her, and when she came to the dead end, where the walkway was built above the FDR viaduct, I could see her turn right. South. Good enough. All I had to do was keep moving in the same direction, and eventually, after she turned around to come back, we'd meet.

A steady roar came from the viaduct beneath my feet, the cars clogged in rush hour. Exhaust drifted up. Trees in Carl Schurz Park, which extended several blocks downriver, were at a fall foliage peak, orange and red and yellow.

I went into the park and found an unoccupied bench. Not so many people out. More than the crummy weather, it was the end of the workday, when everyone wanted to get home. Children no longer seemed to have unsupervised time outside. And the nighttime crowd hadn't emerged yet.

If the mayor still lived at Gracie Mansion, which was in the park, I'd have had plenty of company. But laws preventing the use of taxpayer funds on private citizens meant that unmarried partners could not be accommodated at Gracie, and the current mayor prefers to bunk with his girlfriend. The mansion was available for city functions, but mostly unused. I sat and waited.

By the time Clara returned it was well into dark. The river was shadowed, and lights glowed in the low Queens skyline on the other side. A few streetlights had come on, along the pathways in the park behind me. She must have run for an hour.

When she was thirty feet away, I raised a hand in a wave, but kept to my seat.

"Clara!"

She slowed but didn't stop, instead swinging her head left, right, checking the entire area before focusing on me. Good reaction.

"Just me," I said.

After a moment she halted, putting her hands on her hips, breathing a little hard from the run. "Silas? What on earth are you doing here?"

"I *live* here, as you well know. Have a nice jog?"

"A little wet."

I'd noticed that. Her shirt was soaked, from drizzle or sweat, clearly showing the dark outline of a sports bra underneath. The nylon shorts, equally wet, were plastered to the long, clean muscles in her legs.

"Want my jacket?"

"Don't be silly."

We were at the edge of the park, alone. Somewhere a siren rose and fell.

"You're almost home," I said. "Long run? Why don't I walk you. We can catch up."

"Since six hours ago?" But she was smiling. "You've been working, if you've got more to report already."

I got up from the bench, feeling stiff. I have to say, my ass hurt from sitting so long—people were smaller or tougher or something in Olmstead's day.

"Marlett's death is more and more suspicious," I said, as we started down the path.

"You mean apart from the fact he was assassinated by a sniper, on his doorstep, in the most expensive county in Connecticut?"

I looked sideways at her. "Foul play does seem to be involved, yes."

"Good to know."

"There've been two others," I said. "So far."

"Others?"

"Betsy Sills and Jeremy Akelman."

She was slower than Johnny, but only by a second or two. "*Three* suspicious deaths. All money managers of some sort. Oh my God."

"Yes."

"I can't believe this isn't news yet."

"Nothing connects them directly." Not exactly true, but I didn't see any reason to bring Ganderson into it. "It seems . . . odd."

"Shit, I wish I had my phone. I sort of remember Akelman—got hit by a car or something. And Sills drowned. Do you have any proof they were murdered?"

"No."

"That's okay, I can still use it. What an awesome lead! It's perfect—just what I need to follow up my stories on Marlett."

Which was, in fact, what I'd been hoping for.

"I saw you made the big time today."

"Thirty thousand hits, as of midafternoon."

"Incredible."

"Better than anything else I've written, by far."

"Akelman and Sills, though—that's no more than rumor. Utterly unsubstantiated, far as I know. Can you post it unsourced?"

"Sure. It's online, I can write whatever the hell I want."

"Is *that* how it works?"

"Close enough." She pushed at her hair, which had begun to escape the ponytail and stick to the sweat on her face and neck. "Though it would be nice to have some official statements or something."

"They'll arrive fast enough, once you publish. It's too good a story for the press to ignore."

"The *rest* of the press." But Clara was all action now. "I can't wait. I have to get back and write this up before someone else figures it out."

"Can we talk when you're done?"

"Yeah, yeah." And she was off—skipping up the path, on the way to her next huge scoop.

Okay, I admit I'm lazy.

Ganderson wanted a quiet inquiry. Maybe he was right that the Beardstown Ladies had gone vigilante. Maybe Wall Street was now facing armed rebellion, and every underperforming investment adviser was going to need an SUV full of Xe bodyguards. On the other hand, maybe it was just coincidence, bubbling and burbling in Ganderson's paranoia. I certainly had no idea—and I didn't feel up to the endless drudgery of an actual investigation, trying to figure it out.

Instead, I could just kick over the anthill. Once Clara wrote up the rumor, it would be everywhere. If there *was* a gang of anticapitalist bomb throwers, the publicity might drive them closer to the open, where they'd be easier to find. If not, well, I'd still done Clara a favor. And if Ganderson was ticked that his fears were now front-page news, oh well. I hadn't exactly signed a nondisclosure, and how would he know it was me anyway?

Up ahead, Clara was already almost gone, lost in the shadows of the park, where the pathway curved out of sight around a forested slope. Her legs and arms, paler than the dark running clothes, were visible, moving steadily. I wondered how easy it would be to keep up with her, over the long distances.

A scream.

From the trees to Clara's right, two dark figures appeared, step-ping into her path. At a hundred yards, I couldn't see much. Shad-owy motion, and Clara fell, tumbling to the ground.

Before my brain finished processing, I was at a sprint.

Another shadow—three attackers, now. Clara yelled again, cut off as one seemed to kick her. She rolled left, into range of another. By then I was close enough to gain some detail. Sweatshirts, loose pants, white faces. White hands, too, meaning no gloves. I couldn't make out any weapons.

They saw me coming, at the last moment.

"Shit!" One swung my way, trying a slant kick, but he was too slow. I slammed into him at speed, putting my elbow into his torso, protecting my head. He went down hard, and I rolled off, keeping the momentum, coming back to my feet in a combat stance.

S-S-SHHK.

Uh-oh. A nasty, familiar sound—a telescoping metal baton, flicked out into its locked position.

The man to my right swung at me. Two feet of coiled, slightly resilient steel—it would have crushed my skull if it hit, or snapped my arm. I twisted aside. The baton grazed my shoulder, and I reversed, punching at the attacker's arm.

Missed.

"That's enough, motherfucker!" His voice was rough, not loud enough to carry beyond our little melee.

The first guy kicked Clara in the head.

A swish, I ducked again, the baton flashed past. I went inside, striking the man's wrist to deflect the weapon. He lunged sideways, and I chopped his forearm, this time connecting. Hard. The baton spun away into the grass.

The third man was on me from the left. I blocked one punch, took another in the ribs. But he lost some balance, and I put a knee into his hip, followed with an open-hand strike to his collarbone, and shoved him sprawling.

"Stop! Stop now!" The leader's voice again. I spun to confront him.

No baton now. He held a pistol, two hands, pointed right at my midline.

"We're done," he rasped. Apart from the weapon, he could have been a roofer or a plumber, something like that—lean, not too tall, a little stubbly.

Nobody moved for a moment. Bad odds, even with one of them bleeding into his eyes, the second just getting up from the ground.

"Remember what we said, bitch." The leader glanced at Clara, limp on the grass, then back to me. "Next time, kid, we use the gun first."

They backed off, the pistol steady on me, then faded around the trees and were gone.

Clara lay unconscious, limbs sprawled. I did an immediate first-responder check—airway, breathing, circulation. Respiration okay, mild trauma, abrasions. The real problem was the likely concussion from that kick to her head. If you don't wake up in a minute or so, the docs start worrying about permanent damage.

Too bad I had to burn another new cellphone on its very first call, but this wasn't a time to hesitate. I dialed 911.

"A girl just got jumped in Schurz Park," I said. "Three guys. She's hurt bad."

The operator began her interrogation—where are you? What's your name, sir?—but I just said, "Near 86th Street" and hung up.

Then I picked up the baton and followed the attackers' path into the trees. Sherlock Holmes would have found clues in the dirt, bits of thread caught by twigs, partial foot prints, all that. I just wanted to disappear. I didn't see anyone else around, but who knows? There might even have been a surveillance camera somewhere, though with the city's maintenance record, it probably wasn't working.

I waited until the patrol car arrived. Less than a minute. Impressive. Maybe they'd been on duty at Gracie Mansion. They came directly up the bike path, lights on, the second cop shining his spotlight. When they saw Clara lying on the ground, one went right to her side, pulling on latex gloves, while the other radioed for an ambulance on his portable.

Time to go. I slipped backward through the trees, through the shadows, and picked up the pace after a few dozen yards. This was going to be a big scene—one siren already approaching on First Avenue, and more surely on the way. Clara would get decent care.

It was killing me to leave, but I couldn't do anything more for her.

Maybe I could stay out of the story. Talking to the police was a complete no-win, even though I'd done nothing wrong—hell, the *Post* would probably call me a hero, and even the *Times* would inevitably use the word "samaritan." But any attention is bad attention for someone who lives in circumstances of, shall we say, tenuous legality.

Odds were good the detectives would come calling anyway. Clara would tell them she'd been talking to me, of course; a bystander could have seen it all happen; or they might even catch the assailants, on a tip maybe, and *they* would give me up. But none of that was absolutely certain—not nearly as certain as if I hung around and ended up in a Nineteenth Precinct interview room.

Clara had just complicated my life enormously. I can't do my job *and* be a citizen. I might even need Walter's services myself soon. What a dreary thought: having to flee to Central America or Uzbekistan or God knows where.

What's worse, I'd brought this attack on her myself.

"Remember what we said." They'd been delivering Clara a message, and it wasn't rocket science: stay away from the Marlett story. Whoever had started plugging Wall Streeters, they wanted no interference.

I strode out of the park, wondering where I could dispose of the baton, feeling guilty and angry, wishing I'd hit that smug bastard harder when I had a chance.

Much, much harder.

CHAPTER ELEVEN

T he cops didn't show.

I'd even made it easy for them—went home, went to bed, set the alarm for seven. They could have called or shown up or accosted me when I walked out to buy a paper in the morning.

Yeah: *too* quiet.

The weather remained lousy. A day or two of Indian summer is all we can expect, I suppose. Rain was pocking the window glass when I awoke, and the temperature had barely crawled above forty. I wrapped the comforter around me and maneuvered from bedroom to office—that is to say, the five feet separating the pine futon bed from the Ikea desk half blocking the kitchen alcove. Four hundred square feet and it *still* cost $2,450 a month.

I unsleeped my laptop . . . hang on. No more argument about the death of civilization: that sentence confirms it, right there. No wonder ten-year-olds today are illiterate.

Never mind. I started with the *Times*, then the other papers, then the neighborhood micronews blogs, of which Manhattan has, predictably, many. Some are rather good. One had even reprinted the police statement verbatim, and I discovered why I wasn't in stir that very moment.

"Dawson remains under observation at St. Joseph's Hospital, recovering from traumatic amnesia attendant to the concussion suffered in her attack. She has spoken at length to investigating authorities but is unable to remember much of the incident. Detectives are nonetheless aggressively pursuing forensic and other evidence, and expect to . . ."

My first reaction was relief: Clara was okay. Losing a little short-term memory after a head knocking is more common than not—I should know. She was up and talking and doing fine.

On the other hand, it seemed she'd blacked out our entire conversation. I yanked at the comforter, freeing it from a snag on my chair-back. Some mixed emotions here. Wonderful that she was recovering, excellent that my role had been kept from officialdom. But honestly? Disappointing that, apparently, she'd also completely forgotten I was even there.

I checked *Event Risk* and found a new entry, posted only an hour earlier. More good news because it meant Clara had to be nearly recovered from the physical effects of the head injury—and even better, she'd written up the Akelman-Sills-Marlett connection. Sure, she'd hedged it with "speculation that" and "possibly" and "one may presume," but the story was clear. Ganderson's media-suppression strategy could now be marked a definitive fail.

And seventy-six comments already. She'd be hitting the most-forwarded lists by noon.

I know, perhaps better than most, how terrifying an unprovoked physical assault is. Twelve hours after being jumped and battered and hospitalized, Clara was practically daring them to try again.

Alone in my room, listening to the rain, I found myself smiling. I was *proud* of her.

Except—wait a minute. The amnesia *also* meant she'd forgotten the threats the attackers had made. Or that they had anything to do with the story at all. Clara might have no idea that it was her reporting that had drawn the attack—that it wasn't a random mugging.

I stopped smiling. Now I was worried.

I thought about calling, but cellphones were banned in hospitals, weren't they? And the cops would probably be paying close attention to all her communications for a while. Instead I clicked my browser over to a secure routing, set up a one-off Twitter account and friended Clara, using the link I found on her social-networking page. As I'd hoped, she'd set her account to auto-follow, and when the notification came through a few minutes later, I was able to send a DM directly.

"Thank god you're OK. need to talk—Silas."

I threw the comforter back on the bed, put my head under the shower for a moment and started to get dressed. I had one sock on when it hit me: Clara had lied to the police.

Twenty minutes of amnesia would have wiped out our entire conversation—she'd never have recalled seeing me at all. And yet she'd run the Akelman-Sills story, just like I'd asked.

Maybe she'd lost memory of the attack, but she had to have remembered us talking.

Could it have been her subconscious, working it out down in the lizard brain while the rest had shut off? Hardly likely. No. She knew exactly what she was doing.

Protecting me, just as I had protected her.

Damn, I was smiling again.

I decided to get out and do some real investigating. Those assholes weren't just whacking the Street's best and brightest, they'd gone after an *innocent*. It was time to make them pay.

And I was just the detective to do it.

"You're a detective like I'm a poodle groomer," said Goldfinger, and laughed. The laugh turned into a cough, then hacking, and then a big goober into the wastebasket by his desk.

All this time, I'd never known he had a room of his own—a utility space, off the parking garage. An "office," he claimed, but it looked like he might have moved in. Shirts hanging from a wire along one wall, toothpaste tube sitting atop a half-empty case of water bottles, a couch I thought I remembered seeing at the curb a few weeks ago.

No wonder he was never in the booth anymore.

"Yeah," I said. "I know how you groom poodles."

"You can groom *my* poodle."

Et cetera. What can I say? Goldfinger had skills and access unavailable to the rest of the world—at least, the world outside legitimate law enforcement. I had to put up with him. And he wasn't a terrible guy, if you could ignore the affect.

His real name was Ernie, but we called him Goldfinger on account of the absurd collection of rings on both hands. He said it was instead of brass knucks, so he could at any moment seriously damage someone in the face. Fourteen-carat knuckle dusters. That was all bullshit, he just liked the Gambino look, but what the hell.

The pair of CZ .45s he kept under his jacket were more of the same.

A car squealed down the ramp to the lower level, just outside the door. Fumes drifted in. No natural light penetrated this far, just the buzzy fluorescents.

Last night, on my way home, I'd left the baton in a plastic bag tucked behind the dumpster at Amir's. This morning the bag had still been there, wet but undisturbed. I had planned on finding a permanent disposition today, but now I had a better idea.

"I need this printed," I said, showing Goldfinger the baton inside the bag.

"Yeah." He didn't reach out to take it.

"And run through IAFIS."

"Uh-huh."

"In the next thirty minutes or so."

"What? Get the fuck outta here."

"Come on. You're the *man*. Help me out."

"Yeah, yeah. Ask for the fucking moon, why don't ya?"

And so forth. The dickering was going to take as long as the actual job, but that was Goldfinger for you. I noticed he'd installed his technical equipment on a table by the desk—hood, lighting, tool rack, dirty unlabeled jars.

See, he hadn't always been a parking clerk. Not long back he'd been a forensic technician—sorry, *criminalist*, he gets annoyed if you disrespect him like that—for the Manlius County sheriff's office.

Despite a personality that any normal person would find tedious at best, he apparently made plenty of friends among other forensi— *criminalists* throughout New York and, more important, the FBI. He'd be there still, despite an inclination to drink, except that Goldfinger was a really lousy drunk. *Really* lousy. Even your friends will overlook only so many D&Ds. Pissing all over the sheriff's shiny new Interceptor one night was the last straw.

For a while he'd done okay as an independent consultant— serving as an expert witness in criminal cases, with a nice sideline in freelance forensics. Here's the thing: anybody can learn to take fingerprints or sample DNA. That's the easy part. But to find a match, you need access to the databases, and those are firewalled, quite securely, by the Department of Justice.

Goldfinger's stroke of genius was to get himself deputized. Because he's not a "peace officer," no matter how broadly defined, it wasn't easy. The loophole he used came from Section 654 of New York County law, allowing sheriffs to deputize "agents of societies incorporated for the purpose of prevention of cruelty to animals." It's trivial to sign up with the New York SPCA. God knows how much the bribe was, but when he emerged from the smoky back room of the sheriff's office, Goldfinger was now Deputy Dawg, and he'd parlayed that into a remote subscription to the FBI's fingerprint repository.

Over time his consulting dwindled away, ruined by too many missed court dates, fucked-up reports and incoherent, raging phone calls. The alcoholic's usual trail of wreckage. But he kept a few clients like me—not choosy, off the record, cash paying.

"Are you sure there are latents on here?" Goldfinger had removed the baton from its damp plastic bag, holding it gently with purple nitrile gloves. Sober, he was as good as anybody.

"Mine, for sure. I'm more interested in the original owner's."

"It's not a half-hour job." He looked up. "Tell you the truth, more like a day. They're not fast, in Washington. And it'll cost."

Ganderson was paying, but still. I sighed. "As soon as you can."

He opened it, slowly, and examined the entire length. "No blood."

"Not for lack of trying. They beat up a girl pretty good, but this didn't come out until I arrived, and I took it away."

"Nice."

For a moment my chest had hollowed out. I wasn't about to let Goldfinger know about Clara, but I shouldn't have mentioned her.

"If it's there, you'll find it," I said.

We agreed on a price, and I gave him a dead-drop email address—one I'd signed up for anonymously, and would use once. I always keep a few on tap, for convenience at times like this. I didn't want to have to chase him down if he decided to go on a bender.

When I left, Goldfinger was at his desktop vacuum chamber. The baton rested on two wire supports, to prevent further degradation of what prints might be there, and he had begun to fume it with cyanoacrylate. He looked comfortable, at home in his dank cinderblock cave.

"What should I do with it when I'm done?" he asked.

"Send me the results."

"No—the baton. Is it evidence?"

Hardly. I'd completely mucked up the chain of custody. "I'm not building a court case," I said. "Scrub it clean and sell it at the pawn shop."

———

Outside, the morning's off-and-on rain had slowed. Puddles shifted and flowed, rippled by occasional drops, gray under a lowering sky. Still, after Goldfinger's underground burrow, it felt like freedom. I set off for the Deaconess branch library, happy to walk the six blocks in open air.

I wanted to check my email. As usual, the operative constraints of my profession—that sounds better than paranoia, doesn't it?—turned a mundane task into a notable pain in the ass. Casual news reading is one thing, but I couldn't access personal accounts on any of my mobiles. Not without throwing them away afterward, because none had proxy routers installed and I didn't much trust the carriers anyway. Home had a laptop running up-to-date anonymizing software off encrypted memory, but that was too far in the other direction.

So I had to rely on that fading memorial to the printed word, the public library.

Deaconess was a small, vertical, brick-faced nonentity tucked between two apartment blocks. The tables were more than half filled, and I had a half hour wait for a computer. Browsing in the periodicals—for a small branch, they had a surprisingly well-stocked collection—I noticed the *Post*'s headline: "I SPIT ON YOUR GRAVE: AVENGER TARGETS BANKSTERS."

Whether from Clara or not, the story had come to life. I wondered what the mood was like on Wall Street that morning.

I finally got a computer around eleven. Too many job seekers and people who could no longer afford high-speed home internet, so the library terminals were always crowded. But there's no better place to borrow a connection that no one's paying attention to, and isn't recorded, and therefore even if subpoenaed is useless to prosecutors on fishing expeditions.

Librarians—the final defenders of our liberty.

I ended up with a homeless guy on one side, checking out spring fashion at **neimanmarcus.com**, and a junior high-schooler researching homebuilt bongs. Fortunately, I didn't have to be there long, just a few minutes to check my various addresses.

A hectoring email from Ganderson: "CALL ME NOW!!!!!" I guess he'd seen the papers, or maybe even read Clara's blog. Delete. Other useless messages, delete. Too much spam. Delete, delete, delete. A short message from Johnny—him I'd call back as soon as I could.

And finally, the one I was really looking for: "doing better. out of hosp tonite 7 they say. pick me up?? -c"

Absolutely. I sent back a simple "yup" and signed out.

Somehow, Clara had won me over. She was a looker, no denying, and smart, too. But this is the big city—four million women to meet every day, and plenty of them are sharp. Certainly I'd never had to go far whenever the room began to seem too empty.

Of course, few of them ever learned about the other half of my life. Maybe it was simply that Clara had been the first to get damn near all the way in. A relief, I had to admit, not to be constantly managing the lies and evasions and misdirection that made up my interaction with the civilian world.

But it was more than that. Clear-eyed, independent and making her own way in a difficult world—I'm not much for introspection, but Clara reminded me of, well, myself.

Minus all the deadly force stuff, presumably.

Leaving the library, I had a positive bounce in my step.

CHAPTER TWELVE

"Akelman wasn't an accident," Johnny said.

"We knew that."

"But it wasn't anarchists, either. Not the kind who despise personal property, anyhow."

I looked up from my burrito. "You know something, don't you?"

"If the government has any halfway-smart investigators, they'll be on it too."

"So we can count that out. What'd you find?"

We were outside, walking through Battery Park after buying lunch at the burrito cart parked across from MTA headquarters. The rain had stopped, replaced by another fine mist that dampened the tortilla no matter how I tried to keep it sheltered in its foil. The temperature hadn't budged past forty. The park was nearly deserted, except for soggy tourists near the ferry terminal.

"Akelman was a commodities trader," Johnny said. "Specializing in obscure metals. Like you said, last spring he bought up all the neodymium he could find."

"High-tech motors." I scoured my memory for details from the article or two I'd read at the time. "Disk drives."

"And lasers." Johnny took a huge bite but kept talking. Kind of disgusting. "And that's all I know, except that demand was strong and growing. Akelman could have come out quite nicely, but for the Chinese."

"Who announced a major new find in Inner Mongolia, about the same time."

"Right. Suddenly, supply wasn't tight at all. The price plummeted. Akelman lost his shirt." He was more than half done with his burrito already. "Or his investors did, anyway. They weren't happy."

"That was months ago. Long before he got hit by a car."

"Not so long. But Akelman sold mostly to second-tier institutional investors—midwestern pension funds, small-school endowments, that sort of thing. Bad news for them, of course, but you wouldn't expect a manager to jump up in a rage, drive two thousand miles, and run him over."

I rubbed my forehead, wet from the drizzle. "What are you telling me? It really was an accident?"

"Maybe not." Johnny fell silent for a moment while we passed one of the few other people in the park, a man in a Burberry raincoat glaring at his iPhone. "Akelman almost went under, and he seems to have made one last, big gamble, trying to win back the table."

"On what?"

"Cobalt."

I thought about that. "If he lost so much money on neodymium, he wouldn't have had the scratch to take a big position—and a small position wouldn't save him. I don't see it."

"That's true if he were buying the actual metal." He paused. "Is cobalt really a metal? I don't even know."

"Who *cares*?"

"Not me. The point is, cobalt was over the counter only, until a couple of years ago. The London Metal Exchange introduced futures in 2010, and there's a liquid market. That's where the action took place."

"Aha." Futures were simply a contractual promise to buy or sell product later—not the product itself. The advantage was leverage; using borrowed money as a multiplier, Akelman would have been able to place a dangerously large bet without having to stump up the entire purchase price at the beginning.

"So he went long on cobalt."

"Very, very long."

"How do you know this?" The exchanges report aggregate trading data at almost real-time intervals, but the names of the traders are concealed behind high walls of secrecy.

"It wasn't easy. They don't *want* people knowing this shit."

He wouldn't tell me, of course. Probably he paid someone off. We all have our sources, our cloaks of mystery.

"Okay, whatever. Akelman had bought up a huge stake in cobalt." I stopped. "Wait a minute, I see where this is going."

"Exactly."

"When he died, unexpectedly—did his fund really have to close it out?"

"Looks that way. Akelman Advisers, LLC, ran on the bone. No

other partners, hardly any analytic staff, just a couple of accountants, a secretary and Akelman's nephew, who'd taken a leave of absence from Carleton College last semester. When he died, no one was around to pick up the reins. They pretty much had to shut it down, and quick. Fiduciary duty. If it were the S&P 500, maybe they could have let it ride, but the cobalt was pure speculation. A huge liability if it tanked while nobody competent was in charge."

"They sold it *all* off? At once?"

"Yeah." Johnny shook his head. "At the opening bell, next business day. Every last contract, in one go. It started a minipanic, and cobalt went straight off the cliff."

I could see that. "Algos?"

"Mostly." Algorithmic trading, done entirely by computers at microsecond speeds, dominated every market now. Every program was different, conjured up by secretive teams of quant PhDs, but they had broad similarities. One was an extreme aversion to unusual or unexpected developments. When the Akelman fund's sell orders hit, hundreds of microprocessors simultaneously took that as a sign that something was wrong in cobalt, and they all must have immediately issued their own exits.

Not so long ago, human traders, yelling at each other in the pits, would have figured it out. Or at least not been so quick to pull the trigger. But those sepia-toned days are dead history.

"I get the picture," I said.

"Yeah." Johnny nodded. "*Someone* was short. In the previous forty hours, someone had bought a shitload of deep out-of-the-money puts. When Akelman died, someone made a fucking killing." He choked briefly on his *carnitas*, and I realized he was laughing. "I mean—"

"I know what you mean."

"Interesting, huh?"

"You haven't gotten to the useful part yet."

"Yeah, well, as to that—"

"Wait. You don't know who *did* it?"

"Not exactly." He finished his burrito and crumpled the wrapping. "Same as whoever profited off York when Marlett kicked the bucket. Small transactions, through the electronic markets. Hard to track. Option trades are easier to hide anyway, and they burned a lot of brush behind them."

"A subpoena would pry a name out of the exchanges fast enough."

"Yeah? You got one of those?"

"I mean, if the CFTC takes an interest, it won't be secret for long."

"The FSA—the Exchange is in London."

I knew that. "Point is, I can't believe the Riddler is whacking Wall Street whiz kids just for an edge on a long put. It's too obvious. Trading records would lead straight back to him."

"The firm executing most of the trades was Whyte and Fairlee."

"So you *did* find out who it was!" I swear, Johnny could be a pain in the ass.

"And the IB was Riverton Commodities."

"Well, shit, why didn't you just say so? Game over."

"Not so fast. The trail stops there. The options were held in a street name."

"Oh." For all record-keeping purposes, in other words, Riverton was listed as the nominee—even though the company was only serving as a broker for the actual owner. A convenience for the file clerks meant a solid wall of anonymity. "So all you've got is the broker."

"I looked Riverton up—they're a small shop. One of thousands. You could try a phone call, maybe."

"Maybe."

"But even if you found a single entity profiting from the Akelman selloff, so what?" We passed a trash can, and Johnny tossed in his spent wrapper. "It doesn't prove he killed anybody. It's hardly even circumstantial."

Good point. "Hmm."

The mist had gradually turned to light rain, which was now threatening a downpour. I turned up my collar, once more wishing for a hat.

"Still, if you're right—" I started.

"If?"

"I need to know who these guys are. A pissed-off Bolshevik is one thing. Cold-blooded murder for a few points of alpha, that's something else."

"Yeah." Johnny didn't seem to notice or mind that we were getting soaked. "It makes more sense, for one thing."

At the entrance to his building, we stopped under the awning before Johnny went inside.

"You seem a little distracted today," he said.

"I do?"

"Or not." He shrugged.

But he was right. Johnny watched the world around him far more closely than most people realized, and far more objectively than most people could manage. It might have been why he was such a good trader.

Well, that and a totally ruthless need to win at all costs.

"You got me," I said.

"What's up? Besides the girl?"

I just couldn't keep secrets. Not from Johnny. I looked at him. "I have a brother," I said.

"No shit? Really? You've never mentioned him before."

"I didn't know." The letter was still in my pocket. "His name's Dave. Separated at birth. He tracked me down through Children's Services records."

"How about that." Johnny thought about it, then grinned. "What's he do? Sharpshooter? Pool shark? Puts out oil rig fires? With your genes—"

"Auto mechanic. But, yeah . . . he races, too."

"I knew it. So, you talked to him?"

"Not yet."

A woman in a trench coat walked out of the building, collar clutched against the rain, on her cellphone. Taxis splashed past in the street. Johnny must have sensed I didn't feel like talking about it.

"Hey, I forgot," he said. "I meant to ask you something."

"Shoot."

He laughed. "Right. That's the question."

"Huh?"

"Three of my guys came in to work with guns today."

"Real weapons? Don't you have a policy on that?" I thought about the locker-room antics in Johnny's bullpen. "No offense, but your traders seem to be at the wrong end of the impulse-control spectrum. Do you really want them waving pistols at one another?"

"Oh, I made them lock up the guns before they started working. And they have legitimate permits. All you have to do is go down to One Police Plaza in a nice suit, show them proof of employment, and you're in."

"I hope this isn't some kind of trend." I zipped my wet jacket all the way up. "Life is going to be a lot more dangerous if every asshole banker who thinks he's the Terminator now has the hardware to prove it."

"It's the news, Silas. The guys are worried. They want to be ready if they end up in this avenger's crosshairs."

As if Wall Street weren't the OK Corral already. "So what do you want me to do about it—offer them a firearms safety refresher?"

"Nah, I was hoping you could give me a recommendation."

"A rec—" I stopped. "Oh, Johnny. You too?"

"They're all carrying Glocks. The seventy-seven model or something. Is that a good one?"

I sighed. "Seventeen. It's not bad. You could kill your girlfriend with it, by accident, real easy."

It took a few minutes, but I think I persuaded him to hold off. Handguns ought to be left in the hands of professionals, not hyperactive testosterone-driven alpha dogs. Maybe Walter had the right idea—retiring to a fisherman's shack on Little Torch Key was sounding better and better.

"Keep on Akelman," I said, in parting. "I need names."

"I'll see what else I can dig up."

"I'd appreciate it."

"But if you get to them first . . ." He hesitated. "Or if you just have some ideas even before you catch them, let me know, okay?"

I stared at him for a moment. "Jesus, Johnny." I shook my head. "I can't let you front-run a murder-for-money scheme."

"Why not?"

"Why *not*?"

"I mean, if we try our best to stop them." A thought occurred to him, and he pointed a finger at the air. "In fact, it would be better if you *did* prevent the next one."

"Of course it would."

"No, really."

"What do you mean?"

"Then we could just buy up the other side of their positioning trades—right before you shut them down! We make out like bandits. They lose everything, and go to jail."

"Um . . . got to think about that one." An ethics puzzler. Maybe I could write up a business-school case when this was all done.

"They lose, we win. What's more all-American than that?"

"You're right." I had to agree. "It's in the Constitution."

CHAPTER THIRTEEN

Riverton Commodities didn't look like much.

After leaving Johnny, I'd stopped in at an office services shop to copy, scan and email the copies I had of Hayden's forged identity documents. Walter had outdone himself, as usual—the work was beautiful. I was sure the DA would lock up Hayden immediately, and good riddance. One less crooked hedge fund manager to blight the world.

While I was there I bought some small rolls of tape in different colors. My cellphone collection was getting out of hand, and I figured marking them with color-coded tags might help me remember which was which.

Next, I stopped off at my apartment for a change of clothes. Finally, the trip to Riverton. They'd fronted the rigged trades on cobalt that had earned someone an extra-special payday when Akelman got run over, and I wanted to know who.

I wouldn't get anything by asking, naturally, but at least I'd get to see the place.

They had a suite somewhere in an eight-story building on Ninth Avenue in Chelsea, fifty-year-old brick and pressed cement, not far from the 23rd Street station. Coming up from the subway, I watched the pedestrian flow—people in suits, a few deliverymen, women wearing low black heels, not stilettos. A workaday neighborhood, more business than residential.

The lobby was tiny but nicely trimmed out, with buffed terrazzo floors and a shiny brass elevator. The Near East–looking woman behind the desk didn't speak much English and didn't want ID before waving me on. Friday afternoon, a courier coming out, another suit coming in—a typical, one-of-a-thousand office building, too far from any terrorist's ground zero to worry about.

I did notice a screen behind the guard's desk, though, with a four-panel surveillance camera view.

On the sixth floor, three suites. Doctors Hartzfeld and Logan were clearly dentists, from the fresh mint smell and—how unpleasant— the faint whine of a drill. Transoceanic Services, Ltd., might have been anything, but their windows were dark. Riverton's door, with custom dark-wood molding and a brushed-aluminum sign, indicated the upscale tenant here.

As did the access control panel: silver steel with an aqua-blue LCD. I pressed a large button next to it marked "Please Ring." A moment later the door clicked and I pushed through.

"Can I help you?" Riverton's receptionist was young and pretty and not too busy, unless she did all her work on the pink iPhone lying flat on the desk before her.

"Sure. You buy gold, right?"

"Um, yes . . . you mean gold contracts?"

"No. Gold. The real thing? The metal?" She looked at me blankly. "You know. It's heavy. And, well, gold colored?"

When I'd stopped at the apartment, I'd changed into business casual: permanently creased slacks, open-collared shirt, navy jacket. Also dark-framed, tinted eyeglasses, bronzer and a really heavy dose of Panzer cologne.

No one ever mentions it, but smell is a remarkably effective component of disguise. She'd remember the scent of Panzer forever, but forget what color my hair was in thirty seconds.

"We're a trading firm," she said. "Would you like to open an account?"

"Not really." I glanced around. "See, after the divorce, I ended up with some jewelry. Earrings and like that. Part of the settlement when we divvied it all up. What the freaking vampire lawyers didn't take, I mean. So I'd like to sell it."

"Oh, we don't buy actual gold." She smiled. "Just like contracts and futures and stuff."

"But the sign said—"

"That's not what it means. Not what you think."

"Oh."

Three more doors were visible, but one opened into a conference room with an empty walnut table. A dead-end hallway held four fire-safe file cabinets, all locked. An open closet at the end of the hallway seemed to be the server room; I could just make out a rack with several pieces of installed equipment, a mess of cables, and two keyboards stacked atop each other. LEDs glowed.

The interior office doors had keypads, same as the entry. I could see a pair of motion detectors, one covering the waiting area and front door, the other the hallway and one office. They were discreet, up in the ceiling, but not hidden.

And two cameras. One seemed to be pointed directly down at the receptionist, which might be why her shirt was buttoned all the way up.

The door to the corner office opened, and a big guy emerged. About forty-five, really good hair, a rugby-every-weekend sort of physique. His suit undoubtedly cost more than my car, though that might not have been saying much.

"What's up, Kels?" he asked. Short for Kelsey, I figured.

"I was just explaining we're not a retail store."

"Frank Riverton." He turned to me with his hand out.

"Mark Wilson." I gave his overly firm grip right back. "I got some gold jewelry to sell."

"I'm afraid you'd be better off up on 47th Street for that." He smiled. "But what are you planning to do with the proceeds? Because, I'll tell you, I've got some opportunities here you wouldn't believe."

His pitch ran almost three minutes, despite my obviously increasing uninterest. I finally extricated myself when even Riverton couldn't ignore the twitches, shuffling, glances at my watch, and so forth.

"Keep us in mind," he said. "The stock market's for suckers. Buying and selling *real* things—grain and metal and oil—that's how you make your fortune."

I decided Riverton had started as a pit trader and never

really left the rough-and-tumble. "I'll do that," I said. "Sorry to bother you."

"Not at all."

"Have a good day, now," the receptionist added.

"Thanks." I turned to go, and as I approached the door, a faint click sounded. "You, too."

CHAPTER FOURTEEN

I hate hospitals.

For all the usual reasons—horrifically ill or injured people you can only avert your eyes from, fear of death, lousy food, et cetera. But also because of my profession. If I'm on a patient ward, then either I screwed up and got hurt, or I screwed up and someone *else* got hurt. Either way, no fun and bad associations.

Maybe Clara picked up on that.

"Relax," she said. "It's not like someone's waiting for you with a bonesaw."

"Sorry."

"I think they checked me out already, but I should stop at the nurses' station on the way."

She was dressed in street clothes. A light leather jacket over an Avalon Shrike T-shirt, jeans and sandals—not the running outfit I remembered, which she must have arrived in. The same faded laptop carrier weighed down one shoulder.

"My roommate brought me my things this morning."

"Good of her."

"Him, actually. Yes, it was."

Him? I felt an odd ping in my chest. "You look good for an over-night patient." Her face was unmarked—the kicks must have been to the back of her skull—and her eyes were lively.

"There's wi-fi, so I was able to work most of the day."

"Really?" I followed her into the hallway. "Whenever I get a concussion, I seem to spend two or three days in blinding pain."

"I'm not sure why they kept me. I felt fine when I woke up."

St. Joseph's, unlike, say, some of the uptown teaching hospitals, tends to cooperate with the police. If the detectives wanted Clara boxed up for a day, for reasons of either protection or suspicion or both, they might have mentioned it to the supervising physician.

Or maybe they were just worried about cranial trauma. I should stop being so paranoid.

"We'll get a cab," I said. "Let me carry that."

"Sure." She shifted over the carrier bag.

"Jesus, what do you have in here? Cinderblocks?"

"Documents, books. You know. Work stuff."

"So much for the paperless office."

Outside, the evening air was cool and damp. The rain had stopped in late afternoon, and the sky had cleared halfway. Down York Avenue, up above the lights and noise, I could make out a misty gibbous moon.

"You're really feeling okay? No double vision? Loss of balance? Pain?"

"Just tired from being in bed all day." She tipped her head up and breathed deep. "Feels great to be out of there, actually."

"The reason I ask is, I've got something to do tonight—"

"Oh." She brought her face back down. "No problem."

"No, I . . ."

"I can make it on my own."

"That's not what I—that is, I mean." Christ, I sounded like I was fucking thirteen years old.

Which was annoying. Maybe I'd gotten spoiled. Being a veteran—especially of the black-ops sort—is kind of like being a firefighter after 9/11: women tend to be really interested.

I found my tongue. "Uh, do you want to come along? With me?"

"Sure." She smiled. "Where?"

"BitCon."

"The big con? What?"

"No. A hacker convention." I raised a hand, waving over a taxi from the row of them on 71st Street.

"Hackers?"

"They're not all social misfits. And some have useful skills."

"I bet."

"Anyway, I need to see a guy." I opened the cab's door for Clara, then followed her in. "It might even be fun."

In the backseat, Second Avenue flowing past outside the windows, I said, "You didn't tell the police about me."

"No." Clara shook her head, face dim inside the cab. "I thought about it, and decided you might not want me to."

"Thank you. It's . . . helpful to me that you didn't."

"You had nothing to do with it. You weren't anywhere around when they jumped me."

The concussion. If she'd remembered I'd come to her defense, she'd have told the detectives.

I started to thank her again, but that would just sound stupid. Instead I covered the moment by leaning sideways to check the cabbie's ID placard—a good habit even if you aren't dodging the law, what with the *Post* reporting at least one egregious scamster behind the wheel every week. "Omar Amirana," and the photo looked like him. So we probably weren't headed to the convention hotel via Queens.

"What do you remember?" I asked Clara.

"Of that attack? Almost nothing." I could see her tensing up, and I regretted the question. Her voice became higher and a little hoarser. "After we finished talking, I started off again. I'd been running for maybe thirty seconds when two men appeared from the trees. Then another. And then they started—punching me."

"I'm sorry." Which didn't make much sense, and seemed inadequate to boot.

"After that, it's just sort of blurred. Pain, I remember that, for sure. I must have blacked out, because the next thing I saw was the paramedics. One was shining a light into my eyes."

"Did you notice what they looked like?"

"No."

"Or anything they said? What the voices were like?"

"They were angry about the story."

She sat straight in the cab's seat, almost rigidly so.

"I'm sorry," I said again. "This is too painful. Forget it. Let's talk about something else."

"No, it's all right. The hospital sent in a therapist—I've talked it out. What I have to do is stop running it over and over in my head, like a tape loop. So it doesn't get burned in."

"I think that's right." I almost reached over, to take her hand or something. But I hesitated, and the moment was lost.

"Never mind." Clara shook her head, this time as if to clear it. "Change of topic?"

"Sure." Safer ground. The mood shifted.

"Akelman, Sills and Marlett."

"I saw your posts."

"There's more to it."

"Of course. Who killed them?"

"No." She braced herself as the cab turned a corner, then relaxed somewhat. "Start with, what did they have in common? Finance, sure, but that job description covers a lot of ground."

"Especially around here."

"I spent a few hours digging up performance data. They weren't just three money managers. They were three *really bad* money managers. Each one lost tons of money before they died."

"I might have heard that."

"*Tons* of money."

"I know."

She shook her head. "After the S& L crisis—like twenty-five years ago, when there was still some pretense of the rule of law—thousands of crooked executives were prosecuted. Hundreds actually did hard time. You know how many prosecutions the Justice Department has initiated *this* time around? After Wall Street drove the entire world economy into the ground?"

"In fact, I—"

"None. Not a single one."

"Really?"

"Zero," she said. "And if someone's upset about that statistic and is trying to even things up, well, all I can say is the cheering section is going to be huge."

"Big story, huh?"

"Massive!"

"I'll see it in the paper tomorrow?"

"The paper? It's all *over* the internet right now. Fox Business might run a segment. I had a call from *Hong* Kong."

Ganderson was not going to be happy. I hoped he didn't have any guns lying around when he started hearing the reports.

Clara touched my arm. "Why are you smiling?"

"Nothing." We were in one of Mayor Bloomberg's hybrid taxis. I'd never noticed how small the rear seats were. Clara and I were bumped right up against each other. "Nothing," I said again. "Just thinking."

She waited. "About?"

"Everyone is figuring this as a vengeance play, right? *Death Wish* on Wall Street."

"Like I said." She frowned. "You have to admit it makes sense. Motivation-wise."

"There's a counterparty on every trade," I said. "*Every* trade."

Silence for a moment. Omar slowed for a stoplight, then accelerated as it turned green.

"I don't believe it." Clara's voice was soft.

"Congress has some trouble with the idea, but you can profit just as easily on the way down as up. You *know* that."

"Holy jump." She went from zero to sixty in half a second, scrabbling through her bag for the laptop. "You're serious. It's not Charles Bronson, it's Gordon Gekko."

So she was an old movie fan, too. "Could be."

"Killing these guys just to puff up returns. *Awesome.*"

"Well—"

"How can I verify it? The commodities trader—okay, I could see that. But a mutual fund? Too liquid to matter, I'd think."

"Sills was batting a thousand a few years ago. So Freeboard closed the fund. Her death caused a lot more volatility than you might expect."

That is, the number of shares was fixed, unlike most funds. As a result, their value could rise and fall more steeply on what the economists like to call exogenous events—like, say, her murder.

"Who's doing it? Give me a name!"

"Whoa, hold on. I'm just speculating."

"No, I'm convinced. Come on, I've got to get this out before anyone else does." Clara had snapped open her ultrabook and was tapping the keys impatiently, waiting for it to boot.

I'd begun to regret my bush-beating strategy. If there was a murderous conspiracy behind the deaths, Clara's reporting would help flush them out—and could make them nervous, too, which might mean mistakes, all good for me. But they'd gone after Clara much faster and harder than I'd expected.

The warning attack, on her, was already too much blowback.

"Get some facts first," I said. "Okay? The story will be that much better if you've got proof, not just speculation. Look, it might be total coincidence after all. People die every day. Plain old law of averages means you'll always see some suspicious, but completely spurious, correlations."

"There's no such thing." She glanced at me. "'Law of averages.' Nothing but innumerate superstition."

Somehow my hand had come to rest on her shoulder. "That vocabulary. Wow."

Her eyes were about six inches from mine. She started to say something, then just smiled instead. The whole world narrowed in a great *whoosh*, and all I could see was her face. All I could hear was her breath. All I could feel was her leg, pressed against my knee, and her shoulder, under my hand.

Time stopped—

—and so did the cab. Abruptly pulling over to the curb.

"Flagstone Marriot," said Omar.

CHAPTER FIFTEEN

BitCon had spilled over onto the sidewalk.

Bemused bellmen watched as groups of twentysomethings smoked, argued and shoved odd bits of technical flotsam at one another. Those who weren't hunched over their phones, that is. People wandered in and out the revolving doors, new arrivals with their laptops and rucksacks, bored attendees taking a break from the sessions. A couple of young guys were selling something, maybe their startup, pushing business cards onto strangers.

It could have been any midtown convention—orthodontists or bond salesmen or philatelists—except for the general scruffiness of the attendees. And the death-skull RFID badges. And all the portable hardware, including at least two augmented-reality headsets and one guy with a flexible keyboard taped onto his jacket sleeve.

"Your friend is here?" Clara seemed amused but dubious.

"Acquaintance. Yeah, he's around somewhere."

"Are you registered?"

"No."

Indeed no. The authorities were here, too, undercover and

otherwise. In the old days, at DefCon or HOPE a decade ago, they weren't very good at blending in, and spot-the-fed was easy. Now the three-letter-agency crowd was experienced enough—or they'd simply hired enough of the hackers themselves—to conduct their surveillance more successfully. No way was I risking the micro-cameras and electronic profiling we'd encounter just walking into the ballroom.

"Hendrick doesn't come into the city often," I said. "And he barely leaves the hotel when he does. We'll find his room."

"Hendrick?"

"Dutch, I'm pretty sure. That annoying accent they have."

"He's a hacker?"

"No. Not like them." I pointed at two teenagers with BitCon T-shirts, each holding a tablet with one hand, typing with the other, and not saying a word. "Hacking isn't just about computers. Phone phreaks, biopunks, digital artists, you name it—they're all here."

"And Hendrick's part of that."

"In a way."

"So what does he do?"

"Locks." We pushed through a side door, and I looked around the Flagstone's lobby. "He's very, very good at locks."

I found a house phone and called the front desk—yes, it was only thirty feet away, but why not make it hard on whoever might look at the security videos someday? Hendrick, unworldly naïf that he was, had registered under his own name, which kept it simple. The operator connected me, and a woman answered.

"Hendrick's busy." Noise in the background—voices, music, sudden laughter.

"Tell him it's Silas."

"Whatever." She hung up.

I looked at Clara. "They're having a party, I think."

"Are we invited?"

"More or less."

"So . . ."

"She forgot to give me the room number."

Clara nodded. "Let me try."

She took the phone, went through the operator, and waited through what must have been seven or eight rings.

"Hendrick? No? Who are you? Listen, I found Hendrick's, like, backpack on the floor down here. I dunno, he left it on the table or something, it was just lying there. Some stuff was falling out, like tools and all, but I put it back in. Well, yeah, I think he'd like it back, that's why I'm *calling*, okay? You want me to bring it up?"

She put the receiver down. "Fifty-four-eighteen."

"Hey, that was pretty good."

"Journalism 101."

"They teach social engineering in J-school?"

"No one will ever tell you what you want to know unless you ask."

"A profound insight." We walked over to the elevator bank.

The fifth floor hallway was quiet, though we could hear the party noise closer to Hendrick's door.

The woman who opened it wore an orange badge on the chain around her neck, identifying her as one of BitCon's organizers. Apart from that she looked like a community-college student in from Great Neck—straight blond hair, Hollister jeans, a rumpled linen jacket over a plunging purple silk top.

"Silas," I said. "We just spoke."

"He does know you." She sounded like this had been a surprise. "You have his backpack?"

"Backpack?"

"Never mind."

Inside a half-dozen people stood around the room's desk, which had been pulled away from the wall. Two men were seated, across from each other, working intently. Brass, tools and mechanical parts littered the desktop. Music thumped from a docked iPod. Bottles and beer cans and half-empty cups seemed to occupy every spare surface.

"Hendrick," I said to Clara, pointing. Hendrick, who'd grown out his vandyke to an even more impressive point and apparently curled the mustache ends with wax, looked up long enough to glance at me, then went back to the lockset in his hand.

"Seven minutes," said a guy standing next to us, "and forty seconds, so far."

"What are they working?"

"Medeco. Right out of the factory box."

I made an impressed sort of grunt.

"It's a race?" Clara asked.

"Unofficial," said the bystander. "The public competition is tomorrow. They're just having fun."

Each of the seated men held an unmounted cylinder in one hand, with the tension wrench, and manipulated a pick in the keyway with the other. Hendrick's motions were sort of jerky, the pick moving in staccato twitches, while his opponent had a more deliberate style.

"It's not very realistic," said Clara. "Shouldn't the locks be installed on an actual door or something?"

"Think of it like fencing." I found a plastic bottle of soda and two cups. "Stylized. They're not pretending to be burglars."

"It's purely about the locks," said the man next to us, checking his stopwatch again.

"Medeco markets these as unpickable." And just as I said that, Hendrick's wrench hand twisted the cylinder. He swung the lock in the air and called, "Done!"

"8:52," said the timekeeper. "Not a record, but close. Fucking A, Henny."

The noise level rose as the bystanders called congratulations, refilled their drinks, slapped Hendrick's shoulder. His opponent scowled for a moment, then withdrew his tools and dropped the lockset onto the desk. The scowl turned to a grin. "We'll see what you can do tomorrow," he said to Hendrick. "Under pressure."

"Even faster." The words were accented, like I'd told Clara. He wore a bush jacket, covered with buttons and zips and epaulets.

"No way."

"Yes? You will put some money on it, then?" Hendrick rolled his shoulders. "Let us say, ten dollars for every second under nine minutes."

They stared at each other, Hendrick kind of smiling, his opponent frowning.

"No thanks," he said, finally.

Hendrick shrugged and stood up. When he turned around, he saw me again. The smile didn't go away, but it didn't widen, either.

"Silas Cade. What the fuck." Pronouncing it *fohk*. He stepped forward.

"Long time, Hendrick." I turned. "This is Clara, she writes for—"

That was it for introductions, because Hendrick took a short, savage swing at my face.

I hesitated, twisted a second too late, and the open heel of his hand grazed my jaw.

"Hey!"

But he didn't stop, following up with an elbow strike at my ribs. This time I reacted—block, counterstrike and a trap, catching his arm under mine and locking his elbow.

An ounce of additional pressure would have broken the joint. He grunted.

My free hand was on Hendrick's face, one further motion away from snapping his neck. For a moment we stood, not moving, in some sort of intimate embrace.

Then Hendrick laughed, and I shoved him away.

"You fucked up my mexican," he said, and tweaked the end of his mustache, getting the curl back right.

"*My* fault?"

"Thought you were better than that, man."

I looked at him. "What was that *about*?"

"Just to see if you are still in the game."

"Jesus, I could have broken your fingers." But he'd started with an open-hand blow, and the elbow. The piano player wouldn't really risk his hands.

People around us were staring.

"My friend," said Hendrick, gesturing at me and talking to them. Conversation slowly started up again. Someone took a heavy security padlock from the table—an Abus Granit, the sort you'd need a jack-hammer to break—and started working it with a shim. Attention drifted away from us.

"Pleased to meet you," said Clara, like this was all normal in her world. Who knows? Maybe it was.

"Yes." Hendrick looked her over. "A writer, Silas says? Perhaps I have read you. What do you write?"

"Financial opinion, risk management, that sort of thing."

"Perhaps not."

But they had more in common than I would have thought. Hendrick had a real estate broker's license—locksport didn't pay the bills—which meant he followed the big Manhattan developers, which meant, in turn, that he had to know something about the money flow. Clara had written up some shady deals, and she knew someone at some REIT whom Hendrick had run into once, and did she ever talk to Charley Cox? Who was doing that fifty-story mixed block in Brooklyn? Why sure, Charley was a good guy! Apart from that business with the lawsuit and the restraining order, but hey. Charley's partner was a dickhead, right, so there you go.

And so on. They were chattering away like stay-at-home moms at the playground. After a few minutes of standing around, I drained my soda cup and went looking for another.

"You know Hendrick long?" The woman who'd let us in poured us both another Sprite. She must have been another lock enthusiast—the computer guys could drink themselves blotto, but anyone serious about skills that relied on physical dexterity tended to be careful with the booze.

"Years."

She nodded. I observed, in a detached way, how her top's neckline gaped.

"He cracked an Abloy Protec last year," she said. "First time ever. The company didn't believe it, even after he put up a video on YouTube."

"He's good."

She drank from her cup and then held it at her mouth, looking at me over the rim. "What do you do, Silas?"

"Tax consulting."

"How interesting."

"The new FASB ruling on amortization—did you hear about it?"

"Um."

"Goodwill write-offs are going to have to be marked to market well within the acquisition window. My clients are furious."

She smiled. "I'm sure they must be."

Okay, I cheated. Any normal, sane person would have found that comment incomprehensible and uninteresting—unless they were in the business, which this woman sure didn't seem to be. So she was pretending. Why? Had she figured out how I really knew Hendrick? He and I had done some jobs together; you can probably figure out what kind, given our respective skill sets. Had he talked about them? Was I burned?

"Are you competing?" I asked.

"In the locks?" She laughed. "I'm not very good."

"Oh."

"Some of these guys, they're so *impressive*." She leaned forward, and I could clearly see a delicate pink bra.

"Um." I started to feel totally paranoid.

"How about you?"

"Me?"

"You don't look much like a locksmith." She smiled up. "More like mixed martial arts."

"I hit the Y now and then." I finished my Sprite, just for something to do.

"Oh, I suspect you do more than *that*."

It says something about my current state of paranoia that the obvious reason for her curiosity didn't occur to me until Clara appeared.

"I lost Hendrick," she said. "See that guy in the green sweater? He said he had a Zamok 37."

The woman shifted her gaze to Clara. "A Zamok? You're kidding."

"Some old lock. He claimed it came straight from a decommissioned Russian nuclear silo, but how believable is that?"

Pretty darn believable, apparently. The woman's eyes got big, and she practically ran to the cluster of people around Hendrick. Clara watched her go.

"Amazing."

"What?"

"That she found that lock more interesting than you."

"Huh?"

"I mean, she was all *over* you. Did she manage to fall out of her shirt? Not for lack of trying, not with that neckline."

Oh. I must have looked kind of stupid, with my mouth hanging open. But I recovered.

"They were kind of obvious, weren't they? Not like yours." I made a pointed show of checking.

Clara didn't blush. "Maybe you'll find out someday." She looked into my eyes, not blinking.

Another long moment.

Clara broke it with a laugh. "Anyway, Hendrick said he'd be happy to help you out. With whatever it is you asked him about."

That was the message I'd left him earlier that day. He'd called me back, saying he was in town, but we never connected directly. Thus the trip here.

"Which is what, exactly?" Clara continued.

"Huh?"

"What possible job might you have that requires a highly skilled locksmith?" She glanced over at Hendrick, gleefully disassembling the top-secret Soviet hardware while his fan club offered suggestions and comments. "Someone who can pick a Medeco in eight minutes?"

"My front door key sticks all the time," I said.

"Uh-huh."

"Sometimes it takes three tries before I can get in."

"That many?"

Damn it, there we were staring into each other's eyes again.

"Are you ready to go?" I asked.

Clara grinned. "Always," she said.

My phone rang.

Or rather, one of my phones. I'd put on the colored tape markers but already had forgotten which was which. Ganderson? Walter? Someone else? It took several rings as I checked pockets and pressed the wrong buttons.

Not exactly suave, and a little too distracting, considering the surprises my job was always offering up. I really had to figure out a better way of keeping in touch.

"Hello?"

"Cade? Is that you?" Ganderson's voice was so loud the cheap speaker got buzzy. "What the fuck are you doing at this hotel?"

I instinctively clapped my hand over the phone and looked around, wondering if he was somehow in the room. Clara watched, amused. I whispered to her, "Just a minute, let me get rid of this," then uncovered the handset.

"Ah, which hotel do you mean?"

"The Flagstone, you idiot. I can't believe you're there for the Galician Cooking Association Gala, so it must be BitCon. Aren't you too old for that?"

Classy, my clients. "Personal errand," I said. "Unrelated. How did you know I was here?"

"Following your phone. I'm outside. Something's come up, I need you out here—now."

Fuck. "Five minutes."

"Don't screw around. We're triple-parked." He hung up.

I looked at Clara. "Where were we?"

"On our way out of here." She crossed her arms. The Avalon Shrike logo—all lightning and fireworks—pulled across her breasts. Jesus.

"It's a client," I said. "He apparently needs some hand-holding."

She didn't say anything, just uncrossed her arms and held out her own hand. A moment passed.

Oh, I was torn.

"Dammit, he's paying cash money."

Clara shrugged. "Your business."

"Look, what would you do if Warren Buffet called and offered the exclusive of a lifetime?"

"Invite you along, of course."

Oops, walked into that one. "Sorry, too dangerous. It won't take long. Wait for me."

"Sure." She put down the cup of Sprite. "Not here, though. I'll be in the bar."

"With *this* crowd?"

"Don't worry, I'll buy my own drink."

"Just let me say good-bye to Hendrick," I said.

CHAPTER SIXTEEN

I got out of the elevator on the mezzanine, found the fire stairs, and exited on 54th around the block from the main entrance. It was turning into a pleasant evening, still damp but not too cool, and enough people were on the sidewalk that I could drift anonymously back to 53rd.

Ganderson's limo was obvious, even with blacked-out passenger windows. It was a silver Range Rover LUX, waxed and gleaming in the street's neon, with aftermarket chrome on the wheels. The Connecticut livery plate read "GANDY."

Like it was still 2008. I sighed.

I stepped into the shadows of the building, close to a group of smokers, and watched for two or three minutes. The Range Rover just sat there, and if another team was in place, they weren't moving either, so I couldn't spot them.

What the hell. I pulled out the G-phone and hit redial.

"You said five minutes!"

"I got held up. Are you driving?"

"What? Of course. I *told* you that."

"Come round to 54th Street, by Ezra's Bagels. I'll meet you there." I clicked off as he sputtered.

After a moment the Rover's turn signal came on, and it moved slowly into traffic, heading for the corner. I went the other way, faster now. By the time Ganderson's ride appeared on the back side of the block, I was already there, across the street. When the SUV slowed in front of Ezra's, I ran across the traffic lanes, dodging yellow cabs, and rapped on the rear window, behind the driver.

The lock clicked, so I opened the door and stepped up and in.

"What was *that* all about?" Ganderson had to slide over, but the interior had only one seat row, so there was plenty of room. I scanned for weapons, bombs, other hazards—didn't see anything. The driver was on the other side of a heavy glass window, watching me in the rearview mirror. I waved hello.

"I think that's my question," I said.

Ganderson grunted, then said to the air, "Drive around for a while."

"Yes, si—" The driver's voice, over an intercom, was cut off as Ganderson jabbed a switch on the seatback in front of him. But the vehicle started up again, toward the left turn lane.

"There's been a development," Ganderson started. He seemed even bigger in the closed space of the vehicle. His chalk stripe looked like a Brioni, five figures easy.

"Hold on." I adjusted my jacket, making sure the Sig was handy. "Tell me again how you tracked me down. I deliberately disabled GPS on that phone."

"The carriers know where you are." Ganderson rolled his eyes. "They have to, that's how cellphones *work*."

Yeah, yeah. "I know that. But it's not public data."

"No." He chuckled. "But we're not the public. Anything's available if you know who to ask. And how much to pay."

"Fuck this." I shook my head. "I'm going back to carrier pigeons."

"What?"

"Never mind. What's so important you drove into Manhattan chasing after me?"

"Not chasing you. I was leaving the office, not far, and it seemed easier this way."

Interesting, that he felt a need to defend himself. Ganderson wasn't quite the taipan he wanted to be.

"Well, here we are. You said frog, et cetera." I waited.

"The story's out."

"Story?"

"The three dead guys? That you were supposed to be solving? *Before* the entire world put the puzzle together?"

"Oh." I nodded. "Well, it was always going to be hard to keep secret. There're still a few smart people left in real journalism."

"Not real reporters," he said. "Blogs and crap like that. But it'll be all over CNBC soon enough."

"How's it playing?"

"What you'd expect. A few coincidences and Drudge is already talking Earth Liberation Front."

"Huh?" Ganderson was making less sense than usual. I noticed a discreet minibar tucked behind the driver's seat and wondered if he'd been drinking.

"You know what I mean. Left-wing terrorists."

"Okay."

"And that's the responsible media." *Drudge?* But he didn't let me interrupt. "It's just what you'd expect everywhere else. Most of the liberal news is making it sound like Akelman, Sills and Marlett were the *bad* guys, and the killer was doing the world a favor."

"Well, I wouldn't go quite that far—"

"Damn right not." Ganderson patted his suit jacket. "I'll tell you one thing, the bastard better not come after *me*. I'll blow the fucker out of his boxers."

Jesus Christ. "You're not carrying, are you?"

"Fuck yes, I am!" He pulled out the .45 he'd lent me at the range, laser sight and all. "Me and every other banker I know. We're not going down easy."

He must have had a hell of a tailor, to disguise that monster under his arm.

"Put that away." I'd begun to think the most dangerous place in Manhattan was the inside of this car. "Let's not have any accidents."

"I'm *ready* for the son of a bitch." Ganderson grinned but reholstered his cannon.

The Rover trundled along. I still didn't see what was so important. "What do you want me to do? Go after the reporters?"

"Let's have a status update. How close are you?"

"Following some leads. Look, I know you want the guy duct-taped and on your doorstep yesterday, but it's going to take time."

"We need to get out ahead of this." Ganderson drummed his fingers on the door's windowsill. "If the perp walk happens tomorrow morning, that's one thing. If it's going to be next week, I need a whole different media strategy."

"I'm not exactly scheduling Amtrak arrivals."

Ganderson nodded. The Rover slowed for a light, then started up again on the green. The interior was remarkably quiet.

"Media strategy isn't my area," I said. "But what if you suggested it's Muslim extremists? Lakshmi-al-Jazeera or whoever the hell. Say it loud enough and some wannabe radical cell will claim responsibility, just for air time. That buys you a couple of days."

"Why would al Qaeda care about investment banking?"

"Well, they probably got wiped out like everyone else in the crash."

"Oh, for——"

"Or how about . . . isn't loaning money with interest contrary to the Koran? But who cares? It's not like TV pundits need actual facts to work with."

"Hmm."

I considered telling Ganderson about the attack on Clara, but professional habit kept me quiet. It never does any good to let clients into the process. They already think they're smarter than I am; there's no need to give them chances to prove it. Anyway, given his current mood and the fact that she was the source of the stories, the further away he stayed, the better.

"Motivation seems important, though," I said. Time to move the ball downfield. "Is it possible the killings have nothing to do with terrorism at all?"

"What do you mean?"

"Maybe someone's taking out players to rig the game." He looked at me blankly. "For money," I said. "To screw up the markets in predictable ways. To *trade* on."

"That seems unlikely." But his expression—what I could see of it, illuminated only by the signs and headlights we passed—was thoughtful.

"Just an idea."

"Tell me what you have so far."

And we went round that mulberry bush for a while. I don't know why. Do they demand updates from their accountants, checking while the ledgers are reconciled? Do they call down to their factories, asking how the lines are running? You'd think CEOs, of all people, would understand how to delegate, step back and let the experts get their jobs done, but no.

I prevaricated and offered generalities, and finally Ganderson tired of the game. I noticed we were back in front of the Flagstone.

"I want results," he said in parting. "You've pocketed half the fee already, and so far you've got shit."

"That was just walking around money." I scanned the block as best I could before opening the door. "Don't worry. I'm one hundred percent on this case. Nothing else has even one iota of my attention."

"What? That's not—"

I cut him off by slamming the door, then moved to the curb without looking back.

The hotel bar was surprisingly uncrowded. Too expensive for the hackers, I suppose, and the Galician Cooks must have been preparing their own drinks. So it only took about ten seconds to determine that Clara was not there.

"Avalon Shrike? Sure, she was here." The bartender remembered her a little too well for my liking. "Are you Nesbert?"

"Um." Nesbert?

"You look like she said, but . . ."

I caught up. Clara was being careful, not using my real name. "Yeah, that's right. Nesbert." Ugh. Her little joke on me.

"She left you a note." He pulled a folded paper from his apron pocket.

"Thanks." I slipped him the first bill I found in my pocket—a five. His lucky night.

New lead—have to file. Sorry couldn't wait. Call me

I couldn't remember the last time I'd been stood up—or the last time it mattered, at least. I felt annoyed, then almost had to laugh at myself.

"She leave with anyone?"

"Nope. Just up and gone." The barkeep looked sympathetic. "Sorry, dude."

Outside, rain had begun again. People scurried along under umbrellas, heading for home. It was late and dark and wet.

I needed a good night's sleep, anyway.

CHAPTER SEVENTEEN

Next morning, sunshine.

I did some isometrics and core exercises on the floor beside my futon, thought about a shower, decided not to bother, and pulled a fleece jacket on over the T-shirt I'd slept in. The refrigerator yielded some old yogurt, a half head of green leaf lettuce, and a Japanese red-bean bun. Good enough.

The bachelor life is nothing to boast on, really.

When I finally got around to turning on my many cellphones, I had three messages. All from Clara.

"I thought this was the hotline! Answer the damn phone, already. I'm sitting on *news* here."

Okay, okay. I glanced at the number—it matched what she'd given me three days ago, check—and hit redial.

"What's up?"

"Where have you been? It's nine-thirty—I've been outside here for two hours."

"Another power breakfast. Outside where?"

"Simon Faust's building. They won't let me in, and now there's a

WNYJ truck setting up. Some beauty queen moron from *NewsFlash Six* is going to scoop me."

"Simon Faust." It took a moment. "Neon Rain Capital?"

"Of course."

"Sorry, he's not in my Rolodex. I don't think I can help with an interview."

"No." She sounded impatient. "He's *next*."

Talking to Clara, I was always two steps behind. "Next?"

"Just rumor, but everyone seems to have heard it this morning. The Banker Buster's got him in his gun sights."

"Shit."

I hadn't heard that nickname for the killer, either. The Street just moved too fast sometimes.

But Faust? He made sense. Neon Rain was infamous for buying up GM debt at its nadir in 2008, right before the government stepped in and bailed out Detroit. With federal guarantees, the bonds shot back up. Faust went in at pennies on the dollar, and sold at eighty-seven cents six months later—an almost pure transfer of taxpayer dollars from Uncle Sam to Neon Rain's accounts. That put Faust right up into the megayacht class of billionaires, briefly made him every congressman's favorite whipping boy for soulless Wall Street greed, and brought in some eight billion from eager new investors.

Then he went all bullish on the euro, and lost damn near every penny. Widows, orphans and college endowments across the country were flattened. If the Banker Buster did shoot him, the cheering would be audible in North Dakota.

"So who says he's the next target?"

"Everyone. No one. You know how rumors fly on Wall Street."

"Exactly. Some dope makes a joke on the squawk box, and suddenly it's the lead headline on Bloomberg."

"If Channel 6 thinks there's a story, there's a story."

"Where are you again?"

"Faust's loft in Tribeca, at the corner of Halston Street and Washington. Guards at the door are keeping everyone out."

"Is there a crowd?"

"Not really. A couple of other freelancers I know, and some passerbys."

"Passersby."

"What*ever.*"

And she was the writer, not me. "You called me three times," I said. "Once would have done it, if you were just passing along gossip."

She laughed. "I was hoping you'd help me get in."

"Are those guards armed?"

"Mace, sticks, radios and handcuffs. But no guns that I can see."

So she was paying attention, at least.

"And you're thinking, what, I'll just punch them out and you can step over the bodies?"

"More or less. Come on, Silas, we'll manage something."

I'd been planning to work on Riverton today, but Clara's offer sounded more fun, if nothing else. "Twenty minutes," I said. "I'm not that far away."

On Faust's plane of existence, there'd be several houses: a seaside monstrosity in Sagaponack, a compound on St. Bart's, a castle on the

Loire, and so forth. But he'd need a pied-à-terre in Manhattan for those nights he didn't want to take the helicopter back to Long Island. On Halston Street he'd be a few blocks from work, two doors from Meryl Streep, and safe from striving riffraff everywhere else in the city. With nice river views over the Hudson, too.

Indeed, his address was a converted industrial building with Deco trim and beautifully pointed brickwork. Halston was actually blocked off by a pair of stainless-steel posts set in the blacktop—the kind of barrier you find at the mayor's mansion or on alleys on Sutton Place. In theory the street was still a public thoroughfare, but wads of cash had effectively privatized it.

Two television vans were now parked in front, dish antennas raised and pointed to the sky, cables already snaking this way and that on the sidewalk. A small group eddied nearby: nannies with Peg-Perégo strollers, a pair of runners, businessmen in casual jackets. The day was sunny and clear, washed by yesterday's rain, not too cool.

A patrol car had arrived as well. One officer was at the building's shaded entrance, talking to the guards, who were just as Clara had described, and a blond woman who was eye-catching even at fifty yards. The other officer leaned against his door, scanning the crowd.

I gave him some distance and found Clara near the Channel 6 truck.

"Silas!"

"Hey, Clara." Sunlight gleamed in her hair and on her aviator sunglasses. She had one of those bluetooth earpieces in place, indicator LED aglow, and a two-handed grip on her phone, rapidly thumbing in text. "Anything happen yet?"

"It's on Fox local. Chatter's picking up online."

"Do you really think something's going to happen *now*?"

"The police wouldn't be here otherwise. They must know something."

"No more than you, I bet." I looked around. "Those uniforms are just community relations—the kind you get in neighborhoods like this. If they really expected action, there'd be a tactical van and a SWAT team. Not to mention the mayor."

"Maybe." She didn't look convinced.

More bystanders were drifting in, along the periphery. I heard a helicopter, but it kept going and disappeared.

"I can see why Faust would be a nice target," I said. "But what about the theory that someone's actually trying to make money off his death?"

"I don't know. All he's done lately is get divorced."

"Yeah, that's right." Celebrity-news fodder. When a billionaire like Faust decides it's time to move on, the tabloids move in—and his soon-to-be-ex-wife had obliged in spades, being much younger, beautiful and ruthlessly determined to annul the prenup by selectively leaking discreditable stories about their married life until Faust caved. She wanted fifty million. So far she'd made public his abuse of servants and pets, the bondage room, and his racist disparagement of half the New York political establishment.

Faust was hanging tough, though.

"I think he's mostly in cash." Clara glanced at me. "Too many distractions for deal making."

I could understand about distractions.

"Where were you going after last night?" I asked.

"It didn't pan out." She shrugged. "Sorry about that."

"The bartender seemed to like you."

"He was sweet."

It was just about impossible to imagine anyone ever saying that about me, but I tried for a moment anyway.

"How about—you want to try again tonight? I'll buy?"

"Sure." She smiled.

I banked that, then looked around. "Anything else happening?"

"No." She turned toward the television truck. "Hey, Darryl, you on yet?"

A young man poked his head from the van's rear door, which he'd left open. He had an Amish-style fringe beard, a bowling shirt and a wired headset, one earpiece in place and the other pushed up his head.

"Taping."

"Are you broadcasting?" I peered past Darryl, fascinated—like everyone—by the racks of electronic equipment and camera gear.

"Nah. Just another stakeout. Vivianna thought she might be able to talk her way in, though."

The woman at the entrance, no doubt. Good strategy to send her over to the cops, rather than Darryl.

"She's your talking head?"

"Vivianna's smart," said Darryl. "More than most on-air reporters."

"Uh-huh. I can see that." I stepped away from the truck, letting Clara follow, moving out of Darryl's earshot—not that he'd hear much over the multiple broadcast and sideline channels he had running.

"Friend of yours?" I asked.

"We met in school. He's a nice guy."

"And a good contact, to be sure." I squinted at the building's upper story. "Let me guess—Faust's got the penthouse."

"Of course. Fifteen thousand square feet, four full baths, three fireplaces, and a private deck with rooftop garden. LEED certified, very green. The taxable value is twenty-one point four million." Clara was deep into her phone.

"On the assessor's database, are you?"

"No, the realtor that sold it to him last year. The video tour is still online."

"I'm sure it's gone through a tear-out since then."

"Maybe."

"Guys like Faust need to piss on their trees."

"I thought you didn't know him."

"They're all alike."

In the sunshine I was getting warm. I took off my jacket and held it over one arm. The pockets sagged, heavy from my cellphone collection.

Across the street Vivianna disappeared through the entrance, one guard taking her in and the other resettling himself across the doorway.

"She got in," I said.

"What?" Clara looked up. "Hey, you're right." She quick-stepped back to the van. "Darryl? Do you have visual?"

He'd pulled out a camera trunk of ballistic aluminum to sit on, focused on the raft of controls and slider boards. He gestured meaninglessly and didn't say anything, other hand pressing the head-set to his ears. On the largest screen, right in front of his face, a low-res feed showed vague and unrecognizable shapes in a jagged bounce.

"I didn't see a cameraman with her," I said—quietly, not to disturb Darryl's concentration.

"Spy tech. The audio's easy—pinwire mic and a Nextel. But cameras have become so small recently that people have started carrying them in, too."

"Right." Darryl had one ear for us after all. "She's got a filament lens inside the jacket pin. The transmitter's on her belt. Looks like a cellphone holster if you're not paying attention."

"Is that even legal?"

"She tells them they're on the record." He shrugged. "And shows them a little microcassette recorder, twenty years old. They draw their own conclusions."

"That seems just over the line from entrapment."

"We're not taking pictures for court." Darryl worked some buttons, and the screen view sharpened. "Honestly, we're not even taking them for on air—the video quality is too poor. But it's nice to have a record, and this way Vivianna doesn't have to write notes."

Knowing what I was looking at, the picture became a little clearer. Not moving much, a shiny surface with a line down the middle and a panel to one side with a block of round buttons—just as I figured out Vivianna was inside an elevator, the doors slid open in front of her.

It was odd, watching with no sound. The scene was open and

bright, with indistinct objects lurching this way and that as Vivianna walked and turned. When she stopped, it seemed to be in a
living room—white everywhere, long black couches, color on the
walls that must have been art, and floor-to-ceiling windows, drapes
pulled all the way to either side.

"What are they saying?" asked Clara, but Darryl ignored her,
still working the board, apparently trying to improve the reception.

Now Vivianna had turned to face a new figure: a trim tall man,
middle-aged, graying hair cut almost but not quite too short for
fashion. He reached out to shake Vivianna's hand—the pinhole
camera lens distorted everything around the periphery of its view,
and it looked even more bizarre when he abruptly raised her hand
to brush his lips over it.

"Did he just kiss her hand?" Clara shook her head. "Yech!"

I filed a mental note under Clara, Preferences, Physical Contact.
"Is it Faust?"

"Probably. The picture's not great. But who else would be up
there?"

They were standing next to the loft's vast window now, and Faust
swung one arm, displaying the view. We didn't need audio, the dialogue was easily imagined: "You can see all the way to Connecticut
from here." "Amazing." "I'd call it a million-dollar view, but—"
chuckle "it cost a lot more than that!"

Vivianna dutifully turned to look out the window. Instead of the
Hudson, it faced north, across the other loft buildings of the neighborhood, then uptown. Most of New York's spires were visible.

"Lean down," I murmured.

Clara looked at me. "What?"

"If Vivianna were to lean forward, the camera would see the street below the window—where *we* are. We could wave. Wouldn't that be fun?"

Well, Darryl laughed, at least.

Inside, Vivianna and Faust seemed to be talking—or he was, gesturing widely, face animated.

"Can't you put them on speaker?" Clara said. "This is kind of pointless."

"Oh, sorry." Darryl reached to the controls.

CR-ACK!

For a second, cognitive dissonance—the shot came from outside, up above us, but I saw the window behind Faust, on-screen, go opaque with spider crack. Then another shot, this one blowing out the window, and the image became a tumult of motion and noise as Vivianna fell or dived for the floor.

"What the fuck?" Darryl, staring.

"Someone . . . what . . . shit . . . *gunshots?*" Clara, ducking into the van, looking back and out.

I spun, eyes raised, searching for the shooter. In my peripheral vision I noticed the cop by the cruiser doing the same.

A third shot, and I had him. Directly across from Faust's building, an old warehouse, four stories, with rows of nineteenth-century windows on each floor. At the top, one was open—all the others reflected sun or blue sky, but this one was black and empty.

"Up there!" I tossed Clara my jacket. "Stay in the truck!"

The patrolman and I arrived at the sniper's building simultaneously. He had his sidearm drawn, holding it pointed down, finger outside the trigger guard. We crashed through the door into a marble-and-mirrors lobby. Two uniformed doormen had come around the security desk, both staring. One held a cellphone like a walkie-talkie, the way construction workers do, midcall.

"Stairs?" The cop shouted at them. One pointed to a door alongside the elevators. "Back entrance?"

"Through here." The other gestured behind him, to a corridor leading away from the desk.

The cop looked at me. "Who are you?"

"I'm just—"

"Stay here! Don't do *anything*." He glanced at the doormen. "I'm going after him. Can you shut down the elevators?"

"Sure."

"Do it now. Freight elevator, too, if there is one." The man with the phone clicked off and went to the desk, reaching for an unseen panel. "No one's a hero, right? Backup will be here in a minute or two. Someone comes down the stairs, you just watch him go."

The officer disappeared into the back corridor. The remaining three of us looked at each other.

"All residences up there?" I asked.

"Yeah." The shorter doorman had dark circles under his eyes and that worried-about-my-green-card look. He appeared willing to assume I was authority of some sort, and I was willing to let him. "And the landing pad."

"*Landing* pad?"

"For the private helicopters."

Of course. "Who's on the fourth floor, about halfway down that way?" I pointed, more or less in the direction of the open window.

"No one. Three units and they all remain empty."

"Unsold?" The building looked too clean, too sparkly, to have been renovated more than a year ago.

"I think that is right."

I could hear sirens now, but not close.

"You should stay behind the desk," I said. "Keep—"

A sudden crashing from the back hallway, then an unintelligible shout—and three gunshots, almost inseparable.

"Fuck." I moved toward the hall, while the doormen sensibly dived for the floor.

The sniper came out just as I cleared the edge of the desk. For an instant we stared at each other.

It was the man from the park—the lean, stubbled one who'd led the attack on Clara.

He wore a button-down shirt and khakis, straps of a small backpack over both shoulders—and a handgun held in both hands, right in front of his chest, pointed outward.

His surprise at seeing me may have slowed him down, a fraction of a second, just enough. I was still moving, at speed. He got a shot off, but I'd already begun to drop and the round went high. I hit him hard, midcenter. We tumbled, his torso catching the corner of the desk.

Wiry as a snake, he somehow managed in that halfsecond to twist, elbow me in the head, and land on top when we hit the floor.

Another blow to my stomach and he rolled away, already coming to his feet.

Jesus, he was *fast*.

BR-A-A-APPPPP!

The front windows of the lobby exploded inward, bullets shredding the plaster wall just to the sniper's left. He jerked his handgun up, tracking the new threat, and fired back twice. I lunged off the floor, punching toward his groin, but he moved just enough to deflect the blow with his hip.

Another fusillade came from the street.

Perception shifted to frame by frame. I could almost see him thinking it through—an instant of indecision—as I punched with my other hand. He blocked my second strike as easily as the first, then abruptly spun backward and somehow flipped back into the hallway. Like we were in some Jet Li sequence—fucking *ballet*. And then he was gone.

No movement. Noise came down the long tunnel of my blown hearing. The doormen were huddled behind the desk, but no blood was visible so I figured they were unharmed.

I got up and ran after the gunman.

Stupid? Positively, in retrospect. In the moment—training, adrenaline, anger, who knows why—I was going to apprehend the cocksucker. He'd been within a whisker of killing me, and I'd slipped the bonds of rationality.

The policeman was lying fifteen yards in, crumpled in front of a steel exit door, under the red alarm connected to its push bar. The sniper couldn't have gone over him and out because the alarm would be ringing. That meant the other way:

Up.

I hit the stairwell running. If he was one floor up and waiting to shoot me, *fuck* him—but he wasn't.

Four flights—twenty seconds. Breathing hard when I got there, yes. The metal door in the headhouse was only slightly ajar. Finally, some sensibility returned, and I stopped for a moment to think.

The walls appeared to be utilitarian cinder block, which could certainly stop handheld calibers. I stepped to the hinge side of the door, reached up and—while flattening myself against the wall—shoved it open from the top corner.

No reaction.

The roof—what I could see of it—was black membrane, with a walkway of duckboards meandering over to a set of huge, beige, humming HVAC units. A three-foot parapet covered over with patinized copper walled the edge.

My hearing had begun to return, and that's when I noticed a slow whine, gradually accelerating and getting louder. I stood still, puzzled. A dynamo? An engine? A motor of some sort . . .

A *helicopter.*

I recognized the sound just as the rotors began to turn, slowly whipping the air.

A private helipad, the doorman had said. Either the assassin had arrived by air, or he was taking advantage of someone else's ride.

But if he was operating a helicopter, he wouldn't have two hands on a firearm, covering this doorway. Right?

I went out in a combat tuck, low and fast, off the edge of the duckboards and rolling behind the air conditioners. No shots. The chopper's noise rose to full pitch, overwhelming the rooftop, while rotor wash began to blow dirt and bits of debris my way.

It was a—shit, I don't know, I've always hated the fucking things. A little executive model, dark blue, with a bubble cockpit and a tiny passenger area behind the pilot. Inside the plexiglass I could clearly see a single occupant—the gunman—who was indeed too preoccupied to think about shooting at me.

On the other hand, the bird was about to fly. One skid lifted from the roof in a tentative way. The engines whined even louder.

I sprinted toward it.

The next seconds were a fractured blur.

The assassin saw me coming and jerked the cyclic. The helicopter surged upward just as I arrived. Instead of crashing the door, I collided with the skid, even as the entire craft began to glide horizontally above the roof. Knocked off balance, I grabbed wildly, not thinking—

—and a moment later I was yanked into the air, the skid in my armpit, dangling like a hooked fish as the chopper shot over the edge of the roof.

My whole body swung wildly, this way and that, as the gunman bobbed the helicopter. He must have known I was there, my weight screwing up the flight vectors. A kaleidoscope of the buildings, the street, the tops of cars, the white faces of people staring upward, all flashed past my eyes.

We seemed to be over the West Side Highway, but on top of everything else, some sort of inner-ear dislocation had completely bollixed my sense of up, down and sideways. Wind and the roar of the chopper's turbines overwhelmed my hearing.

I thought I saw flashing lights below, maybe a fire truck or a police van. Just a glimpse—

The landing gear jerked under my arm, and I almost slipped off.

I yelled and couldn't hear myself, grabbing at one arm with the other to lock my grip on the skid. Pain flared down my side as I tightened the death grip, squeezing it into my armpit.

Uptown? My thoughts were broken and unconnected. Heading north.

The helicopter dived, and for an instant I felt weightless. Cars and light poles rushed up—then the pilot yanked us into a screaming climb, and the skid was almost pulled from my hold. I gasped, swinging wildly, a monkey on a bucking rope.

I looked up, and saw the pilot's door start to open. Not good. One-handed, he could easily point a pistol down and fire until he hit me. I was in no position to do anything except cling and pray. The helicopter's turbines screamed.

Ahead I saw that monster parking garage on the river, at Houston. We were only a little higher—I could see the bizarre brilliant green of the soccer fields on its roof, white lines forming a bull's-eye in the center.

Uh-oh. The pilot apparently had a very bad idea, because we immediately lurched, dropping to a height that would skim the fence around the artificial turf.

It rocketed toward us at a hundred miles an hour.

He was trying to scrape me off, like mud from his boots. I yelled and swung my legs up, twisting away from the steel spikes. The chopper bucked again, the lunatic pilot taking us right between two light poles, no more than two yards of clearance on either side. Ten feet above the roof—if we hadn't been moving so fast, I could have almost stepped off, as if I were disembarking from a train.

We cleared the far side, rising slightly, and I looked up again.

Above me the madman's door swung wide, opened by centripetal acceleration as the helicopter turned sharply. His hand appeared, holding the pistol.

I looked down and saw the bank of the Hudson, dropping away to blue choppy water.

I let go.

CHAPTER EIGHTEEN

"Ouch."

"Sorry."

"Hey . . . fuck! That *hurts*!"

"Try to stop moving around."

"Ow!"

Me, embarrassingly enough. Shock endorphins had worn off long before, and all I had now was pain and self-recrimination.

"I don't see anything except this bruise." Clara gently probed my ribs.

"It's a *big* bruise."

"If anything was broken, you'd be hurting worse."

Not much of a bedside manner, though I had to agree with the diagnosis.

"It must have been fifty feet to the water," I said.

"You were lucky."

And that was the understatement of the year.

I'd landed only about twenty yards from the shoreline, slamming into the water like a rock. But I didn't lose consciousness, so I struggled to shore and dragged myself up onto the boulders that formed the base of the river wall. Then I just collapsed, utterly spent, for about five minutes, until I realized nobody knew I was there.

The parking garage that had almost been my doom was three stories tall, sitting in between the greenway and the Hudson's edge. The entire incident, from the gunman's first shots at Faust all the way to my swan dive, had lasted a few minutes, tops. No one on the West Side Highway saw me fall, because the garage was in the way, and no one else noticed or realized what was happening or believed their eyes if they did see it.

Emergency responders were focused on the dead and the wounded back at the scene. Clara and anyone else thinking about me would be trying to track the helicopter, which was probably headed across New Jersey, at top speed, toward the wilds of eastern Pennsylvania.

While I figured this out, I began to shiver. I pushed myself to my feet, walked over to the cycling path and stood, watching bicyclists and joggers and traffic go by.

Home was too far to walk, if I even wanted to go there. Official attention would be keenly focused on my role in the escapade. Clara had more sense than to start lying outright about who I was, so it would only take a question or two before the police had my name and address. Detectives were probably talking to my neighbors already. It didn't matter that I'd been on their side. Unless they had evidence revealing the assassin's identity, they'd be chasing every other lead, with all the urgency that only a spectacular attack on the very rich could command.

I still had my wallet, and the money inside was usable—nobody likes the look, but all that new anticounterfeiting technology makes for surprisingly durable polymerized paper. Close to seven hundred dollars. Because I avoid traceable payments whenever possible, I tend to carry more cash than most people. Muggers aren't really a concern.

The sun shone bright in a cloudless sky, and even by the river the breeze was light. I was cold, but a brisk stroll would warm me up and help dry the clothes at the same time.

So it was decided. I waited for the pedestrian signal at Watts Street, then set off crosstown, heading for one of the small, not-quite-awful, almost-cheap SRO hotels scattered throughout the East Village. In the anonymous company of drunks, doghouse husbands, European backpackers and midwestern tourists who really shouldn't have booked the cheapest place possible, I'd dry off, rest up, and plan the next step.

Clara showed up four hours later. I'd checked in, left her a message from the front-desk phone and barely gotten the soggy clothes off before falling into the bed. She woke me up by banging on the door, carrying a takeout container of steaming hot ramen noodles—almost as good as chicken soup.

"The Mallory Arms," she said, watching me eat. "It sounds nice, but I don't know . . ."

Scratches and holes in the plaster, a gritty floor, one thin blanket on the bed—she had a point.

"Cheap, though." I watched her watch me. It was *good* having her there. "What happened?"

"Faust died."

"Sorry to hear that."

"Want to bet the ballistics are the same as Marlett?"

"You don't know?"

"NYPD isn't like Old Ridgefork. A box of donuts doesn't get you anywhere."

"I'm sure you're right." I splashed broth in the plastic container, not adept at eating the slippery noodles with chopsticks. "The chief himself was probably on scene."

Clara handed me all the napkins from the paper sack. "You might need these."

"Nah."

"The detective interviewed me for half an hour," she said.

"Oh?"

"You, they'd *really* like to talk to."

"They know who I am?"

"I couldn't tell them much."

I was in the middle of drinking off the dashi and didn't reply.

"Because I don't *know* much."

On the room's small flat-panel television—bolted to the wall in an aftermarket steel frame, thank you very much—CNN was showing the fireball footage yet again. The sniper had landed the helicopter, only a few minutes after losing me, at an oil-tank farm just over the Hudson in New Jersey. He set down directly on top of one of the tanks, shot up the pipework until there was oil and gas spewing everywhere, then fled down the access ladder. Before he escaped, he set it all on fire—possibly with an explosive charge, since fuel oil doesn't actually ignite all that easily.

The tank was forty feet tall, so he might have used a grenade launcher, though I wasn't sure how it would have fit into that book-pack he'd been carrying. In any event, thick smoke from the result-ing conflagration shut down three highways, two rail lines and enough air traffic to snarl flights across the country.

Of course he'd also burned the entire helicopter down to a few carbonized fragments. No forensic evidence there. I almost had to admire the choice he'd made. He could have snuck quietly away, at the cost of leaving a few clues behind. Instead, he'd completely oblit-erated his tracks—and was now the target of every law enforcement agency on the eastern seaboard.

Not to mention he'd stolen the helicopter in the first place, once he realized his first escape route was problematic. Improvisation and luck, working together.

His actions were effectively insane, but the fuck had style.

"I'm a tax-planning consultant," I said.

"You mentioned that."

"But I've taken on a few other assignments. Over time. In cer-tain specialized areas of expertise."

"I gathered." Deadpan.

Sometimes you have to trust people. I spend too much time with sociopaths as it is—most high-ranking Wall Streeters are awash in psychopathology, unsurprisingly. You can't lie all the time and make any kind of normal human connections. A relationship that has any value requires honesty, which may be why I don't have many.

I didn't want Clara to slip away.

"You could think of me as a forensic accountant," I said. "Except written for TV—more guns, fewer spreadsheets."

"I got some interview tape from those doormen who saw you

take on the assassin. They made it sound like Jason Bourne, watch out."

"Oh, that wasn't anything."

"No." She shook her head. "You saved *my* life, too—and three against one."

Pause.

"I thought you were unconscious during that."

"I figured it out."

"Well, I—" Wait a second. No lying. "No. You're right."

"Yes?"

I thought about the attack on her, in the park. "The thing is, they could have killed me then, easy. Once he pulled out the pistol, standing over you, I was dead—except he didn't feel like it, I guess."

"He had a gun?" She sounded surprised.

"Yeah. Probably the same one he was waving at me on the helicopter."

"What? It was the *same man*?"

Oh, right. I forgot—nobody but me knew that. I sighed. "Let me tell it again," I said. "I'll try not to leave out anything this time."

And I did. Clara listened, and the few questions she asked were keen and to the point.

When I was done, she picked up the takeout container and the chopsticks and carried them to the bathroom's wastebasket. I was still sitting in bed, against the headboard, blanket pulled up. The river's chill was slow to dissipate.

Clara came back and sat on the edge of the bed. She'd brought my fleece jacket, the one I'd tossed her before taking off after the mad sniper. I put it on. The room was small, with no additional chairs.

"You're a hero," she said.

"Ah, fuck."

"No. Even the detective interviewing me thought that, though he didn't say it. I could tell."

This was too depressing to think about. The TV vans were probably all outside my door now.

That's the problem with being a hero—you lose the rest of your life.

"I'll never be able to work again," I said. "Assuming I don't go to jail."

"Not necessarily."

"No. Once the cops start digging around, they're going to find out far too much about me. Then some department blabbermouth will call the *Post,* and I'll have to hire on with some merc company and ship out to Yemen."

She put both hands on the mattress and leaned forward, facing me. "I didn't tell them your name," she said.

My turn to stare.

"Or where you lived. Or anything."

"But, I thought you said—"

"I told the detective I'd run into you on another story, just a face in the crowd. I didn't even remember you when you came up to me outside Faust's building—but I try not to alienate potential sources, so I was polite. It was just chitchat, mostly with Darryl. Then the shooting started, and you ran off, and that's all I could tell him."

"That wasn't smart. You lied to a cop."

She lifted her hands to shrug, and sat back. "I told him I needed to go through my notes, see what I could find that might help with details about you. I have to call him back later."

"Uh." The situation did give her total blackmail control over me, but we could worry about that later. "Why? Why would you do that?"

"Because you saved my life," she said. "Don't you listen?"

"Not enough, I guess." I wiped my hands and face and chest, and blanket and pillow, too—somehow the ramen had dribbled everywhere—and tossed the wadded napkins vaguely toward the bathroom. "Not enough."

"Work on that."

Conversation faltered.

I noticed smudges of dirt on Clara's cheekbone. Her hair was no longer neat, strands falling across her forehead and over one ear. Her collar had folded under.

The kiss was sudden and hard, both of us going in simultaneously. Her arms around my back, pulling me forward, while I caught one hand behind her and the other swept aside the blanket. A groan, mine—a moan, hers. Our faces switched sides, then again. Pain from my bruised chest was distant and unimportant. We started to fall onto the mattress, conveniently placed beneath us.

Clara pushed back.

"Not now," she said.

We were both breathing hard.

"Not *now*?"

"It's not the right time."

"Yes it is!"

"No it's not."

"But—" Wit seemed to have deserted me.

"I don't . . . I've rushed into a few too many things. You know?"

I was thirty-five years old, single, formerly in the military and now nine years resident in Manhattan. Of course I knew what she was talking about.

"No," I said. "What are you talking about?"

"I don't know." She stood up from the bed, sort of pulling herself back together.

"Don't know what?"

"How big a mistake you are," she said.

And five seconds later she was gone, the door closing gently behind her.

CHAPTER NINETEEN

The night proceeded through degrees of ache and discomfort. Painkillers seemed like a bad idea—even the informal kind, the sort that comes in a flat glass bottle—since I was worried about being found. I needed to be sharp if the police showed up. Or the press. Or Ganderson.

Or my death-from-the-sky mad sniper.

My chest sure was sore, and movement was stiff and slow, but I had to get out. Hardly any bruising on my face, fortunately, so no second glances. I rode the subway uptown, the Sunday-morning passengers mostly quiet, all of us keeping to ourselves. Some kids on the platform were horsing around, a hundred feet away. A middle-aged couple shared a *Times*, dumping unwanted sections onto the train's floor as it rattled from one local stop to the next. Everyone else sat deep in their cellphone shells.

The garage booth was empty, but when I hammered on the utility closet's door—metal and solidly locked—Goldfinger opened up. He was dressed and awake, holding a radio in one hand. Sports talk, the usual posturing and jabbering.

"Hey, funny you showing up," he said. "I was gonna call."

"Good." I pushed in, pulled the door shut. The room smelled of food going bad and open liquor, though I couldn't see any. "What's up?"

"I got a match."

"A match?"

"Yeah. I'm the CSI *king*, motherfucker. Ralph Waldo *Emerson*."

My ribcage hurt. My head hurt. I took the radio and dialed it down to inaudible. "What are you talking about?"

"Nothing escapes the giant eyeball."

"Have you been drinking?"

"Fuck you. Want the name or not?"

"What name?"

"Your friend with the baton, and I don't mean the fucking drum major, you know?"

"Baton—hey, that was fast."

"No shit." Goldfinger coughed. "Truth is, it wasn't that hard. Clean print, and the guy was in the service, so his records are in good order. IAFIS kicked it out straightaway."

"Uh-huh."

"You picked a hardcase to fuck with, I'll tell you that. His 201 was mostly redacted, and you know what that means—black fucking ops."

"Name?"

"And he spent ten years in. Hey, what's MOS stand for again?"

"Military Occupational Specialty. His job in the army. Come on, Gol—I mean, Ernie. Tell me what you know."

"What's an 18B?"

I paused. There are hundreds of MOS codes, but I happened to know that one: Special Forces Weapons Sergeant.

The guy who's so good with every kind of firearm, he teaches and maintains them for his teammates.

"I'm dying here, Ernie. Give me the *name,* already."

"Joe Saxon. Ring any bells?"

None, but I hadn't recognized him in person, so no surprise.

"I'll email you the sheets," Ernie said. "No printer here. The last current address is Kentucky."

"Is it an APO box?"

"Yeah, at Fort Campbell. Does that mean anything?"

"No, not much." I gave him one of my disposable email addresses, and he sent it while I watched.

"Thanks, Ernie. That was nice work."

"Give me a challenge next time."

I didn't hang around long. "I came over to get my car," I said on the way out. "Anybody been by asking about it? Or me?"

"No." He looked at me, sharp. "Why? Should I be expecting something?"

I didn't figure the police to have backtracked me this far. My arrangement with Goldfinger was unofficial and cash-based. The car itself was registered to a corporation that had no existence outside a PO box in White Plains.

"If authority shows up," I said, "you don't have to cover for me. Tell them what they want to know."

Which he'd do anyway, of course. Goldfinger was no dummy. But this way he'd feel better about it.

"What are you involved in?"

"Righting wrongs. Making the world a better place. What I'm always doing."

He laughed with that deep rasp you get from a lifetime of abusing your metabolism. "You and me," he said. "You and me both."

I drove back downtown—it was downright pleasant on the avenues, light traffic, no delays. Too bad it can't be Sunday morning all week. Even parking wasn't too bad. It only took about five minutes to find an on-street spot a few blocks from the hotel, and I could leave it there until Wednesday, the next street-cleaning day.

Back in the room with takeout coffee and muffins, I crawled back into bed, like a wounded animal going to ground. I really had taken a beating the day before, and time was the only cure. Staring at the wall, I thought about what Goldfinger had dug up.

Fort Campbell was, among other things, the headquarters for the 160th SOAR—the Night Stalkers. The Army's special forces aviation unit.

No wonder Saxon could steal a helicopter like he was hot-wiring a Chevy.

Which suggested another point. If Saxon had a decade of SOF experience, he'd be drawing six figures easy on the private market. Even more if he was hiring out for gray-area assignments, like terrorizing young women bloggers.

I was starting to see big money in the mist. Johnny's theory seemed to be gaining ground—anarchists and guerrilla-theater impresarios generally don't have bankrolls like that. Ganderson's nemesis might be just one more capitalist enterprise.

The room's single window had only a torn shade, but the glass was dirty enough to serve. The dim airshaft, eight stories deep, meant a permanent, murky twilight.

One of the phones I was carrying around had more than basic functionality—not quite a smartphone, but I could do basic web surfing. The proprietary browser was awful, and the rates extortionate, but that didn't matter. I logged on and picked up Ernie's email. It was buried amid twenty Viagra pitches. How do the spammers do that?—the address had been active for only a week, and I'd never used it for *anything*.

Good thing building botnets pays more than, say, designing microprocessors, or those Russian hackers would eat America's high-tech lunch.

Anyway, Ernie was right, Saxon's 201 was as heavily redacted as every other Bush-era intelligence document. One solid block of black overprint. But the basics were there: dates of service, unit information for Saxon's first few years and a discharge summary. It looked like a typical climb up the spec-ops ranks: infantryman, airborne certification, a tour with the Rangers, specialized aviation training—and then nothing. Blankness, all the way to the end, followed by the separation date and a list of badges and combat decorations.

Three separate Purple Hearts. Expert Marksmanship Badge, with six component bars. Two Silver Stars. Blah, blah.

And a Distinguished Service Cross.

The motherfucker was a *hero*.

I could have gone after him on the internet. As Clara proved by demolishing my own careful walls, it's really hard not to scatter electronic bread crumbs—not if you live a halfway normal life. But she was the researcher par excellence, not me. I didn't have the patience for all that time online, especially on a three-inch screen

Instead, I started calling around.

Even though the SOF numbers have skyrocketed in the last decade—even Gates loved us—we're still a small community. Especially the guys who've actually been outside the wire. Small-unit activity in hostile territory creates bonds stronger than anything on earth. We don't exactly have conventions, but we keep up.

Among other reasons, you never know when you might need a favor.

"Joe Saxon? That prick? If you find him, first thing—before *anything* else—shoot his balls off."

That was call number six, when I started to close in.

"Had a problem with the guy, did you?"

"Only when he breathed, moved or opened his mouth." This was serious criticism, coming from a sergeant who'd spent months with Saxon in Afghanistan. "Political as all hell, and useless with the hajis. He'd have done ISAF twice as much good working directly for the Taliban." The man paused. "Good shooter, though."

"Sniper?"

"Some. He didn't really have the patience for that. But in close-quarter combat . . . Saxon's a total raving asshole, but there's no one I'd rather go through a breached wall with."

"Because he—"

"Completely cool under fire. In the worst firefights—you know, three-sixty incoming, nothing visible, just mud and rubble and your guys dying around you—Saxon never lost it. He'd just keep on doing his job, putting every round where it counted."

"So why didn't you love him?"

"He cheated, lied, stole, gobbled go pills, backstabbed us with headquarters and sucked the major's dick."

"Literally?"

The sergeant laughed. "All but that last one, and he might as well have. The major wrote him up for about fifteen citations."

"I saw the medal count."

"Yeah." He hesitated. "I'll say this, though—Saxon deserved at least half of them. Absolutely."

More than one call went like that. Saxon seemed to have had a genius for alienating his comrades. Which bolstered his reputation for exceptional competence—you have to be twice as good to survive if even your *friends* hate you.

No one had kept up with Saxon after he left the service. Unsurprising, but not helpful to my search—until the very last call, going on evening, when I talked with a lifer who happened to have been injured, and on desk duty, the day Saxon filed his discharge papers.

"Yeah, I remember," the man said. I'd reached him in Hawaii, at Fort Shafter, where it was still the middle of the day. "Saxon couldn't wait to leave."

"Where was he going?"

"Private security, of course. No one else would be crazy enough to hire him."

"DynCorp, Blackwater, like that?"

"No. Stateside. Joe boasted how he was making a perfect soft landing—no more shooting it out with the hajis for him."

"Kind of ironic, if that's all he was good at."

"You're telling me. I was just glad he was gone."

"So what was the company, do you remember?"

"Sure," the man said. "A-Team Tactical Dynamics."

I had to laugh. "They weren't bidding for DOD contracts, were they?" Only civilians would take a name like that with a straight face.

"State Department, maybe."

After I hung up, I checked online. A-Team's website was defunct, but enough PR Wire puff clips, press releases and brief news stories in the trade press were out there to assemble a picture. A-Team had lasted five years, then faded away. Saxon's name wasn't mentioned anywhere, which wasn't a surprise—he wouldn't want the publicity, and A-Team would minimize the sort of information that could make things easier for the lawyers they'd inevitably attract.

Before I shut down, I remembered how easily Clara had found me. A quick search for "Joe Saxon" turned up ten thousand hits— the name was too generic.

But "Joe Saxon A-Team" immediately struck pay dirt: ". . . three years with A-Team Tactical Dynamics, where he specialized in executive protection and counterterrorist operational consulting. Joe Saxon served ten years in the U.S. Army Special Forces, earning commendations including a Distinguished Service Cross for actions in combat zones around the world. As Blacktail Capital's new Director of Security, Saxon will be responsible . . ."

Aha.

And what was Blacktail Capital? Their website was pleasantly designed but minimal, the interesting content probably all behind the client login. "We achieve consistently market-positive returns," read the mission statement, "through advanced technological implementation of complex and proprietary mathematical structures."

A hedge fund, that is, almost certainly focused on high-frequency, high-velocity trading—the kind where powerful computers, programmed by the best MIT and Stanford PhDs available, might buy and sell thousands of instruments every *second*. Sure, Blacktail and similar operations had almost crashed the market multiple times. "Complex mathematical structures" also meant uncontrolled volatility and liquidity flight beyond the capacity of human brains to comprehend, still less to keep up with. But so what? They practically minted money—for themselves.

A little odd that they'd hire someone like Saxon, perhaps. Blacktail was probably no more than a few dozen employees, and "security" at an organization like that usually meant IT—keeping competitors and viruses out of the computers. It's not like they needed an armed perimeter and active-measure counterintelligence.

Unless they were dabbling in their own form of direct action, of course.

In which case it all made sense. Saxon's personality would fit right in at a firm like Blacktail. The partners, raking in hundreds of millions for themselves every year, would have long ago left behind law, morality and the social compact generally. I should know, because men like that—always men, of course—were ninetenths of my client base. It was no stretch at all to imagine them realizing how a few convenient deaths could ramp up returns even further. I wondered how cheaply Saxon's overtime services had been bought—a percent or two of the net?

I erased, emptied, deleted and cleared the phone's browser memory, then shut it down. No need for records—Saxon's and Blacktail's details were burned into my brain.

Maybe the vast wrecking of the entire world's economy, by plutocrat financiers as venal and greedy as Blacktail's, had finally caught up with me. Maybe it was the utterly amoral calculus of their strategy. Maybe it was the direct nature of the killings—for all the suffering they caused, bankers usually didn't contract actual hits themselves. Or maybe the tattered shreds of my conscience had finally had enough. Whatever, I was surprised to find myself *angry*. What Blacktail had done was evil, plain and simple.

And here I was—hired to make them stop. Again: I was getting *paid* to do the right thing.

The situation was so novel that I dozed off still grinning.

CHAPTER TWENTY

One end of City Hall Park had been taken over by the farmers' market, parallel rows of sawhorse tables under white tented awnings. At one-thirty, lunch-hour office workers still flocked around, picking over heaps of greens and fall raspberries and the season's last corn. The bakery was busiest; a line stretched out past the Laotian co-op's table with its bitter melon and tatsoi. Sunlight streamed through the trees, their leaves golden and red.

The location was Ganderson's suggestion when I'd called him at dawn. I've yet to meet a hard-driving Wall Streeter who doesn't boast of rising at five a.m. to run ten miles and catch up on the European markets, and lazy *Today*-show-watching slugabeds would never admit otherwise. Sure enough, Ganderson had rather groggily said he was "just getting out of the pool," and suggested he might slot me in midday.

But I had to join him for an errand.

"He's so damned picky," Ganderson said now, at the stand of an upstate organic co-op. "Has to be exactly the right *kind* of burdock."

"They all look the same to me." Who'd *want* to distinguish one long, dirt-encrusted root from another—let alone eat them?

"I got the wrong eggplant once." Ganderson shook his head.

"Why not just have your driver stop at Whole Foods on the way home?"

"Brandon would know. Somehow. Not worth chancing it."

It was a side of Ganderson I hadn't expected. The guy probably hadn't been inside a grocery store for twenty years, but here he was, hands dirty, sorting through organic vegetables in wooden bins.

For his son, who liked to cook. Apparently Fairfield County roadside stands didn't have the range and quality Brandon required.

"One less thing to fight about," said Ganderson. "That's all." He settled on a handful of the roots and paid the weather-beaten woman behind the table. "Thanks, hon."

We walked through the market. I had Dunkin' Donuts coffee from the Fulton Street stop, where I'd gotten off the subway, and I admit I tried to obscure the logo on the styrofoam cup. Embarrassing.

"You were right," I said. "A serial killer *is* stalking the mean streets of Greenwich. I found the son of a bitch."

"Run it down again."

"Ruthless, amoral, outside the law and willing to do anything to make money . . . and those are his *employers*."

"Haw."

I worked through the evidentiary chain, starting with Saxon's fingerprint and connecting the dots, all the way to Blacktail—minimizing mention of Clara, though.

This wasn't a court of law.

"All right." Ganderson stopped, set the plastic bag of burdock on a park bench and rebuttoned the cuffs of his white-on-blue pinpoint. I noticed veined muscles in his forearms. Maybe he *had* been in the gym at first light. "We'll take care of it."

"How?"

"I'm not the only principal here." He flicked his jacket over his shoulder. "We'll talk it over, decide what to do."

True, he had used the plural pronoun in our first discussion, but I hadn't figured on getting hired by a committee.

"The guy's a menace," I said. "Dangerous."

"A little more proof would help."

"Proof?" I snorted. "Hire Kroll if you want a lawyer's report. I don't *do* proof."

"I get you." We started walking again, under the dappled shade of the trees. "Believe me, if Blacktail's involved, we'll call in a Predator drone strike. Just don't go setting fires before we've got the extinguishers lined up, okay?"

Metaphor central, but I started to see what he was worried about.

"I'm not talking about calling the cops," I said. To say the least. I *couldn't* call them. If I tried to explain what I knew about Saxon, and how, they'd end up just as interested in me. "But I could handle this in other ways. Suppose Saxon just disappears? Completely and forever?"

"Nothing's that simple."

"Or I could just put Blacktail out of business for a few weeks. One of their prospectuses mentioned the provider they use to mirror their server farm." Yes, the internet has made *some* parts of my job easier. "A few explosives would take them down, hard."

Ganderson took a moment to respond. Either he was considering the idea seriously, or his eye had been caught by some NYU girls kicking a hacky sack on the grass.

"Not now," he said. "Draw attention to Blacktail and we all suffer. Every time some hedge fund cuts corners, the entire industry goes in the doghouse." He shook his head. "People are stupid, you know that?"

I did know that, in fact. It's why I could make a living. But I could see Ganderson's point. "I guess you don't want to risk inspiring imitators, either."

"Exactly."

"Keeping it quiet . . . you're going to talk to them, aren't you?"

"Yes."

I considered. "Can I be there?"

"What?"

"That's going to be a really fun conversation."

"No." Ganderson laughed. "No you can't, and no it won't be."

We reached the edge of the park, back in the direct sun. A warm smell of grease and potato drifted from the knish vendor parked at the corner.

"Maybe you could lay the groundwork, though," Ganderson said.

"Groundwork?" Set up his meeting? I wasn't following.

"I don't know. Reconnaissance, supplies, like that. In case we decide to green-light a more, ah, direct response."

"To Blacktail."

"Yes."

That was more like it. "Sure."

"Just precautionary." He gave me a sharp look. "Don't do anything without an authorization. From me."

"Of course."

We were in familiar territory now—or so it felt. Ganderson wanted to control what happened, but also *when*, and orchestrating press releases probably wasn't the only reason. He was looking for angles, and in his world that meant looking for ways to make money.

Just like Johnny, he wanted to trade against Blacktail.

"Good." He reached out to shake hands, a clear dismissal.

"By the way," I said, "how about a progress payment?"

―――――

The ATM tapped out at three grand, at least until tomorrow. Unless the police found me out, got the Feds involved and closed down my bank accounts. I did have go-bags stashed in a couple of locations— a safe deposit box in Chinatown, or if I was completely blown, one buried in the wall of an abandoned building in Brownsville. But they were for extreme circumstances, and I didn't want to show my face at any of the institutions that held my invested savings. For now, I'd try to live out of pocket: Ganderson had only laughed and promised a bonus, and I was going to have to wait.

This meant a problem with Hendrick, however, because I couldn't guarantee a cash payment—or, indeed, give him anything up front.

"How long have I known you, Silas?" His accent was almost gone today. Maybe it was the hangover. We were in Grand Central Station, amid the noise and bustle and flow, watching midday commuters clatter through the main hall.

"Ten years? But that's *my* question. In all that time, have I ever welshed? Even once?"

"No, which reveals my point. In ten years, we have always agreed on certain mechanistics. The first of which is that I receive sixty percent in advance, in clean currency." He glanced at the schedule board. "My train is in twenty minutes."

"You'll make it."

"I am looking forward to a comfortable night in my own bed."

He looked it too—badly shaved, red eyes, rumpled clothes. He'd won the locksport open, apparently, and cleaned up in off-venue wagers as well. Only after all that had the serious drinking begun.

"How about free access to everything except the single file I need?" I said. "Anything at all you find in the office, it's yours."

This was not, in fact, a serious proposal. I needed to be in and out without anyone ever discovering, and letting Hendrick rifle the safe would clearly ruin the game. Still, I wanted to convince him of the offer's sincerity.

"If this firm is as shady as I suspect," I continued, "they'll be running significant business off the books. Odds are strong that pleasing volumes of untraceable instruments are stashed in there."

"I don't do percentages." Hendrick was grumpy, his breath stale and acid. "I let you in, then I leave. As always."

"All right." I shrugged. "I simply don't have access to adequate working capital right now. If you can't work on spec—for once, the only time in our entire, heretofore perfectly satisfactory, relationship—then there's nothing to be done."

"Tell me this," he said. "Why don't you have the cash?"

"That's a reasonable question." Yes, it was. "Truth is, I met a girl . . ."

And I let my imagination take over. Not Clara—well, only as

inspiration—but after a minute of improvisation, Hendrick was just shaking his head and muttering.

"No, no, no," he said. "That is all bull crap you are telling me."

I sighed. Deep. "Yeah, you're right. You got me, Hendrick. Look, I took a job I shouldn't have. Now lives are at stake, and you're the only person I know who can jump the locks in the way."

And that was all true.

It still took fifteen more minutes, and Hendrick probably agreed only to prevent me from physically detaining him past his train's departure. But in the end we had not just a handshake, but a plan and a time, too.

"Who's going to be downstairs?" Hendrick asked, before he ran for Track 26. Meaning someone watching out, prepared to call an alert or defend our backs if something unexpected appeared.

"I'll let you know," I said. "I hope he's not as hard to convince as you were."

CHAPTER TWENTY-ONE

"**F**uck you," Zeke said. "And the horse you rode."

Walter had been wrong—it was one pitcher in front of him, not three. Beer signs glowed in the window, their colored light barely penetrating the murk. At eight p.m., Volchak's was moderately busy, the bar area filled with young professionals who'd gotten off the Lex and stopped in for drinks. But in the booths, on ancient wood carved over with decades of graffiti, it could have been twenty years pre-gentrification.

If you squinted hard.

"Rode *in on*," I said. "You got it wrong."

"Is that what you think?"

Zeke had never been much to look at: barely five-eight, a hundred-forty maybe, thinning hair badly cut. If you looked closer, you might notice how callused his hands were or the faded scars poking out of his collar or the taut, banded muscles. If you were smart, you'd then move very carefully.

Unlike in video games, elite soldiers—Seal Team Six, Delta, whatever—tend to be small runty bastards. Forty-mile runs in full kit are tough if you're carrying twice as much muscle mass. Not to mention the bigger a target you are, the more likely you'll attract hostile fire. Combat isn't about trading haymakers or wielding a SAW machine gun in each hand. Not in real life.

Zeke's battle decorations would fill an army rucksack, if he hadn't thrown them into a four-star's face after his court-martial—acquitted, but kicked out all the same. He and I had been on operations together a few times, here and there. We got along okay, and it's fair to say we'd each probably be dead more than once except for some action by the other.

Some of those occasions had been after we'd both returned to civilian life, in fact.

"Keeping busy?" I sat down with the cranberry juice I'd gotten at the bar before coming over. Lemon twist and crushed ice. Zeke kind of sneered, then realized that was exactly why I'd chosen it.

"This and that."

"Walter said he ran into you here."

"Reference check."

"Oh?" Was that an explanation or a non sequitur? One of the things I liked about Zeke was you could never be sure.

"Someone gave him my name," Zeke said. "Walter crosses his *t*'s."

You'd be stupid, albeit only for a very short time, if you used Zeke's name without his permission.

"So," I said. "You like the Jets this year?"

"You need something from me?"

I drank some juice. Too sweet. "I know, I know," I said. "Endless small talk and casual banter. Drives me nuts, too."

"I only got a few minutes. My show's coming on." He glanced at the television screen above the bottle rack, behind the bar. "GRITtv."

"Tivo on the blink?"

"I do without electricity at home."

See? Almost believable, knowing Zeke . . . and yet.

"Come on," I said. "Let's take a walk." When he didn't move, I added, "I paid you up already."

Outside I turned left, away from the brighter lights of Third Avenue. For a neighborhood that had paparazzi-worthy nightclubs and one-bedrooms selling well into seven figures, this edge of Gramercy was scruffier than outer-borough tourists might expect. The sidewalk dipped and sagged, patched roughly with asphalt. Heavy grates were pulled down over the darkened windows of shops like Huangpao Trading Ltd. and Deepwater Maritime Services. I felt right at home.

I laid out the job. Unlike most guys, Zeke needed the backstory, too. A habit from his days in dusty third world villages, where understanding clan politics and local feuds was the only way to know who'd be shooting at you. A few times I'd tried to convince him it not only didn't matter if he had my employer's name, he'd probably be better off in the dark, but Zeke was adamant. A twenty-minute intel briefing or he wasn't interested.

"The whiz kid yesterday, he was number four. Faust." Zeke wasn't much on the news, usually, but apparently the inescapable, wall-of-noise coverage had seeped through.

"That's right. And he'd almost wiped out *his* investors, too. So far the targets have all been, ah, notable subperformers."

"It's like Batman in reverse."

"What?"

"Your killer isn't avenging the poor, the helpless or the down-trodden. He's taking out enemies of the superrich. They're the only ones who could afford to invest with these bozos."

I rolled my eyes. "Hey, don't go all ideological on me."

"Just saying."

"Because it doesn't pay. Little kids getting beat up for their lunch money can't afford your rates."

He shrugged. "Maybe I should check in with the other team. Seems like they're having more fun."

I glanced sideways. Zeke's face was expressionless, as usual, shadowed in the street's poor lighting. "If you happen to be implying you know who they are," I said slowly, "we could avoid a great deal of tedious gumshoeing. I'll even split my fee."

"No idea."

Good enough. Zeke could be a pain in the ass, but he never, ever lied.

To me.

Well, that I knew of.

"Remember Akelman? The hit-and-run, not long after he bet his firm on cobalt."

"Commodities." Zeke said it the way he might have said "dog-shit" or "health insurance executive."

"Yeah. So when he died, his successors sold off the holdings, like, the next day. The dump drove prices into freefall."

"Tough."

"Not for everyone. In particular, not for the smart money that had bought up a boatload of deep puts about a week earlier."

"Shorts." He brightened. "Who was it?"

"That's what we need to find out. This little company Riverton Commodities was the introducing broker, but that's where the trail goes cold."

"Okay."

"Riverton was the cat's-paw, buying and selling what he'd been told to. We need to find who was using him."

"I thought you said Riverton was an IB."

Zeke, autodidact. Ninety-nine point nine percent of the country—and most of the people on Wall Street, for that matter—wouldn't know what that meant.

I had to explain the most arcane trading intricacies to the guy I was hiring to stand around and watch for police cars.

"You're right. Riverton places the orders, but structurally he has to delegate floor operations to an arm's-length entity. In this case, Whyte & Fairlee. They work so closely, though, they might as well be partners. How do you know this shit?"

"I read. Don't you?"

"Just YouTube."

We crossed 13th against a red light, forcing a speeding yellow cab to veer out of our lane. Farther down the street a handful of people stood outside a nightclub—the Portico—under colored lights. Closer, we could see velvet ropes holding the queue, and two large men in double-breasted suits standing before the metal doors. A red-uniformed figure supervised the valets driving off in Escalades and Beamers.

As one mind, Zeke and I crossed the street, to pass on the far side.

"I don't see what you want out of Riverton," said Zeke.

"They made pots of money off Akelman's fund."

"So you think Riverton's the button man?"

"'Button man'? Who are you, Robert Mitchum?"

"Doesn't make sense." Obstinate.

"Look, every dollar lost by Akelman's fund, after he died, went into someone else's pocket. Get it?"

Zeke was still thinking while we walked opposite the nightclub's entrance. Just as we passed, the doors were slammed open, knocking one of the two bouncers aside. The crowd outside parted as a scrum of men in dark suits scuffled out onto the sidewalk.

It wasn't much of a fight. Not a fight at all, in fact. Seven large men, a majority with shaved heads and all wearing black, hauled six other guys out. The offenders were at least average size and seemed fit, but they looked like kids in comparison to the professionals.

Of course we stopped to watch.

"Fuck you, motherfucker! You're a fucking piece of fucking shit!"

"Out you go, gentlemen."

Zeke gestured with his chin. "He's using a police come-along. Nice."

"Tricky to get it right without practice." I peered more closely. "That guy looks familiar."

"Friend of yours?"

"Don't think so . . ."

"Might not be the best time to say hi."

On the other side of the street, the security chief looked around. "Any of you gentlemen use the valet service? We can get your car for you."

"*Fuck* you!"

"No? Fine." The chief nodded to the small crowd enjoying the show. "Sorry to disturb you folks." He turned back to his crew. "Down the block, please."

The bouncers pushed the miscreants halfway down the street, then set them free. More "fuck you" this and "motherfucker" that— a good sign none of them had been in the service, where if nothing else you learn to swear properly—and the security staff walked back to the club. All in a night's work.

The street quieted down. The suburban teenagers might not have gotten into Portico, but they had a good story. The chief shuffled his staff around, replacing the door guards with two others, and the rest returned inside. The half dozen men who'd been kicked out muttered at the end of the block, but it was obvious they wouldn't be going back for more, and they soon disappeared around the corner. Zeke and I walked on.

"It wasn't Batman," he said, returning to our conversation. "That's what you're telling me."

"Right."

"Akelman got killed so someone could scavenge the carcass."

"Not just roadkill—they walked away with twelve million when the fund cratered."

"Okay, I get it." He sounded satisfied. "You want to find out who was on the winning side of Akelman's death spiral."

I nodded as we turned the corner. "All makes sense now? Every question answered? Any other little details we need to cover before you tell me whether you're in?"

"I don't think—"

A sudden shout from across the street broke our attention.

"Hey! Hey! It's the motherfucker who robbed me!"

"What?"

"It's *him*! Come on!"

We looked up to see the six bounced louts starting across the pavement toward us.

"I'll be damned," I said to Zeke.

"You *do* know him."

"Yup," I said. "His name's Hayden."

And like a sick blessing it was. The DA was taking her sweet time locking up the son of a bitch—I'd sent her Walter's documents days ago.

They converged, surrounding us. Hayden got right in my face, jabbing at my chest with one finger.

"You owe me, motherfucker," he growled.

"Don't you know any other bad words?"

His pals muttered. We were out of sight of the club, and this block was deserted—shuttered buildings, dark windows. Zeke had stepped slightly behind me and to the left, facing out.

"You sucker-punched me the other night." Hayden paused, then reached into his jacket and in a flash drew a semiautomatic pistol. Before I could react, he'd pointed it right at my nose, three feet away.

"Shoe's on the other foot now, huh, shithead?" He grinned so wide it must have hurt his mouth.

I didn't move. "What do you want?"

"What was it?—both knees, both elbows, and one ear?" His face twisted. "But first, we're going to pound the shit out of you and your fairy fuck buddy."

Zeke made a small cough that I recognized as a chuckle.

"Our business is over," I said. "And that's all it was—business."

"You fucked with me, and I'm going to fuck with you!"

I breathed—once in, once out, deep. "Walk away, Hayden."

"Fuck you!" His face went red.

I waited a second, until his next breath—then dropped, turned half left and launched myself straight at his midriff, shoulder first.

The gun went off and missed. If he'd had the sense to aim at my center of mass, it would have been harder, but the face is only a few inches wide—even from three feet, it's easy to duck.

I hit him hard. As he started to fall back, I brought up my left arm, locked his gun hand, and twisted sharply. At the same time I punched him right under the floating ribs, in the soft tissue, with my knuckles bladed.

The bruises I'd taken from the fall into the Hudson hurt. I hoped Hayden hurt more.

He sagged, but the gun was still in play. I struck again, this time his face. His nose went splat, blood flying.

Another shot. Someone yelled. I twisted Hayden's arm farther, forcing him down, and finally yanked the gun free of his weakened hand.

And at that exact moment, one of his pals kicked me in the side. *Oooof.* That *hurt.*

Since I was already falling, I went with it, watching the guy wind up another kick. I let him in, then caught the leg, crouched slightly, and flipped him up and backward. Tendons and ligaments tore. The man screamed as he tumbled to the ground.

I kept moving, turning around, spinning Hayden's pistol into a firing grip at the same time. It was familiar—one nine-millimeter or another, the good ones all have that confident, competent feel to them.

I didn't want to shoot anyone, but this had gone way out of control. I was ready to put down the entire litter if necessary.

Not necessary.

It was over.

Zeke stood pretty much exactly where he'd been a moment ago. Hayden's four other friends lay on the ground around him, groaning. Two were unconscious. I straightened up.

Zeke put his hands in his pockets. "You got blood on your neck," he said. "And that shirt's ruined."

I dabbed at the scrape. He was probably right. "You want to go through their wallets?"

"What for? They were just being assholes."

"That's what for." I started with the unconscious ones, emptying billfolds and dropping them onto the ground. When I got to Hayden he glared up at me through tears of pain. Broken noses hurt.

"This is a nice stack of cash." I held the wad I'd collected. Hundreds, maybe a few thousand dollars. "I'll set it right here."

I laid the bills on the ground, between the bodies. The ones who were awake stared at me.

"You might need it at the hospital. I'm sure you all remember who had how much, so you can divide it up."

Zeke made that coughing sound again.

"As for the ID and credit cards . . ." I looked at the stack of plastic in my left hand. "I guess it'll be a race. Can you cancel everything before I sell them over in Alphabet City?"

No one said a word. I went back to Hayden and leaned down. He had both hands on his face.

"I'm keeping the pistol," I said. "You're a loose cannon."

"Fuck you." Barely more than a whisper, but consistent to the end.

"Oh well."

Zeke and I walked off, no particular rush, but no reason to wait around either. The cops were going to have fun interviewing the only potential witnesses: the clubgoers and bouncers. I didn't think there were any surveillance cameras to worry about. This wasn't Times Square. But even if there was one between Volchak's and here, the light was too dim and the video quality too low-res to be a problem.

A block away I wiped down the handgun with my shirt, ejected the magazine and dropped the pieces down two different storm drains.

Zeke nodded. "You're not really walking over to the Alphabets, are you?"

"No." I wiped the cards where I'd touched them. Another two blocks and we found a blue USPS mailbox, and I put them through the slot. "They'll get them all back tomorrow."

Zeke shook his head. "Petty."

I kept back Hayden's license and Amex. Those I'd send to the DA.

And I'd started to wonder. Earlier, Hayden had seemed like just another prick, the kind you run into all the time south of Park Place. But he was comfortable with that pistol, and entirely ready to murder two strangers over, well, not all *that* much.

Maybe Walter had been right to be suspicious. Could Hayden have somehow been involved in Marlett, or even the others?

The night was pleasant, cool and finally dry. My chest hurt, but more from the fall into the Hudson yesterday than from the kick I'd taken. Not a bad day.

"So, this job," I said. "Are you in, or not?"

"Sure." Zeke flexed his hands. "You obviously need someone to watch your back."

CHAPTER TWENTY-TWO

"I'm sorry," I said, holding the phone awkwardly while I pressed ice onto my neck. I'd bought a bag at a mini-mart on the way. The Mallory Arms didn't provide amenities like ice machines.

"Why? It's not late," Johnny said.

"Not about that." I knew he lived on four or five hours of sleep a night, like Edison or Napoleon. Or Lady Gaga, for that matter. Energetic successful people could do without.

Myself, I need a good nine hours, at least every other day.

"No," I said. "About Simon Faust. I would have called if I'd had any idea he was on deck."

"Oh *that*." Johnny made a dismissive snort. "I heard about him hours before Green Goblin rappelled into his loft."

"Rappelled? What?"

"Isn't that how it happened?"

"Jesus, can't the reporters get *anything* right? It was a sniper, across the block."

"And he got away by jetpack." Okay, he was pulling my leg.

"Spiderman could have followed, except the Hudson was in the way."

"You were there, weren't you?"

I grimaced. "Let's talk about that some other time."

I'd walked the fifteen blocks to the Mallory after leaving Zeke, unwilling to hail a cab with blood on my neck and shirt. Drivers remember things like that. Once I had finally got in I kept thinking about dialing Clara. I knew it was a bad idea. I understood clearly that she needed time to decide. Far and away the best thing would be to wait, of course. But my reptile brain had other ideas, and my hand kept drifting to the phone. Finally, in a defensive maneuver, I'd called Johnny instead.

"So if you heard about Faust beforehand, did you, ah, trade on the event?"

"No." He sounded frustrated. "I couldn't figure anything out. And neither could anyone else, apparently. I've been watching the wire all day, and zero has happened in Neon Rain. The usual trickle of trades, some in, some out, but nothing else. None of the investments have moved significantly."

"Interesting." I considered. "Maybe that's why the assassin was okay with leaking the rumor ahead of time."

"Or maybe we figured wrong, and he *isn't* doing it for money."

"Do you believe that?"

Johnny laughed. "Not in this world."

"Me neither."

Melting ice dripped down my torso. I shifted so less would run onto the pillow. It was a crummy bed in a crummy hotel, but it would only be worse sopping wet.

"Hey, are you going to the target competition next weekend?" Johnny asked.

"What?"

"My guys were talking about it this morning. A shooting contest at some firing range on Long Island—the 'First Corporate Challenge Target Competition.' They're excited."

"A Saturday crowd of ramped Wall Streeters with guns? No thanks."

"Rifle, pistol, trap and ten-meter running target." Johnny started laughing. "I like that last one. How do they find someone to be the runner?"

"They pick up day laborers from the Home Depot parking lot."

"No, really?"

"Unless it's Olympic sanctioned. Then it has to be a union guy."

After my run-in with Hayden, I was starting to think maybe Johnny *should* arm himself. Lower Manhattan had apparently gone completely gun crazy.

"Change of topic," said Johnny.

"Sure."

"What have you heard about Plank Industrials?"

"Ah . . ." I thought. "Old-line manufacturing?"

"That's the one."

"I think they used to be part of the Dow, years ago. I don't know what they actually make."

"Now that you mention it, I'm not sure either. Crucibles for steel mills or something."

"And they're still in business? I though all that moved to China and India in the eighties."

"Fortune 600."

"Huh."

"And a byzantine stock structure to keep control in the founder's family. The CEO is the grandson, Terry Plank."

"Okay, I learned something today. What's the point?"

"I might have heard Terry's next on the list."

"Really?" The cabal had changed tactics, for sure, if they were now leaking everything ahead of time.

"Maybe. Someone mentioned it."

"How many someones?"

"Right. Good question." I could imagine Johnny nodding to himself. "Only one, a trader I know. Long-term, value, focused on industrials. Plank's in his area."

"Where'd *he* hear it?"

"At the gym. Pickup basketball, someone was talking. He says."

Interesting, but I didn't know what to do with it. "News to me."

"The stock's started to go down. Off two percent at close of business."

"Are you in?"

A long pause. The line sounded dead, the way digital does when no one's talking. "Johnny?"

"I can't decide."

"What's the short interest?" That is, how many traders were betting that the stock would go down further.

"Five-point-one. Up a little."

"So if the assassins have gone short—"

"The market apparently thinks that Terry Plank dead would be bad news for the company," Johnny said. "Which is not always the case."

Especially in closely controlled family firms—and doubly so at the third generation, when killing off entrenched leadership would usually kick the stock *up*. "But if it's true here, then buying a big short position and shooting Plank might be a really good move."

"Enough to retire on."

"So what are you waiting for?"

"I dunno. Feels funny, that's all."

Like I said, Johnny relies on instinct.

"We're not in well-charted territory," I said. "Popping CEOs like ducks in a fairway gallery. I can't believe traders are taking it all in like just another BlackBerry news alert."

He laughed. "You need to spend some time on the floor, then."

I got up, carrying my phone, to drop the ice in the bathtub. It was almost midnight.

"Terry Plank must have heard by now," Johnny said.

"His personal-security expenses are about to skyrocket, I imagine." I examined my neck in the mirror. The bleeding had stopped, and the swelling was minimal. Even the bruise on my chest was only slightly discolored. "Maybe I should call, see what he's willing to pay."

"The killers would expect that, though." Johnny kept going, ignoring me. "Making it all the harder to get at Plank. So why would they say anything?"

"They're being sporting. Who cares?"

"Well, that's why I'm not in. The pieces don't fit."

"I wonder . . ."

"What?"

"Nah." I went back to the bed and flopped down. "Can't see it."

"What are you thinking?"

"How was Plank doing before today? Business good? Decent press? Rising stock price?"

"Normal. Spinning the hamster wheel, no more. His company's a backwater."

"And now?"

"Whoa." Johnny was silent for a moment. "You think he put the rumor out *himself*?"

"It's going to get noticed. Really noticed—like dominating-the-news-cycle noticed. And CEOs do seem to like being the center of attention."

"Fuck." An even longer pause. "I can't think how to play that."

"Who says you have to?" I felt some late-night philosophy bubbling up. "Life is about more than just the next trade, you know."

"Not a life worth living." He might have been serious. "Let me know what you hear tomorrow."

It was late, and five busy days had caught up with me. I fell asleep thinking about Clara.

CHAPTER TWENTY-THREE

I n the morning, I continued charging all my phones, two at a time, using the replacement adapters I'd picked up at a bodega yesterday. As they powered up I turned them on and checked for messages. Only the red-tagged phone had any, and I returned them immediately.

Unlike me, Clara picked up her phone on the first ring.

"What were you waiting for? I called five times."

"I know," I said. "I heard them all when I turned it on just now."

"Maybe it's how I live." She didn't sound *too* annoyed. "Online publishing, you have to be available around the clock. Digital sweatshop and all that. But it seems like you'd be working inside the same set of parameters."

"Parameters."

"Life of danger? SMERSH operatives everywhere? If your job is to solve problems with guns, don't enemies come looking for you?"

"They don't usually bother calling first." I sat down on the Mallory's squeaky bed, phone propped at my ear, and started pulling on my socks. "I like to think of them as counterparties."

"What?"

"Not enemies."

"Whatever. Hey, I'm working at the athenaeum this morning. Want to meet me for lunch?"

I looked around the depressing hotel room and saw nothing remotely edible. "How about breakfast instead?"

"It's already nine-thirty. Just getting up?"

"A life of danger tends to run to late evenings. Brunch?"

"Sure. Call me when you get here, I'll come downstairs."

Of course I wouldn't be allowed into the Thatcher by myself.

"And read my story if you get a chance. From this morning. It's running hot."

"Oh?" But she'd already hung up.

I took the train downtown. Not too crowded, midmorning, which is an advantage to being self-employed. If you set your own schedule, you can avoid the awfulness of rush hour.

Outside the Thatcher, Lockerby was just getting off his bicycle—another commuter on his own schedule.

"Hi, Silas." He was wearing khaki cutoffs and a sleeveless undershirt—okay for riding, maybe, but thin for the cool weather. His muscles were kind of wiry all over, like you see on those Tour de France dopers. He looked surprised to see me.

"I'm meeting Clara. Where are you coming from?"

"Bushwick."

"How's the ride?"

"Not bad, actually. And the Williamsburg Bridge is a decent way to enter the city."

His bike looked typical: a road frame, disguised in dull, mottled second-coat paint, with bullhorn handlebars and alloy, not carbon, rims. The fenders indicated a more mature sensibility, however—image-conscious riders would never use them—as did the ancient "Bikes Not Bombs" sticker on the down tube.

"Tough in the winter, though."

He shrugged. "I used to see peasants in Panjwai pushing their bicycles over dirt roads in the mountains, loaded down with the harvest. This is nothing."

"Harvest?"

"Opium, mostly. We were refereeing a civil war, not doing inter-diction."

"I hear you."

A pair of men in business suits went past. Lockerby watched them, then turned back to me.

"I was going to call you."

I thought about my throwaway collection. "That's harder than you might think. What's up?"

"I'm worried about Clara. After she got mugged and all . . . I thought I saw someone staking this place out."

Now that was disturbing. "When?"

"Last night. There was a car down the street, someone sitting in it."

Vehicles were parked all along the block. I raised a skeptical eyebrow. "Lots of innocent explanations for something like that."

"It was there earlier in the day. That time with two heads visible."

Lockerby stooped to finish chaining his bike to an iron fence around a tree in the sidewalk.

"All right."

He stood up. "You ever ride mounted patrols?"

"Sure."

"Remember how it was, watching for IEDs? Pretty soon you're so paranoid, every little pile of dirt looks like death?"

"Yeah."

"So I know what paranoia is. But I also learned how to pay attention to all the tiny details."

"Like a plate number?"

"Yup." He recited it. "New Jersey."

"Model?"

"A silver Cadillac of some sort."

"Kind of fancy and memorable for a stakeout."

"They drove off when they saw me approaching."

If it weren't for Clara's involvement, I would have dismissed the whole thing. But Lockerby wasn't a typical bystander, and Clara had already been attacked.

"I'll have the plate run," I said. "Might take a day."

"Thanks."

"And let me know if you see them again—or anything else." I gave him an unused phone number.

After Lockerby went in, I surveyed the block once more. Nothing seemed out of place. I waited for Clara to emerge.

A sausage-and-dog vendor was setting up at the corner, his grill smoke a reminder of how hungry I was. A claque of students went past, on break from the photography college down the avenue, most of them staring at their cellphones and talking to their friends simultaneously.

"Silas!"

She bounced down the steps, hair loose, a jacket tied around her waist, the ever-present courier bag in one hand.

"You look great," I said, and I meant it.

I was ready to leave my entire life behind, right then.

"Um, not you." She laughed. "What happened to your face?"

I guess the dings I'd taken from Hayden were more obvious than I'd hoped. "I'll tell you about it, but let's get that food first."

"This way."

We went up a couple blocks to a chrome-and-linoleum diner, the kind I never seem to find outside the city. The lumberjack special appealed, especially since a peek at the other booths suggested the owner had chosen "good food" over "huge portions" as a menu strategy. Clara ordered coffee—"And keep it coming, please."

"So what's your big story?" I asked when the waitress disappeared back around the counter.

"Plank Industrials. You didn't read it?"

"The Mallory Arms doesn't provide en suite internet, surprisingly. But I heard last night—Plank's in the batter's box."

"I think that metaphor works only if the pitcher is throwing nothing but beanballs."

"Or grenades. You're the wordsmith, not me. Anyway, where'd you pick up the rumor?"

"It broke in London, about nine a.m. their time. Middle of the night here, of course. But I happened to be up early. Far as I can tell, I was first out the gate on this side of the pond."

"Congratulations. Are you getting source credits from Fox Business?"

"Of course not. But plenty of links and hat tips in the feeds. Traffic is ticking over really well today." She looked pleased. "The hosting provider says I may have to pay up a level—I'm hitting the monthly bandwidth limits in like four days."

"Will you still remember me when you're famous?"

"You can be a guest," she said. "On my syndicated morning cable show."

She opened her laptop, found some wi-fi, and let me read the headlines. Maybe it was slow in the business bullpens—no bank collapses, huge fraud cases, or absconding fraudsters to talk about—but the Plank story dominated everywhere.

Except print, since it had come too late to make it into the morning editions.

Ill-informed pundits were pounding the airwaves—and the internet—competing to propose the most outlandish, yet believable, "analysis." Predictably, the "main street is mad as hell and won't take it anymore" meme was leading, with anticapitalist direct action a close second and "al Qaeda financial jihad" a distant third. Clara's explanation—rational profit maximization—was the dark horse, a topic for odd corners of the blogosphere that seemed to understand how Wall Street actually worked.

Our food arrived. I poured hot sauce over the egg-and-ham side of my plate and syrup over the rest.

"Why aren't you camped out at Plank's offices?" I asked, mouth full. "The attack on Faust came less than ten hours after the rumors appeared. An assault team is probably parachuting in as we speak."

"No one knows where he is."

"Really?"

"Believe me, I've tried. But no surprise, right? After seeing what happened to Faust, Plank would be stupid *not* to disappear."

I'd read the *Times* that morning as I sat on the subway. They were too slow for the Plank story, but they had plenty on Faust's sniper. The usual PR dynamic was at work, fortunately: NYPD and the FBI, both involved but each intensely resentful of the other, therefore willing to leak anything and everything that might demonstrate the prowess of their side of the investigation. That meant plenty of detail, the sort that really ought to have been kept in-house. You could almost follow the detective work in real time. If they ever got a solid lead on the sniper, the TV vans would probably get to his hideout first.

Though that looked unlikely to be any time soon. Saxon had burned his tracks well.

I wondered if I should drop an anonymous dime.

"What I was thinking," Clara said, raising her empty coffee cup toward the counter, "was that maybe you had access to other resources."

"Huh?"

"To find Plank."

"He's gone. Like you said."

"But you're an investigator. Aren't you?"

And a damn good one, I felt like saying, but of course it wasn't so. The sad truth of our profession is that mostly you just ask the same questions over and over, to more and more dull-witted participants, until you get lucky. I had a little more leeway than my state-licensed colleagues—I could hit someone in the face if they needed it, for example—but that helps less than you might think.

Apart from internet databases, the job hasn't changed much since the Pinkertons were tracking the James Gang.

The waitress swung by with refills.

"I could call around," I said. "But it won't get us anywhere. Plank has good reason to dive into a bunker. No one's going to see him until he's ready to come out."

Clara wasn't giving up. "If you *do* find Plank, you call me first, okay? I'll even cut you in on the exclusive, if you want. It'll be worth a fortune."

Ganderson, Johnny and now Clara. Everyone wanted me to do their legwork for them.

"You're star-one on the speed dial," I promised.

Some syrup slopped, and I wiped my face with a napkin. I'd forgotten about the scrape from last night, and I must have winced when I rubbed over it.

"So what happened?" Clara asked. "Fall off another helicopter?"

"Feels like it." I told her about running into Hayden, and the fistfight.

"He was going to *kill* you? Did you call the police?"

"He wouldn't really have done it." Shows how much perspective I was losing around Clara—I'd forgotten she was a civilian. "I wouldn't have let him."

"But—"

"And no, I didn't call 911. The matter was settled."

She frowned. "Are you sure?"

"Well . . ."

"Anyway, I thought you said the district attorney would put him in jail."

It *was* curious that Hayden was still out wandering around, waving a pistol at semi-innocent people on the street.

"I'm not sure what to think about Hayden," I said. "He couldn't have shot Marlett. For that matter, he didn't even know Marlett was coming after the money Hayden lost until I braced him that night. The timing doesn't work."

"What you're describing, though, he sounds fishy."

"Fishy."

"Crooked, even. He could be the kingpin."

"*Kingpin*?"

"The criminal mastermind." She laughed. "Who hires gunsels to do the wet work."

"You don't watch movies made later than 1940?"

A group of kids came in, truants from some stratosphere prep school, and jammed themselves into a booth at the window. Two mothers dawdled over their coffee, children asleep in a double stroller blocking the aisle. A beam of painfully bright sunlight reflected off a glass skyscraper across the street, falling across one of the babies, who woke up with those tentative, prewailing coughs. The mother lifted him out and calmed him down.

"I had a letter a couple days ago," I said. "Out of the blue."

"A letter?"

"You know—paper. In an envelope."

"And this is unusual, for you?" Clara didn't seem surprised.

"Right, well, he says he's a long-lost brother I never knew about."

"No!"

I told her the story Dave Ellins had written, and about looking him up online.

"You think it's true?"

"His picture—it was like looking in a mirror. I don't know what to think."

"Seems like there are only two alternatives. Either someone's running an awfully complicated scam—"

"The photos didn't seem faked, but any idiot can use Photoshop."

"It's not that easy." She finished the last of her grapefruit. "The other option is he's for real. Nothing complicated."

"No," I said. "No such thing in my life. *Everything's* complicated."

The letter had been on my mind. The more I ran the sentences through my head, the more ominous they became. *I was out there, few years back. Guess I know what kind of accountant that makes you, huh?*

Dave could be my brother, or not. Either way he was a problem.

"So write him back." Her eyes were on mine. "Sometimes life is obvious."

"Maybe."

It was close to noon when we finally left the diner, forty bucks lighter but, at least in my case, completely stuffed. I wouldn't need to eat for three or four hours.

"I'm going back to the Thatcher," Clara said. "I need to get a follow-up posted, maybe try to run down some interviews."

"Plank?"

"I wish. Would you . . ."

"What?"

"I could get you into the Thatcher."

I smiled. "Sit around while you hammer away at the keyboard? Sounds exciting."

"The antiquarian map collection is quite good."

"You know, I'd love to." In Clara's company I could watch grass grow and be happy. "But I've got some errands this afternoon, before a job tonight."

"What's that?"

I hesitated. I'd told her about Hayden, but Riverton was different— she didn't need to be an accomplice to outright, no-gray-about-it, illegal activity.

"Running down a lead. I'll let you know if it goes anywhere."

"Okay." She turned toward the steps of the athenaeum. "Stay safe."

"Yeah, right." I smiled. "You, too."

CHAPTER TWENTY-FOUR

Zeke and I sat in the back of Hendrick's car, which he'd driven into the city from his house in Westchester. Remarkably, he'd found a parking space exactly where he wanted, two blocks down Ninth Avenue from the Riverton Commodities office. It was dark, a little before eight, and the sidewalks were almost entirely empty. The district included office buildings and lunch restaurants and small businesses. The homeward commute cleared it out like a neutron bomb.

"You have the supplies?" Hendrick asked, from the front.

"Yeah." Moonsuit, plasticuffs, utility clothes, and so forth. It had taken me hours, all the way to Newark and back, for most of the stuff. But out there you could pay cash and leave no trail.

We checked our kit.

"After I open the door," said Hendrick, for the third time, "you wait at least *twenty* minutes. All understood?"

"Yeah."

"I can't be anywhere nearby when you go in. Not in my own car."

"Don't worry about it," said Zeke. "Silas is a professional."

We pulled on unmarked, identical black ball caps, gray Dickies coveralls and light latex gloves in the color closest to skin I'd been able to find. I turned on a cellphone, connected to the other two on a conference call, and checked reception on the bluetooth earpieces. We then taped the phone's switches to lock them on.

Tactical Comm Gear for Dummies.

"Right," said Hendrick, and we all got out, slamming the doors simultaneously.

The office building's security was good enough to keep out panhandlers, ex-employees and the occasional midday con artist. But we weren't in the diamond district, say, or on Fifth Avenue, where determined burglary gangs were a likely threat.

At the head of the alley behind the building, I indicated landmarks in a whisper. Then Zeke shot out the neighboring wall's camera with a pellet gun. It was accurate enough at twenty yards, and far better than any kind of real weapon, legality-wise. Those mandatory minimums for possession are a genuine deterrent.

See? Gun control works.

Of course, I had my Sig Sauer, but that's because I'm a nonconformist thrill seeker.

The metal utility door into Riverton's building barely slowed Hendrick down. He scanned for alarms, double-checking my assertion that there weren't any. Most management companies wouldn't bother—too much expense, and individual tenants generally bought their own security systems—and this building was no exception. Satisfied after about ten seconds, Hendrick slipped his tools into the Sargent keyway, raked it, and pulled the door open faster than someone using a key might have managed.

"Nice," I mouthed at him, soundlessly, and he waved me in.

Zeke disappeared back to the head of the alley, to keep an eye on both front and back entrances.

"Go," he said, his voice clipped, coming through the earpiece.

"Right."

The emergency stairs were quiet, the air still and stale inside the closed stairwell. At the sixth floor Hendrick studied the heavy metal fire door for a moment, then simply slipped the latch with a strip of flat spring steel. He held it while I eased the door open, just enough to peer through the crack. The hallway was empty.

I gave a thumbs-up, but followed that with one finger raised: *wait a moment.* Hendrick stood patiently while I unrolled the disposable Tyvek bunny suit from its plastic pouch and pulled it on. Elastic held the cuffs down over the latex gloves, and I tightened the hood drawstring enough to pull it around my cap. The thing was designed to OSHA hazmat standards, nice and snug.

The plan was that no one would ever know I'd been inside the Riverton suite. Nothing stolen, everything put back and, to all appearances, undisturbed. Like the emperor's ninja, I would vanish unseen. I needed information—not a posse saddling up. Still, if something went wrong, and some painstaking forensic team went through afterward, I didn't want them sweeping up my DNA.

Running into someone unexpectedly in the hallway was a chance we'd take, but a small one. The building appeared deserted, and I'd only be in public areas for a minute or two.

Hendrick pulled the door open, then closed it silently behind us. He wasn't going in, so he didn't need the protective gear.

The Riverton Commodities door was halfway down the hall. Hendrick bent to examine the buffed keypad for a long moment, then knelt and put his head all the way down to the floor, peering at the door's base.

"Are you ready?" he whispered.

"Yup."

"I will bypass the alarm first, then open the door. I think tape will hold the latch fine. Then I leave. Where will you wait?"

"In the stairwell."

"Please remember, twenty minutes."

"Cross my heart and hope to die."

He gave me a funny look. Dutch schoolchildren must not use that expression.

"I mean, I pinky-swear."

Hendrick just shook his head. He took a coat hanger from under his jacket—yes, a regular, laundry-service wire hanger. Same reason as Zeke carried a BB gun instead of a real weapon. He untwisted it and bent the wire into a big L.

"Okay," he muttered, then punched a four-digit code into the keypad. The lock clicked.

I didn't even have time to be impressed by the speed before Hendrick had knelt again and fished the coat hanger under the door. An instant later he reached up, turned the knob—

—and stood up, like a satisfied butler, gesturing with a sweep of his arm and a small bow.

"That's *it?*" For what I was paying him, it should have taken longer than a few fucking *seconds*.

"They never reset the administration password," he whispered. "And when the motion detector saw movement inside, it thought someone was exiting, so it unlocked the door automatically."

"If it's that easy, I'll do it myself next time."

"Sure." He shrugged, then cut a strip of metal tape from a small roll and placed it over the latch. "Go ahead and try."

Back inside the fire stairs Hendrick clapped me once on the shoulder and started to walk down.

"Thanks," I said.

"Twenty minutes, don't forget." And he was gone.

I stood and waited, beginning to sweat inside the plastic suit.

Ninety-five seconds later Zeke's voice came through the earpiece.

"He's gone."

"All the way?"

"Saw the car drive off." A pause, then, "All clear otherwise."

"Good." I checked my gloves one last time. "Fuck the twenty minutes, I'm going in."

"Fine." Unsurprised.

I went back down the hallway. In the building's dense, after-hours silence, my Tyvek rustling seemed painfully loud. At Riverton's door, I didn't stop—just pushed it open, and stepped through.

Assuming Hendrick's analysis of the security system was accurate, all I had to do was find the camera's controller, almost certainly in the equipment closet I'd seen during my reconnaissance visit, and turn it off. He'd given me a USB stick, preloaded with Russian cracking software, that would go to work automatically. Kind of like a pick gun for a PC. I didn't mean what I said before—the guy was a genius.

I felt like whistling as I headed into the executive suite. This was going to be a walk in the park. I could just feel it.

———

"Good God! Who the hell are you? What's going on?!" Frank River-ton jumped up, yelled and scrabbled for his console phone all at the same time. Papers went flying. Somehow he knocked his laptop off the desk, and it crashed to the gleaming hardwood floor.

So much for all that stealth ninja shit. I should have just kicked the door in.

Of course my Sig was *inside* the zippered moon suit. I jumped over to the desk and grabbed the phone out of his hands, yanking the cord so hard it broke.

"Shut the fuck up!"

"What *is* this shit?!"

"What's up?" Zeke's voice in my ear. My yelling had probably deafened him.

"An asshole working overtime."

Pause. "Is this a situation?"

"I don't think so. I'll let you know."

We were in the biggest office, with corner windows and heavy teak furniture. Riverton stared at me, finally quiet but twitchy.

"We found sarin in the ventilation system," I said.

"*What?*"

"I'm sorry. You'll probably be dead in five minutes."

It only threw him for a few seconds, but that was enough. I finally extracted the P226 and pointed it at him.

"What do you want?" He fell back into his big executive chair, suddenly nerveless.

"Are you Riverton?" Of course I knew the answer was yes, but I wanted him to think we were meeting for the first time—one more bit of distance from the idiot who'd stopped in yesterday, trying to pawn his ex-wife's jewelry.

"Uh—"

"You run this bucket shop?"

He hesitated, then: "No. He went home already."

I pulled the trigger. The blast was stunningly loud in the room. The bullet passed just over his shoulder, shredding leather and padding and knocking the chair backward. Riverton fell off, hit the floor hard, and came back up slow. We were both half deafened.

"Shit," I said. "I missed." I took the handgun in both hands, aiming more carefully at the center of his face.

Zeke's voice: "You never miss. Stop fucking around up there."

"Don't shoot me." The man's voice was hoarse.

"Let's try again. Are you Riverton?"

"Yes. Yes!"

"Very good." I kept the Sig motionless, locked on his eyes. "I have one question. It's a very easy question. Will you answer it?"

"Yes!"

Researchers on hostile interrogation—makes you wonder where they do their fieldwork, doesn't it?—have discovered that getting your subject to say they'll help, even under duress, actually increases the likelihood of truthful answers. Hard to believe, but true.

Our own brains are usually our worst enemies.

"You conducted a number of related trades recently," I said. "I'm going to briefly describe the transactions, and then you'll tell me the name of the client. All clear?"

He nodded.

"I *said*, all clear?"

"Yes!"

"Okay." I allowed a brief, dramatic pause. "July. Cobalt. The counterparty was Jeremy Akel——"

I could have stopped at the second word. Riverton's face was so obvious I wondered how he'd ever worked the pits.

"You know what I'm talking about, don't you?"

"Yes, but . . ." His voice trailed away.

"Good, that makes this easier. So who was it?"

"I don't know."

"Excuse me?" I gestured with the pistol, drawing his attention back to the mouth of the barrel.

"I don't know!"

"What do you mean? Twelve mil didn't walk through here in cash. Who the hell signed the checks?"

"All I had was a company name. Everything was transacted via bank drafts. Final disposition was a SWIFT transaction to a foreign account."

Skating the edges of regulation, that. "Uh-huh. What was the company?"

"Blacktail Capital."

It took me a second, and then I felt that electric thrill of discovery. The jigsaw puzzle, assembling itself. The case was *moving*.

Riverton had given it up so fast that I decided he'd actually been playing the game straight. He would have filed all the proper reports with both British and U.S. regulators, kept good records, maybe even called the police himself when Akelman died, just to keep his nose clean.

If he wasn't dirty, then he wasn't involved.

And if he wasn't involved, he'd do the right thing again, and call 911 as soon as I was gone.

"Boo-Boo Bear?" I said to Zeke. "Might be code red after all, when I finally leave."

"Make it soon."

"Yup." I turned my attention back to Riverton. "Okay, that's fine, we're done."

"Really?"

"Oh, one thing." I almost forgot. "You've got cameras running in your foyer. I'm afraid I can't leave that video behind."

Indeed not. Riverton wouldn't be a good eyewitness. The outfit I was wearing—hat, scary suit, hood—along with the handgun, which kept his attention pretty much every second, would make it very difficult for him to provide the detectives a useful description. But the cameras could. I needed to eliminate that footage.

"I don't know anything about that."

The son of a bitch was trying to be sly. I felt affronted.

"No? Fine. Option two."

"Option . . . ?"

"I'll have to assume that camera server is located in your computer room down that hall, with all the other equipment."

"I don't know," Riverton said again. But I watched him closely, and it was like a textbook illustration of tells: quick swallow, eyes cutting to one side, a short breath.

"I don't have time to figure out which server is which, though. Instead, I'm going to have to destroy them all." I reached into the moon suit. "A couple of thermite charges will melt every hard drive in there down to slag."

He blanched. "Wait—"

"Oh, don't worry. You've got offsite backups for the critical data, right? All your trading information, like that?"

Zeke in my ear: "What is he, a total moron?"

"Yes," I said.

"No." Riverton, sweating visibly, held up a hand. "Maybe I remember."

In the utility closet, he showed me the camera computer, and I probably could have figured it out myself: its dedicated monitor showed a view of the waiting area, and the only external connections were two coaxial cables that entered the wall just below the ceiling. Still, nice to have the confirmation.

"Thanks," I said, and cracked the box open to extract the drive. Fortunately it was one of those toolless builds.

"Yo." Zeke, so quiet I barely heard him. "Hurry up."

"Almost done." I yanked the drive free, tearing its internal connectors.

"Sirens."

"On my way." To Riverton: "Sorry." I tapped him on the head with the pistol and spent an extra moment to flexicuff him to the server rack. It would take the police that much longer to find him here—seconds, or maybe even minutes, that I needed.

"Broomstick," said Zeke.

"Broomstick," I repeated. Not exactly NSA cryptography, but

we'd just agreed to meet at our second—B for 2, get it?—prearranged rendezvous. A few blocks farther away. I had no doubt Zeke would be there, too, despite the increased risk to himself.

It makes you feel good having people you can trust.

"Good night moon," I said, and let myself out.

CHAPTER TWENTY-FIVE

One of the oddities of my profession is how difficult it can be to arrange a face-to-face with the client.

"I could swing by your office."

"Absolutely not!"

"Coffee shop nearby?"

"No coffeeshops."

And so forth. Of course we couldn't discuss business on the phone. And I understood why Ganderson didn't want to be seen with me, at least not anymore. Conditions were volatile, the case out of anyone's control. Hiring your own off-the-books Annihilator could draw attention Ganderson didn't need—the IRS not least, always interested in those missing 1099s.

Still, even to someone as paranoid as myself, this was ridiculous.

"How about outside? We can take a walk."

"It's raining."

"Not more than a drizz—"

"And there are cameras everywhere. You can't go anywhere outside without someone watching you on video."

Fair point.

"How about you pick me up in the limo again?"

"I don't want a driver involved."

Of course he wouldn't drive the damn thing himself. "Well, what do you suggest?"

A minute later, Ganderson came up with an idea original enough to impress even me.

"A hospital waiting room," he said.

The more I considered, the better it sounded. "No cameras, because of health-care privacy law. No one else paying attention, because either they're in pain or their friend is. Constant background noise to keep a conversation private. I *like* it." Ganderson had just had a genius moment.

A few more and he wouldn't need me any longer.

So here I was, in the half-filled, reasonably clean vinyl seats of St. Joseph's. It hadn't been my first choice, because I'd come through just four days ago with Clara. But it was convenient to Ganderson's office, and he wouldn't consider going farther.

The waiting area seemed crowded for a weekday, with more than half the chairs filled and background chatter punctuated by children crying and an occasional siren. Of course Ganderson had to make me wait, thirty-five minutes past the time we agreed. Fortunately there was an amusing little mishap, at the swinging doors between the ambulance dock and the emergency wards, when a gurney collided with a scrub nurse carrying an open Starbucks. The coffee must have been hot, because the patient screamed and jerked around and tore out his IV line. Everyone got so busy yelling at each other they nearly forgot about the victim.

I was still chuckling when Ganderson walked in.

"No, don't get up," he said, dropping into the chair next to me. Not that I had made any move to. "Let's get this over with."

"Don't sit there," I said, but he was already up again, slapping at the seat of his nice charcoal suit. "What is that? Blood? Mother of God!"

"No," I said. "Baby puke, maybe."

A satisfying start to the meeting, all the way around. We finally settled in across the room, Ganderson wiping at his ass with wet paper towels.

"I'm still working," I said. "I'd have reported anything new. What's up?"

"That last time we talked, the body count was still at three. Now it's five."

"Everything I know about Faust and Plank has been in the news already. And Plank's still alive, isn't he?"

"Faust and Plank." Ganderson shook his head. "Simon Faust was a friend of mine."

Different circles, all right. "I'm sorry," I said flatly.

"Maybe 'friend' is overstating the case. Business acquaintance, anyhow. We did a deal or two together."

"Still."

"That's right. Still." Ganderson stared at the triage desk, the kind of stare that doesn't actually see anything. "He called me."

"That morning?"

"Yes. About an hour before he was . . . before he died."

"He knew he was being targeted?"

"Of course. About fifty people had contacted him, he said."

I wondered who. Other traders, I bet, thinking the same as Johnny: *Interesting rumor—what can I do with it?*

"But Simon said he'd seen it first on the *Today* show," Ganderson continued. "Can you imagine that?"

Hearing on national television that I was next on some mad killer's to-do list? "No," I said. "I can't imagine that."

"Me neither." And just like that, the eulogy was over. Ganderson cleared his throat and swung his gaze back to me. "Terry Plank is different," he said.

"Yes." Among other things, as mentioned, he was still alive.

"The press has abandoned all forbearance on this story. It's everywhere."

"I might have noticed."

"In other words, sorry to say, exactly what you were hired to *prevent* has now occurred."

"Well, not exact—"

"These deaths," Ganderson bored on, "are now the single biggest news story in the country."

"Really? Bigger than Lindsey Lohan?"

"That's a different audience."

We paused while a middle-aged woman shuffled past, supported on either side by a younger version of herself, the two daughters muttering at each other over her head.

"Did you have that conversation with Blacktail?" I asked.

Ganderson nodded. "I'd have to say they were . . . evasive."

"Gee, really?"

"They had a lawyer in the room, the whole time. Phil Tarbari, you know him?"

"Only by reputation." Powerful, downtown, well connected—a silver-haired fixer, decades on the Street, the sort of guy whose client list was more or less published in the Forbes 400 every year.

Blacktail had brought a howitzer to a knife fight.

"Did they tell you *anything*?"

"We discussed the weather. And the Giants."

I shook my head. "Joe Saxon works for Blacktail, as their director of security."

"They don't deny it."

"Saxon is a Special Forces veteran gone very bad."

"They showed me his service record." Ganderson laced his fingers over one knee. "They've got a certified war hero on the payroll."

"Yeah, yeah. Why do you think they need him? To walk around the office at night, checking the windows? Come *on*."

"Honestly?" Ganderson smiled. "He's part of the sales pitch. 'We're so important, even our support staff includes Medal of Honor winners.' Same reason they hire models and strippers for IR."

Investor relations, that is—the public face of the firm. Actually, I kind of doubted the stripper part, but it was undeniably true that many hedge funds had tall, blond twenty-four-year-olds issuing their press releases.

"He didn't get a Medal of Honor," I muttered.

"Really?"

A beeping sounded over the waiting room's loudspeakers, followed by calls for a doctor on level three. A patient was coding somewhere, presumably. I waited until the din had died down.

"The sniper on Faust's roof?" I said. "It was Saxon."

Ganderson took his hands off his knee and straightened in the chair. "How do you know that?"

This wasn't judicial. On the other hand, I wasn't going to implicate myself to Ganderson. "Inside knowledge. Trust me on this one."

"I'm not sure——"

"Blacktail specializes in the kind of high-frequency trading that would be perfect for taking advantage of these fund managers' deaths. I think they just went the next logical step, and arranged for the deaths beforehand."

Ganderson grimaced. "They're up to something. For sure. No one hires Tarbari before skeletons are falling out of closets everywhere. But I'm not sure your idea makes sense."

"You hired me to find the killer, and I think I have."

"Why? There's no evidence tying them to any of the trades— or even that there *was* opportunistic trading around those events. Anyway, they make so much money as it is, I can't see them risking felony murder for an occasional goddamn boost in the spread."

A good point. But people aren't the rational calculating machines of neoclassical economics, not all the time. "You said it yourself. People do stupid things."

"Employing mercenaries to kill businessmen all over Manhattan goes a little beyond stupid, don't you think?"

"Well . . ."

This would have been the moment to bring up the connection I'd discovered between Akelman, Riverton and Blacktail, but I hesitated.

"You know what I do for a living," I said. "Real life actually *does* get comic-book, sometimes."

Ganderson smiled. "Never mind. I sat with Blacktail's managing partners for two hours, Tarbari jumping in about every third sentence. Look, I can read people. I have to, you can't survive as a trader otherwise. What I think's going on is that it's not just Blacktail. All the HFT firms are getting hammered. Congress held hearings, and even the SEC is making noises about systemic risk. They've probably got some pigshit trades they're covering up—everyone does—and they're being extra careful. It'll pass."

No, this wasn't the time to bring up my little talk with Mr. Riverton. Ganderson was in a parallel universe, one gradually diverging from reality. I'd have to think about how to bring the two back together—or if doing so was even necessary.

"What about Hayden Pennerton?" Ganderson said. "Fucked up his hedge fund, and now he's tied to Marlett, somehow, according to the cops. I saw it on the wire."

I'd noticed that too, catching up on my feeds that morning. One Police Plaza was as leaky as the mayor's budget.

"I've heard of him," I said, cautiously. "But a connection to Blacktail, I dunno, that seems really farfetched."

"Maybe. Hard to see why they haven't arrested him yet."

"Indeed."

"Anyway, Terry Plank." Ganderson leaned back in his chair. "The fact that the killers have announced he's the next target is very interesting."

"Yes," I said. "Certainly to Terry."

"Haw."

We watched a pair of EMTs run in another gurney, staff in blue scrubs meeting them and taking over on the fly. Rapid talking, paperwork back and forth. I noticed they left the ambulance door hanging open.

"At first, the deaths went unconnected," said Ganderson. "By the time they shot Marlett, though, we noticed. And we thought it was going to be about attention seeking—a kind of bizarre Marxist attack on the foundations of capitalism."

I didn't feel like rehashing our first conversation, so I just grunted agreement.

"Then we realized the motives might be more sinister. It seemed like someone was trying to profit from the killings. Maybe it was an actual conspiracy, a despicable plot to manipulate prices by assassinating particular market participants."

You can see why Ganderson was a go-to for industry quotes. "That's what we discussed, yes."

"But now we have to rethink completely. Again. Whoever the murderers are, if they're announcing their attacks in advance, they get no advantage in a trade against the targets."

He was right. The way you beat the market, about 90 percent of the time, is by exploiting inside information. The forthcoming death of an important player would do the trick—but not if the whole world knew ahead of time.

Leaking Faust's and Plank's names did seem to undermine the Chicago-School Cabal theory.

"So we're back where we started," Ganderson said. "Nutcases, out to make an ideological point."

Outside the exterior doors, a man in a sweatsuit and an arm cast noticed the open ambulance door. He looked around, then leaned forward to peer inside the vehicle.

"What do you want from me?" I asked.

"We need to shut them down. Sling a ton of bricks onto their towel-wrapped heads."

"Like I said, I'm working on it. Although there's no reason to assume an Islamist connection—"

"Whatever." Ganderson waved one hand. "Maybe they're ecoterrorists or antiglobalization agitators. Doesn't matter."

"Uh-huh."

"So it's good you're going after them. But, in parallel, we need a countering narrative. We need to demonstrate that we're unafraid of these bomb throwers—that we're willing to do whatever it takes to defend our liberties, our way of life and the free markets that have enriched more people than ever in history."

I've noticed that high-level executives use a lot of abstract language. That's okay. Usually I have some idea what my clients are talking about. But Ganderson had me baffled.

He realized that, and lowered his voice, looking me directly in the eye. "We're going to leak what you're doing," he said.

"What *I'm* doing?"

"Don't worry—we won't use your name. Or anything that might identify you personally."

"Hold on." I fought an urge to seize Ganderson by the suit lapels and shake some sense into him. "This is *not* part of our arrangement. This is *not* okay. My entire *modus vivendi* is to operate in the shadows, unseen."

Ganderson raised his eyebrows. "Don't you mean *modus operandi*?"

"No!" It's not a good sign when clients begin arguing latinate subtleties. "I live my entire *life* this way—and it can't be otherwise. If people know who I am, I simply cannot do my job."

"Well, no problem, because no one will ever find out. We'll make sure of that."

Said Haldeman to Nixon.

"Let me guess," I said. "You've started the whisper campaign already. Selected journalists, a few bloggers—"

"People who know how to be discreet." He smiled. "Exactly."

I stared at him bleakly. "Why are you doing this?"

The smile turned into a steely glare. "So the world knows we're serious. No one can start gunning down investment professionals and expect to get away with it. We're fighting back, on their home ground, in the shadows."

"The deterrence of assured retaliation."

"Precisely."

"Sort of like, the partisans ambush an *Oberleutnant* and the SS comes back and massacres the entire village."

"Yes, ri—" He stopped. "No, wait a minute."

I looked away in disgust. Through the window I saw the guy with the cast slip furtively out of the ambulance, tucking a bulky plastic sack under his sweatshirt. He turned the corner and disappeared just as the EMTs came out.

Nice to see that *someone* was still on his game.

I turned back to Ganderson. "You had better be right about keeping my name out. Completely."

"Or what?" He didn't sound worried.

"Or I'll come for you," I said. "You, personally." I got up to leave. "Think long and hard about that before you wave me around like an Amex black card."

He started to say something, but I walked away.

Rule number one: clients *always* fuck you up.

CHAPTER TWENTY-SIX

So Ganderson's media strategy had gone from "keep this secret at any cost" to—a picosecond later—"I want a billion eyeballs." By the time I'd found a pizza shop with wi-fi, twenty minutes after leaving the hospital, it was already on *Gawker*. *Deep City* was close behind, and then, like a piñata exploding, it was everywhere.

DealNote: THE CATTLEMEN HAVE HIRED SHANE

Alpha Insider: THEY FUCKED WITH THE WRONG BILLIONAIRE THIS TIME

StreetWire: BOND VIGILANTES!

AP: FINANCIAL EXECUTIVES RUMORED TO BEGIN PRIVATE INVESTIGATION

New York Times: AGGRESSIVE TACTICS MOOTED IN HUNT FOR FINANCIER'S KILLER

Post: DON'T BAIL THEM OUT; *TAKE THEM OUT!*

Ganderson himself was quoted: "Of course we have complete confidence in the authorities who appear to be working on the case. It is absurd to suggest we would take justice into our own hands simply because four people have been shot down in broad daylight and not a single arrest has been made. We would never consider trying to find this insane murderer ourselves—and we certainly would not try to stop him before he kills, kills and kills again."

And so on, for a few more paragraphs.

I threw away the pepperoni slice I'd bought and stomped out of the shop.

"I was worried about you," Clara said. "You idiot."

She'd visited my apartment, looking for me. Jesus.

"You shouldn't have gone." In the middle of this crisis, my gaze kept drifting back to the short black skirt she'd chosen to wear today.

"*You* should be answering your phone."

Okay, that was my mistake. There had to be a better way to keep my office open than carrying a dogweight of cellphones around all the time. I'd turned on three, but somehow overlooked the fourth—which, of course, was the only one that mattered.

"You really didn't notice anyone?" I said.

"Your neighbor the ex-convict was at the mailboxes," she said. "Nothing to worry about."

"How do you know?"

"He hit on me." She glanced at me. "In a low-key, subtle way. No one else was around."

Low-key and subtle. I decided not to believe this was a back-handed comparison. "What does an ex-con look like?"

"Shaved head? With tattoos on his skull? Not very good ones, either."

"Oh yeah, that's Gabriel. He's all right."

The drizzle had never stopped. I'd caught up to Clara in a chain copy shop on Second Avenue, after I finally collected her messages. Over a row of self-service Xerox machines I could see umbrella-wielding pedestrians slogging past outside, dim in the murk.

The steady clacking buzz of a half-dozen copiers at work provided more than enough white noise to conceal our conversation.

"Your name hasn't appeared anywhere." Clara continued feeding pages from a long printout through the intake tray. "I looked, and set some search alerts. No one I talked to mentioned you either. The story totally owns the cycle, but you're not in it."

"Not personally. Not yet."

"I walked back the reporting. Which wasn't that hard, because after three links everyone's basically repeating the same source." She finished the stack of documents and waited for the machine to spit them out. "I'd heard of Ganderson, maybe even met him once— he spoke at a conference I was at, back when I could still get press credentials. Did he really hire you?"

I didn't say anything for a moment.

It's not true that I never discuss what I do. I shouldn't, of course. Professional ethics—not to mention self-preservation—demands discretion.

They called Matt Helm everything from The Silencer to The Demolisher, but never The Blabbermouth.

On the other hand, I'm not some psychotic loner. Half of being human is conversation. Sports and real estate will only take you so far—eventually you end up talking about your life. Still, I'd always kept it compartmentalized. Colleagues, one-off teammates, acquaintances in the business, sure. Civilians—including those I really, really wanted to sleep with—never.

So what the fuck was I doing, unspooling to Clara?

"Yes," I said. "He's the one who hired me. But not to lead some hunter-killer vengeance squad."

"Have you ever done that?"

"What?"

"Killed someone."

I blinked. How did we come to have this conversation, here of all places? We were standing in a FedEx office, for Christ's sake, under fluorescent lights, breathing ozone and toner fumes. We should be in a confessional, or a schul—or at least a badly rumpled bed, at four a.m.

"I was in the military for eight years."

Clara shook her head. Her copier had fallen silent, waiting. "After that."

Pause. "Yes," I said.

Eventually, just audible over the room's noise, she said, "It would be one hell of a story to write."

I couldn't respond to that, only shook my head once slowly.

"Too bad I never will." She smiled, just a bit. "Ever."

An even longer pause. "Thank you."

"Ever," she said again.

I guess I'd forgotten what it was like to trust someone, utterly, outside a firefight.

"By the way," I said, "every last one of them deserved it."

"Are you still working for him?" Clara said.

"Ganderson? He owes me money, so I guess I am."

"You don't sound enthusiastic."

"No." I nodded. "Not after he hung me out like that."

"What, then?" Clara punched some buttons on the copier's payment module, retrieving her credit card and a receipt.

"Everything." I picked a topic. "I can't see why Faust was targeted. He'd pulled out of the markets almost entirely, with the divorce going on. Too much garish publicity to get anything done, or just too much of a distraction—who knows? But nothing's happened to his assets since his death. If the idea was to make money, I just can't figure the payoff."

"I think you answered your own question."

"Huh?"

"Heaps and *heaps* of cash."

"Yes . . ."

"And who gets it now?"

Suddenly I felt very dumb. "The wife!"

"Sure." Clara grinned. "Whatever she might have gotten out of a settlement, it would have been less than a hundred percent. This way she walks away with everything. The entire estate."

"She *hired* it done."

"Makes sense to me, that way." Her smile faded. "Not that I can hint about it, online. She's not a public figure—libel suits would come raining out of the sky, and it wouldn't matter if I won, in the end. I'd be bankrupt ten times over."

"Post it anonymously, on some obscure blog's comment section," I suggested. "Then report the comment. Public domain, right? You're safe."

"Not from a determined law firm with an endless budget. It's not worth it."

I watched a scruffy older man photocopying what seemed to be an entire book, three machines over. One page at a time, seven cents each . . . the digital revolution hasn't come to everyone yet.

"The cabal, the assassin's league—they're more than versatile," I said. "Akelman, commodities. Sills, a huge mutual fund. Marlett, private-equity M&A. Faust, a simple contract hit."

"And Plank."

"Right—something else entirely, a major public company. The only constant is the payday someone earned on every one."

"We think. What I'd really like is a smoking gun. Documentary evidence."

"You and everyone else."

Clara packed her papers into the courier bag, removing and replacing items until it all fit. The flap barely closed, but she yanked the latches and tucked everything in, protecting it from the rain still falling steadily outside.

I leaned on the copier. "You know these machines are like self-contained computers? Every copy they make is scanned, and stored on a hard disk inside. Since overwriting doesn't eliminate the files, anyone can read what you were copying, later."

"I do know that, in fact. But I choose not to obsess about it." She looked up at me. "Ready to go?"

I couldn't keep anything from her.

"The men who attacked you," I said. "The ninja in the helicopter. Same guy."

"You told me that."

"I know who he is."

She quickly straightened up, hauling the bag onto her shoulder. "Are you going to tell me?"

"You can't publish it."

"Of course."

I still hesitated, then found my mind going down a little-used path: if things went bad, and I was no longer around, it might be nice to have someone like Clara to speak for me . . . to give Saxon's name to the police.

"He's an ex-serviceman. Army Special Operations, with years of top-secret missions in the Long War."

"Like you."

"No!" I lowered my voice. "Never like me. He's no more than a cheap gun for hire."

We walked out, pushing through the glass double doors into the rain. Water dripped off the rooflines from somewhere far above, spattering the sidewalk. Not yet five, it was dark as night.

"Not that cheap," Clara said. "Not for what he's been doing."

"You're right." I zipped my jacket and wondered when the hell I'd ever remember a hat, or an umbrella. "But if I know him, he probably knows me. Or he will, soon enough. And that's a problem."

"I see."

"It's not a job anymore," I said. "It's self-preservation."

CHAPTER TWENTY-SEVEN

We took the subway together, uptown—and being neighbors and all, we got off at the same stop. It was the most natural thing in the world for Clara to invite me up to her apartment for dinner.

"Rondo might be around."

"Rondo?"

I'd seen the building, when I followed Clara out on her jog, but hadn't gone back. It had only been five days but seemed like a year. She shared a two-bedroom on the upper floor: prewar moldings and solid wood doors, but cramped and worn from years of rental use. A bathtub had been installed in a tiny alcove off the kitchen, which itself was only about six feet square. When we came in, a man was sitting at the table, eating from a plain blue plate.

He was *big*. Not wide, but tall and powerful, even seated in the chair. A robust biker mustache flowed down the sides of his jaw.

"Nice to meet you," he said, standing to shake hands, towering over me.

"Silas is here for dinner," Clara said.

"Really? Who's cooking?"

"I'll find something."

"I bet." To me: "Keep your expectations in check." He sat back down. The plate before him held a large, off-white block, densely sprinkled with brown and red flecks. "I have a class at six-thirty. You can have some of this if you want."

"I thought you were off on Wednesday," Clara said.

"Sensei's out sick, so I'm filling in."

When we shook, I'd felt the callus on the edge of his hand and across the knuckles, and he'd moved with a kind of grounded fluidity you only get after years of disciplined training.

"Karate?" I said.

"Tang soo do." He didn't seem offended. "You?"

"Level Four Combatives." Pentagon bureaucrats could never use a simple phrase when polysyllabic jargon would do.

Rondo grinned. "Uh-huh. And?"

"Life experience."

"Must be an interesting life."

Of *course* Clara's friends wouldn't be self-absorbed dullards. I looked at his dinner. "What are you eating?"

"Lao tofu, with togarashi pepper and nori. Want some?"

"Got any steak?"

"No, but you could put A.1. sauce on it if you want."

When you meet a woman's male friends, it can be awkward, especially when the parameters aren't clear—no matter what anybody says, there are always boy-girl complications lurking. But I wasn't getting any of that from Rondo. No posturing of any kind, in fact.

Maybe if I was so good at some martial art that I could substitute for the master, I'd be more self-confident, too.

"Kimmie went out," Rondo said. "And not back anytime soon, judging by the outfit she was wearing."

"Kimmie?" I looked at Clara, who had dumped her bag on a chair and was rummaging in the refrigerator. "You live with your coworker?"

"We were roommates first. She introduced me to the supervisor at the athenaeum."

"You know Kimmie?" Rondo cut a slab of tofu and shoveled it in.

"We met. She seems very quiet."

"*Kimmie?*"

"He's putting you on." Clara returned to the table with eggs, pepperoni, mustard and a Chinatown sack of lychees. "There might be an omelet in there somewhere."

"Cook much, do you?"

"Only coffee."

"Like I said." Rondo stood up, rinsed his plate in the enameled sink, and pulled a jacket from a hook on the back of the door. "I have to go."

"Did you read my story today?" asked Clara.

"Every word." He paused, and looked over at me. "Are you——?"

"No," said Clara.

"Ah." He nodded. "See you later."

When the door had closed, we looked at each other, across the table.

"Hungry?" Clara asked.

"Yeah, but not for raw eggs and mustard."

"Maybe there's bread around for toast."

Someone had music on somewhere, loud. Bass tremors drifted through the building. The kitchen was well kept, considering three unrelated twentysomethings lived there: the floor swept, dishes in the drainer, counterspace cluttered but clean.

Clara found an English muffin and some bread heels in the freezer. Pepperoni stretched it out, and lychees for dessert.

"Sorry," she said. "I didn't think—we could have stopped at the market."

"It's fine. I've had worse." Like on four-day infiltrations into Indian country, nothing but water and crumbled energy bars, but no need to mention that.

"Blacktail Capital," said Clara. "They're central. That's where the story is."

She was right, but I couldn't go break into their offices, too. They'd be Fort Knox compared to Riverton. "Saxon, maybe," I said.

"What do you have on him? Besides what you've told me?"

"Nothing."

"Nothing? In the digital age? You just haven't looked hard enough."

"All right, you tell me." I looked around. "Where's your computer?"

She got it out, pushing our plates to one side on the table. I swung the keyboard my way long enough to log into one of my one-off email addresses and pull down the file Ernie had forwarded.

"I know his name and employer," I said. "And scraps from this—his service record."

I turned the computer back to Clara, showing her Saxon's Official Military Personnel File, the 201.

"They blacked out just about everything, didn't they?" She scrolled down. "Birth date, Social . . . wait. There's one address, Fort Campbell. Where's that?"

"Kentucky. I'm pretty sure that's his last service posting."

"It's not current?"

"He's been elsewhere for years."

That was it for the 201. A straight Google search yielded nothing except some press releases more or less identical to the one I'd found, when Blacktail hired Saxon. They'd never publicized anything after that.

"Which suggests something about what he does there," I said.

Clara called up Blacktail's webpage.

"Not much here, is there?" she said, looking at the same minimalist presence I'd found earlier.

"No, but that's typical for a hedge fund. They're not trolling for customers or trying to sell anything. And they mostly want a low profile regardless. It's just a splash portal for their investors."

"Where are they located?"

"Chalder, New Jersey. Up in the north, close to where 287 crosses into New York."

"Suburbia."

"Which makes Saxon an anomaly. You don't need SOF skills to check employee badges in a New Jersey office park."

"We know Blacktail was on the other side of Akelman's losses. Saxon attacked me after I wrote about Marlett, and he killed Faust. Seems definitive to me."

"Yup. I just wish we knew more about him."

"All right." I noticed that Clara's mouth thinned as she confronted obstacles. "Time to get serious."

"Good." She was the digital detective; maybe she could work some magic.

"We'll start with the identity theft arenas."

"Identity theft?"

"Carding forums, hacker tool startups, you know. East European warez chat rooms. That sort of thing."

I watched her type, much faster than anyone I'd ever seen. "Spend a lot of time on the dark side, do you?"

"Anyone with money can buy a LexisNexis subscription. This stuff you have to work for, and most reporters don't bother. Gives me an edge."

"Hmm."

"So . . . let's see. How about the VA? Saxon's a vet."

"You're going to break into Uncle Sam's *mainframes*? On your home network? Are you nuts?"

"No, no. But the VA has outright lost tens of thousands of veterans' records," she said. "Mostly on misplaced laptops, that sort of thing. The key data is for sale if you know where to ask."

And Clara did know, apparently. It cost some money. "They like Bitcoin," she said. "Liberty Reserve was popular for a while, until the Europeans cracked down. It's all anonymous."

Learn something new every day. The high-finance criminals I usually deal with have far too much cashflow for fly-by-night digital-gold schemes—they launder their money right through Citi or Bank of A. This ground-level hawala was something I hadn't seen before.

But no results—another empty net. "What next," muttered Clara, thinking aloud.

"How about tax returns?" I asked. "He's Blacktail's director of security. That's not an under-the-table kind of position. There must be a W-2 somewhere."

"You're right," she said. "But not even the Feds can get at those. The IRS is mandated to protect privacy, and they do a damn good job of it."

"Better than the military? We got his 201, after all."

"It's their systems, believe it or not. Congress has deliberately underfunded the IRS for years, which means they're still using these, like, fifty-year-old System/360s running Fortran and storing data on punch cards. Hacking their data is like trying to crack Linear B—it's so ancient, modern technology is completely frozen out."

How about that? Maybe I could start filing my own returns again.

"What about professional groups?" Clara asked. "I don't know, the NRA maybe? What kind of affiliations does a corporate security officer have?"

"I can't see Saxon going to ASIS conventions in Vegas. And he doesn't need to read their bulletin." We tried anyway. There must have been twenty organizations for guys in this sort of job, but we couldn't find Saxon in any of them.

Close to nine o'clock Clara gave up. "I hate to say it, but I think he's defeated the internet."

"He works in New Jersey, lives somewhere in the tristate megalopolis and has taken himself completely off the grid?"

"Apparently."

"I'm impressed." Too bad he'd tried to kill me before we had a chance to talk shop. "What now?"

"We know where he works, right?"

"Yeah."

"Well . . ."

Of course it was the obvious next step. "I'll drive up in the morning."

"By yourself?" She frowned. "Given what this guy seems capable of, is that a good idea?"

I felt an odd reaction, defensive and grateful at the same time. Having someone worried about me was not a common occurrence—really, since I got out of the service.

"Maybe I'll call Zeke."

"Don't take stupid chances." Clara put her hand on mine, next to the laptop.

A long moment passed. I couldn't look away from her eyes.

"I . . . have a question," I said.

"Hmm?"

"I can't figure out why I'm a mistake."

She laughed. "Let's see. Mysterious past, check. Violence and mayhem, check. No job, mortgage, car, children, dog, 401(k) or any apparent signifier of conventional life whatsoever, check."

"Actually, I do have a car."

"Oh? Well." She leaned across the small table, still looking right into my eyes. "In that case . . ."

CRASH!

The front door banged open, hitting the wall. I rolled off the chair, diving left, reacting without thought. Plates fell from the table—

"Silas!"

I hit the base of the counter, spun to my feet. Dishes shattered on the floor, shards bouncing.

"Hey!"

Kimmie stood openmouthed in the doorway. Her short leather jacket was dark and shiny from rain, her black boots soaked.

"What are you *doing*?" Clara stood up now, too.

"Um." I straightened. "Hi, Kimmie."

"You remember Silas," Clara said.

"Sure." She continued to stare.

"He stopped by for dinner."

"Oh."

"Rondo said you were going out for the evening."

Kimmie shrugged. "Too wet. Everybody's at home or whatever."

We cleaned up the broken dishes, righted the chairs. Kimmie shucked her boots at the door, dried off, then offered to share the takeout General Tso's she'd picked up. Which was generous, for three people. I tried not to have more than a few mouthfuls.

But the mood between Clara and me had fled once more, lost in the shift to normal domesticity. When we'd finished, I found my jacket myself.

"Let me know what you find at Blacktail," Clara said, seeing me off at the door.

"I might have to embargo the details."

"Even if they're really, really good? And could totally make my career?"

I smiled. "You don't need my help for that."

"Call me." She ran her fingers over the uninjured side of my face—a bare, fleeting touch.

"First thing," I said, and got out of there.

Clara was totally rewiring my life.

CHAPTER TWENTY-EIGHT

"We don't even know he's here." Zeke, grouchy.

"That's why it's called surveillance."

"Seems like better recon would help."

I couldn't argue with that. We were sitting in a white Ford Fusion, a car as bland and unappealing as its name, which of course is why I chose it at the rental desk in Newark Airport.

Leaving the Mallory in the morning, I'd bought a MetroCard from an automated kiosk in the Second Avenue station—the uptown side, with no attendant present. Because I still had it, I'd tried Hayden's credit card. It worked just fine. I guess he hadn't gotten around to canceling it.

With that confirmed, I'd gone ahead and taken the train all the way out to Newark. On the way I studied Hayden's driver's license. He and I were just close enough in age and hair color that I could probably use it, and the Amex, to rent the car, pretending that I'd just flown in. Why not? He'd caused me enough aggravation. I might as well take a little back.

Not to mention I was still suspicious. If Hayden was involved somehow, it couldn't hurt to fuck with his identity. Leave some unexpected clues for the government trackers. Shake him up, he might make a mistake.

As one more precaution for myself, I swapped license plates with an identical Fusion in the next spot. In the vast rental lot the switch took less than a minute.

This was as close to bulletproof anonymity as you could get on the road nowadays, at least without a fully forged identity. If, God forbid, the police ever had reason to run the plate, it would show the proper make, model and owner; the chance that they'd notice a discrepancy in the handwritten rental agreement was effectively nil.

All dressed up and nowhere to go. Zeke and I were parked along the far boundary of the Spruce Hill Office Park, off Route 118 in Chalder. A sprawling, two-story, faux-brick building housed a dozen companies with names like Everspritz Technology and Human Potential Corporation. We hadn't gone into the lobby to check, but from Blacktail's suite address we deduced they were on the second floor.

The windows formed silver-blue reflective bands around the building. We couldn't see in. Occasionally someone walked in or out, to or from a car. A narrow strip of scraggly grass separated the parking lot from the six-lane roadway.

"What if he goes out the back?" said Zeke.

"Seems unlikely. There's no car parking in the rear." Just asphalt up to the loading dock, dumpsters and a windowless utility building. I'd checked earlier, when we arrived. "He'd need to roll up the dock doors, too."

"I'm going to have to piss soon."

"There's a peanut butter jar in the backseat."

"Empty?"

"Mostly."

"I'll try to hold it."

He wasn't really grumbling. Waiting behind a mud wall in hundred-degree heat and full armor, wondering whether it was going to be mortar rounds or just sniper fire when the anticipated engagement finally began—*that* was something to complain about. This was about as challenging as a nap on the couch.

"What kind of support does he have in there?" Zeke said.

"I don't know. It's not like Blacktail has piles of cash to worry about or two hundred employees to keep an eye on. From their website it seems like they might have two dozen people, tops, and a roomful of PCs."

"So why do they need a Director of Security in the first place?"

"That's the question." I shifted in my seat. The sun had been going in and out of clouds all day, and at the moment it was shining too brightly through my side of the car. "Millions of dollars flow through there, but it's all electronic."

"I thought all the trading happened down at the stock exchange. On Wall Street."

"No. The NYSE floor's more than half empty now. I think they keep a few guys running around just so it looks good for the tourists. Everything else is in the ether."

"I guess."

"The exchange set up its big new data center in Mahwah, about five miles from here. Blacktail must have a direct feed—probably through a massively armored cable pipe, underground."

"If we knew where it was," Zeke said, "we could cut it. That would invite their attention."

I looked at him. "That would invite a full-scale assault."

"Yeah?"

"In any given second, Blacktail might account for ten percent of total trading volume—ten percent of the entire market! Fuck with that and commandos will be rappelling out of the sky."

"Amazing." Zeke had a glint in his eye.

"No," I said. "Stop thinking like that."

He studied the building. "Saxon better show up soon, all I have to say."

The afternoon wore on. Eventually enough people would drive away that we'd be too conspicuous. I drank some bottled water, ate a granola bar. Zeke seemed to have entered a zen state of watchful stillness. Or possibly he'd fallen asleep with his eyes open. Hard to tell.

I drifted into my own road hypnosis. Spruce Hill was perhaps the dullest architecture on the planet—a brick-shaped block, made of brick. Traffic motored past. Clouds drifted slowly in the sky. Somewhere, paint dried.

I put in the bluetooth earpiece and called Johnny. The markets were open, but he made a few minutes to talk.

"How's Plank Industrials doing?" I asked.

"Down, down, down. It's a feeding frenzy. And not just the stock—guys are starting to short the bonds."

"Really?" Short selling bonds was a notably riskier way to bet on a company's downfall, mostly because the market for them was much less liquid. The best position in the world is worthless if you can't buy or sell out of it. "So everyone's totally convinced that Terry Plank is going to die."

"Not necessarily. If he has to spend the next few months in hiding, it's almost the same thing—his business still suffers."

I thought about that. "Still seems ghoulish."

"It's just a trade." Hairsplitting ethical philosophy was not Johnny's forte. "Where are you?"

"Chalder. The salt flats of American culture."

"Jersey." His dismissive shrug was clear in that single word. "What's happening there?"

"Waiting for the killer to show up." I explained Blacktail's connection to at least three of the deaths so far.

"Blacktail Capital? The flash traders? They're huge. You're saying they're *involved*?"

"Maybe. Probably."

"And you *didn't tell me this*?" Johnny sounded upset.

"Well . . ."

Gunned motors sounded in the parking lot. I caught a glimpse of a black truck roaring up the aisle toward us.

"Holy sh—"

Brakes slammed and wheels screeched. A second vehicle—an SUV—bounced over the grass strip behind us and scraped along Zeke's side, jolting our car and banging it forward a few inches. The truck slewed around in front, stopping at an angle across our left front.

I'd started the engine in an instant, but we were boxed. Zeke couldn't even open his door.

"Silas?" Johnny's voice in my ear. "What's going on?"

I ignored him.

One man leaped from the truck. Gray body armor, flat cap, combat boots—and a SCAR assault rifle. Black-tinted windows concealed however many others remained in the vehicles.

Zeke drew his handgun and fired without hesitation. Four shots in an instant, right across the windshield. The safety glass fractured into a million spiderweb cracks but held together. He shoved forward, out of his seat, going right through and rolling across the hood. The shattered sheet of glass fell aside.

The attacker was on my left, swinging his weapon up. I opened my door fast, levering off the floor, and slammed him in the torso. The rifle stuttered. Unaimed bullets cracked into the car's metal and fiberglass.

Zeke was gone. I heard a couple of shots.

"Drop your fucking *guns!*" The truck had a bullhorn.

I didn't even have mine out. I jammed the transmission into reverse and bucked backward, but the Fusion's bumper scraped and jammed on the curb. Okay—forward, then. I struck the truck, budging it left a foot or two.

Another guy jumped out, leaving his door hanging. He had a handgun in each hand, like some idiot Hollywood hero.

Good news, because it's near impossible to aim either one that way.

On the other hand, his range was about six feet. Both pistols came up, pointed at me. I hunched, involuntarily.

A shot, and the man jerked, then fell.

Thanks, Zeke.

I rammed the car backward, then forward again. More gunfire.

The Fusion's side windows blew out in a spray of glass. I kept going. Neither vehicle could be pushed out of the way, but daylight opened up between them. Side panels screeched and tore as I scraped through.

"Stop! Stop!" More yelling through the bullhorn.

As I cleared the truck, I looked right and saw Zeke coming out of the SUV.

Out? He must have gone in the opposite door, shot his way through, and kept right on going.

One hostile vehicle out of action.

The truck suddenly moved, leaping forward and sideswiping the row of parked vehicles in front of us. I spun my wheel right, gaining room but destroying the front of a Prius.

Zeke yanked open the rear passenger door and dived into the backseat.

"Go!" he yelled.

"I know, I know!" I put the accelerator on the floor, and the Fusion shot ahead.

"Fucking *bumper* cars!" Zeke laughed.

"Silas?" Amazingly, Johnny was still on the line.

We rocketed down the long row of parked vehicles. The truck pulled close, then struck the Fusion's rear corner, throwing it into the beginning of a spin, but we ricocheted off a minivan and I wrenched the wheel back into line.

"They're wearing armor." Wind through the absent windshield blew bits of glass into my chest and made my eyes tear.

"Go around the corner." Zeke reloaded, leaned around and fired twice at our pursuers.

"Right." So far none of the collisions had been at speed, so sensors had not blown the airbags in our car or their truck. But if we arranged for them to plow into us, that might change. "Hold on."

I sped up as the end of the parking lot approached, letting them think we were heading for the exit. At the last car in the row, I pulled the wheel sharp right, then immediately back left. The car swayed, its centripetal acceleration amplified by the one-two, and slid into a smoking left turn. I hit the gas, hard, and the rear tires whined, still in their skid. We cleared the corner just as the rubber finally caught traction, coming out of the turn and accelerating into the alleyway behind the building.

"Yawww, motherfucker!"

Zeke's battle zone war whoops could be downright embarrassing.

The service way was barely one truck wide, the loading dock on one side and the utility shack on the other. I hit the brake pedal with both feet, throwing the car's nose almost to the ground, and we screamed to a halt sixty feet in.

"Brace!" I shouted and threw my arms in front of my face.

The truck took a few extra seconds coming around the corner. The driver must have been good, because they appeared going almost as fast as we'd been.

Really good. In one second he saw us, realized I'd set up the collision—and decided to avoid it.

He feathered his steering, just enough to pass us. The truck had to be going forty, fifty miles an hour. It flashed by, a blur of black metal. I could see it start to turn in again, the driver calculating he had barely enough room to slide in between us and the utility shed.

He almost made it.

A stepdown transformer was bolted onto the shed's exterior wall, several fat power cables routed overhead. The truck was inches clear of the wall but struck the big metal box, breaking it free of its mount and dragging the cables.

The driver slowed, too late. His truck caromed off the wall, bouncing up on two wheels, completely out of control. Cables snapped, and masonry cascaded down where the junction box was torn free.

"Uh-oh," said Zeke.

The utility shed exploded.

One instant—I saw huge sparks, and flame and blast debris blowing out from the epicenter.

Then something struck the front of the car, and the airbags detonated. I was punched in the face hard enough to lose consciousness for a moment.

When I swam back a few seconds later, the bags had deflated. With no windshield, I had a nice clear view of the destruction still raining down in front of us. The utility building had half collapsed, metal and wood sticking into the air, while flames leaped from the transformer. The truck was crumpled against the loading dock, where it had finally come to rest, one door sprung open. Even as I struggled to get moving, a man lurched out of the cab and stumbled several steps.

Zeke grabbed my shoulder.

"Come on! Gonna blow!"

We ditched, scrambling out and running back the way we'd

come. At the building's corner I glanced back. A fireball exploded from the wreckage, engulfing the Fusion and ticking our way.

The truck was on the other side. I could see it dimly through the white heat. Whether its occupants had escaped was, at least for the moment, irrelevant—there was no way for them to reach us through the inferno.

A hundred yards away we stopped. People were already coming out the front door, some running. Every single person we saw had a cellphone pressed up against their ear, shouting.

"Shit," said Zeke.

"That was *too* fucking CGI." I brushed grit from my face. "What the fuck were they storing in that shed, Tovex?"

"The transformers. Loaded with insulating oil, flammable as all hell."

"I guess so." I watched thick black smoke pour from behind the building. The first siren was just audible.

"Those guys—Saxon?"

"No. Not the two I saw. I think I recognized one from the attack on Clara, but not for sure."

"Might be time to go."

I took a moment to look him over, while he did the same for me—shock could make you unconscious of all sorts of injuries. We both seemed to have nothing worse than some scratches and grime.

"The car's fucked," I said.

"Good." The more damage, the slower CSI would get anything useful out of it.

"Yeah, but I don't think there's a subway nearby." I pulled out my phone, and realized that I still had the earpiece in place. "Johnny? Are you still there?" The display indicated the call was still clocking, but I didn't hear anything. I hit the red button and dialed a new number.

"Calling a taxi?"

"No, we're going to have to walk." I gestured, and we set off, trying to look normal, strolling through an increasing flow of gawkers headed inward. "I thought maybe I ought to report the Fusion stolen."

"That's courteous."

"For Hayden's sake—to keep him out of it a few extra hours."

"Why bother? You said he was dirty."

A second explosion boomed behind us. "Maybe you didn't notice, but we're kind of *implicated* right now. Let's at least make a getaway before we go back to fucking with Hayden's life."

Zeke nodded. "Think the false ID will hold up?"

"Not unless we're luckier than we deserve. But they might not be able to make a connection to me. Or you, for that matter."

"Hope not."

"What I can't figure is, how did they notice us?"

"Sitting in the car all afternoon? Any dummy could have seen us from their window."

"Maybe."

We watched a police car make its dramatic entrance, lights and siren and horn all going. It was green and tan—must have been Chalder local cops. The first fire engine followed close behind, and then the rush started: staties, ambulances, unmarked Interceptors.

Overhead, helicopters began to appear, rerouted from their watch over the afternoon commute.

"You know," said Zeke, "there're times I'm happy to work for you for *free*."

"That's convenient," I said.

CHAPTER TWENTY-NINE

"Awesome." Johnny leaned back in the cracked vinyl booth. "That is a literal description. I stand in awe of what you did."

"You're sitting."

"I was standing when I heard, though. *Four hundred seventy* points off the Dow. Fucking amazing."

Seven p.m. in Dan's All-American, a little place down in Soho. Zeke had let me stay at his place for a few hours, to clean up, watch the news, make some calls. I even napped for an hour. But Zeke really *doesn't* have electricity, so at six it got dark.

Zeke might have been fine with an oil lamp, but not me. He fell asleep before seven, and I arranged to meet Johnny. I'd drained one cellphone talking to Clara earlier, and at Zeke's I couldn't recharge the batteries. Obviously. Here in the diner I had it plugged in to one of the outlets Dan provides for laptop users.

"At least this time there's a clear explanation for the crash," I said. "So the market should come right back up again."

"It hadn't as of close. Volatility's through the roof overseas, too. I think this one's going to reverberate for a while."

Johnny was practically rubbing his hands, like some gleeful Victorian. Traders love a high volatility index more than anything. So long as the market's moving, up or down doesn't matter.

It's Flatland where the experienced guys go broke.

"It wasn't just the sudden outage," he continued. "Blacktail was running some sort of microarbitrage on a slew of old-economy dinosaurs. When you knocked them offline, they had something like six thousand open positions—that one instant!"

A lot. More than enough. Several of Blacktail's major orders were for stocks in the actual Dow industrials index—which is only thirty companies, not the entire exchange. As they plummeted, panic set in, first as other traders' automatic sell orders were triggered, then as humans started making split-second decisions to get out. Everything spiraled out of control even faster than last time, despite the array of system tweaks the regulators had put in place.

When a bubble bursts, no safeguards in the world can keep it inflated. No one should even try.

I watched Johnny bulldoze through his snack: pan-fried steak, sweet-potato fries and red gravy.

"You heard it start," I realized.

"Mm-hmm." His mouth was stuffed.

"On the phone. And I'd just told you I was outside Blacktail's offices." I started to laugh. "Damn, Johnny, you were in, weren't you?"

"Twenty seconds." He swallowed, drank some Nehi out of the bottle. "I heard the blast, and you yelling, and I figured—no way that's a good thing. Maybe neutral, but certainly not good. I got in twenty seconds before everyone else started realizing that Blacktail had gone dark."

It doesn't sound like much, but in the hyperkinetic world of modern market flow, twenty seconds is an eternity.

"What'd you make?"

Johnny looked at me. "Tell you what, tonight's on me."

"Oh, come on."

"Two point six."

"For twenty seconds of trading."

"Isn't life grand?"

Outside young businessmen and women, leaving work, wandered toward the Soho bars. Dan's was half full. A steady buzz of plates clanking and conversation and WPKN on the radio kept the background lively.

"Are they going to let you keep it?"

"That's a good question. We'll see."

"I thought—after the flash crash and the last October surprise—they put policy in place. Sixty percent. Sounds like you exceeded that."

Dominated by unregulated and totally out-of-control high-volume trading, all the markets—not just the NYSE—had become disturbingly unsettled in the last few years. Unexpected events seemed to occur more and more often, each time precipitating jaw-dropping swings in value. And it usually only took a few minutes, or even just a few seconds, for shockwaves to hammer through the entire universe of tradeable assets.

Instead of fixing the root problem—a simple half-percent transaction tax would have done the trick—the exchanges and the regulators tinkered with marginal solutions. One was to declare, arbitrarily, that any trade executed on a price swing exceeding 60 percent would be subsequently canceled.

"Sure, they put the rule in place," Johnny said. "And about five minutes later every trader on the Street had reprogrammed his stops at fifty-nine percent."

"You too?"

"What do you think? I mean, it's like the state police announcing, in advance, every one of their speed traps. Of course I made the limits automatic."

Although, in truly panicky situations, stop orders can miss by a mile. In the end, human intervention is always best, as I think Johnny was trying to tell me.

"It's something to be proud of," he said. "How many people can say they crashed the *total fucking market* all by themselves?"

"Ugh."

"Hey, you're not eating. How about some grits and gravy?"

Zeke and I had left behind a dramatic crime scene. Saxon's operatives had apparently fled—or if they were talking, the cops were being remarkably closemouthed about it. I had no idea where VINs and registrations on the truck would lead, but the Fusion's rental record was not obscured well enough to hold off the two hundred FBI agents reportedly on the case.

Trying to blow up Times Square is one thing. Taking down the foundation of American capitalism is quite another.

When they caught up with him, Hayden Pennerton was going to have some explaining to do.

"By the way," said Johnny, "why are you even out in public?"

Good question.

"If my number's up, my number's up," I said. But the truth was, I figured Zeke and I were still pretty well covered. At the airport rental desk I'd worn driver's gloves, a ball cap, the tinted glasses and another slug of Panzer cologne. The explosion at Blacktail would have burned off other prints, DNA, and so forth. The forces of order might get lucky, but we hadn't posted suicide videos on a jihadist website or left behind a wadded-up utility bill or bought our guns a week ago in Virginia and signed our real names to the paperwork— which is how these cases always seem to get solved.

Unless Johnny was an FBI informant, it would be an uphill investigation.

Still, for a moment he almost looked concerned. "Maybe I shouldn't be seen with you."

"Dan doesn't pay attention."

"Dan died a year ago."

"What?"

"Didn't you know that? Some Korean family bought out the estate."

Now that he mentioned it, I realized the food had improved lately.

"I didn't cause the damage," I said. "*They* were shooting at *us*. You want villains, talk to Blacktail."

"Uh-huh. I'm sure the cops are."

I pushed some hash around my plate, trying not to check the doors and windows too often or too obviously.

"I could use some help," I said.

"Yeah? Judge Dredd time?"

"Well—"

"Kidding." He raised his fork briefly. "Whatever you need."

"See if you can find Blacktail's fingerprints on any of the others.

Even Plank. I know he's not dead yet, but there's all kinds of action in the stock. Do you have any sources that can read the order flow?"

"That's not legal."

"Not realtime, for Christ's sake." I paused, realizing Johnny had not actually answered the question. "Wait a minute."

"What?"

"Are you telling me you *do* have someone inside?"

"Of course not." He looked at me, innocent. "If I did, I'd be retired. Motoring out to my private island on a three-hundred-foot yacht."

True—or in jail. That was one kind of insider trading the SEC had a genuine zero tolerance toward.

"So ask around. See what you can find out. I need something to take to the authorities when I give myself up."

"When's that going to be?"

"Why, you want to be there?"

"Just wondering. You know."

I watched him vacuum up the last of his grits. "You see a position, don't you?"

"Well . . ."

"Why don't you hire a band to dance on my grave, too?"

"No, listen." He wiped his face with a paper napkin. "Suppose the DA announces they have a suspect in custody? In about ten seconds, everyone's going to realize that means Terry's out of danger. Plank Industrials will rebound, big time."

"By 'suspect,' you mean *me*."

"In fact, we might see a serious short squeeze." His eyes got a distant look. "I told you—one-fourth of the entire float has been sold short. If the stock price began to go up unexpectedly . . ."

He didn't have to finish. Short investors had, in effect, sold shares in Plank that they didn't actually own. If the price dropped further—as everyone expected would happen when Terry caught the Jackal's bullet—these guys would simply buy some of the newly cheaper shares to close their positions, and pocket the difference as profit.

But if the share price rose, the value of the short position would decline, and then go negative. Brokers hate it when their clients are suffering losses, even only on paper, and they generally insist that the traders post additional collateral to cover the potential deficits. If the investor didn't have cash lying around, however, he'd have to close out his position, by buying the now more expensive shares to cover his short sale. See what happens? The rising price forces more buying, which pushes the price higher, which squeezes more shorts to close—and so on, in a vicious cycle that can cause share prices to skyrocket. The greater the short interest, the nastier the squeeze, and the higher the price might go. Fundamentals become irrelevant.

The shorts get killed, always a big crowd pleaser. The stock price shoots upward, which delights management and regular shareholders. Trading volume is huge, making the exchanges happy. Win-win, except for the losers who'd gone short in the first place.

Johnny wanted in on the "win" part.

"I'll think about it," I said.

"I'll cut you in for ten percent beneficial interest."

I had to laugh. "That's too cheap. Fifty-fifty."

"You're not putting up a penny!"

"No, but I'll be the one getting Mirandized."

"Twenty-five."

A minute later we'd agreed on thirty, and I still wasn't sure if Johnny was serious.

"In a perfect world," I said, "this won't be necessary. The proper authorities will find the real killers first, and I'll never be part of the story."

"A perfect world?"

"I know." I closed my eyes, tired. "That's not the one I live in, either."

Johnny mopped up the last of his food. "I might get dessert. Lime pie?"

"No thanks."

He flipped through the plastic menu, then called an order to the counterman. Turning back to the table, he said, "You need a place to stay tonight? I'm going home, but you could use the apartment the company keeps downtown. I don't think any of my guys are using it tonight."

"A trader's crash pad?" Visualize the wildest frat party imaginable, followed by an earthquake. "No thanks."

The pie came, a slab of nuclear-waste green under fake whipped cream. Johnny slid it in front of him.

"The narrative is getting all twisty," he said. "First it's dead bankers. Then we hear that other bankers—the ones still standing, that is—have paid a hired gun to hunt down the outlaw gang. Now a trading firm gets blown up. Everyone seems to believe the bad guys did that, too, but when you think about it, it doesn't really make sense."

"I know, I know."

"What's funny is that you're at the center of all of it."

"Funny—" I stopped.

Johnny looked up, utensils suddenly still in his hands as he stared at me. "What?"

It was like a door slamming open, hitting me right in the face.

Akelman and Sills happened before I was paying attention. But Marlett?—I was about five minutes from being there when he was shot. Faust?—on the scene. Blacktail, Hayden, they happened *because* of me. Even Plank, who wasn't dead yet, but it was for his sake that Ganderson had outed me, to draw fire away.

And Clara.

I'd put her square in the line of fire. She was a target because she'd published leaks that I'd given her, despite knowing how dangerous they were.

"I have to go." I was already sliding out of the booth, grabbing the first cellphone I found in my jacket.

"What's going on?"

"Collateral damage." Dialing.

"I *told* you, I'm getting the tab, no need to—"

"I'll see you, Johnny."

I pushed through the crowded booths, mumbling excuse-me's, phone jammed to my ear. Outside, as the diner's glass door swung shut, voices and clatter faded into Soho traffic noise and the city's constant background hum.

"Hello?" A male voice.

"This is—who are you?"

"Rondo. Who's calling?"

It sounded like him. "Silas. Is Clara there?"

"In the shower. She got home twenty minutes ago."

"She's—" I stopped. *A hunter-killer team has her in their gunsights. They could show up any second with breaching charges and fully auto assault weapons. They want to kill her, you, me and everyone in the vicinity.*

Lunatic talk. Rondo would think I was nuts.

"She's in danger," I said. "Put her on."

"In the *shower*, I said. Look, she told me a little about it. We're fine."

"No." My jaw was so taut I could barely talk. "You are *not* fine."

"We're on the third floor." His voice was calm. "Kimmie's out, probably for the night. You've seen our entrance—the foyer doors are as old as this building, two and a half inches of solid mahogany. Ten minutes ago I pulled the electric cable at the junction box, so the intercom works but it's impossible to buzz the door open. Right now I'm sitting at the window, and I can see the entire block."

"Well . . ."

"We're secure."

"I'm still coming over."

"Yeah, fine. But you don't have to rush."

Another minute and I actually believed him. Even if Saxon's cowboys showed up, they wouldn't get in easily, and Rondo had the phone in his hand, 911 on speed dial.

"Okay," I said.

"It's covered." And I think what convinced me, in the end, is that he didn't sound excited. Most people, situation like this, they're going to be amped up, thrilled to be part of something big, feeling the adrenaline—and consequently even less useful, if not downright dangerous to their own side. Rondo was in control of himself, and therefore in control of the situation.

All that time in the dojo, maybe.

"I'll be there soon as I can," I said again, and we hung up.

Through the diner's glass I could see Johnny, across the booths, joking with the waitress as he paid the bill. A group of women came out, laughing. A taxi rattled over asphalt patches in the street, headlight beams juddering.

Clara was safe, for the moment. But she wasn't the only person connected to me, and thus now in the crosshairs.

I stepped around the corner and dialed Walter's number. It rang. Five times . . . six. And then it stopped.

No message, no click. Just an abrupt nothingness on the line. I looked at the phone, a bad feeling starting in my chest.

"Call ended," the screen said. But I hadn't heard an answer.

I tried again.

"I'm sorry, the voicemail box is full. Please call again later."

Not good.

Walter and I had some characteristics in common—and not just shady résumés, dubious jobs and paranoia. We both depended on clients. For reasons I've already been tedious about, a single, anonymous phone number was more or less our only connection to these clients. Which meant keeping it in good order—taking messages, answering promptly. I would never, ever let a line get crammed up like that.

And neither would Walter.

My phone's display read 8:07. Walter's place wasn't far, over in the Lower East Side. I hesitated.

Saxon couldn't be in two places at once. If something was going on at Walter's, Clara was probably okay for now.

I crossed the street and headed up Houston.

CHAPTER THIRTY

Too many sirens.

A blue-and-white had screamed past me, going the same direction. I jogged south to Stanton, then turned east again. The night was cool but pleasant, people out and about on the sidewalks.

At the corner of Kent, a narrow, older street, a group of girls in skirts and boots were talking and staring and holding up their phones to take pictures. As I approached, I thought I smelled smoke, and apprehension bloomed into fear.

Walter's place was on Kent.

Fire engines blocked the street. Two ladders were up, pairs of fire-fighters on each pounding the building with water cannons. Flames had engulfed the top floor, flaring through rents in the brick walls. Smoke and spray and gusting ash filled the air, obscuring detail.

I stood with the girls, twenty feet from a uniformed police officer holding the perimeter, his back to us.

I'd seen Walter's sanctum once—an airy, modestly sized, top-floor loft. Now it was nothing but wreckage.

My phone rang, the same one I'd just tried to call Walter on. The caller ID meant nothing. I raised it to my ear and stepped away from the gawkers, moving back around the corner, back to the relative quiet of Stanton.

"What?" The voice on the other end was hoarse, unrecognizable. I frowned. "Who's this?"

"Silas?"

"Walter! You're—" *Alive,* I almost said, but cut it off. "What happened?"

"Forced retirement." He coughed. "They came in the front, some bullshit about neighborhood watch, but nobody visits me. Ever. I was already on my way out the back when the shooting started."

"It looks like they used incendiaries."

"Are you *there*?" Another cough. "No, that was me. I had to hit the burn switch."

Walter was too careful to leave evidence lying around. Unlike mine, though, his work was tangible—papers, documents, computer records, card blanks, passports, all sorts of material to make a prosecutor's day. He'd clearly prepared for a potential raid by rigging a self-destruct button.

But that meant that everything he used in his job was gone.

Forced retirement, indeed.

"I'm sorry, Walter. I'm really sorry."

A taxi dropped someone off at the corner, a young woman with a real camera and a laptop bag. She ran toward the fire. A reporter, probably, some kind of stringer or freelance blogger or just someone trying to break in.

"This life," he said. "It catches up to you."

"I know." More than Walter realized, perhaps. "Are you—when are you coming back?"

"Never."

"Aw, come on."

"I told you, bonefishing. I'm tired of this shit up here."

"Where are you?"

"Linden."

It took me a moment. Linden was a small, private airport in New Jersey, more exclusive and much less well-known than Teterboro. Walter was flying under the radar, almost literally.

"One thing," he said. "You got any idea who it was?"

"It's tied to Hayden." I explained how the Blacktail bomber's Fusion had been rented with Hayden's ID. "I don't know how they got on to you."

Walter paused. "Doesn't have to mean it was him. I've been doing other work, too."

"You keep your clients happy, I thought."

"It's not your normal type of business, and they're not your normal type of client." That seemed to strike him as funny. "As you know. Anyway, there've been a *lot* of them lately. All rush-rush. Yesterday I was here seventeen hours straight. Could be someone didn't trust me—thought he had to clear the tracks on his own."

"The Street *has* gone all Wild West this week. Snipers, assaults, killings." With me at the middle of too many, but no need to go into that. "Maybe you're right."

"One thing for sure, everybody's worried. Most of them are carrying guns now."

"I've noticed that."

"I wonder what a negotiation is like when you've got a squad's worth of small arms in the room?"

"I hope I never find out."

"Makes me all the more happy I'm leaving."

Another fire truck came down Stanton, siren whooping, and I had to cover the phone's mouthpiece for a moment. It was a hazmat unit, with a department Blazer right behind, carrying more crew.

"You use chemicals in your work?" I asked. "Vats of acetone, like that?"

"No. Why?"

"Never mind." I glanced around the corner. The fire still seemed out of control. "So you think it was one of your new customers did this."

"I don't know." He sounded frustrated. "Not that it would do much good. The smart ones don't give me their names."

I decided I'd seen enough, and turned to leave. "Get many dumb ones?"

"Well, I'll say this—you got to have *something* upstairs to make a hundred million dollars."

"And something else to try and steal it. What are you telling me?"

"A couple of the current buyers were smart. John Smiths. But I might have recognized one."

"Who was he?"

"I don't know." He coughed again. Got some smoke before he left, maybe. "I've seen him somewhere. In the papers? On TV? I'm just not sure."

"No name?"

"No."

That didn't seem to help me any, but I said, "Thanks."

"I generally don't pay much attention. I do my job, I do a little fishing, I don't care much about the rest of the world."

"So—"

Noise came over the phone for a moment. "So if I *have* seen the guy, he must be famous. Or he's not, but I ran into him somewhere, and don't remember."

"I get it." Someone who thought Walter knew him might perceive a threat. "I hope you got paid up front."

"Always." He almost chuckled. "You know that."

I let him go.

Whoever torched Walter's life, it didn't have to be Saxon. Ruthless opportunism was always the essence of successful business dealings in our part of the economy; now that freewheeling violence had apparently been green-lighted, potential shooters were everywhere. Dogs eating dogs.

I looked around for a cab. I needed to get to Clara's as fast as I could.

CHAPTER THIRTY-ONE

"I don't know," said Clara. "Should you even be *telling* me this?"

Nine-thirty, her apartment. Rondo had seen me in, then left. Kimmie was still out, not expected back until late.

We sat at the kitchen table, finishing off some grapes Rondo had bought that morning. Tap water and stale crackers rounded out the meal. I hadn't eaten much at Dan's, but I still wasn't hungry enough to notice.

The rush of relief I felt on finding her safe had been short-lived, and then it was right back to worrying and—though I didn't much want to deal with it now—guilt. Clara was in this situation because of me.

"Probably not," I said.

No, I shouldn't be talking to Clara, implicating her, jeopardizing myself. If she was ever compelled to talk—or just decided to, voluntarily, for some reason—I was in big, big trouble. Stupid. *Beyond* stupid.

I told her everything.

"I don't know what to think," she said. "I mean—it's like a

movie. Action, corruption, criminal activity at the highest levels."
She looked at me. "A hero."

"Oh well, you know."

"And I can't write about it. Any of it."

"Um . . ."

"You've given me the story of a lifetime, and I can't use it!"

"Sorry."

She laughed. "Jesus, Silas."

Music drifted faintly through the window, thumping from another apartment down the alley. Only the light over the sink was on, leaving shadows at the kitchen's ends.

"You're still wearing the same clothes," Clara said. "From, like, days ago. Haven't you been home at all?"

"Not since the attack on Faust."

"Are you still checked into the hotel?"

"Yeah, but I'm not sure I should go back."

The question hung in the air between us.

"Maybe Rondo can lend you something to wear." Clara punted.

"Where did he go?" I'd had mixed feelings when Rondo left. He seemed more and more like someone useful to have around in . . . situations.

She shrugged. "Meeting someone. He's kind of private about his personal life."

I could hardly complain about that.

But after a moment, Clara shook her head. "Actually, I asked if he could find something else to do for a few hours," she said. "Kimmie, too."

That wasn't a punt.

She leaned back in her chair, stretching her legs out to one side, past my ankles. Her presence seemed to fill the tiny space, driving out all other claims on my attention.

I reached out, brushed the hair back from her face and let my hand slide gently down her neck and shoulder.

It's glorious, that long endless moment when certainty finally arrives. You lean in and she's there, and you're there, and everything, *everything* is possible in the whole world.

Her mouth opened under mine, and I started to pull her close. The damn table was in the way—then somehow it wasn't, and we were grappling, tearing at each other, one chair falling and the other screeching across the floor. I felt her arms around and under my shirt, raking. I slipped one hand under the waistband of her skirt, cupped and lifted her into me.

We broke for air, an instant. She found my belt buckle the same moment I identified her bra snap. I stumbled, off balance, and my hip banged the counter. The dish drainer slid into the sink, crockery crashing.

"Oops. Sorry."

"Not here. Ridiculous. Come on." Clara pulled me toward a door off the narrow living room.

The bedroom had one small futon frame and one bed, clothes and towels and books piled everywhere. Clara clicked on a tiny Art Nouveau nightlight, and pushed me toward the bed.

"Two—?"

"Kimmie and I share this room. Rondo gets the other."

"Kimmie?" I looked at the futon in some alarm. "When is she coming home?"

"Don't worry." Clara disappeared out the door.

And Jesus, I was on *fire*. "Wait, what—"

She was back in a few seconds. "Rondo won't miss these."

A tear strip of condoms.

"Excellent. You sure?"

"He has plenty lying around—he's always bringing *his* boy-friends home."

Oh.

"How long is he going to be gone?"

"Long enough." She sank onto the bed, and I pulled her in and down. "More than long—oh!"

We lay in the tangled mess of clothes, sheets, books, paper, power cables and other stuff of daily life that Clara might have kept in a dresser or a wardrobe or a desk if the apartment had been large enough to accommodate such furniture. I could feel the beat of her heart, its rate still elevated—though no less than mine. She had one hand on my chest, lightly exploring the muscles.

"*Another* one?"

"They're mostly from the same incident."

"I thought you wore armored vests and like that."

"Not always." I remembered the outpost, far up a desolate, scorching valley, our only supply line a twice-weekly Chinook. The Talibs attacked at least every day, and after a few months, it was one long blur of battle, cold food and bad dreams, never enough sleep. By the end, all discipline had collapsed. We'd sometimes jump into fire-fights wearing nothing but boots and underwear. Visiting officers had trouble with that, but too many of us were dying for them to make anything of it.

"I'm not all post-traumatic or whatever," I said, "but let's talk about something else, okay?"

"I'm sorry."

The window was open a few inches, and a chill night breeze blew through, cooling the sweat on my back. Clara had pulled a blanket half over us.

"Last I checked," she said, "Terry Plank was still alive."

"Beating the odds."

"I don't know. Intrade hasn't set up an explicit contract for that outcome. But Plank Industrials stock is still in a nosedive."

"I saw. Down twenty-one percent at close. Hard to believe the market rates the entire company on one man."

"It's all short interest. Something like a sixth of the float has been sold short now."

"They're convinced Plank's a walking dead man." I settled more comfortably alongside her. "Which isn't a bad bet, considering the shooter's track record."

"So much for Ganderson telling the world he'd hired the Lone Ranger. You'd think that might have made Plank seem a little safer."

"In one sense." I ran one hand down her side. "On the other hand, Ganderson's announcement also confirmed the entire scenario. No doubters anymore."

"What are you going to do?"

"I don't know." I raised up on one arm. "I can't make the story add up right. I'm not saying all these bankers deserved to die—but there are so many possible motives, and so many possible suspects, it's too hard to sort out."

"On the other hand," said Clara, "they're no more than a drop in the bucket."

"How's that?"

"People willing to take your money and blow it on bad invest-ments? I mean, that's what Wall Street *does*. All of them. The real question isn't why Marlett and Akelman and the others were killed—it's why the thousands of others weren't."

"Hmm. That's a good point."

I could almost see it . . . but the understanding slipped away again. "I'll figure it out," I muttered. "One of these days."

"Anyway, like I said, what are you planning to do?"

"This second?" I lay back down. "I dunno. Maybe . . . drift slowly off to sleep?"

"No." Clara batted my chest. "About Saxon and his killers."

"Oh." Since she was right there, I brushed my nose against hers, then settled back. "Walter's not sure, but I think we have to assume they're the ones who destroyed his building. Which suggests they're sweeping up. Taking care of loose ends."

"What about going to the police?"

"Uh-uh. The only way to convince them I'm not a crank would mean incriminating myself, far more than I can tolerate."

"Can't *I* tell them? Or just send in an anonymous tip. They have an 800-number set up."

"That's the FBI. But, no—they're getting thousands of wackos a day. Plank would be dead ten times over by the time they took it seriously."

"You can't just let it go!"

"No." I sighed. "No, I can't."

A door opened, out in the apartment. A moment later light came on, shining under the bedroom door. Clara listened for a moment, then said, "Rondo."

"Thank goodness." I'd pulled the blanket all the way up to my chin without thinking.

"Don't worry. I put Kimmie's pajamas on the couch in the living room. She'll know what that means."

"Really?"

"Sure." Clara nestled.

After a moment, the nestling became more active.

"Hey," I whispered. "Keep it quiet."

"Don't worry about Rondo."

"No, I mean—"

"Let's just do . . . this."

"This?"

"This."

". . . this . . ."

CHAPTER THIRTY-TWO

At four a.m. I couldn't sleep anymore.

Clara mumbled and shifted when I disengaged myself, moving slowly and gently, but she didn't waken. I pulled on my boxers and slipped out of the bedroom.

Kimmie was zipped into a padded sleeping bag on the couch, only the top of her head visible. In the kitchen I drank a glass of water. Someone had cleaned up the dishes Clara and I had flung to the floor. LEDs glowed on electronic devices here and there, including my cellphone collection, all plugged in and charging. I leaned over to study the radio sitting on the microwave, wondering if I could turn it on quietly enough to listen to WBAI.

"Silas." A whisper.

I spun around. Rondo stood in the opening from the living room, wearing cotton shorts and an unbuttoned shirt with its sleeves torn off.

"Sorry," I whispered back. "Didn't think anyone was awake."

A shrug. He had a dominating presence in the small kitchen—taller than me, muscled, that absurd Fu Manchu. Every other guy who tried it would look ridiculous, but on Rondo the mustache was hip, even dangerous.

"Couldn't sleep."

"Me neither."

"Want coffee or something?"

"I'm good."

We sat at the table, lifting and setting down the chairs so they didn't make noise.

"Something I want to ask," said Rondo quietly.

"What's up?"

"I've known Clara, jeez, forever. Three years, almost. Kimmie was advertising for roommates, and we showed up at the same time."

Okay, I could see where this was going.

"She's a great person," I said.

"Yes." He watched me, not blinking. "She is."

"And you're wondering what she's gotten mixed up in." I waited for a nod. "You're wondering about me."

"Clara's important to us."

"And to me." I sighed. "The guys who attacked her in the park? I ran them off. We encountered one of them later, and he damn near killed me. Wait a minute." Rondo had started to speak, but I raised my hand slightly. "He'll be trying again. Absent other considerations, I'd probably just go home and wait for him. The issue is he obviously knows who Clara is."

He frowned. "You're drawing him here, instead of to you."

"He might come here first anyway."

"Risking Clara's life!"

"Protecting her."

We glared at each other for a minute.

"You're dangerous," said Rondo, finally.

"Not to Clara. Not to you or Kimmie, either."

"Anyone can tell." Rondo gestured slightly at my hands. "You've been punching the heavy bag for years. What do you weigh, Silas—one-eighty? Eighty-five?"

"In there."

"I've got forty pounds on you, then, and a third-*dan* rank. And I bet you could walk straight over me."

"Probably." I nodded. "It wouldn't be easy, though."

And somehow, that broke the tension. Rondo kind of laughed, without making any noise.

"No," he said. "It wouldn't."

We sat for a while longer. Rondo offered me a banana. Kimmie muttered and tossed on the couch.

"I need to talk to someone," I said. "Which means I need to leave for a while."

"I'm here until noon." He stood up. "Hang on."

While he disappeared into his room, I collected my cellphones, packing up the chargers and distributing the phones themselves into the pockets of my jacket.

"Here." Rondo offered me some folded T-shirts, underwear, a pair of pants. "Clara said you could use a change."

"Thanks." I guess I could roll up the cuffs—no time to be picky. "You don't mind staying with her?"

"I won't let anything happen to her."

I pulled on one of the shirts, switched my belt over to his pants, found a pair of socks.

"I'm sorry," I said. "I shouldn't have gotten her involved."

"Ah, forget it." He waved it off with one hand. "No one tells Clara what to do."

"I'm figuring that out."

He let me out, latching the door silently behind me. I stood on the landing for a moment, listening for the clicks of the double bolt and the security bar.

Then I headed downstairs, checking my watch: 4:50.

Ganderson should just be getting to his pool.

———

Outside, the city was still dark, the air damp and metallic with coming rain. One or two other people were on the street—a college kid on his way home, an older man leaving for an early shift. A bus trundled down the street, lit up inside, passengers staring blankly out the windows.

No public transit for me today. Ganderson was in Connecticut—I needed my car. I zipped my jacket, pocketed my hands against the dawn chill and walked quickly to the garage.

The concrete ramp smelled of old exhaust and oil. Goldfinger's booth was brightly lit, as always, and empty. No surprise—it was barely past five a.m.

But the wooden gate bar was lying on the ground, broken.

I stared. From the look of its position, the bar had been smashed by someone driving in, who'd knocked it off to one side. No tire marks, no panic braking.

Deliberate.

I ran to Goldfinger's utility cubicle. The metal door was closed, but a faint glow came from underneath.

"Ernie? Ernie?" I hammered the door, which abruptly opened under the blows.

A single ceiling bulb cast the only light, but it was enough to see the destruction. Every single item in the room had been tossed, and most thrown into the center of the floor in a big heap—broken shelves, soda cans, papers, old clothes. Goldfinger's computers were in pieces, along with his forensic equipment. The couch had been overturned, its upholstery completely ripped out.

Ernie himself lay on the concrete floor, shoved into a corner. His body was broken and unmoving, obviously dead.

For a long moment I could only stand motionless, shocked into immobility.

A hum from HVAC in the building, but no other noise in the garage. I looked back across the floor. All the cars seemed empty and still. And why would the attackers wait around? They had no reason to expect anyone—say, me. They were long gone.

No surveillance video. I'd asked about cameras, the first time I talked to Ernie and negotiated my own parking space. Building management was too cheap, and couldn't see a reason for it anyway. Not in a small mid-income, mixed-use facility.

Keeping my hands in my pockets, I stepped carefully into the room. Just to be sure, I leaned over Ernie, but there was nothing I could do. He was beyond help. It looked like a shooting—small entry wounds, big mess in back of his head and chest—and a sting of pro-pellant hung in the dank air, over the smell of blood and death.

But he had his guns out. One in each hand. And they'd been fired, too. I glanced backward, guessing at trajectories, and saw bullet holes in the wall, along with two obvious dents inside the door. There was some chance that not all of the blood was his.

He'd gone down like the OG he'd always wanted to be.

The rubbish of his small life lay strewn everywhere. I pushed at a torn cardboard box on the floor, uncovering a splayed paperback and a crumpled takeout sack. At the desk I saw a cordless telephone and an answering machine, both broken open. It looked like their chips had been pulled.

This was pointless. Whatever his attackers had been after, either they'd found it or they hadn't, but I certainly wouldn't learn anything by picking through the wreckage. And if it was a setup—unlikely, but always possible—then I needed to vanish.

Enough.

I couldn't take my car—the risk that it was connected, or that the killers had booby-trapped or marked it somehow, was too great. I ran, pulling a phone out as I went.

The emergency dispatcher must have just come on shift. She listened to the details, alert and no-nonsense, and I could hear a keyboard clacking as she started asking who I was. Of course I hung up, but hopefully she'd have the police on scene in a few minutes. It was the least Ernie deserved.

I wished I had more to give him.

CHAPTER THIRTY-THREE

I t had to have been Saxon.

Somehow he'd known when his military records had been accessed. Not too hard, now that it was all computerized in St. Louis—he'd have had no trouble bribing a GS-3 clerk to keep an eye out. Or just asking for a favor. Civilians were always happy to help out a bona fide war hero.

And if the records request was connected to the IAFIS search, well, where else would Saxon's fingerprints have come from but the baton? Which is what Ernie's killers must have been after. Saxon was eliminating all possible leads that might point in his direction.

A light misting rain had begun to fall, making the weary dawn even gloomier. Streetlights were half on, half off down the block. At the far corner I saw a street sweeper turn left and disappear, its clatter and roar fading.

I didn't want to go back to Clara's. Rondo was there keeping watch, but more important, my primary objective now had to be Saxon and his kill team. I could find them, or they could find me—either way, I wanted it to happen as far away from Clara as possible.

I had no leads, of course. But as I walked along, leaving the neighborhood, wondering where I could get a car, a realization hit.

My name wasn't the only one connected to every one of the dead Wall Streeters. There was another person, right at the center—and he'd been there all along.

I didn't stop walking. Too much undirected anger not to keep moving. But I found the right phone and hit redial.

"Yeah?"

"It's Silas."

Ganderson didn't sound surprised, or sleepy, or annoyed, or anything else I might have expected at five-thirty in the morning. Some kind of background noise—banging, voices—made the line a little unclear. But if anything, he sounded . . . distracted.

"What do you want?"

"We need to talk," I said. "Now."

"I'm in the middle of something here."

"*Right* now."

"Sorry, this isn't a good—"

"Are you at home?"

"No." He barked, not a laugh, but more than a grunt. "No, I'm at the fucking Eighth Precinct."

That brought my pace to a halt.

"Are you—did they arrest you?"

"Arrest me?" Angry. "What are you talking about? No, it's Brandon."

"Brandon. Your *son?*"

"Lawyer's on the way. Listen, do you know anyone here? Anyone in the cops at all? I just want him out!"

I was on 79th, almost at Second Avenue. A taxi waited at the light, going the other way. I waved to the driver, and he cut a U-turn against the red.

"The Eighth?" I said. "Lower East Side?"

"Yeah. You know it?"

"I'll be there as soon as I can." The cabbie coasted to the curb in front of me. I grabbed its door handle. "Don't go anywhere."

The Eighth Precinct is headquartered in the East Village, west of Tompkins Square Park, a four-story bunker of stone and exposed girders painted white. I'd never been inside, but I make it a point to scout all the lower Manhattan police stations at least once a year. I even visit the cop bars now and then, pretend I'm a wannabe, see what they'll tell me. You never know.

So I was familiar with the building. When the taxi had driven off, leaving me across the corner, I tried Ganderson's cellphone but got no answer.

I looked at the station. A half-dozen police vehicles were parked under "No Parking" signs along the street—unmarked blue-and-whites, a supervisor's SUV—and some of the other cars were obvious, with Fraternal Order of Police stickers in the windows or reflective vests on hangers in the rear. But no people were standing around, not in the rain, and the dark windows stared blankly back at me.

Not a happy-feeling place, but maybe that was the point.

Fortunately, I found Ganderson quickly enough, in a public waiting area to one side of the concrete reception desk. Plain steel benches sat along the opposite wall, under stained acoustic paneling. The officer behind the desk gave me the eye, but I nodded at Ganderson and walked over.

"They won't let me see him," he said, skipping right past the hi-how-are-you-thanks-for-coming bit.

"A good attorney will have you in straight away."

"Really?"

"Sure." Probably not, but it wasn't my problem. "What was he doing?"

"I don't know! I called the son of a bitch an hour ago. The retainer I pay him, you'd think he'd be here in his pajamas."

Behind the desk sergeant, an open space had some cubicles, with glass-fronted offices along the wall. A metal detector stood unused in front of an elevator bank. Two uniforms were talking in low voices at the stairwell, both holding styrofoam cups of coffee. Office noise—keyboards, the occasional cellphone, a copier—drifted from the bullpen. The holding cells were probably in the basement, hidden away, and the detectives would have their own unit somewhere else.

"I meant Brandon," I said.

"Oh." Ganderson grimaced. "He was being an idiot, as usual. He didn't say much on the phone, maybe because cops were listening in, but it sounded like he was hanging out at the park after midnight and one of his friends mouthed off to someone and it got out of hand."

"Which park?"

"Tompkins Square."

"Ah." The notorious after-hours drug market had been cleaned up and the homeless largely evicted, but it still wasn't exactly a frisbees-and-hot-dogs greensward. Not in the middle of the night. "Anybody hurt?"

"I don't think so."

"Doesn't sound like more than a misdemeanor, then. They're probably keeping him a few hours just to make a point."

"I hope you're right."

"Want to sit down? Go get a coffee or something?"

"No." He shook his head. "I need to wait here."

Ganderson wore a nylon shell over a plain polo shirt and jeans. His hair, which had always been exactly combed, stuck this way and that—buzzcut short but unruly. He had on a pair of eyeglasses, squarish titanium frames. Woken in the middle of the night, he must have skipped the contacts.

It was hard to square this worried father with the suspicions I'd begun to have.

On the other hand, I thought I noticed a bulge under his jacket.

"Hey," I said. "You're not carrying, are you?"

"What?"

"That handgun of yours. Did you just walk into a city police station *armed*?"

"Yeah, so?" He shrugged in annoyance.

"Jesus." I looked around, suddenly feeling like a focus of attention from every policeman in the building. "Someone sees that and we'll *both* be sitting in a cell, waiting for the lawyer."

"Calm down. It's licensed. And I contribute a nice packet to the PBA every year. They won't give me any trouble."

"Why do you have that cannon, anyway?"

"Four dead guys and another on deck, that's why. If those terrorist madmen come after me, they're going down first."

I glanced at the sergeant again, but he seemed to be ignoring us.

"And now they've struck again," said Ganderson. "Though nothing like the pattern so far."

I brought my attention back. "Is Plank dead? I hadn't heard."

"Plank? What are you talking about?"

"You said——"

"Blacktail." He frowned. "The terrorists hit Blacktail yesterday. Don't you get the news?"

"Oh, that."

"Plank's still alive and well. CNBC did an interview this morning—asked him what *he* thought about the car bomb."

The cabbie'd had his radio on during my ride down the length of Manhattan. The world seemed to have decided that the anarchist cell was floundering, and Terry Plank too well hidden, so they'd struck a different target instead: another hedge fund. But instead of one of the principals, they'd taken down the entire operation—and by an unfortunate chain reaction, the rest of the stock market, too.

It was the sort of story that almost made sense.

"Look at this." Ganderson held up a copy of the *Daily News*. The headline read, "BLACKTAIL DOWN."

"What do you think?" I asked.

"I think this has to end, is what I think. We can't live on the Kingda Ka roller coaster." He tossed the paper onto the metal bench. "What will they do next, nuke JP Morgan?"

"I'm sure that's been discussed at the Fed." I kept my voice down,

hoping Ganderson would do so as well. "The coincidence seems a
little too . . . uh, coincidental."

"What coincidence?"

"Blacktail. I matched their Director of Security to the attack on
Faust, and you talked to them on Tuesday. Two days later, the Expend-
ables blow up their office. See what I mean?"

"You think they attacked *themselves*?"

"The timing's funny, that's all."

We eyed each other for a few moments. I broke first.

"Terry Plank escaping, apparently," I said. "That seems funny
too."

"He's lucky to be alive," said Ganderson. "The way these terrorists operate."

"Not if they don't know where he is."

"How hard could it be? CNBC found him."

"Good point."

"In fact, I think he's the best bet."

"Huh?"

Ganderson rolled his shoulders like a fighter trying to get back
in the match. "There's no clue about where they'll strike next. You
haven't found anything to lead us to them—your one lead, Blacktail, ended up being a victim itself. The way I see it, all we have is
Plank."

I couldn't figure Ganderson's angle. "Maybe . . ."

"I'm going to try to contact him. And when I do, I'll get you in."

"What? And why on earth would he agree?"

"To save his life, that's why. You seem to be a lousy detective, but everyone I've talked to says you're the best, ah, security contractor available."

"Well, I don't know about—"

"True or not, I don't care. You're good with a gun, and you're closer than anyone else to the case. It might be the edge Plank needs."

So there: no longer an independent, crackerjack investigator, I'd just been demoted to bodyguard, the lowest form of hired gun. What was Ganderson up to?

I protested, a little, enough to renegotiate the rate upward ten percent. Then he stepped aside to call his attorney again. I watched, Ganderson apparently hearing nothing but rings, wondering how he could possibly be involved with the bad guys.

The main problem with fitting Ganderson in as villain was that I couldn't see how it made any sense to put *me* on the payroll.

He came back. "Voicemail. Again. Maybe I should try someone else."

"Sorry."

A woman came in, older and Chinese. She began a long discussion with the desk sergeant, gesturing, but not loud. He nodded, commenting occasionally. It looked like they knew each other, like they'd had the same conversation before.

"The industry can't take much more of this," Ganderson said.

"Of what?"

"The murders! This killing has to *stop*."

Oh, that. "Look at it this way—how many private investment firms are there in the U.S.? Plus the prop traders and mutual funds?—it's got to be thousands. Statistically, that's a robust ecosystem." Clara's point.

"What are you talking about?"

"I mean, the anarchists. They're going to have to seriously ramp up their numbers to make a dent."

Ganderson didn't find that funny. But I wasn't sure I was joking, so call it even.

"Every thumbsucker in America seems to think it's open season on bankers," he said. "We're being dragged behind the pickup truck of public opinion."

"It's not so bad." Actually, I liked that one. What hardworking American, seeing his retirement account mismanaged into toxic waste, *hasn't* wanted to wrap a chain around some guy in chalk stripes and hitch him up to a flatbed?

"It's not working, you looking for the assassins," Ganderson said. "Now we're going to let *them* come to *you*."

I finally figured out what we'd been talking about.

"Hey!" I said. "This is a setup, isn't it? You think Plank's a staked goat, and you want me there to shoot back when they finally make their move."

"Not exactly." He shrugged. "But if it works out that way, I think everyone would be happy."

I wasn't even a bodyguard, I was a fucking leg breaker.

And I was angry about it. I realized just how angry when I barely stopped myself from striking Ganderson—right under the sternum, knuckles half folded, a killing blow if done just a fraction too hard.

Ernie's violent, terrible death, on top of everything else. I desperately needed to find Saxon, beat the truth out of him, and tear my way to the heart of the lunacy.

Ganderson could wait.

The station's door opened, pushed wide by a tall man in a suit the color of midnight, over brilliant white pinpoint with a blue silk tie that probably cost more than my car. He strode over to Ganderson, no hesitation, not glancing once at the sergeant.

"Good morning, Quint," he said, and the voice was deep and powerful and perfectly pitched.

"It's about time." But Ganderson straightened up. "Let's go spring my boy, all right?"

"Why I'm here. We just need to go over a few things first." He looked my way, one eyebrow raised.

Ganderson could take a hint—at least, coming from this guy. "We're done for now," he said to me.

I was still working on controlling my adrenal response. Catecholamines had flooded my system.

"Call me when you reach Plank," I said, jaw tight.

"You got it." Ganderson made it sound like he was doing me a favor.

The lawyer nodded a dismissal my way, and they walked off.

I guess I knew *my* place.

CHAPTER THIRTY-FOUR

When I walked out of the station, the sky was lighter but the rain heavier. At seven-thirty the morning rush hour was under way, cars splashing down the street, pedestrians hunched under their umbrellas. The commuters looked sullen—nothing like starting out your workday wet and cold.

I passed by two Starbucks on general principles before finding an independent breakfast place closer to NYU. It was crowded, most of the tables filled, busy and noisy. A waiter pointed me to a two-top near the restroom doors, and I sat down, trying not to drip on the table.

"Coffee?"

"Sure." I ordered an omelet, extra mushrooms, double toast, oatmeal on the side.

It felt like it was turning into that kind of day.

Ernie's death continued to weigh on me. I wanted to call Clara, but that wasn't any kind of conversation to have over the phone, in a public space. Just to hear her voice . . . but I couldn't *not* talk about what had happened. Best leave it be for now.

I took my time. Every table probably turned over twice before I finally finished eating, especially the fruit bowl and yogurt. But it was worth it—I had dried out, warmed up and started to come to terms with the violent scene I'd walked into four hours earlier.

I'm sorry, Ernie.

I paid up, thought about but decided against an umbrella from a display that had been opportunistically set up at the register, and stepped back out into the day.

Ganderson's motives were puzzling, but one thing was clear: I might need some backup.

Under a block of construction scaffolding, rain dripping through two-by-sixes overhead, I called Zeke.

"What do you want?"

"Jeez, is that how you always answer the phone?"

"So?"

"If you're rude, people won't want to call. They'll avoid you."

He just snorted.

"Yeah, yeah, okay, I get it," I said. "But someday money is going to call, and you'll be an asshole, and it'll go somewhere else."

"Good riddance. Why are *you* calling?"

"I might have some work. You busy?"

"Are you kidding? After last time?"

"I *said* I was sorry."

"Naw. I just wish all my jobs could be so fun."

"You're the only one who sees it that way."

"Yeah," Zeke said. "Listen, I'm working tonight, but—"

"When?"

"Afternoon, then probably late. Celebrity event. Some rich guy's worried about paparazzi. He wants a few more secret service in the perimeter."

"Try not to shoot the wrong one."

"It's nothing important. You need me? I can skip this."

"No, no. Just lining up the ducks, in case."

"Sure?"

"Yeah."

"Call anytime."

"Thanks."

People pushed past me, between the scaffolding columns and the Jersey barriers along the street's gutter. Buildings are always being renovated downtown—feels like every single block sometimes. A workman twenty feet from me bent to cut pipe at the back of a truck, his circular saw flaring sparks like an oversize flint toy.

The noise of the saw was painfully loud. I started walking again.

I thought about what Walter had told me last night. When the noise stopped, I switched phones and dialed again.

"What?"

"Johnny, it's me."

"I'm in the middle of something."

Click.

Well, fuck that. I hit redial.

"Don't hang up!"

"I *said*, I'm in the *middle* of a fucking—goddamn it!"

"Sorry. Listen—"

"I just lost a penny and a half!"

I had no idea what that meant. It was too wide to be the spread on an individual price. Maybe it was shorthand for 150 thousand dollars.

Or a million and a half.

"So make it back on the next trade," I said. "This is important."

"Better be." He subsided, grumbling.

"Someone famous is about to flee the jurisdiction."

"Who?"

"I don't know."

"What'd they do?"

"Don't know."

"How much money?"

"Um—"

God love him, Johnny started laughing. "What the hell *do* you know?"

"It's a good tip."

"And utterly useless. Why are you telling me?"

"I was hoping you'd heard something. So I could start connecting dots."

"The NASDAQ dropped a hundred fifty points at open, then made it all back, plus another fifty. The VIX crossed forty an hour ago. Volume is off the charts."

"You're having an exciting day?"

"Good enough. Better than over at Wetherell Stark. One of their options strategists dropped dead at his desk. Massive coronary."

"Anyone notice?"

"They had one of those portable defibrillators on the wall—you know, like on an airplane? Didn't help, though."

"You might want to get one, for your boys."

"Hah!"

"No, really."

"Would you give a chainsaw to a five-year-old?"

I could see Johnny's point. Last year one of his traders, celebrating, had grabbed the fire extinguisher and sprayed half the room. He'd shorted out three keyboards before they wrestled it away from him. The damage somebody could do with four thousand volts didn't bear imagining.

"Hey, I followed some crumbs on Marlett this morning," he said. "Once I knew who to look for, it was obvious. The major counterparty on those York Hydro trades was Blacktail Capital."

"No shit?"

"And they're implicated on Sills, too. Blacktail bought shares in her fund, which as we mentioned was doing really, really badly. As soon as she was dead, though, the price jumped up. Investors must have figured that *anyone* could do a better job at it—which maybe wasn't too hard because it was actually trading at less than aggregate book value. Blacktail cleaned up."

"So that's it!—every one of these killings was done for profit."

"Seems clear to me, but I don't know that a jury would buy it. Or understand it, for that matter. Could have been just luck. And there were other parties in every transaction—Blacktail could be simple coincidence."

"It's good enough for me," I said. "Can you pull together some documentation?"

"Piss off. What am I, your research assistant?"

Okay, I didn't think he'd go for that. "At least point me in the right direction if I'm going to have to do it myself."

"I'll email you something later. After close."

A ringtone. For a moment, confused, I stared at the phone in my hand, wondering how it could ring if I was talking on it. Then I realized it was coming from a different pocket.

"Gotta go, Johnny."

"Your mystery absconder? You get a name, call me back."

"In a heartbeat."

I hung up, dug out the other one. A horn blared, some asshole driver in a Lexus giving me the finger, and I jumped back onto the curb as he roared past.

"Hello?"

For a moment I only heard random noise—bangs, splintering. Loud. Then, "Silas!"

"Who's this?"

"They shot everyone and grabbed Clara!" His voice cracked.

"Rondo?" I stopped dead.

"They attacked the *library*!"

"What's going on?" I was shouting.

"They've got—" The call cut off. For a moment I stood, stupidly. Then I started to run.

CHAPTER THIRTY-FIVE

The athenaeum was twelve blocks up and two over. Call it a half mile.

I dodged a woman carrying an umbrella, rebounded off another man, and landed in the street. Fine. Fewer obstacles.

In ten seconds I came up on the Lexus, slowing for a red light. The street was black with rain. I glanced right, into the cross street, and was momentarily blinded by headlights.

As I passed the Lexus I struck it with one fist, on the roof. The driver looked up, astonished. He swore and accelerated, trying to cut me off, and we all entered the intersection simultaneously. Horns blared on all sides.

A taxi, crossing with the green, slammed into the Lexus, punching it into a spin.

My perceptions went into overdrive, and the cab's front swung toward me, slow motion. I leaped, on instinct and terror, and hurdled the corner of the hood—just as a third car struck the taxi. Metal crunched. Skidding and small explosions sounded as airbags detonated everywhere.

I landed on my feet and kept going.

At St. Marks I caught the light but was almost clipped by a truck turning left. More horns. A cyclist wanted to play chicken, flying straight toward me, the wrong way down the street. I raised an arm, ready to bodycheck. At the last possible moment, he swerved and hit the curb. For an instant I saw him start to tumble. Then I was past, the first shouts rising from bystanders.

Crossing 15th, a slight downhill, and I moved even faster. Cars, faces, buildings—all fragments, the barest impression.

On the last corner I grabbed a light pole, jerking myself violently left, to make the turn. Halfway down the block I could see the Thatcher's facade. A fire engine had just pulled up, firefighters hopping down from the cab. A dozen people stood in the street and on the sidewalk. More were drifting in. Sirens approached.

The huge front doors were pushed open partway. Shards of transom glass glittered on the stair.

"Don't go up there!" A firefighter yelled, but I shoved past, hardly breaking speed, and leaped up the stairs.

Inside was a horror show.

The elderly desk guard had been shot in the face, his body sprawled across the security table, blood spattered over the wall and floor. Across the marble lobby another body lay at the arch leading to the reading room—a patron, perhaps, in heavy tweeds, a book on the floor near his hand. He'd been shot too, twice it looked like. The killer, or one of them—I had no idea how many were inside—had stepped in the blood on his way through the archway. Smeared prints led onward, then faded at the first rug.

I took a couple of seconds to check the guard's body. Not for signs of life, but to see if he'd been armed.

No luck. My jaw hurt and I realized it was death lock clenched. I forced my face to relax. I needed a weapon, and this was a fucking *library*.

Nothing.

I ran to the side door Clara had shown me, the employee stairs. No weapon, no backup, no plan—all I had was speed. I slammed through without stopping and sprinted up.

At the top, another library worker—a young guy, T-shirt, sitting backward against a copy machine in a mess of blood and gore. Gut-shot, staring, barely alive.

The copier had taken a bullet too, and whined and groaned as its rollers turned uselessly inside.

"Which way?" I whispered fiercely. "Where did they go?" But the man was past hearing.

I couldn't stop. Down the hall, which I recognized. The supervisor's office, still an impossible mess but no one inside. The storage closet, empty.

Lockerby's restoration room, and signs of a struggle—a bench turned on its side, books and paper and tools scattered everywhere. A puddle of blood, spatters on top of the disarray and a trail leading out the door.

I grabbed a chisel from the worktable and went back out, holding it in a knife fighter's grip, close to my side. Not much against jacketed hollow points, but better than what I'd had a minute ago.

At the fire door—

I couldn't help it, I screamed, an involuntary cry of rage.

Kimmie had been thrown sideways, lying in the corner, her blood everywhere. She'd been shot five, six, shit, *many* times, rounds going through her chest and neck and legs. Her eyes were open and dead, and she still held one of Lockerby's knives in both hands.

She'd fought back, and died.

Clara.

Through the door I heard a noise—a thump, then a small groan.

I hit the door running, and it slammed against the wall inside the cinder block stairwell—the utility stairs, down the back of the building. Blood spots on the treads headed down. Another faint noise below.

No shots. I leaned enough to see down to the next level, not quite, and saw nothing. No movement.

I gripped the chisel, pointed it away from my body, and vaulted over the rail.

With my left hand on the bar, I twisted in midair, controlled my fall just enough, and came down hard a few steps above the landing. I swept the chisel forward, partly for balance, partly just hoping someone would be there, but no one was.

A loud *clack* echoed off the concrete walls, and the lights went out.

I immediately repeated my vault, one more level down.

If they knew where I was, they'd shoot me. If I kept moving, the darkness might help. In the red glow from emergency exit signs, I saw movement at the street-level door.

I'd have killed him, but he was lying on the floor, trying to push himself up, clearly wounded. I might get a question in.

It was Rondo, not one of the killers. Blood ran down his face, black in the reddish light.

"Rondo!" I lifted him to a sitting position, one handed—I wasn't letting go of the chisel. "Where's Clara?"

"They took off. Grabbed her." His voice was hoarse and weak.

"Who?"

"Men with guns. I don't know."

"I thought you were staying in the apartment!"

"Clara felt cooped up. You know how she is. I tried, Silas." He attempted to straighten, groaning. "I tried."

A phone rang, loud in the dark, closed stairwell, and I started. Rondo raised his hand, the mobile folded inside his large fist. He must have called me on it, but been hit after the few words he'd managed to get out.

Now he was having trouble answering. I took it from him.

"What? Who's this?"

Pause, then the voice at the other end said, "No. Who the fuck are you?"

I recognized him. "Lockerby? It's Silas. I just got here."

"What—"

"Rondo's alive. Where are you?"

"On my bike. I'm following them. Shit!"

Silence. "Lockerby? Lockerby!" I was shouting.

He came back. "Sorry, hit a hole. I'm hurt, Silas. I'm hurt."

"Where's Clara?"

"In the van." His voice strengthened, but only a little. He was breathing hard. I imagined him on his bicycle, bleeding, trying to ride and talk. "They took her, in the van, but I'm following."

"*What* van?"

"White . . ."

Rondo was coming alert, pulling himself together. I tipped the phone out, so he could hear, too.

"Where are you? What street?"

After a moment of noise, Lockerby's voice returned. "Seventh Avenue."

Southbound, then. "Cross street?"

"Fourteenth, coming up. They're fifty, sixty feet in front of me. Not speeding. Moving with traffic. No windows in the back. I can't see anything."

"Any turns?"

"What? No. Don't think so. In the middle lane."

"Seventh and 14th." I looked at Rondo. "What's—? Fuck, the Holland Tunnel!"

"*Jersey?*"

"If they get off Manhattan, we'll never catch them. Bike can't go through the tunnel, can it?"

Lockerby, listening in: "No."

Out front, sirens, louder now. Police would be coming in, riot gear, shooting to kill. They'd take us down, all questions for later. We'd never explain fast enough to get them out after Clara.

"What do we do?" Rondo stood up, swaying slightly, but he'd gotten his shit together.

"Outside. How bad are you?"

We pushed through the exit door, me first. The alley behind the Thatcher was clean and paved with perfectly flat blacktop, dumpsters shiny and neat lined up along the building. Rain bucketed down, spattering broad puddles on the pavement. Just inside from the street, a silvery midsize was stopped crosswise, two doors hanging open.

"I'm not shot." Rondo pulled a hand away from his skull, looked at the dark blood. "They had their hands full with Clara. One of them rammed me into the wall, I hit my head."

"That has to be their car."

"Hey." Lockerby's voice, tinny on the phone.

"Hang on." I looked at Rondo. "I'm going after them. Sit on the ground, put your hands up, don't make any sudden moves—then tell the cops everything."

"No, I'm—"

"And be *convincing*." I ran for the car.

But Rondo beat me there, sliding into the driver's seat like a NASCAR pit crew.

Shit.

It was a Cadillac, engine still running—you never risk an ignition fail, not in a commitment situation. I glanced in, saw black metal glinting in the rear seat.

"You sure you can drive?" I said, but Rondo was already yanking it into gear. I scrambled into the back, barely in time. He didn't pause a moment, just hit the accelerator, swung the wheel and let the jackrabbit acceleration swing both our doors shut.

I still had the phone. "Lockerby?"

"Yo."

"We're moving."

"Right."

A pain in my hand, and I realized I was still clutching the chisel—so tightly my fingers had gone white. I forced them open, dropped the tool, and covered the phone's mouthpiece for a moment. "Hey, Rondo. He's on a bicycle. How can he talk on the phone?"

"It's a fixie. You know—fixed gear. No brakes."

"He doesn't have any *brakes*?"

Rondo cornered onto 19th so fast I tumbled across the seat. The Caddy scraped something—newspaper box, the curb, I couldn't see—but he didn't hesitate. Horns blared all around.

"Turn on the wipers!" I yelled.

"Oh yeah." Like that the windshield was swept clear. He also found the seat adjustment and slid backward, giving him more legroom—all without lessening speed.

Into the phone: "We're four, maybe five minutes away."

"They might hit the tunnel by then. We're already in the line."

Outbound traffic, waiting to enter the Holland, queued up on Varick. It would slow them down, but Lockerby was right. Midday, it wouldn't take long.

"We might not make it."

"Yes, we will." Rondo put the accelerator down. The ride went from dangerous to terrifying.

I hesitated, then pulled out one of my own cellphones, dialing one handed while I kept the other at my ear.

"Police emergency." The woman sounded bored. "We are recording."

"Listen closely." I spoke loudly and slowly. "I have packed a vehicle with seventeen hundred pounds of explosive, arrayed for spherical penetration. It has just entered the Holland Tunnel portal. I expect to reach the middle of the tunnel in one minute. At that time I will stop. Exactly five minutes after that, I will detonate the explosives. Do you understand?"

"Sir? Where are you?"

"*Sit dakaek min el-janna, ya hayawanah!*" A little rude, that, but the dispatcher wouldn't be insulted, only the Arabic translator presumably kept on call for situations like this.

"Sir? Sir! What—"

I clicked off.

Rondo had slowed slightly for a red light, then sped up again, swerving behind one taxi and just in front of another. Both of my feet hit the floor in an unthinking reaction, automatically seeking the brake pedal. Somehow we squeaked through, skidding on the wet street.

"That won't stop them!" he yelled. "You didn't even describe the van!"

"No."

"But—"

"They'll close the *tunnel*. They have to."

He hesitated. "In time?"

"Yes." It took 9/11 to bring them together, but the city's feuding agencies—transportation, emergency services, police, even a token federal liaison—had implemented serious counterterror response plans. No-fucking-around plans. If they thought there was a weapon of mass destruction under the Hudson, the operations center would be in full screaming red-alert mode.

"Lockerby, you get that?"

"I heard you." The connection was poor, his voice weaker. "They're still in line. About two hundred yards to go."

"Traffic moving?"

"Uh . . . not so much. Stopped, maybe."

"Don't go any closer! Wait for us."

"Right."

What I'd seen on the backseat was an unzipped, oversize nylon duffel filled with familiar armament. While Rondo pretended we were in the Monte Carlo Rally, I found three Glocks, extra magazines, a Mossberg 590 and a half-dozen M84 flashbangs, still in their plastic packaging.

"Whoa." A bonus, underneath. "These motherfuckers are *serious.*"

"What?"

An M2—a Browning .50-caliber machine gun. "My new long gun."

Rondo slammed the brakes. I looked up to see the intersection gridlocked, cars in all directions stuck. Honking. Swearing audible even through the now steady rain. The lights were red all the way around.

"How about that," I said. "It worked."

"We're still ten blocks away."

"Lockerby? What's going on?"

Through the phone I thought I heard sirens, but maybe they were closer to us.

"Dead stop. Nothing's moving. Red and blue lights flashing at the portal, I think. Wait . . . a police truck, coming into that little service lot on the north side. Motorcycle cops. Damn."

"The van?"

"It's sitting there, with everyone else."

The breakneck pursuit had drawn to a complete halt. We were in the right lane. Cars all around us, and more stacking up everywhere. Smug pedestrians wove their way between vehicles on the street, carrying umbrellas. Rain hammered the roof of the Caddy.

"Decision time," I said to Rondo. "Call 911 back and tell them about the van? Or handle it ourselves?"

He looked over the seat, seeing the cornucopia of weaponry for the first time. "Jesus Christ."

"We stole the right car."

"Only one thing matters," he said. "Clara comes out alive."

"Agreed."

"And I don't know if guns blazing is the best way to do that."

"Yeah." I was truly torn. "But a siege isn't much better. SWAT teams tend to suck at anything that doesn't involve mass casualties."

We looked at each other, uncertain.

"Silas?" Lockerby's voice, through increasing static.

"Yeah?"

"I think they're moving."

"Already?" I couldn't believe they'd checked and cleared the tunnel that fast.

"The truck's kind of shifting back and forth, trying to get out. . . fuck, he's jumping the curb into the police lane."

"Which way?"

"Back—moving fast now. One block. He turned onto Canal."

"Can you follow them?"

"On my way."

"Keep the phone on!"

Rondo was staring at me. "What? What?"

"The truck bailed. He's headed south."

"Downtown? There's no way off the island that way."

"The Battery Tunnel."

"Shit!"

Long pause. The cars all around us were unmoving. Lights and signs glowed in the darkening rainfall.

"Silas? The truck's on West Broadway now. Traffic's lighter—the jam is mostly the other way."

I looked at Rondo. "They're getting away. Down West Broadway."

He pounded the steering wheel in frustration. "Fuck! Fuck!"

"I know."

For a moment I thought Rondo was going to jump out and start sprinting. Instead, he growled, then shoved the transmission into gear.

"Hey," I said.

"We're getting *out* of here." He twisted to look behind us, backed up, then went forward, back once more. "They're not giving me enough room."

I could have waved one of the Glocks out the window, but I wasn't sure what good it would have done. No one had anywhere to go.

Rondo swore once more, then hit the gas. We slammed backward into the car behind us, jolting and rocking in the crash. Without stopping he accelerated forward, smashing the bumper in front.

If Zeke were here, he would have been whooping. I covered my face with both arms.

Twice more and we were out—onto the sidewalk. The tires crunched going over the curb, all the way to the rims.

"Always *wanted* to do this," Rondo muttered. I looked in the rearview mirror and saw him grinning like a mad bastard. He hit the gas and we shot down the sidewalk, scattering the few pedestrians in our way.

We struck a small tree, a sapling that had been planted by the street. It splintered, disappearing under the car. Ten yards farther, a parking sign. It scraped down the side of the car and tore off the mirror. The corner loomed in front of us—

"*Cocksuckers!*"

The intersection was equally jammed, cars backed up in all directions. We couldn't have gotten through with an MRAP armored truck.

Rondo yanked the wheel right, and we got around the corner, still on the sidewalk. It was a tight fit, and a mailbox did serious damage to the car's side panels. But somehow Rondo kept us moving.

"If all the corners are full of vehicles," I said, "we're going to end up circling the block. All the way around on the sidewalk."

"No." Rondo's jaw was set. "At the next one, we're going through." He sped up, and we banged past light poles, flattened a wire newspaper rack outside a convenience store, and knocked over a hydrant. By the time we hit the corner we must have been doing thirty or forty miles an hour.

Doesn't sound like much, but *far* too fast for a sidewalk.

Fortunately, this cross street was more or less clear. Waiting cars hadn't edged much past the zebra stripe, so Rondo was able to fly through. He even aimed the left wheels through the curb cut on the other side.

Every police officer in the city must have been headed for the Holland Tunnel. No one appeared interested in pursuing us.

"Are we going to drive all the way to Battery Park like this?" I asked.

"If necessary."

Lockerby's voice came over the phone, which I'd returned to my ear.

"Where are you?"

I glanced at a street sign as we knocked it over. "Lafayette and . . . White."

"We're almost at Barclay Street."

"What's down there?"

"I think . . ." Random noise sputtered on the line. "They're going into the marina."

"*Marina?*"

"South Cove Private Facility Keep Out Members Only."

"Are you a member?"

"No guards at the gate. Looks like anyone can walk in."

I looked at Rondo. "South Cove Marina. You know it?"

"Rich people's boats. Sure. I had a client there once."

The street ahead was almost normal—full of cars, but moving at regular speeds. Rondo roared off the curb, right in front of a bus. The Caddy's nose banged into the asphalt, the entire car juddering. I had an instant's glimpse through the bus windows, astonished passengers staring out, then we were in front, the diesel horn diminishing behind us.

Rondo accelerated, pushing the car hard now that we were back on intentional pavement.

"Full exercise room," he said.

"What?"

"On the yacht. Weights, machines—you'd think it would have sunk the damn thing."

"Pay attention to the road!"

We swerved. Just missed an SUV pulling out of a parking garage.

"Relax." Rondo seemed a lot more comfortable on an actual street.

And we were flying now, blowing past taxis and trucks and black livery cars. I turned my attention back to the armory, reloading several magazines, checking slides and actions. All the machinery was well kept—cleaned and oiled within a day or two. Saxon ran a tight ship.

Rondo caught a lucky green at the end of North Moore and we swung onto the West Side Highway for a few blocks. Other cars gave way before us. I wondered just how bad the dents and scrapes looked. Ground Zero passed on the left, cranes and construction dumpsters visible through netting above the Jersey barriers. The site was dismal in the October rain.

Another quarter mile and Rondo turned right, tires screaming, almost flipping us over. We slid to a halt alongside a row of silver bollards set into the sidewalk. Apparently the blank, modernist office cube behind them needed protection from car bombs.

"The entrance is right up there," said Rondo.

"Lockerby?" I spoke into the phone. "Where are you? We're in front of . . . fuck, I don't know—wait. Malvey Street."

"I'm under the walkway. Should be right in front of you."

I looked down the street and saw Lockerby limp from behind the colonnade fronting the next block. He waved halfheartedly, then went back to shelter from the rain.

"Let's go." I grabbed the duffel, fully loaded, and we exited into the downpour.

CHAPTER THIRTY-SIX

Outside a pair of diehards stood huddled next to a doorway, shielding their cigarettes from the rain. They stared at us. I glanced back at the Caddy. The side was caved in, side mirror torn away, metal detail hanging loose. The rear bumper was gone, under a deep dent in the trunk. The front grille was entirely smashed.

"Don't worry—my friend's a Student Driver," I said to them. "Some rain, huh?" We ran down the street.

Lockerby was drenched. A streak of grit and mud ran up the back of his pants and shirt. But he was wounded, too—blood on his neck and both legs, pants dark with it. He was hunched, one arm held close to his torso in that way that meant broken ribs or internal damage or both. His bike was abandoned on the ground, dropped where he'd finally dismounted.

"How the hell did you ride this far?"

"Couldn't lose her." His voice was whispery, but he didn't look at me, kept staring at the marina's entrance.

"Where are they?" Rondo said.

"The van's there."

This whole area, a dozen landfill blocks sticking into the Hudson, was several feet above the river's waterline. From our vantage at the end of the office block we had a view over the fence surrounding the boatyard. Past the parking lot and a cedar-shingled boathouse, a dock extended along the water's edge, then out into the river along the jetties on either side. A large fuel tank sat in a neatly painted cradle at the top of the dock. The slips held a row of power yachts, big sailboats and various other seagoing palaces. At the very end, a vast, four-level behemoth towered above everything else, interrupting an otherwise stunning view of the Hudson.

The van sat at the far end of the parking lot. No people were visible anywhere. One or two of the boats had lit windows, cheery in the gloom. Atop the big one, white-covered radar antennas turned slowly in the rain.

"Let me guess," I said.

"Yeah." Lockerby kept his gaze fixed. "The monster yacht. You can just see the name on the bow—*Tangible Assets*. I saw two men drag Clara into it through a door at dock level. Two others with them."

"How long ago?"

"Five or six minutes."

"Okay."

I lowered the duffel to the ground and knelt, zipping it open. Lockerby glanced down, then looked more closely.

"What's this shit?"

"Boy Scout motto."

"Damn."

"It's theirs—they left it behind when they jumped into the truck."

"Amateurs."

"No." I put one Glock in my belt, set another aside and put two magazines each into my hip pockets. "But I think they're improvising. Something went wrong for them. What exactly happened back there?"

Rondo took a moment to draw a breath.

"I stopped in the library when I walked her over. Too much rain, and I had some time. We were walking through the reading room when I heard a crash, and bangs." His voice trailed off, throat working.

"They came in hard," said Lockerby. His voice was bleak. "I heard the same sounds—you know, it's true, you never forget. Knew exactly what it was. I ran out, like an idiot. Got hit as soon as they topped the stairs."

"It was—I don't know." Rondo wiped his head again, but it was more rain than blood now. "Chaos. I barely remember running through the library. I saw them shoot someone on the floor, just a guy reading a book, an instant later he, just . . . an explosion. Of blood."

"They separated Clara at the utility corridor," said Lockerby. "Hauled her off. Rondo hit one, and the guy whacked him back, ran him into the wall. I followed them out, but they were already getting in the van when I came through the door. So I got my bike."

"Recognize anyone?"

"No," said Rondo.

"Me neither." Lockerby was fading, almost bent over in pain. "Soldiers, though. You can tell. Motherfuckers."

"Why did they take her?" Rondo raised his hands. "I don't mean—just, I don't get it. Why is Clara still alive?"

"That's a good question." But I knew the answer, even if I didn't say it out loud: they were using Clara to come after me. Ruthless exploitation of an opponent's weakness. Saxon didn't want to waste time chasing me around—now he could sit back and wait.

Of course I'd shown up a little faster than they'd expected, and things got messy. But Saxon's basic plan was fine.

My karmic meter was deep into the red.

We stood for a moment before I shook myself back into motion. "All right."

"What are you doing?"

I stood up and offered Lockerby the .50 cal. "You in any condition to handle this?"

He straightened, a little, and took the rifle. "Sure."

"You know how to use it?"

He hefted the M2 for a couple of seconds, then quickly ran the bolt and checked the action. A spark of vitality returned to his face. "It's been a few years."

"Like riding a bike."

Rondo had been watching with a frown.

"What are you doing?"

"I'm going in." I looked at him. "Clara and I are coming out."

"Is that—maybe we should wait for the police?"

"What if they drive that boat away?"

We stood in silence for a few moments, staring at the vessel.

"All right." Rondo wiped his face one more time. "I'm going with you."

"No. They're killers. You have no idea—"

"Stop wasting time."

Lockerby was visibly struggling to pull himself together, barely able to walk. Rondo looked like a video game poster, all cut muscle and steely glare, blood trickling down his face. Rain fell heavily behind us. On the boat were an unknown number of ruthless and experienced soldiers, almost certainly ex-military, probably including a man who'd nearly killed me twice.

"I know what I'm doing," I said. "You don't."

"Clara's my friend." He said it with absolute finality.

I sighed.

"Fine," I said. "Ever fired a handgun before?"

———

We didn't have much of a plan. We probably couldn't even count on surprise, though Lockerby swore they hadn't seen him because it was open terrain between us and the boat.

I found my bluetooth earpiece and we rigged the phones, same as Zeke and I had used at Riverton. I gave Rondo one of my extras. No use worrying about calls being traced now.

"If you have a chance, drop it in the water when we're done," I said.

Lockerby picked out a firing point behind the car parked closest to *Tangible Assets*. "I could pitch the stun grenades in," he said. "But that seems kind of dumb, with you two inside."

"I'll take the flashbangs. If you decide to pick someone off, make sure you're aiming at the right targets, okay? No Pat Tillman bullshit."

"Yeah."

"And stay behind the engine block. They're carrying SCARs—those rounds will go right through the rest of the car."

He chose to look offended. "I *know* all that."

"Rondo, your only job is to haul Clara out. I'll handle the crew."

"Yes."

We could go over it one more time, or we could get it done. "Right," I said. "Let's go."

Lockerby went first, long gun concealed in the duffel bag. He walked like an old man, limping, bent at the waist—none of it an act. No security appeared. He made it across the parking lot.

Nothing happened.

"Okay," I said, and Rondo and I stepped out. We walked together, shoulders hunched, moving fast like we just wanted to get into our dry cabins. Rain fell steadily. An air horn sounded from the river. Ahead of us Lockerby suddenly disappeared, dropping out of sight.

On the dock we kept moving, then slowed at two boats distant, like we'd reached ours. The whole way I'd scanned *Tangible Assets*, seeing nothing—no faces, no cameras, no one standing guard.

On the other hand, it was 150 feet long and there were four decks, most of which had long swooping stripes of reflective black windows. An entire company of infantry could be hiding inside, watching, fingering their triggers.

Rondo stepped back from me, and I gestured at him. We pretended to argue for a moment. Then I stomped off, heading further out the dock. Rondo watched me go, standing still, then shook his head and jogged after me.

I know it was weak, but *I said* we didn't have time to plan.

He caught up to me just as I reached the edge of the dock, a foot from the hull of the huge yacht. It rose steeply, a wall of white and blue—and that was the idea, because we'd now be much harder to see from anywhere on board.

We immediately went left. The stern had a low platform, almost at waterline, where passengers could swim and put on their scuba gear and cast fishing lines. This was to be our egress.

"All clear," said Lockerby in my ear. Rondo should have been hearing the same thing, on conference. "I'm not seeing any movement."

I looked at Rondo. We were on no-unnecessary-noise protocols. He shrugged. I nodded, pointed . . . and we went over the edge of the dock, dropping onto *Tangible Assets*.

The open-planked decking held two pool chairs, a cocktail table bolted in place, and a stainless-steel gas grill. Under an overhang, double doors of dark, smoked glass led into the lowermost deck of the yacht's interior. The rain was a constant noise, splashing and draining out scuppers below the gunwales.

"All's quiet." Lockerby, barely audible over the rainfall, even with the earpiece jammed into my ear canal.

So far so good. Maybe this would be easy. I stepped toward the door.

CHAPTER THIRTY-SEVEN

THUMP!

A shape leaped from the second deck, just above us, landing alongside Rondo and pulling him down. Simultaneously the door in front of me slammed open. Another man bowled through, bringing his assault rifle up to my center of mass.

"Shit!" Lockerby.

I dived forward and right. Bullets tacked across the deck. Since I was close, I punched out and struck the man's leg as I skidded on wet planks. He stumbled.

I crashed into the other door. As I rolled to my feet, I glimpsed Rondo in midthrow: he'd somehow spun his assailant into the air, the man aimed headfirst for the rail.

The glass above me shattered, shards blowing inward. Lockerby?

"Careful!" I screamed.

"No problem." His voice was calm.

I could barely hear anything else amid the drumming rain. The rifleman was up, swiveling, seeking a target, five feet away. I went down again as he fired, this time stitching the dock next to us. But no good—he was tracking my fall, the barrel less than a second from lining me up.

The gunner jerked and fell, arms flying out. Lockerby must have found his range. The SCAR continued to fire, his finger caught in the guard, as it swung wildly across the deck. Bullets spanged off metal, chunked into wood, shattered plastic.

"Holy shit!" I went forward, trying to get under the rifle— anything to avoid the full-auto spray.

An enormous splash, audible even over all the other noise. I glanced sideways, saw Rondo in a crouch. Nobody else. His opponent must have gone into the river.

Then I collided with the gunman, the two of us banging into the door, falling. I landed on top, jammed an elbow into his throat, grabbed the weapon's barrel. It burned my fingers, but I yanked it free and tossed it away.

"Down!" Lockerby, louder. I didn't move, confused—wasn't I *already* down?—then I saw Rondo leap for shelter under the over-hang. Flashes of gunfire from deck two, above. Wood chips exploded from the deck boards. I rolled away.

"Two men up there." Lockerby was in control again.

"No shit," said Rondo.

"Lost my pistol," I said, more to myself. I'd dropped it some-where in the melee. I started to rise.

"Body armor," said Lockerby in my ear. "And concealed behind the pillar. Can't sight them."

Sudden shooting from inside the doors. Rondo and I were

trapped—couldn't go forward, couldn't go backward, and in about two seconds the firing would cross on our positions.

"Lockerby!"

WH-O-O-O-MP!

The grill's propane tank exploded. The fireball blasted one recliner completely off the deck, but that was fortunate, because the chair struck me on its way, shielding me slightly and knocking me down again.

"Fuck." Rondo's voice, in the earpiece, not loud. I couldn't see him. "Good one, Lock."

Being in the open, right under the shooters above us, was certain death. I went forward instead, crouching and sprinting toward the shattered door.

And as I did, I glimpsed Rondo, in peripheral vision, leaping from behind the other chair, upward. The second deck was eight feet above us, the top of its rail three feet more. Rondo went up like LeBron James, grabbed the rail and in one motion chinned himself, kept pulling, and rolled over the top.

No time to be amazed. As I went through the door, a figure came into focus on my left—gray, armored vest, submachine gun. If he hadn't still been stunned from the propane blast, I would have died. Instead, I had an extra fraction of a second to get close. I went low, under the weapon, then slashed up with one arm, knocking the barrel aside.

Guns are better, but once you're inside, they become a hindrance. Still, the man was good. He brought his knee up, hitting me sharply in the chest. I kept my arm strike going, over and down, catching his gun's stock and yanking it into a brief hold.

He pulled the trigger, and I felt the burst course through the weapon. The noise, so close to my body, was deafening. Somewhere, more glass shattered and fell.

Desperate, I grabbed him around the waist, shoved, and tumbled us both to the floor. By pure luck his head struck the hard tile first, and I sensed him go woozy. I released the submachine gun, raised slightly, and smashed him in the temple with my forearm.

My brain, running behind, realized that several single shots had been fired above us.

"Lockerby?" No need to maintain radio silence now.

"You all right, Silas?"

"Is Rondo still alive?"

"Sure."

And as if coordinated, the man himself landed on the deck right outside the door, dropping like a paratrooper from the sky. He didn't roll, but took the shock entirely in his thighs, grunted, and swung around, looking for me.

I stared at him. "What happened?" He'd jumped into the laps of two experienced warfighters, both shooting to kill with automatic weapons. I couldn't understand how he'd survived.

"One guy popped up when I came over the rail, and Lockerby shot him." Rondo shrugged.

"Yeah." Lockerby's voice. "And the kung fu master here disarmed the other one like he was pulling a weed. Fucking beautiful."

"Where are they?"

"They had plastic handcuffs, so I tied their hands to their ankles. Lockerby hit the one guy in his vest—he's still breathing."

"Five down, then. That has to dent their force."

"Where's Clara?"

"I don't know. This boat's *huge*."

We were standing in a lounge, just inside the broken fragments of the glass doors: marble tile, ornate and heavily padded furniture, gold-framed mirrors on both walls. Fluffy towels were stacked three feet high in a brass rack. A tiny, bluish safety light glowed at ceiling height.

I picked up the last guy's SCAR, swapped the magazine for a full one from his belt, and lifted it into a forward ready. Rondo wiped his face and arms with one of the little bar towels.

"Let's go," I said.

"Wait up." Lockerby broke in.

"What?"

"Activity." He paused. "There's a door at waterline, about five feet toward the front from where you are. It's opening."

"Waterline?"

"Facing the marina, not the dock." Another pause, and I could hear a faint buzzing whine through the yacht's bulkheads. "It's a, a . . . a garage, I guess. Small boats inside . . . it looks like they're launching one."

I turned back to the deck. "How many? Armed? What?"

"Three . . . four? One's carrying—" He stopped abruptly.

"*What?*"

"Fuck—"

BAMMM!

A car in the parking lot exploded.

"Lockerby!" I was yelling.

A moment, then, "I'm okay." But he sure didn't sound it. "RPG, I think."

"Get out of there!"

"Yeah."

Rondo and I stared through the rain at the parking lot, a hundred yards away. I saw Lockerby appear, stumbling for the boathouse.

Even over the pounding noise of the rain I could hear automatic weapon fire. Lockerby stopped, fell forward, then rose and continued, more slowly, in a crouch.

"Go," I whispered. "Go."

He almost made it.

Just as he reached the corner of the boathouse, another RPG round struck, demolishing half the structure in an explosion of wood and metal. Lockerby was tossed like a rag in a gale.

I started to run toward the dock—and the fuel tank caught fire, bursting into flame from the pipe connections at its top. Lockerby disappeared in a shockwave of fire.

"Oh my God." Rondo seemed to be entering shock.

I couldn't blame him. I was more and more wobbly myself.

"Okay," I said. "Okay, okay, okay." Trying to calm him and me both. "Come on. We're here to save Clara." I took his arm. After another moment he looked away, then down at my face.

"I'm going to *kill* them," he said. Low voice. "All of them."

"Forget that. Clara. She's all that matters."

I ran to the next door inside, through the lounge, and kicked it open. The hallway beyond was lit by crystal sconces over teak paneling and a Persian runner on the floor. The buzz was louder, coming from behind another door directly opposite.

Rondo reached for the knob, and I grabbed his arm.

"Me first," I said. "If there's gunfire, stay out here until it stops."

Without waiting for him to argue, I stepped to the side and tested the door's latch. It depressed easily, not locked. I held it down, glancing at Rondo. He went to the other side and nodded. In one motion, I shoved the door open, tucked the assault rifle to my chest, and dived through in a tuck roll.

Bright light. I slid across the floor, came to my feet in a crouch, and swung around.

It *was* a garage. A Zodiac inflatable hung from a gantry mounted in the ceiling, pointed toward a wide-open door in the yacht's hull. A Jet Ski sat alongside. Two workbenches held tools and grease and a stack of Day-Glo life vests. Just beyond the small boats, water lapped below the edge of the door.

The Zodiac was moving, the hoist rolling it toward the exit.

CH-H-H-H-CKKKK!

Bullets shattered plastic and boat parts all around me. I went to the floor again, getting behind a tackle locker against the outer wall. I looked back, saw Rondo peering in, and waved him away.

I couldn't fire back, not without a firm location for Clara.

"Give it up!" I shouted. "Police will be all around this barge in two minutes!"

"Fuck off." Another burst of gunfire. I hunched into my narrow shelter.

The gantry's whine stopped. A moment later, I heard the Zodiac drop to the deck, then slide out, splashing into the river.

"*Assalamu alaykom, keef halak?*" I called out in my grade-school Arabic.

"Silas? *Matha?*" Clara's voice, weak.

"*Ayna anta?*"

"*Fi ep markeb.*"

In the boat. I risked a look over the top of the locker. The inflatable bobbed just outside. Clara lay inside, silver binding her legs and arms. Duct tape. And at the doorway, about to jump aboard, was Saxon. In one hand was an M4, the military's standard assault weapon. In the other he held a small box, connected to the bulkhead by a cable.

"All I want is the girl," I yelled. "Put her back inside, you can go."

Instead, Saxon fired all his remaining rounds at me—one long burst. The wall overhead basically imploded, demolished by the fusillade. The locker rocked as it was slammed by bullets that, fortunately, were stopped by the steel facing. Dust and shards of plastic showered over my head.

A *clunk.* I looked out again, warily. Saxon had tossed the carbine into the Zodiac. As I emerged, he tore the cable from the wall and threw it and the box into the river.

"Don't come after me." He wasn't even breathing hard. "I'll kill her if you do."

"No—!"

Too late. He hopped into the inflatable, and a moment later the outboard roared into life.

"What's going on?" Rondo, calling through the door.

Saxon glanced up at me, a pistol in one hand. I ducked back inside, followed by two shots cracking into the wall, wide and wild.

It's impossible to aim a handgun from a small boat.

"Clara!" Rondo appeared beside me. Outside, the outboard rose in volume, and we could hear the Zodiac start to move away.

"We can't chase him with the *Queen Mary* here," I said. "By the time we find the bridge, he'll be in Nova Scotia."

Sirens rose in the distance, getting closer.

Rondo and I saw the Jet Ski at the same time.

"Get it into the water!"

Rondo ran over and bent down, looking at the little mechanical sled the Jet Ski sat on. A track led to the door.

"I can't see any way to make this *move*." He looked ready to tear the machinery apart by hand.

"Shit." I remembered the cable box Saxon had thrown to the fishes. "Saxon wrecked the hoist before he left." Smart.

Rondo stood up. "We can't let him get away!"

"That thing must weigh five hundred pounds. How can we get it out?"

He glared, started to say something, then bent down and tried to push the Jet Ski toward the door. It didn't budge.

"Come on, let's talk to the police. Maybe they can get a helicopter over here."

"Not in this weather." Rondo set his feet, braced, and gave a tremendous, vein-popping heave. The Jet Ski moved, about a quarter inch.

"Fuck!" His face went dark with effort. He tried again—and the craft abruptly jerked out of its cradle, crashed to the deck, and slid forward. Breathing like a steam engine, Rondo kept moving, shoving it forward, until it tipped over the sill and dropped into the river.

I pulled on a dark green life jacket, slung my rifle over it and looked through the doorway.

"I'm going!" Rondo said.

"No. It's a one-seater."

"I want to go!"

"I'm sorry," I said. "Look, have you ever killed anyone? Do you even know how to use this thing?" I tapped the rifle at my side. "Stay here. You want Clara back, let me handle Saxon."

I stepped out, got a foot onto the Jet Ski, and almost toppled into the river as it slid away from the yacht. I jumped, banging onto the seat, nearly losing the SCAR. The key was in the ignition. I turned it, punched the start button and the machine rumbled to life.

"Tell the cops everything," I hollered. "Get a lawyer, but don't play games. Not worth it."

If he had any sense, Rondo would do exactly that: surrender, spend a day in an interrogation room and then go home. He'd probably start getting movie offers five minutes after his picture showed up in the news.

Or at least reality TV. He'd be fine.

I accelerated into the river, after Clara.

CHAPTER THIRTY-EIGHT

A squall of rain pelted down so hard it knocked the earpiece out. I squinted into the murk. Saxon was just disappearing around the end of the jetty, accelerating in a high plume of river water. Jersey was a thousand hazy lights in the distance. The Jet Ski was absurdly loud. I couldn't even hear the rainfall on the river. I twisted the throttle, all the way, and the craft sprang forward with such a lurch that I almost fell off.

How fast were we going? It felt like ninety miles an hour—Saxon a few hundred yards ahead, me on an intersecting tangent, catching up but barely. Even the middle of the river seemed crowded at that speed. Rain stung my face. We swerved around a Circle Line tourist boat—what's a little precipitation to the midwesterners?—dodged a bedraggled sailboat, shot past a maniac in a rowing shell. I think our wakes swamped him, but he shouldn't have been out anyway, the idiot.

The Manhattan skyline flashed past on our right. Long docks, mostly empty. Thank God for the rain—otherwise the news helicopters would be all over us, live video streaming to millions.

As we passed the Chelsea Piers, I finally closed enough distance to shout at Saxon. He saw me, but there was too much noise for any kind of communication. Instead, he raised the M4 and fired a burst in my direction.

When the hell had he reloaded?

Missed by a mile, of course. I couldn't risk shooting back, not with Clara in the boat. She wasn't visible—lying on the bottom, I assumed—but my bullets would go right through the canvas pontoons.

I didn't know where Saxon was going, but he must have had a destination, and there was a good chance he'd have backup waiting there: Friends? Guns? Or friends *with* guns. No matter what, another bad outcome.

Only one thing to do. Grind my teeth and keep the throttle as high as possible. The Jet Ski hydroplaned, almost out of control. Bucking and pounding on the waves, I pulled a little ahead of Saxon. Ten yards, twenty . . . I glanced back. He was glaring my way. I raised one hand, just long enough to give him the finger, then yanked the steering bar sideways. The Jet Ski reared like a horse, didn't quite swamp, and after a split second, when it recovered its footing, roared straight for the Zodiac.

It was a truly stupid move, the only positive aspect being that every other option was worse. Saxon may not have believed I'd do it, at first—he didn't turn away for a couple of seconds.

And then it was too late.

I struck the inflatable dead center. By chance, at that instant, the waves had slammed me down and bounced the Zodiac up—so instead of riding up and over the pontoon, the Jet Ski smashed its nose and stopped as abruptly as if we'd run into a seawall. I rocketed off the seat, thrown forward like a crash-test dummy, and about as gracefully.

It was only luck that I didn't fly right over the damn boat and land in the water on the other side. Instead, I slammed into Saxon himself, standing conveniently in the way. We collapsed onto the bench. The Zodiac almost tipped over as the steering swung wildly. The outboard's screw came out of the water, screaming.

The action got a little hazy for a few moments. Saxon and I had both been half knocked out, and we grappled and punched at each other on autopilot. He landed a pair of useless strikes on my chest, which the life jacket absorbed. I tore at his ear, and he tried to bite my hand. Blood was running down his left arm. We both had sub-machine guns but couldn't spare the seconds it would take to find the trigger and point the barrel.

Saxon recovered faster. Despite the bending, rocking surface of the Zodiac's bottom, he managed to stand up, then kicked me in the neck. I went down hard. He kicked me again, lost his balance as the boat swayed, and recovered by bracing against the steering column.

"You crazy motherfucker," he said, and pulled the M4 from behind his back, where our struggle had tangled it up. "They said you'd be *easy*."

Unfortunately, we weren't going to have a long, chatty discussion. Saxon gripped the carbine, aimed at me and started to pull the trigger.

For an instant, I saw Death.

But we'd both forgotten somebody.

Clara, trussed like Houdini, had wormed her away across the

base of the boat. On her back, hands and legs taped together. Just as Saxon corrected his aim, she curled her legs to her chest, then kicked out, as hard as she could—right at his knees.

He collapsed. The carbine jerked toward the sky, and I saw a trail of bullets in the rain. With one last, volcanic surge of adrenaline I launched myself at Saxon, struck his hip with my head, and knocked him clean off the boat.

I scrambled up, slipped, grabbed the steering wheel. The Zodiac swerved sharply. I straightened and stared at the water.

Where *was* the bastard?

Clara kicked me in the shin. Oh, right. I bent down and tore the tape from her hands. She undid her legs herself, as I went back to searching the waves.

"Thank you," I shouted, over the spray and rain and engine noise. "You are amazing."

She pulled herself up and grabbed me around the chest.

"I thought I was going to die," she said into my ear.

"Me too."

It felt like she was crying. I held onto the wheel with one arm and hugged her with the other. "You're all right now," I said. "We're safe."

"Where is he?"

If I knew, I'd have tried to run him over, wouldn't I? I kept searching the dark water. "Don't know."

A sudden blast of engine noise. We swung around, and there he was—on the goddamn Jet Ski. Fucking Christ, the man had more lives than Jack Bauer. I fumbled for my SCAR, wondering if we were about to go through the same crap again, in reverse.

But no. Maybe he was hurt. Maybe he realized Clara was loose, and it would be two to one. For whatever reason, he simply turned and gunned the Jet Ski away from us, disappearing toward the west, exhausted by the whole business.

I knew how he felt.

"I think I'm going into shock," said Clara.

"Hang on until we get to shore." I found the Zodiac's throttle, put our backs to Saxon, and headed for land.

We could have taken the boat out at Hell's Kitchen, but who knows what people there might have seen of our high-seas duel? I didn't want to get dragged into explanations, dissembling and police custody just yet. Instead, I motored another two dozen blocks farther north, finally pulling in at the 79th Street Boat Basin.

Before we arrived, I dumped the SCAR into the river. No need for the attention it would draw.

Most of the marina's hundred-plus slips were full. 79th Street is the only city facility willing to let people live on their boats year round, and there was a long waiting list. Myself, I can't see the draw—puttering around your tiny cabin in cold gray weather, cooking on a propane one-burner, trying to sleep to the lullaby sounds of tugboats, barge traffic, foghorns and booze cruises passing by. But for many, the romance of the sea is stronger than common sense.

The rain hadn't let up. Thunder crashed. No one seemed to be outside to see us tie off at the outer dock, though warm light glowed through windows of a number of the docked boats.

Clara was shivering, hard.

"Can you walk?" I'd lifted her from the Zodiac, and stood her up on the slippery wooden boards.

"I'm sorry." Teeth chattering.

"Don't be stupid."

"You told me to stay at the apartment. With Rondo. But I left."

"Forget it." She could barely stand. "You need medical attention."

"No."

"Don't argue." I put her arm around my neck and we shuffled along. "In fact, we need to let the police know you're here."

"You can't!"

"Why not?"

"Once they start asking *you* questions, you won't get out for days."

Which was more true than she knew—or I hoped she knew. "I'll deal with it. We're not putting you on the wrong side of the law."

"But you have to—" She stumbled on the end of a boat's line, sloppily hitched to the dock cleat.

"What?"

"It was the same man. The one who attacked me in the park."

"Saxon. I know."

"You have to *get* him." Clara stopped, swung to face me and held my shoulders with both hands. "He cannot be running around loose."

"The police?"

"You." She stared into my eyes, intense, almost febrile. "You can do it. They can't. Not soon enough."

"Thanks for the vote of confidence, but—"

"You." Abruptly her grip weakened, and she started to fall. "Promise!"

What could I do?

"Okay, fine, I promise. But only if you take care of yourself."

"Thank you." Her eyes closed, and she collapsed, limp. Good thing I was ready, or she might have gone into the river again.

The marina's entrance was a hundred feet up the dock. I lifted Clara into a fireman's carry and jogged toward civilization.

CHAPTER THIRTY-NINE

"Y ou *left* her there?"

"Only once the paramedics took over." I didn't like how defensive that sounded.

"I hope she lives."

"Fuck, Johnny, I did the best I could!" I felt control slipping. I started yelling into the phone. "They killed every one of her coworkers at the Thatcher. Every one! Automatic weapons and *grenades*— she's lucky to be breathing!"

I was in Central Park, in the wooded Ramble. I stopped walking, not even bothering to shelter from the rain under a tree.

"I'm not Superman! What do you want? I should go back and get arrested and spend the next ten years in jail? *That* won't help!"

"Hey, no, I didn't mean that." He sounded surprised. "Calm down."

"Fuck. Fuck!"

I forced myself to be quiet for a moment, ignored Johnny and looked around. A few early evening joggers were out, the hardy ones who liked to ignore the weather, splashing along in reflective lycra.

At four p.m. it felt like night under the drizzling clouds. Thunder rumbled again.

"I'm sorry. I'm having a really bad day." I suddenly chuckled in an involuntary, weirdly hysterical manner.

"I know, man, I know."

"It was just a touch of hypothermia and a delayed reaction to the abduction. She's safe, she's in the hospital, the cops are on guard."

"I hope so." He paused, a moment's silence on the phone. "For your sake, too, not just hers."

Emotion started to bubble up again, but I jammed the lid on. Time enough later to deal with my shit. Right now I *had* to focus on Saxon.

And his masters.

"Can you look something up for me?" I said.

"Yeah, sure. Where are you?"

"On walkabout."

"You might want to keep going."

"Why?"

"Haven't you seen the news?"

"No, I've been chasing heavily armed kidnappers all over the city, remember? Jesus. What news?"

"The FBI tracked down the bomber—the guy who blew up Blacktail?"

"But—" Wasn't that Zeke and me? So much had happened I was losing all the threads.

"Hayden Pennerton, disgraced hedge fund wunderkind. His name was on the rental car's papers. Not the name I expected, actually."

"Oh. They caught him?"

"At JFK. He was actually on the jetway when they arrested him."

"How about that."

"Apparently," Johnny continued, "he was traveling under a false identity, with a complete set of phony documentation. Plus cash *and* a bunch of guns. The FBI is being cagey, of course, but 'unidentified sources' are talking about an anonymous tip."

So the DA finally looked at my mail. "About time."

"There's video up already." Johnny had obviously been spending too much time clicking through news updates. "A SWAT team, running through the terminal—ski masks, big fucking guns, Kevlar, the whole deal. It's amazing how many people seem to have their cellphone cameras waiting for this sort of thing."

"Good for them."

"Traders this morning can't talk about anything else. One of their own—they don't usually go down so spectacularly."

As I crossed one of the park's roadways, four cyclists whizzed past. One wore the clear plastic rain jacket that was standard Tour de France fashion in about 1975. They must have been going thirty miles an hour, despite the rain-slick road. I stepped aside, just in time to avoid wheel spray.

"Is *he* talking?"

"Who, Hayden? Not to the media, that's for sure."

How long did I have? Hayden would roll over immediately, of course, but there wasn't much he could say about me. The bank codes we'd used in recovering Marlett's money were his—Marlett's, I mean—and I'd cleared my own transactions subsequently. That trail would die in the Republic of Overseas Tax Evasion, Caymans Branch.

Forensics on the rental car? The Hooverville labs could be incredibly persistent. Or they might match me some other way. We really do live in a panopticon.

"All very interesting," I said. "And it's now even more important—the favor I need."

"Shoot." He hesitated. "So to speak."

"The yacht Saxon took Clara to. *Tangible Assets*. Who owns it?"

"Good question."

And it was. Theseus's thread through the entire maze, in fact.

Saxon was a nasty piece of work, but in the end, just another hired hand. He certainly didn't have the scratch for a 150-foot supercruiser. Nor could he possibly have orchestrated the slay-to-pay scheme in all its devious glory. A market player with a billion or two to gamble and no morals whatsoever—yes, I realize that doesn't narrow the field particularly—set it up. He was the guy I wanted to see.

He'd be the boat's owner. Saxon had been running to his daddy.

"Nothing's coming up on Google," said Johnny.

"Well, hell, I didn't think it would be *that* easy. There must be databases, though. Boats have to be registered, right? Maybe there are yacht spotters, like the nutcases who track private jets as a hobby? I don't know. See what you can find."

"I don't spend much time in idle websurfing." Which was undoubtedly true. I'm not sure Johnny had any interests at all outside the markets. "You need someone who knows how to do this," he said. "A researcher."

"She's in a hospital at the moment."

"Oh." He paused. "Sorry."

I let a beat pass. The rain had turned pretty in the park, and I just watched it fall.

"Look, it's going to take a few minutes. Call me back."

"All right. Thanks." But before I hung up, I thought of something. "Hey, what's going on with Plank Industrials? Are they still in play?"

"The share price is headed for the moon. No, Alpha Centauri. Up something like seventy percent today."

"Why?"

"Because they arrested Pennerton! Everyone figures Terry Plank is safe now."

"The shorts must be hurting."

"On the *coals*." Johnny laughed. "I'm not sure I've ever seen a short squeeze so pure and clean—not on a Fortune 500 stock. It's beautiful."

"Sounds like you have a piece of it."

"Not much."

Right. Johnny wasn't much of a poker player.

He went back to his computer. "MarineRegistryOnline-dot-com. That looks good."

"Well?"

"They're asking for a credit card number."

"Yeah, that's how it works. Who the hell does your shopping for you?"

"The help." Maybe he was serious. "Give me a half hour."

"An address, too, if you can get it."

"Right."

I tucked the phone away as I came to the edge of the park. A forlorn ice-cream vendor was packing it in, shuttering his cart and folding the umbrella. When the light turned I squished across Fifth Avenue.

I needed dry clothes, but I still couldn't go home—even more so now, with Hayden under the bright lights, Rondo getting all kinds of questions and probably every cop in the city looking for me. This neighborhood had nothing but high-end women's boutiques and bespoke tailors. Finally, in a sandwich-and-gelato multimart, I found a display of tourist gimcrack, including some souvenir clothing. For seventy bucks I got an FDNY hoodie, a T-shirt with the notorious FML subway sign and a huge Yankees umbrella.

"You want a bag for all that?" The girl behind the counter looked dubiously at the damp bills I handed over.

"No, I'm changing into them right now."

Down the street I bought an oversize, overheated coffee with extra whipped cream. The shop was bright and noisy, one of those places that costs four times as much as McDonald's but has the same cheap plastic furniture. I sat in a corner, nipping at the scorching caffeine, and examined my half-dozen cellphones. Remarkably, they all still worked. I was about to turn them all off again when the blue-taped one rang. I looked at the number but drew a blank.

Of course I'd forgotten who I'd assigned blue to.

"Hello?"

"Don't you ever answer your phone? I thought you gave me this number so I could always reach you! I've been calling for two hours."

Ganderson, sounding just like Clara. Was I really so out of sync
with the pace of modern life?

"I turned it off while I went for a run," I said.

"What?"

"Friday's my long day. Fifteen miles."

"Oh. Listen, I've got your meeting with Plank set up. Where are
you?"

Meeting? "I have to take a shower."

"Make it quick."

"But—" I frowned. "I thought Terry was safe. Now that the police
seem to have caught the terrorist."

"So they *say.*"

"You don't believe them?"

"I stopped believing the government the same time I stopped
believing in the tooth fairy."

"Well—"

"More important, Terry himself doesn't think he's out of danger
yet. He wants you on board, PDQ."

I had no idea what those initials meant. Old folks are always giving the new generation shit for textspeak, but they have plenty of
their own inscrutable jargon, IMAO.

"Fine. I'll see him. But let's agree on a minimum, okay?—if I get
there and he's changed his mind, I still get a day's pay."

"No problem. Sure."

I looked at the phone. No *problem*? No nickel-and-dime outrage?
Ganderson might actually be worried.

"So where is he? Some private estate, surrounded by militia? An
underground bunker? Iowa?"

"No, no. He never left Manhattan."

Ah. Not bad. Whoever was running Terry's security had some smarts. The most dangerous times are when you're moving, not when you're hunkered down, so it made sense for Terry to have gone to ground in place.

"He's going to make a public statement," Ganderson continued. "Later this evening. He wants you around to double-check, keep an eye out, like that."

I started to see why Ganderson was concerned. "Public statement? Why bother?"

"Too much speculation around his company. He wants Plank Industrials out of the news, for good. Standing up in front of a crowd, and nothing happening, makes the point that he's safe and the hyenas should hump off elsewhere."

Hyenas? Oh, the press.

"And I'll be there to make sure nothing does happen," I said.

"Exactly. *Absolutely* sure. You and a few dozen other guys."

"I need an hour." I could have headed straight over, wherever Plank was, but it might be a good idea to clean up first.

"The news conference is going to be at the Grand Plaza. You can meet us there. Call when you arrive and I'll tell you where we are."

Nice. The Grand Plaza was a vast, ornately luxurious hotel-slash-conference-center on Broadway. Anesthesiologist conventions, celebrity weddings, Russian oligarchs visiting the Big Apple—an apotheosis of twenty-first-century public culture. I'd heard they maintained a green room just for A-list paparazzi. "Is Plank staying at the hotel?"

"That's classified." Ganderson coughed—no, he was laughing. "Operational security, you know."

"Got to go," I said. "I'll be there within the hour."

"Good." Ganderson clicked off.

It wasn't just the job. If Plank was really still in the crosshairs, Saxon would be holding the rifle.

And if Saxon was ready to kill someone else tonight, despite everything he'd gone through today—well, I could be there, too.

Another ringtone. I shuffled through my collection while taking a long gulp of coffee. This time I was pretty sure whose it was.

"Johnny?"

"Yeah."

"Wasn't I supposed to call you?"

"Were you?"

"Never mind. Do you have a name?"

"It wasn't easy."

"How much did MarineRegistryOnline-dot-com charge you?"

"Don't worry about it. On me."

A long pause.

"Well?" Not that I was impatient or anything.

"Sorry." Johnny was clearly distracted. "Some action in Plank Industrials options. Futures spreads widening . . . there's some serious buying going on there."

Options, because the exchange was closed, and shares wouldn't be traded again, publicly, until tomorrow morning.

"He's doing a press conference tonight," I said.

"The market appears happy to have heard that."

"So what's the name?"

"Name?"

"The yacht!"

"Oh, right. It's registered to an entity called Waterborne Inclinations, LLC."

I waited. "And?"

"So I tried to look them up. They're incorporated by a brass-plate law firm in Bermuda."

"Along with five thousand other tax-avoidance vehicles, no doubt." The tax havens were filled with such offices: one room, one attorney, and one extra large file cabinet. Their only advertising was typically a small nameplate screwed to the door.

"You'd need a big-gun lawyer to hack through the holdings trail," Johnny said.

"And far more time than I have."

"Right. So I googled the bugger just to see what might come up. Turns out they're not trying to hide—or not trying hard."

"You found the owners?"

"Maybe, maybe not." Johnny paused to set up his revelation. "But I turned up some news clippings—maritime trade press releases, that sort of thing. Waterborne Inclinations has done some other business, like renting a yacht club for a reception, chartering a party boat, and so forth. They don't lay out an org chart, but every event was owned or headlined by Aldershot Capital Partners."

It took me a moment.

"Aldershot—that's Ganderson's firm!"

"Yes." Johnny sounded pleased with his accomplishment.

"He hired me to find *himself*?" I was arguing with myself, really, the same conversation that had been running inside my head all day.

"You don't think someone like Ganderson could be behind the killings?"

"Actually, no, I think it would be *just* someone like Ganderson. A ruthless and amoral hedge fund, trying out unorthodox strategies to rig some trades."

"So there you go."

"But every fund manager is like that. The successful ones, any-way. The real problem is that Ganderson *hired* me." Repeating myself.

"Uh-huh. To do what, exactly?"

"To find out who might be assassinating lousy fund managers."

"Why?"

"To avoid bad publicity——"

"Or any publicity at all," Johnny said. "The kind that might, you know, interfere with his scheme."

"Sure," I said. "If he was responsible, he might hire me—but not to find him out. That's just stupid."

"I dunno." Johnny's shrug was clear over the phone. "Ganderson may have written you some checks, but he also owns the boat that the number-one bad guy ran to when he was in trouble."

Indeed. I couldn't work it out in my head, not in any logical way.

"What are you going to do?" asked Johnny.

"Ganderson said Terry Plank wants me at his press conference, in case Carlos the Jackal shows up."

"Still planning to go?"

I thought about it. Around me office workers drank their

end-of-day pick-me-ups, ate stale pastries from the morning delivery, talked on their own cellphones. The novel writers had gone home. The counter staff looked like they wanted their shift to end ASAP.

I knew the feeling.

"Yes," I said.

"Even though——"

"Maybe Ganderson set it up; maybe he didn't. Either way, he's at the center of the whole thing. And he's invited me to show up in the same room with him—armed."

"I guess."

I suddenly wished I hadn't thrown away the SCAR.

"Armed," I said again. "I don't think I can pass this chance up."

CHAPTER FORTY

The Grand Plaza was as imposing as its name. A hundred and twenty years old, built of carved sandstone and brick, it occupied an entire block near Times Square. Ten flags drooped in a row from brass poles extending over the broad entrance. A team of bellmen, valet drivers and concierges briskly managed the traffic in and out the sweeping glass doors. Even the smokers' area was well maintained, with its own Art Nouveau awning, a pair of bronze ash stands and a blower discreetly drawing secondhand smoke away from the sidewalk.

I stood by the entrance to an ATM machine across and down the street, pretending to talk on one of my cellphones while I studied the hotel.

A two-day conference was in progress: "Innovation and Strategic Investment in Distressed Assets, Eleventh Annual Sessions."

Or as the finblogs shorthanded it, "VultureFest XI." You might have expected a lower profile from this crowd, but public opprobrium means nothing to guys whose best deals generally involve mass layoffs, pension stripping and fire-sale liquidation. At six p.m.

they were probably sitting down to dinner inside. Ignoring the keynote, thinking about which strip clubs to visit later. Ganderson would be in his element, but I wasn't sure what Plank Industrials was doing there. Decades-old midwestern factories, big-steel manufacturing—exactly the sort of "distressed assets" that investors like these live to dismember. Imagine a baby bunny, blundering into a pack of dire wolves.

On the other hand, if Terry Plank wanted to make a very public statement, it wasn't a bad choice of venue. Reporters were on standby, hoping to catch examples of vulgar excess and plutocratic disdain, populist titillation for their readers. I even saw two television vans. It was hard to tell at a distance, but Clara's friend Darryl might have been standing outside one of them, thumbing a smartphone.

Otherwise, no action. No police and nothing unusual in the tide of pedestrians sweeping past, mostly workers on their way home in the rainy evening. Cars sloshed along Broadway, honking now and then, but with little enthusiasm. Umbrellas jostled. The doormen whistled taxis. It all looked perfectly normal.

The decoy phone rang, right in my ear. I jumped, half deafened.

"Why aren't you inside?" Ganderson, sounding harried.

"Inside?"

"The hotel. Plank's waiting."

"All right. One minute."

"Good." He hung up.

I gave the street one more long look. If something was screwy, I couldn't tell. I put the decoy phone away and walked briskly over to the Grand Plaza.

As I entered, it occurred to me that Ganderson must have just tracked me down by the cellphone's autolocation. I had to figure out a way around that, someday.

A tall, aloof doorman swept me through the brass doors with a slight bow. Inside, the lobby was warm and welcoming, if dimly lit. A waterfall tumbled two stories down the far wall of the atrium. Recessed alcoves, full-grown trees in planter boxes, and several different levels—up two stairs, down three, and so forth—created a space filled with semiprivate areas to stand or sit and talk and wait and people-watch. As luxury hotel foyers go, it was more than pleasant.

Over near a broad, plushly carpeted stairway leading to the mezzanine, wide-screen monitors listed events and ballrooms. I headed that way.

At the top of the stairs, someone slipped up next to me and said, "Silas."

I suppressed an automatic reaction, barely. The slightest bit more adrenaline and I'd have lit up the entire floor.

"Calm down."

"Zeke?" I stared. "What the hell are you doing here?"

"I told you, I'm on the job. The question is, what are *you*—"

"You're working here?" I felt dumb.

"Like I said."

"For who?"

"A blowhard named Ganderson."

"Fuck!"

"What—" He stopped, seeing my expression. "Shit."

"I don't believe it."

"We're down to zero degrees of separation, aren't we?"

I glanced around. "Can we get off the floor?"

We found an unused facility room down a hallway on the mezzanine. It was surprisingly large inside, dark and quiet, with blank partitions set up across half the floor. Empty desks trailed power cables. It looked like a group of trade-show exhibitors had just left, or was about to arrive.

Behind us the door closed silently.

"I'm just additional security," Zeke said. "Exactly like I told you."

"What did Ganderson say he's worried about? Your rates are too high just to fend off a few overzealous photographers."

"The deer hunter seems to have put everyone on edge. This conference, all that fucking money—these guys are worth what, hundreds of millions? I was watching them in the dining room just now, and you could tell, they're *scared*." Zeke allowed himself a small smile. "Of one man with a rifle. Somehow I thought it would take more than that."

"The soft underbelly of the kleptocracy." I rolled my shoulders. "Ganderson wanted *me* here. Specifically."

"I can't believe you didn't tell me he'd hired you." Zeke was still put out.

"You didn't mention his name either, when we were on the phone."

"Why should I?"

It was true, we'd both kept a secret too many.

"Sorry," I said. "Bad habits." I ran down my experience with Ganderson once more, in case there were other blanks to fill in.

Zeke thought for a moment. "You think Ganderson knows we're connected, you and me?"

"No."

"Me neither." I knew Zeke would never talk about me, just like I would never talk about him. Not to a civilian. "When does Plank come in?"

"Is that who's speaking?"

"He didn't tell you?"

"Just something about a VIP guest." Zeke paused. "Hang on. You mean *Plank*? The deer hunter's *next target*?"

"Apparently, the whole world has heard he's making a statement tonight. But Ganderson didn't give you the name?"

"No." I couldn't see Zeke's face well in the dark room, our only illumination being from light under the doors. But he seemed to be getting pissed. "He should have."

Something rattled in the corridor outside. We stood silent, waiting while it rolled past. A waiter's cart, maybe. The noise faded down the hallway.

"Are you on a permit?" I said. A concealed-firearms permit, that is—in other words, was he strapped.

"Sidearm only."

"That's all it takes." I thought. "How many of you are there?"

"Don't know. A dozen in the briefing. Others—?"

"Anyone we know?"

"No. Basic jarheads. The chief was senior, though. Fort Bragg through and through."

"He say so?"

"Of course not." One clue, that. "Had the look. He'd been scrapping, too. His left wrist was wrapped with bandage tape."

That caught my attention. "Five-eight, all gristle, blue eyes, buzzcut?"

"You know him?" But Zeke wasn't slow. "Shit. *Saxon?*"

Clearly Zeke and I had over-fucking-compartmentalized. I'd forgotten Zeke had never seen Saxon, even though I'd talked about him enough. "Four hours ago he kidnapped Clara, took out everyone at her library, and tried real hard to kill me."

"*What?*"

He was having trouble believing me. I couldn't blame him, but we didn't have time for exposition.

"Tell you later." As one mind, we were out the door, moving fast down the hallway. Zeke loosened his jacket.

"She okay?"

"I think so." I wasn't sure about myself, though. I was practically glowing with adrenaline.

"I don't understand what's going on."

"Where's Saxon now?"

"Don't know." Zeke slowed, checking each banquet room door we passed. Most were empty. "The main group's in the ballroom, down there. Ganderson wanted me near the door. Saxon could be anywhere."

Fifty yards ahead the corridor opened up, into a two-story space, with crystal chandeliers and broad double doors opposite an elevator bank. White-clothed tables, empty now, had been arrayed to form a cocktail area. The room was almost deserted, just a couple of men in suits grimacing into their cellphones. Behind the double doors we could hear banquet noise: someone on a microphone, too garbled to understand; low chatter; glass and flatware clinking.

"If I see Saxon," I said, "I'm going to—"

POP! POP!

And just like that, shooting, inside the ballroom.

"Left!" Zeke sprinted for the far left door, leaving me the right. We hit them at almost the same instant.

We crashed through, and entered bedlam.

CHAPTER FORTY-ONE

tandard fancy-dinner setup: a hundred, hundred-fifty guests at round tables scattered through the room. Older men and a much smaller number of young women. Dais at the front with a speaker's table and podium. Two large projection screens to either side, currently showing a brightly colored bar graph. Vast stacks of identical books for sale, or handing out, at a table in the rear.

And everyone moving. Shouting. Diving for the floor, jumping up, running into one another. All pretty much by the book for a live-fire urban-terror situation.

Except one thing—half the hedge fund motherfuckers had their *own weapons.*

Handguns everywhere! Automatics, mostly—nines, 1911s. A guy in front of me was crouched behind his table holding a polished, silvery Desert Eagle in two hands. A woman next to him had a little pink Cobra .25, waving it the other way. Over there a young man in a classic Weaver stance, wild-eyed.

"Holy *shit.*" Zeke's voice cut through the yelling and crashing, twenty-five feet away.

"Police!" I screamed, as loudly as possible. "Everybody stand down!"

That just drew attention my way, and I was abruptly staring into gun barrels from every direction.

Thank you, NRA. I'm not sure how a total deregulation of firearms equates to liberty, but it was sure as fuck invigorating the rubber-chicken-and-boring-speech paradigm.

"Over there!" I'd spotted Saxon himself, standing at the edge of the dais, scanning the melee. He held an MP5 submachine gun by his side. A few heads swung, following my gesture.

Someone fired from deep in the other side of the room, in the middle of a desperate bunch who had run for the kitchen doors. A scream, the yelling even louder. Another shot, then another.

Suddenly, it was a war zone. Idiots all around the room pulled their triggers. The intense noise stunned a few people and drove the rest into blind panic. Blood and haze filled the air.

What the hell. The lady with the Cobra was screaming right next to me, so I grabbed her arm, closed my hand over hers so she wouldn't pull the trigger, and took the gun away. Then I fired at Saxon, right before he went backward off the dais, leaping for safety. Couldn't tell if I winged him or not.

I hit the carpet myself, elbow-crawling as fast as I could for the book table. The doors were a deathtrap—jammed by people trying to escape, then dying in place as others fought to get through.

Zeke had the same idea, diving behind the three-foot stacks of hardbacks just as I arrived. Bullets thwacked into the books, knocking them into the air and throwing out puffs of shredded paper. We huddled in the slight shelter.

"Insane!" Zeke shouted over the din. "*I* want a broker's license!"

"They can't all be carrying reloads," I yelled back. "This should die down in a few seconds."

And it did. The firing sputtered to a halt, replaced by moans and wails and pointless shouting. In the relative quiet I risked a look around the tumbled heap of books.

Saxon also reappeared, walking cautiously toward the center of the room. We saw each other at the same instant. He had the advantage, raising his MP5 immediately and firing a burst—but I was still protected behind our literature berm, and the bullets pounded harmlessly into the books.

Zeke looked out the other side, raised his pistol and shot Saxon square in the center of mass. He went down hard, falling on his weapon, and didn't move.

Sometimes things are easy.

"Got to find Ganderson," I said. "Figure out what the fuck is going on."

"Go ahead." Zeke ejected the magazine from his Beretta, left the slide open, and wiped all the metal with a cloth napkin from the floor. "I'll try to calm everyone down here."

"Lots of accidental deaths just happened. No one's ever going to sort it out."

"Exactly." He tossed his cleaned weapon onto the floor, twenty feet away.

The shooting had stopped, but everything else was still pandemonium. The first, largely misguided attempts at first aid began—waving air at dying faces, tearing open bloody shirts, tying on improvised tourniquets that would halt all blood flow and lead to unnecessary amputations. Everywhere crying, sobbing, voices shouting.

"Kinda feels like a car-bombed street market, doesn't it?" Zeke stood up.

"Not as well organized."

"These people haven't had as much practice."

Zeke saw someone he recognized, apparently one of the security men, and waved him over. In a moment they'd found another, then started a rough triage, going through the room. Faintly we could hear sirens and fire truck horns somewhere outside.

"What were those first shots, do you think?" I asked. "Before we came in?"

"Dunno. If I had to guess, I'd say some dumbass drew his weapon to show off to his girlfriend. Accidents happen."

"No shit."

Zeke glanced at the Cobra, still in my hand. "Leave that here."

"What?"

"When ESU blows in, they're going to shoot everyone who looks like any kind of a threat."

"Hmm." The NYPD's Emergency Services Unit did have a reputation.

"Look around." He gestured. "Everyone in here who's halfway functioning is on their phone."

He was right. Cellphones were pressed to ears everywhere.

"And they're saying *anything*. First responders will be expecting Mumbai."

"Okay, okay." Look like a terrorist and I might very well die like a terrorist. "It's not mine anyway." I handed him the pistol.

At the center entrance I helped pull a few bodies from the stack— most of them still alive, actually—and cleared the doorway. Stepping through, I found a few other survivors stumbling for the stairs, down to the lobby. A woman in a white uniform, from catering or something like that, looked around the corner near the elevators, hesitated, then sprinted past. I couldn't see into the lobby, too far from the escalators, but it was noisy down there, too—more shouting over the waterfall.

BANG!

The lights went out.

I leaped into a forward roll, automatically, slammed into a wall and kept going. The explosion hadn't sounded quite like a gunshot, but who knows—my ears had been saturated with battle noise so long now I couldn't count on them.

Emergency lights snapped on, battery-powered floods at widely separated points in the hallway.

"Silas! Silas, down here!"

Well, *that* was easy. Ganderson himself, poking out of one of the banquet rooms farther down. He waved me forward, an urgent swimming motion.

"Come on!" His voice was more than a whisper, less than a yell. "What's *happening* in there?"

I rose to my feet, wary, and jogged down the corridor. My feet made no noise on the carpet. The shouting faded a little behind me.

At the door, Ganderson stepped aside to let me in, while keeping watch toward the ballroom. He seemed to be alone. The room inside was almost empty—two flat handcars of chairs, stacked up, and some folded tables along one wall. A single battery lamp in the corner cast a pale light.

"Where's Terry Plank?" I said.

"Don't know. He was supposed to come later." Ganderson came in behind me, letting the door close, and checked his watch. "Actually, in about twenty minutes. He didn't want to take any chances being spotted beforehand."

"Lucky him." I noticed that Ganderson held his .45, the one with the laser mount. Finger outside the guard, pointed properly at the ground and away from both of us, yes. He paid it no attention, but I didn't let my eyes wander. "If he's still out there, he'll soon be surrounded by every duty officer in the city. Safe as a kitten."

"Good."

"Listen, what's with all the fucking ballistics?" The entire world seemed to be better armed than I was. "That roomful of Wall Streeters had more armament than a rifle battalion."

Ganderson shrugged. "Hobby shooters, like me. Plus a lot of guys who saw Marlett and Faust go down and figured if the police can't do their job, they need to protect themselves."

"And a fine job they've done of it, too."

"We had private security. They should have been keeping order."

Right. I'd almost forgotten why I was here.

"Was Saxon one of yours?"

"Who?"

But it was too late. Even in the dim, shadowed murk, I'd seen Ganderson's eyes twitch.

CHAPTER FORTY-TWO

"Fuck, he was. *You* hired Saxon!"

"Calm down, Silas."

Confirmation. Saxon worked for Ganderson, and Ganderson and Blacktail were partners. No wonder his goons had found us outside Blacktail's office—Ganderson had been tracking me all along, with the cellphone, just as he'd found me outside ten minutes earlier.

And the client Walter had sort of recognized? Who else? Ganderson, who was always in the news somewhere. He was preparing to flee, with the millions he'd earned from his spree.

"You were killing your *own*." I still couldn't believe it.

Ganderson didn't say anything. He exhaled, long and slow, then lifted the .45 to aim directly at me.

Maybe he was ready to shoot, maybe he wasn't. Maybe he was just fucking around. It didn't matter now.

My hands were already in front of me, three feet from the pistol. I sprang forward, arms reaching.

Ganderson fired, twisted away and stepped backward, all at the same second. The shot missed. So did the second and third because I'd struck his left arm. I scrabbled for a grip on his wrist as I collided, and we went down, clawing at each other.

A blur. He kept both hands on the pistol, trying to shove it toward my stomach. I kicked with one knee, grabbed his arm, head-butted in the direction of his chin. He squirmed sideways.

For an old guy, Ganderson was *strong*. All those five a.m. swims paying off.

He pulled the trigger three more times, rapidly. The last shot barely missed my head—I felt the sonic crack of a bullet inches from my ear. Desperate, I got one hand on his, over the grip, and squeezed. Hard as I could. Somehow, tearing at the tendons, I caused his trigger finger to spasm, and five more shots flew into the floor.

That was it—the magazine should be empty.

But Ganderson realized the situation as fast as I did and rolled away. In a completely lucky punch, he whacked me on the head with the gun barrel as he went. I phased out for a moment.

A few seconds later I was back on my feet, but Ganderson had retreated to a corner, protected by the two chair racks. With a moment's respite he'd pulled a new magazine from his pocket and tried to ram it in.

"I'm not *part* of this!" I yelled, but that was just distraction.

I was twenty feet from Ganderson, and he'd almost finished a reload. I had no weapon and nothing to prove. I ran for the door, crashing into it just as Ganderson finished, recovered and started firing again. Bullets followed me out.

Sprawling into the hallway, I looked left, right. Still just the battery lights, and no emergency responders in view yet. A couple of people too far away to be any help, even if they weren't blood-covered and shocked. I remained on my own.

In another second Ganderson would be at the door, with unobstructed sightlines and fresh ammunition. The hallway was barren, empty of anything I might use as cover.

In front of me were the double doors to the room Zeke and I had conferred in. Twenty minutes ago and it seemed like a week. Without hesitating, I grabbed at the handle, pushed it open, and leaped through.

The door closed just as Ganderson came up. I could see his shadow in the crack of hallway light seeping under the door. Inside it was still as dim as before—the emergency light was obscured by one of the exhibitor partitions, casting black shadows.

"Come on in, Ganderson!" I stood to one side of the door, near the dais, out of through-fire range. "I finally found my backup pistol. Let's see how good you are face to face."

Pause.

"I don't believe you." He kept his voice down.

"Then walk through the door."

"You're a dead man, Silas!"

We stood in the standoff for a long moment. I don't know what Ganderson was doing—reloading again, if he had any sense. For myself, I was frantically going through my pockets. Knife? Pen? Piece of fucking *string*? No, absolutely nothing—I was purely weaponless.

Except for five cheap cellphones.

"Police will be coming up the stairs any second." I took out one of the phones, punching at the keypad. "When they see you standing out there? Holding a gun and yelling threats? *You* are the fucking dead man."

"They're taking their time." His voice sounded reasonable, barely audible through the door. "You know how the protocols work. We've got all night."

In fact, true. ESU hated running in blind and unprepared, with so many innocent bystanders waiting around to be shot accidentally. The commanders would have to argue it out for at least ten or fifteen minutes. "It's your gamble," I said, "not mine." I finished with the first phone and pulled out the second. I held my fingers over the top, trying to dampen the beeps. "How long are you going to jerk off out there?"

"If you had a gun you'd have used it already, Silas." He was trying to convince himself.

"You never gave me time to get to my ankle holster."

"Bullshit."

"Your call, asshole."

I was on the fourth phone now.

"What happened to Saxon?" Ganderson's voice was almost conversational. "Did you kill him?"

"No."

"Because maybe you're the one who should be worried about the police, not me. What are they going to think about you?"

He was throwing my own tactic back at me, trying to start a dialogue, hoping to put me off guard.

Which meant he'd be blasting through the door any second.

"I gave my lawyer all the details!" I shouted. "Recordings, video, witnessed affidavits—if I die, your entire cabal goes down with me!"

Then I ran. Ganderson said something, but I wasn't paying attention. To the first exhibitor booth—in, out, on to the next. Then to an opposite corner. Back—

"You're *lying*, Silas!" And he kicked open the door.

He came through in a combat roll, the .45 held close, sliding along the wall and leaping for the scanty cover of a folded table. What I could see of it, in the dim light, was nicely done. If I'd had a weapon of any sort, he'd be dead, of course, but I would have had to work for it.

No matter. I dropped off the fourth phone and slipped into my own hiding place, under the dais. I held the last phone close, concealing the glow from its tiny screen.

Silence.

The door drifted shut on its closer, darkening the room again.

Ganderson shifted, crouched, began to examine the surroundings visible from his position. A red beam sprang into life, from his handgun, and switched back and forth around the room.

The laser.

"All right," Ganderson said. "You're hiding."

I kept quiet.

"It won't make any difference. I have firepower. You have nothing. I'm going to walk through here, booth by booth, and as soon as I find you, I'm going to start shooting."

"Are you sure you can find me?" I said, into my hands, which I'd cupped over the last cellphone . . . . . . and my scratchy voice seemed to come out of nowhere, emerging from four other phones. All on speaker. Volume at maximum. All four connected in a single conference call. In fact, slight transmission delays, as the signal bounced among different carriers and different towers, created an odd false-echo effect, disembodying my words even more.

Ganderson spun around, the laser beam swinging wildly across the partitions and tables near him.

"You have no idea *where* I am."

BLAM!

He fired once, blindly. I winced as the round tore into the wall about ten feet above the dais. Lucky guess.

"Tell me one thing," I said. "Why did you even hire me?"

"You're dead." His voice was almost a snarl. "Terry Plank will be dead soon enough. Too bad you're going in backward order, but the story will hold."

Okay, I'm slow. Real slow.

"Son of a bitch." I finally, *finally* understood. "You set me up."

BLAM!

Missed by a mile that time, but almost knocked out phone number two. He was figuring it out.

"You wanted me close to the investigation not so I could solve the murders, but to start implicating *me* in the assassinations."

BLAM!

Ganderson—angrier, or more confident he had my number, or both—strode through the room, turning his head side to side as I talked.

"While meanwhile," I said, despite that, "you go on minting profit on trades ahead of each event. So let me ask—where's your money on Plank? Is he going to die or not?"

Ganderson stopped, ducked down and came up with phone number four, which I'd laid on the table in a corner of one booth.

"Tricky, Silas," he said, then tossed it in the air. As the phone fell, he raised his pistol, the red beam jagging like lightning, and shot it dead center.

From only about a yard, yes, but it *was* moving. The muzzle flash left afterimages dancing in my field of vision.

"Seven point five," I said. "Moderate difficulty, dramatic execution."

"I *hear* you," Ganderson said, and walked straight to phone number one, balanced on the top edge of a partition twenty feet away. This time he simply dropped the phone to the carpet and stomped it with his heel.

"Who else is in it?" I asked. "Is there a whole gang involved? Or just you and Saxon? Oh, by the way, if you didn't see—Saxon's down. Dead, maybe. Took a round right in the chest, and emergency services are having trouble getting into the ballroom at the moment."

He paused. "Silas, you batfucker!—you are a pain in the *ass.*"

"No, I'd—"

"A straightforward deal, and you've screwed up every single step of the way. One little thing! Have you done even *one little thing* the way I asked you to? No!"

Another satisfied client. "Oh well."

By now Ganderson had indentified phone number three, on a stack of chairs off in the other direction. He headed directly toward it, head cocked slightly to track the sound's origin.

This route took him right past the dais.

It would be nice to say I'd planned it all out—the bread-crumb trail of cellphone speakers, a subtle hiding spot, an improvised weapon at hand. But I won't even try to pretend. Unfortunately often, it comes down to plain dumb luck.

When Ganderson passed in front of me, I'd already pulled myself into a tight ball of potential energy: feet flat on the floor, back braced against the floor of the dais. It was held together cheaply, with some bent-pipe legs and plastic bolts. The moment I saw his shoes, I lunged upward, putting every last bit of frustration, irritation and pent-up rage into it.

The rear plastic ties snapped. The floorboard—an eight-by-four piece of plywood—rotated up and out, hinged by unbroken connections along the front edge of the dais. The momentum of my furious shove spun the wood like an enormous riverboat paddle: up, around and down. Down hard. *Smashing* down.

Right onto Ganderson.

Not his head. He was too tall for that. But the edge of the plywood caught his shoulder and raked his entire arm. As I followed through, I sprawled onto the board, hammering it all the way to the floor. It scraped down Ganderson's side, dislodged the pistol from his hand, crushed his foot, and knocked him to his knees.

"Aauugggh!" He sounded hurt.

I tried to stand, lost my balance on the tipping plywood sheet and fell again. I grabbed at Ganderson and took him all the way down with me. The angle may have broken his ankle, which was still trapped under the edge of the board. He certainly screamed, even louder.

The .45 was missing. I couldn't take any chances.

"Asshole," I said, and with two *kenpo* power strikes, broke both his collarbones.

CHAPTER FORTY-THREE

"I never asked," said Johnny, as we drove through the dark tunnels of the Northeast Kingdom at dusk. "Did he pay your bill?"

"Ganderson? Hah!"

"Chiseler."

"Well, I got about half, in progress payments, before everything blew up. And I'm not giving it back—I did what I was hired for, after all."

"I guess small claims is out."

I smiled.

An hour past sunset—which wasn't that late, this far north in Vermont—impenetrable forest crowded the remote county road on either side. Peak fall foliage had come and gone, and most of the leaves had fallen. The blacktop twisted and curved, uphill and down, yellow warning signs reflecting our headlights. We hadn't seen another vehicle since Drakes Mill, seven miles back.

"I appreciate your helping drive," I said. "In case I forgot to mention."

"Oh, I always take a vacation around now."

"Late October? In northern New England?"

"One tires of the same old Riviera beaches year after year."

We were getting close. I examined the map one more time. Paper, not GPS—this wasn't the sort of trip where I wanted even the faintest electronic trail.

"You have to give him points for style." Johnny, the permanent contrarian. "Sets up a foolproof scheme, whacks a few Masters of Doom, starts banking 5x returns—and then hires *you*, just to goose the publicity."

"Not publicity. Or not only. He was already planning ahead. I was the fall guy."

"Which makes a little more sense, I suppose. Kind of underestimated you, though, huh?"

"Yeah." And I have to admit, it was that part that rankled the most. I thought I had a solid reputation, but Ganderson treated me like a Fishkill loser on parole—like a wino you'd hand a gun to, point at the bank branch, and say the getaway car would be around the corner. What the fuck did Ganderson *think* would happen? I was smarter than that!

Wasn't I?

"Don't worry about it." Johnny sounded like he was reading my mind, but it wasn't too hard because I'd been repeating the same complaint since we'd left the city. "He was a vastly overpaid investment banker. Those guys think they can tell the sun when to set. If you're bothered by pathological overconfidence, you need to find another set of clients."

"The problem is, they pay the best." I sighed. "Even worse, though, they're all apparently armed to the teeth now. I still can't believe the shootout at the conference. It was like an Afghan wedding in there."

"It wasn't all random, is what I heard."

"Huh?"

"Once the guns were out, people realized they could start settling scores."

"No way." I had to laugh. "Really?"

"You know—old grudges, resentments over past deals, that sort of thing. I think the whole event was cathartic for everyone."

We slowed to a stop at an unmarked crossroads. I checked my notes.

"Go right. Two-point-eight miles."

Johnny glanced at the odometer and got us moving again. "And Hayden, never part of it. That's still hard to believe."

"He was a thief and an embezzler, and he tried to kill me more than once."

"But not connected to Ganderson."

"Nope. Just another hard-charging dealmaker. Not much more than business as usual."

I opened my window, breathing the cold night air. It had that early-frost smell, the snap of winter. We passed an unlit sign, something about firewood and beer.

"How's Clara?" Johnny asked.

"Out of the hospital." They'd only kept her for a day. "Hammering the blogosphere. Callouts all over the internet. She writes really well, did you know that? I mean, digging up dirt, that's one thing—but her stories are just great to read. That job offer from CNBC ought to be arriving any day now."

"You haven't *talked* to her?"

"Can't." I looked out at the dark forest around us. "She doesn't need the kind of trouble I've got stuck all over me."

The headlights illuminated the trees and brush along the road, creating a tunnel effect. The car ran almost silent on the smooth pavement.

"Did you ever call up your brother?" Johnny asked.

Dave. "No." I'd thought about it, but after all the near-death excitement, the possibility of family I never knew I had was a straw too many to deal with. "Someday I will."

A minute later Johnny coasted, braked and stopped. A slight widening of the dirt verge was the only indication we'd arrived. He popped the trunk release and we stepped out into the night, closing both doors to turn off the dome light.

At the car's rear I pulled out my small pack. I was still carrying an extra water bottle, which I drank off and dropped into the trunk before slamming the lid.

"This is the ass end of nowhere," said Johnny.

"That's the point."

"You'll be lost in two hundred yards, fall into a pitch black gulley, break both legs and die of exposure right before the bears eat you."

"Me and D. B. Cooper." I laughed—not much, but a real honest laugh. "Go make some money, Johnny. I'll be fine."

"Yeah." He hesitated. "Do you think . . . are you coming back, Silas?"

The serious questions always come at the end.

"Don't know."

I inhaled. Pine needles, rock, a bit of rain. It wasn't a Central Asian desert or the jungly forests around Fort Bragg. Still less the clamorous asphalt and lights and crowds of Fifth Avenue. But it felt good.

Almost like home.

"This time was different," I said slowly. "Too much. Too much killing, too much money. I'm having a little trouble getting straight about it all."

"You will."

"Maybe."

"Look, it's like this." Johnny seemed to be trying to find the right words. "You know how long a security is held, on average? Buy to sell?"

"Twenty seconds." I did know, in fact. "But it's all those high-frequency millisecond trades."

"Things change," said Johnny. "Nothing lasts."

Even Johnny's philosophical metaphors come straight from the market screen. But the heart was there.

"Yeah," I said. "I understand that. I'll be all right."

"Okay." He nodded. "Hope to see you, though. That's all."

"Thanks again."

"You, too." We shook hands, just like we were parting after a quick lunch at Delaney's. He got back in the car, turned it around, and drove off without looking back.

In the silence I stood for a few moments, adapting to the solitude and the darkness. Then I found a place to sit, ten feet from the road, against a maple thickly grown over with soft, earthy moss.

The moon would be up in an hour. After that, I'd be able to see clearly enough, and I'd start the night's trek. The Canadian border was only four miles from here, following the long watershed of the Vossen River. I'd get wet once or twice, depending on how much rain had filled the forest streams recently. Then another twenty miles of woods and occasional farmland—abandoned and overgrown homesteads, for the most part—to Stanville-Ost in Quebec, with its clapboard-fronted main street, stone church and bus station. From there, I could go anywhere.

So long as I avoided the marijuana fields, back country meth labs, and—on the U.S. side—occasional gun-toting hermits, I'd be fine.

I'd hiked the entire distance twice and back, last year, keeping the landmarks and hazards clear in my memory. I was already anticipating the coffee at Stanville-Ost's single breakfast diner. I'd sleep on the bus, the deep contented sleep of someone tired from honest exercise.

This wasn't the only bolt-hole I'd prepared over the years. After picking up the emergency cash and ID from my Brownsville cache, I could have gone in any of six or seven different directions. I chose Canada because I liked autumn in the woods, and because the northern border was still fairly easy.

I had to disappear. Didn't matter I was on the side of the angels. There were enough bodies and blown-up buildings and missing millions to keep a federal cross-jurisdictional task force in business for years—and vast teams of lawyers busy in civil court for another decade after that. I'd have to cut deals, submit to depositions, testify and bargain with prosecutors, police, clients and bagmen. I'd never get my life back.

Nor could I just keep a low profile until it all blew over. I'd told Clara not to perjure herself—even if she'd tried, she'd trip up eventually, and then they'd have us both. Not to mention Rondo and everyone else I'd run across in the last week. My life was going to be picked over and reported in the most mind-numbing bureaucratic detail imaginable.

I had no choice but to leave.

At seven-eighteen the moon appeared, glowing through skeletal, leafless tree branches to the east. I got to my feet, pulled on the pack and stepped away, deeper into the forest.

Silas Cade was gone. I was just a nameless accountant now, fading into the woods.

CHAPTER FORTY-FOUR

EVENT RISK

Greed, Guts and Glory—
Commentary from Clara Dawson

< Previous Post   Next Post >

Final Payout for Turncoat Financier

Posted 07:18 Mar 11

According to **NYPDBeat**, Quint Ganderson died this morning, shot down on the driveway of the Greenwich estate where he'd been serving mansion arrest while awaiting trial.

Last fall, of course, Ganderson allegedly masterminded his notorious **first-thing-kill-all-the-bankers** scheme. As the body count piled up, observers noticed that the dead investment managers all had stunningly poor records, having lost hundreds of millions of dollars for their clients in lousy trades and **wrongheaded bets.**

Early speculation assumed a disgruntled investor had taken the law into his own hands—a **Bernie Goetz** for the new Gilded Age. Later events revealed a more banal motive, albeit one fully in tune with the Wall Street mindset: Ganderson had allegedly been setting up trades against the victims' various positions, **profiting handsomely** when their deaths kicked the last props out.

Although the investigation into Ganderson's murder has only begun, sources inside the Old Ridgefork Police Department have described strong similarities to the sniper killing of **Tom Marlett**, the third domino in Ganderson's hit parade. "Tripod marks, .338-caliber rounds, even a half bootprint—it's the same guy, all right," one person told me. "The FBI is full of shit."

Federal authorities are apparently more focused on **Silas Cade**, a mysterious figure who uncovered the first evidence of Ganderson's financial interest in the killings and halted a murderous shooting spree during the **Grand Plaza Clusterfuck**. The FBI is refusing to comment—to me, at least, and on the record—about their interest in the only person who was on top of the situation from the beginning . . .

CHAPTER FORTY-FIVE

C ustoms at JFK was shabby and unimpressive, the walls of the holding pen stained, the floor scuffed, and the armorglass shields at the booths already scratched. But the officials were cheerful and efficient. Mine even smiled briefly as she banged an entry stamp into my passport and passed it back.

"Welcome home," she said.

On the way to baggage claim I tucked the documents back into my jacket. I won't say I was flooded with relief, but I felt good. Walter might have retired, but he was willing to do me a favor, and these papers were top class. When I'd picked them up at poste restante in Lisbon, I'd compared them millimeter by millimeter with the real thing, and I couldn't find a single flaw.

Outside I found an express bus, paid the fifteen bucks, and sat for half an hour inside the vehicle, waiting, before it finally got under way. Sure, a taxi would have been faster, but the bus is the simplest path back into unrecorded anonymity. No cameras, no driver's curiosity, no trip receipt. I had a new name now, and it was going to stay unknown as long as I could manage.

A new name.

My sixth, in fact.

There's no Silas Cade in the Pentagon records. Or the SSN databases or anywhere in the vast Equifax-Acxiom credit-data archipelago. On a birth certificate, somewhere, yes—filed long after the date on it, backfilled by Walter's magic. But "Silas" was as imaginary as any of my other identities, all assumed, used up and shucked over the years.

Sure, it's a nuisance, recreating myself each time. But I operate without the long tail of official existence: no credit cards, no bank accounts, no W-2s, no tax filings, no property registration. No nothing. Most people need a four-drawer file cabinet to keep track of their paperbound lives. For me, a few memorized passwords and a safe deposit box are good enough. In that light, it's not so hard to start over.

At Port Authority I exited the bus and walked down 42nd Street. Late March, and bright sunshine wasn't having much effect against the cold air. I bought a hot pretzel from a vendor, eating it quickly before it cooled. Men went by in topcoats, women in fur. Young people walked briskly, glancing up occasionally from their smartphones. Kids scuffled and laughed and poked each other, oblivious of any other pedestrian over the age of eighteen.

At Bryant Park I pulled out my new cellphone, purchased a day earlier in Copenhagen. I also had a store of fifteen fresh SIM cards. I chose one, snapped it into the phone, and clicked the on button, waiting for a signal.

Yes, I was still tied to disposable technology. But at least the chipcards were more compact than multiple handsets.

"Hello?"

I heard her voice for the first time in half a year. It was a moment before I could speak.

"Hello? Who's there?"

"Hey, Clara," I said. "I've got a story for you."

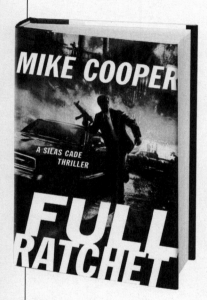